Stolen Pleasure

A little push from behind caused her to fall forward, closing the distance between her heated body and his. Jacob's soft lips covered hers. His warm breath slid seductively over the dampened surface of her mouth.... She gasped at the exciting small intrusion, and felt his arms tighten around her, pulling her closer. She felt her breast crush up against the hard wall of his chest, his hand curved around her buttocks, pulling her hips against his solid thighs. His kiss deepened, stealing her breath. She was drowning in evil wicked carnal desire, and she hated herself for not wanting to be saved....

Praise for Patricia Williams's *Warrior's Prize*:

"[A] vibrant story."—*Rendezvous*

"An incredible work of art. Patricia Williams has boldly gone where no woman has gone before and ... successfully combines action, great characters, and tremendous insight into an African culture. *Warrior's Prize* deserves to be on the bestseller's list." —*Affaire de Coeur*

Titles by Patricia Williams

FREEDOM'S SONG
WARRIOR'S PRIZE

FREEDOM'S SONG

Patricia Williams

JOVE BOOKS, NEW YORK

If you purchased this book without a cover, you should be aware that this book is stolen property. It was reported as "unsold and destroyed" to the publisher, and neither the author nor the publisher has received any payment for this "stripped book."

FREEDOM'S SONG

A Jove Book / published by arrangement with
the author

PRINTING HISTORY
Jove edition / June 1995

All rights reserved.
Copyright © 1995 by Patricia Williams Kanaley.
This book may not be reproduced in whole
or in part, by mimeograph or any other means,
without permission. For information address:
The Berkley Publishing Group, 200 Madison Avenue,
New York, New York 10016.

ISBN: 0-515-11631-9

A JOVE BOOK®
Jove Books are published by The Berkley Publishing Group,
200 Madison Avenue, New York, New York 10016.
JOVE and the "J" design are trademarks
belonging to Jove Publications, Inc.

PRINTED IN THE UNITED STATES OF AMERICA

10 9 8 7 6 5 4 3 2 1

*In loving memory
of my first official fan,
the princess
Barbara Adams*

Prologue

Zululand, South Africa, 1827

Her screams pierced the hot, muggy night. Outside the hut, her husband, Cira, stood rigid at attention, wanting to run, but unable to move.

"Cira, come on now. Leave it to the women." His friend Punga tugged gently on Cira's arm, the muscles bunching and stretching as Cira clenched and unclenched his large fists.

Another scream echoed through the stillness, then faded into a meek whimper. Cira had been through this two times before. Mangoaela was seven, and Godongwana had just turned three. But still, Monase's labor cries terrified him. Childbirth was dangerous, and this time there were twins. He hung his head, clamping his eyes and mouth shut, murmuring a fervent prayer to his ancestors to protect this woman who was everything to him. She was so slight. Godongwana, a big strapping boy, had nearly split her in two. A single tear made a silvery track down Cira's lean cheek. Docilely, he allowed Punga to lead him away. Monase's plaintive cries followed him, vibrating hauntingly through the dark, oppressive skies.

"I'm here, baby. Squeeze my hand. I'm here for you." Sondaba gently stroked Monase's sweat-glistened brow. A brittle, strained smile curved Sondaba's lips, but didn't quite reach her eyes. She loved this little sister and had once been like a mother to her, but the pain in her heart was too great.

She couldn't rejoice with her over the birth of yet another child when she, Sondaba, was barren.

Each cry of pain was a twisting blade in Sondaba's heart, echoing her own cries of sorrow. For six years she had formed the same desperate cry. Month after month she had watched her flow come, the blood draining a little bit of life with it, a little of her spirit, her will to go on. Isanusi, her husband, had been patient and gentle, but season after season she had ceased to live, becoming an empty shell.

Isanusi was a man. He needed an heir. His business had faltered. New competition had halved his previous income. King Shaka, great chief of Zululand, was becoming neglectful since the death of his mother, allowing warring tribes to raid the kraal's grazing cattle without retribution. Isanusi's hide tanning business was not as lucrative as it had once been. With this constant drain of cows and customers, he hadn't the cattle to afford the lobala for a second wife who could bear him children.

Sondaba's eyes burned. The whites shot through with fine red lines, but no tears came. They had all been depleted years ago. Now she could no longer even seek the solace of weeping. With great reluctance, her husband had finally been forced to face the fact that he would have to exercise his right to return Sondaba to her father, in exchange for one of her younger, fertile, unmarried sisters.

Suddenly, Monase squeezed her sister's hand, the grip causing Sondaba's fingers to overlap. Sondaba crooned softly to her, telling her everything would be all right. Monase relaxed, panting, as the spasm left her body. The midwife crowed out happily that the head was visible between her knees. Putting one hand on each of Monase's knees, the woman pushed them wide apart.

"Push now, push. The babies are almost here."

A dry sob caught in Sondaba's chest. It wasn't fair: two

babies at once, and Monase was only allowed to keep one. How could the gods be so cruel? Here she was, a good, obedient wife, subjected to the shame of having to return, unwanted, to her father's keeping, a burden on him forever. Then, as if that wasn't enough, she had to watch another woman, one of her sisters, go take her place, to bear children for her good, kind husband. The blade twisted deeper, rendering an unbearable pressure in her chest.

"It's a boy!" the midwife cried. An infant's hearty wail filled the hut. Monase's grip relaxed in Sondaba's hand. The newborn infant was quickly bundled up by the stout woman and taken from the warm, dark hut, to the waiting arms of his new grandmother, Niamani.

Time passed more slowly now. Exhausted, Monase faded in and out of a delirious consciousness. Sondaba sang a soothing lullaby to her as she rocked back and forth, still holding Monase's limp hand. Then the contractions started again.

The midwife called out, "Push now, push! The head is showing." Monase's beautiful face twisted, her lips pursing, her eyes clamped shut. Her face grew dark with exertion as her chest rose, then fell with a great gush of the breath she'd been holding.

"I can't. I can't. Sondaba, help me please..." Monase's words died on a weak cry of pain. "The burning, the pain. I can't." Again her voice faded. Then her head lolled to one side. Sondaba moved a hand to Monase's damp forehead.

"Come on, you can do it. Give it another try." She whispered.

Monase lifted bloodshot, weary eyes to her. The pupils were enormous, frightened, exhausted. "Please Sondaba, take h—" Her eyes closed in the deep sleep of unconsciousness.

The midwife muttered under her breath. Reaching her hands deep into Monase, she drew out a small, quiet baby girl. Sondaba's voice was barely a whisper.

"Is it . . . Is she dead?"

The woman shook her head. "Were that it were, poor thing." She wrapped the small form in a supple zebra hide and handed it to Sondaba. "Take it around back, put a little clay in her mouth. It shouldn't take long to suffocate her. She is already so weak. It was harder on her than it was on her mother."

Sondaba's eyes grew wide in horror as she gazed down on the small bundle. She knew that among many of the South African tribes twins were considered a birth defect, and the second twin, or female, was always suffocated and buried before its spirit could sap the strength of the other twin. She had grown up aware of this custom, but never had she actually had to witness it, to do it, to be the one to snuff the small life that she so desperately wanted for herself. In a daze she rose, still clutching the silent bundle. The midwife looked at her oddly, then turned her attention to the afterbirth she pulled from Monase's womb.

Outside, Sondaba bent behind the hut. The hut was on the outskirts of the kraal. Fragrant sandalwood trees swayed gently in the heavy night air. Sondaba breathed in deeply, steeling herself for the task she faced. Suddenly, the small body moved. Sondaba peeled back the hide blanket. Two dark, serious eyes stared out at her. Her hand froze, as it hovered over the child. A tiny hand reached out, grasping her finger. The eyes never wavered, the little hand held strong to her finger.

Sondaba's eyes welled with tears—tears she thought had long since dried up streamed down her cheek. She pulled the baby close, burying it in her ample bosom. In reflex, the child began to root. Searching, then finding Sondaba's nipple, she began to suck. The gentle tugging on Sondaba's breast seemed to tug on the very strings of her heart. Her tears rained down on the child, baptizing it with her sorrow. Momentarily, the child stopped, confused at the moisture falling over its face. The dark eyes, large and unblinking, searched around, unfocused, above her.

"Yes, Monase . . . I will take her." A sob racked Sondaba's body. She knew what she would have to do: take the child and run. If they didn't survive, it was all the same. For to stay, they both would undoubtedly die, anyway. Sondaba bent her head, stroking the small, soft cheek.

"My little love. My little Thandawe." The baby smiled, showing pink, toothless gums. Then her tiny mouth formed a silent O and she closed her eyes, drifting off to the sweet, peaceful slumber of innocence.

As the moon rose higher above the trees, Sondaba wrapped the infant tightly in the zebra hide. Never looking back, she slipped into the darkness, heading north. Where she would go, she didn't know, but it didn't matter. Her burden had been lifted, her journey was bright. She had a child. Her little loved one, Thandawe.

One

January 1849, London, England

Amanda stared out onto the dark, dismal scene below. As she pressed her nose against the cold window pane, her breath fogged up the glass, blending the black coats and umbrellas with the dingy snow, making the view a mottled gray. God, how she hated English winters. The spring and summer were all right if you didn't mind the constant drizzle, but the dampness in the winters crept into your very bones. With a small shiver, she drew her shawl closer around her slender frame.

"What's the weather going to be today, child?" The voice drifted to her from a creaking wooden rocker by the tiny apartment's small, glowing fireplace. The words were followed by a burst of harsh hacking coughs.

"Cold, gray, snow . . . no sleet mixed with snow." Amanda moved to sit on a small stool at her aunt's feet. Amanda had been blessed with the ability to read the weather. A lot of good it did her here, as the forecast rarely changed. But her aunt never tired of asking; saying it was her gift from her Zulu ancestors, because she had been a second twin who had survived. Her Aunt Sondaba had told her a lot about the beautiful lands of South Africa and about the Zulu customs and people. She hadn't embellished on her family, her parents, or her supposed other twin. When asked, her aunt would grow quiet and distant, her eyes pools of despair and sorrow, only saying

Amanda's mother had been a beautiful, courageous woman, loved by her father, a brave handsome impi warrior, and that she, Sondaba, had named her Thandawe, the loved one. This hadn't satisfied Amanda's insatiable curiosity, but it was all she could wrest from her frail aunt. Instead, she would beg to hear about her ancestors, the Sans and the Khoikhoi. She also liked to hear about the great King Shaka. The papers these days were full of accounts by missionaries and explorers describing the peoples of Africa. But the people described in the papers were barbarians, crude and savage. Not at all like the gentle, loving, and industrious men and women of whom her aunt talked. In Aunty Daba's stories, King Shaka was a military genius, to be compared with Napoleon, Alexander the Great, even Caesar.

Her Aunt Sondaba had told her a little of how they had come to be in England. She told of her journey north from Zululand. She told how, weak and dehydrated, she and a five-month-old baby had arrived at the mission in Gcalekaland. There, Minister Carrington and his wife had taken them in. The minister's wife, Elizabeth, had taken care of Sondaba and taught her Christianity. Liking the idea of a benevolent God who forgave all sins and who promised to reunite her with her loved ones in an afterlife, she allowed both her niece and herself to be baptized as Methodist.

At that time, Sondaba had been told she would have to choose a Christian name for both herself and the child. Sondaba had been reluctant to give up the very special name she had chosen for Thandawe. Elizabeth had been understanding, drawing out a worn book of Latin names. Sondaba had been delighted when they discovered the name *Amandus*, which meant fit to be loved. So Amanda had gotten her name. Her real name, Thandawe, became her middle initial, T. For herself, Sondaba had been less picky. She had settled on the name Helen, simply because she liked the way the English pronounced it, with a silent H, soft and rolling off her tongue, so different than the clicking, hard sounds of the South Africans.

They had not needed a last name until the summer of 1828. Minister Carrington had come down with the dreaded sleeping sickness, a virus that often attacked the cattle. The missionaries decided to return to England and persuaded Helen to come with them. As the paperwork was prepared, an English last name was needed. It only seemed natural that they should choose the name Smith. After all, Sondaba's father had been an iron smith; besides, her husband was dead to her now, undoubtedly married to one of her sisters.

Resting her cheek against her aunt's knee, Amanda sighed. Her life had been good: boring, but safe. She had received a complete education, and had proven a very apt pupil, especially in mathematics. Mr. Carrington had opened a small religious bookstore when he had recovered, and often allowed Amanda to help him with the accounting, especially since he had never fully regained his stamina. For hours, Amanda would sit in the leather chair behind his big walnut desk breathing in the delightful smell of leather and bound paper. When she finished her work, she would read the endless stacks of available books, papers, and whatever else she could get her hands on. Once, she had found a book of Greek mythology, and had read it over three times before she begged Mr. Carrington to find more for her. The minister was very fond of her, as he had no children of his own. The next week he had managed to get the book *Ulysses*. It was written entirely in Latin. Undaunted, Amanda had painstakingly learned enough of the ancient language to understand the story. Impressed by her tenacity, Mr. Carrington and his friends would lend her books, journals, anything to see her eyes light up and her bright beaming smile. She knew she was not beautiful, but was aware that her smile could twist some of the hardest hearts. Her aunt said she had inherited her father's strong, even white teeth and charming dimples.

It was among these written gifts that Amanda discovered two things that changed her life. One was an article by a young black American named Frederick Douglass. The man was eloquent beyond words. His passion rose like a flame from the pages. She felt her soul cry out with the injustice of the American slave, and her heart bled for the hopeless agony of these fettered men and women. She also found his photograph enticing, and she fell a little in love with him. He looked so different from the men she knew. He was black, and he was also rugged. His hard life could be seen in every nuance of his features. It was obvious that he did not sit around all day smoking cigars, drinking brandy, shuffling papers and discussing the latest news from the papers. This was a man who had learned life the hard way, and who made things happen.

The second discovery was the ever-growing appearance of articles about the Wild West of North America. When she read of the majestic mountains, open plains, and endless space, she felt a thrill shoot through her body. It reminded her of the stories of Africa, where wild animals roamed the land. She would love to go back to visit Africa, but she knew that as surely as she wore white kid gloves and donned three to six petticoats every morning, she could never live comfortably in a land where the women ran around with barely a sheet tied around their shoulders. It wasn't that she was a snob or a prude, it was just that she wasn't of that world anymore. But, as she felt her aunt's knee shake beneath her cheek, and a sharp barking cough rack the dear woman's shivering body, she knew she didn't belong here in damp, colorless London.

"Aunty Daba, tell me a story of Africa. Of the bright sun, blue skies, and wondrous, wide open spaces."

The old woman shook her head, debating whether to chastise Amanda for using her childhood name for her or ignore it. Here in England she was Helen, with the silent H. As she lifted her frail hand to stoke the two long braids trailing down the girl's back, she paused. What did it matter, here in the privacy of their rooms? She lowered her hand, catching one of the thick plaits in her palm. She pulled gently, so her niece looked up into her lined face.

"Is it Africa you be dreaming of, child? Or is it this new western America?" The words were soft, almost musical. Amanda beamed up at her beloved aunt, this brave woman who had sacrificed everything for her. Although she appeared to be over sixty, Amanda knew she was little more than forty-six. Her journey in Africa had aged her, and the English climate continued to deteriorate her health. Sondaba had developed a constant bronchitis shortly after their arrival. Many nights she would sit with her head enclosed by a towel and her face over a steaming pot of water. She had caught pneumonia twice, and she was always coughing. She also refused to eat fish or beef, a mainstay in England. She claimed that like all people of Zululand, she had no taste for fish. She also claimed that it was a waste of cattle to eat them, and instead would mix crushed crackers or bread with a pitcher of cream. She said this was her *amaSi,* the true food of her people. Amanda always grimaced at the gloppy mixture, glad that she, personally, had no such misgivings. The only concession Sondaba would make was to add a large spoonful of jam to the mush, her favorite being the sweet-tart orange marmalade.

"Please Aunty, it is so . . . so colorless here. You know, today I just read about the Wilkes expedition. These American explorers traveled into a huge basin, so far out West that only wild Indians populate the land. You should have heard the description of the land, the Aputaput Falls, and the glorious canyons. The Indians there say it was carved out by a giant beaver who left his claw marks along the canyon walls. Oh, I would so love to see a waterfall, so big that the rushing of the water shakes the very ground you stand on."

FREEDOM'S SONG

Sondaba shook her head and began to tell her of the great waterfalls she had seen on her journey north in Africa.

Amanda closed her eyes, trying to relive the memories that her infant eyes had been too young to absorb. As her aunt's voice rumbled on, she could hear the roar of the water, feel its cool spray upon her face. The sky would have been so blue, the sun blazing, not a cloud in sight. The moment was spoiled by another series of hacking coughs from her aunt.

Breathing with great difficulty, Sondaba rose from her rocker. Amanda's face became serious. "From everything I've read, the far western territories in the United States are very similar in climate and terrain to your beloved South Africa. It would be good for you, your health. Let's go. Let's leave this damp, desolate London behind."

Her aunt sighed, easing herself back in the rocker. "No, child. I'm too old. I left one world to find another, and I haven't the strength to face yet another." Her eyes were sad, knowing. "A story was told to me by your mother." Amanda tensed. Her aunt rarely talked about her mother, Monase. "She said an *iisangoma*, a seer-of-everything, said she would bear a daughter that would go to a different world far across the ocean. I had hoped she had meant here with me, in England." The woman stopped, cupping Amanda's face in her hands. She stared wistfully into the young girl's eyes. "Now I know that is not so." Her voice grew soft, barely above a whisper. Amanda had to lean in close to hear. "May the ancestors go with you. May the spirits of courage be by your side. Never forget, you are the daughter of a great wife, the great granddaughter of a chief's wife." Amanda smiled, nodding, as always confused by the tribal tangle of great wives, first wives, substitute great wives. It was all so foreign. But it mattered to her aunt, and her aunt mattered to her.

* * *

That night, Amanda found a small envelope on her pillow. Underneath it was the beautiful zebra hide that her aunt had wrapped her in on the journey through South Africa. Sitting down on the edge of the bed, Amanda opened the envelope with trembling fingers. She was surprised when she found a thick stack of pound notes. She gasped. It had to be her aunt's whole life savings, and even then, how had she managed to collect so much money? Then she remembered the exquisite ivory jewelry and combs her aunt had in her top dresser drawer. She rarely wore them, saying they were from her ex-husband, and she no longer wished to be reminded of him. But still she kept them, and at times she put them in her hair and in her earlobes. Unaware that Amanda was watching, Sondaba would preen in front of the mirror, stretching her neck, turning her head first this way, then the other. Amanda could envision her as a lovely young wife. Then the sorrow, the hurt would return, etching deep lines of grief in her aunt's face. Sondaba would remove the ivory, placing it gently inside the soft hide bag.

Now Amanda went to the dresser. She and Sondaba each had their own bedrooms, no larger then a closet, so all furniture, other than their beds, was kept in the larger living room. Quietly pulling the wooden drawer out, she peered into the shadowed darkness. Dipping her hand into its recesses, she groped for the bag. She found it. Even before she drew it into the light, she knew it was empty. She crushed the velvety softness between her fingers, and felt her eyes sting with the threat of tears. Sondaba had sold her last treasures. But why? She would give the money back. Tell her to retrieve her prized possessions. Amanda started, as a cold brittle hand grasped her arm. She whirled around, pulling the small thin woman to her.

"Why, Aunty Daba? They were all you had to remember . . ." Amanda's voice trailed off as she sniffed, wiping her nose with a long finger.

"I have you. I have my memories. I don't need such trinkets. Start your new life. Find this western world of yours. I am not long for this world. My spirit will be with you." Her aunt's voice trembled with bridled emotion.

As if true to her words, Amanda's aunt's health began to deteriorate at a rapid pace. By the end of the month, she was confined to her bed. Most days she was incoherent, mumbling deliriously, occasionally calling out to her ancestors. Day after day, night after night, Amanda stayed beside her bed, praying to her Christian God.

Late one night, Sondaba grew restless. She tossed and turned violently on her bed, then was still. Small beads of perspiration dotted her forehead and sunken cheeks. Amanda reached out to soothe her face with a damp cloth. As she lowered the cloth, Sondaba's clawlike hand caught her wrist, holding Amanda's hand suspended above her. Amanda was shocked by the strength in those gnarled fingers, when she tried to continue her ministrations.

"Never give up easily. Your parents were courageous people. They never gave up. You will have great challenges to face in America, and you will show them your pride and strength." Sondaba's voice was surprisingly strong and clear. Her eyes burned with a fanatic intensity.

Amanda felt her heart race with fear and concern. Momentarily, she looked away, contemplating if she should rouse the Carringtons or one of the servants. Reaching up to grab Amanda's chin between her finger and thumb, her aunt turned Amanda's face toward hers again. There, as her aunt lay sick, maybe dying, Amanda caught a glimpse of the determined young woman who had trekked over six hundred miles of dangerous African wilderness to deliver her, Amanda, into safety. As their eyes met and held, Amanda placed her hands on her aunt's shoulders. Pulling her toward her, she pressed her lips against this incredible woman's forehead. Her lips moved softly against the weathered skin.

"I never knew my parents, but they did not want me, and you did." When Sondaba struggled to pull away, Amanda silenced her by placing a finger to her lips and held her tighter. "You, my dearest aunt, are inspiration enough. You are courageous and wise, and I have learned much from you. I will always make you proud. You will get well, and we will go to America together."

Giving up her struggle, Sondaba wrapped her thin arms around Amanda's waist. Amanda felt Sondaba's thin body shake as she struggled to restrain a sob trapped in her chest.

"No, sweet child, but may God and your ancestors go with you, my dear, dear Thandawe."

There, in her arms, Sondaba ceased to live. Unable to release her, Amanda held the wasted, lifeless body, rocking back and forth. That night she made her decision to go to the western Americas. To live in a wild, vital new land.

In the silence of the room, she felt her aunt's presence, and she felt comforted. She knew her aunt's spirit was indeed with her, her own protecting African ancestor.

Two

"Miss Smith," Minister Carrington began, as he rose from his heavy leather chair behind his desk. Amanda could tell from her guardian's formal use of her name that he was not at all pleased with her decision. Coming around the desk, he lowered himself into one of the armless chairs facing hers. He sighed wearily. "Amanda, be reasonable." Amanda smiled at his heavily lined, gaunt face, a face that she knew and cared for so much. For all his stern, ministerly affections, he was still the same man that had hidden gifts for her in his pockets when she was a child. He was older now, his hair whiter, and his pale blue eyes faded, but he was still the only fatherlike figure she had ever known, and she was going to miss him.

"I'm being very reasonable, Mr. Carrington. I have not arrived at my decision lightly. I have given it a lot of thought, and I am convinced that I have decided what is best for me. I know what I want." Amanda reached out to grasp the older man's hands before he could protest further. "My aunt would have wanted this for me as well. We talked many times of my future." Amanda leaned closer to the minister, her grip tightening, her eyes a rich, liquid amber. "I've only heard of my native land, of its beauty and color. I heard of the wide open spaces, the endless blue skies. I would love to visit that land, the home of my ancestors, my family, but you know as well as I do that everything is different now. I am not as I was when I was an infant.''

Amanda's gaze fell to the clasped hands in hers, the long, thin white fingers stark against her brown ones. The minister followed her gaze. Her skin was so smooth, so young next to his old weathered hands. He felt a paternal rush of protectiveness surge through his being. He saw her as the large-eyed, skinny little naked toddler she had been, running full speed across the mission grounds, unable to stop herself except by falling. Then she had been free, a child of Africa, one with the land. He glanced up to the quiet visage before him, watching as the long, spiked sable lashes rose to reveal those same large eyes that he had loved so long ago. He thought of the land where they had both lived over twenty years ago. He remembered it well. He closed his eyes to block out the carnage and destruction that he heard about in the papers. That beautiful land and people they had both been a part of so long ago was but a ghost now, a world on the verge of destruction.

"You are right. You would never fit in. It is not what it once was. It has become much too dangerous a place for you. Just as I feel this new America—"

"I know." Amanda cut him off before he could continue. She couldn't allow him to start extolling the many dangers of a woman traveling alone, of the uncivilized, unsettled ways of western America. It would only make it that much more difficult to convince him otherwise, and it might shake her resolve. When the minister frowned at her rude interruption, she smiled apologetically. "I'm sorry, but I've thought it over carefully. I'm not going to Africa. I want to keep that world the way I know it through my aunt's words: a land of brave and courageous people." Amanda hesitated for a moment, looking off to some distant point. Then her dark eyes moved back to the minister's face, her turbulent eyes of a moment before now gleamed with excitement. "Please try to understand. I want to discover a new land, another land of brave and courageous people. A vast land of openness and color." Now her hands flew wide in exasperation, like startled birds rising from the brush. "This . . ." Her hand swept the room, as she sought the words to describe all the emotions boiling inside of her. "This is not enough. I want more. I want . . . I need to find a place where I belong."

Minister Carrington wanted to shake those slender shoulders, to capture those naive words that floated so innocently about her restless hands. She would not belong in America. Americans would see her as chattel. Her ignorance made him angry. "Take a trip to the continent, Spain, Italy. You have the resources, your aunt's savings and the sale of her ivory and gold jewelry has left you a tidy little sum that I've invested." As John Carrington spoke, his anger turned to pleading. "America is not home for you, Amanda. They do not treat people of your race kindly." His last words were spoken softly, with deep regret.

Amanda clasped her hands together in a tight knot of frustration. She had been afraid of this. His arguments were strong, and they came from the heart, making them difficult to easily brush aside. But from what she had read, most of the western territories were voting against slavery. Besides, she wouldn't be so foolish as to choose one that did allow slaves. She worried her bottom lip between her teeth as she contemplated her finances. It was true that she had some money from her aunt, and to someone like herself who had never paid for much of anything herself, it looked like a lot of money. But, she worried, was it in actuality only enough for an excursion of a month or two on the continent? She glanced up at Minister Carrington's solemn face studying hers so intently. She wanted to ask him, but was afraid to show any sign of weakening of her intentions.

"I appreciate everything you and Mrs. Carrington have done for me, but I'm an adult now. I'm nearly twenty-three. It is my inheritance, and I have made up my mind. I intend to leave in a fortnight for America." Amanda grimaced as she saw the pained look the minister gave her, but she stood her ground.

John Carrington wanted to weep. He had thought better of Amanda. She was a smart, levelheaded young woman, but she was taking a huge and unnecessary risk. He studied her now, her amber eyes ablaze with defiance, her full bottom lip more pronounced in a pout. In the Gcalekalands she would be considered a beauty. Here, where the fashion was pale, porcelain skin, she was more an oddity. He ran his long fingers through his thinning hair. The chances of her marrying here in England were slim at best. Maybe she was right; maybe she'd have a better chance in America, but he worried. Even at twenty-three, in some things she was so innocent. She had been virtually shielded from the prejudice she would undoubtly encounter in the States, and he didn't want to even think about the fact that most likely she knew nothing about men and their sometimes lustful and deceiving ways. He felt a pang of guilt that he had been unrealistic in seeing her raised as a privileged young lady of the upper class. He had not thought that this day would come, and now that it had, he saw that it had been inevitable.

"If you are determined then," the minister started, as he rose slowly from the smaller chair to return to the safety of his throne behind the desk, "at least will you allow me to make a few inquiries, to perhaps help you find a family, perhaps a position?" He had wanted to add *"some protection,"* but he knew that small addition would only get Amanda's dander up and turn her against his suggestions altogether. For all his years, he was not unaware of youth's belief that they were invulnerable. His mouth twitched as he remembered his own parents' concerns and objections to his own call to adventure some thirty years ago.

It took Amanda a few seconds to get the full jist of the minister's words. He had capitulated. She smiled briefly, then nodded her head. She could scarcely believe the battle was over. She had been prepared for much worse. As her gaze followed her guardian back to his chair, she registered the rest of his words. He had offered to find her a position. A warm feeling of accomplishment and excitement washed over her. She was really going. It felt so right, she was sure she had made the right decision.

It took nearly three weeks to make all the arrangements, and the days flew by with alarming speed. The minister had been able to locate a family related to one of his church members that was moving to Philadelphia, and was in need of a governess for their two small boys. Charles and Mary Wall were determined to have an English governess for their children. If they were surprised by the color of Amanda's skin, they made no indication, but instead were more than pleased to learn of Amanda's mathematical prowess and knowledge of Latin.

The journey was an almost complete nightmare. If it weren't for the new friends she made in the boiler room, Amanda doubted she would have gotten off the boat in Philadelphia. The trip was twelve days of seasickness and humiliation. Unaware that it would make any difference, Amanda and the Wall family booked their passage on an American ship.

As the ship pulled away from the wharf in Liverpool, Amanda remained on the deck, the cold wind whipping her tears in frigid streaks from the corners of her eyes. She leaned forward across the ship's railing, waving vigorously to the rapidly diminishing figures left behind. The weather was unusually cold that day, and her two young charges, Matthew and Harold, began to complain in high-pitched, whining voices, causing some of the other passengers to glance down at them with disapproving frowns.

Reluctantly, Amanda waved one last time to the Carringtons, who by this time were little more than dark shapes without faces. She then turned, and with a heartfelt sigh, ushered the boys to their cabins below.

As they descended, they encountered a short, balding ship's steward. Amanda nodded her head and smiled, but when she opened her mouth to ask directions, the man briefly glared at her, then lifted his chin and averted his eyes. Amanda was so stunned at his outright rudeness that by the time she had the wits to close her gaping mouth, the little man had scurried around a corner. It was then that angry indignation surged through her blood, setting every fiber of her being burning with resentment. If it weren't for her responsibility to see the cranky children safely to their rooms, she would have followed that insolent gentleman, if you could call him that, and forced him to apologize.

In frustration, she looked down into the sleepy eyes of the youngest boy, Harold. With a small whimper, he tugged on a handful of her skirt. Scooping him up into her arms, she tried to erase any irritation from her voice.

"Don't worry. We will find our rooms ourselves. We don't need that unpleasant little man's assistance, anyway." Hoisting the little blond three-year-old higher on her hip, she stretched out her free hand to the older boy, Matthew.

"He was rather rude, weren't he, Miss Smith?" Matthew queried in a rather grown-up voice.

"Wasn't he, Miss Smith." Amanda corrected automatically,

then added, "But never you mind about him. Just come along." With that, she leaned to her left to capture his right hand. Allowing her to grasp it without a struggle, Matthew twisted around to stare down the dark corridor, as if expecting the man to reappear around the corner.

"Do you suppose all Americans are so rude? Or do you think he just don't like children?" This time, Amanda allowed the breach of grammar to slip and instead, tugged on the child's hand. She masked a smile with a very serious face, as she fought back the urge to laugh at the boy's interpretation of the encounter.

"I surely hope that most Americans are a good sight more polite. And if that gentleman doesn't like children, then more the pity for him." Having said this, Amanda permitted a genuine smile to curve her lips. Silently, she chided herself for jumping to conclusions. At the time she thought that perhaps Matthew had been right. Looking back now, the only good thing that had come from that encounter had been that at that moment, a special bond was formed with her normally wild and unruly charge. Matthew immediately turned to face her, his eyes wary and disbelieving. He stared intently at Amanda's face, as if searching for verification of her sentiments. As Amanda's smile remained solemn and unwavering, Matthew returned it with a slow smile of his own, revealing a large gap where two front teeth had been.

Amanda's heart went out to the serious but normally energetic boy. She was correct in her assumption that he received little in the way of confirmation that he was both likable and acceptable as a child. This new relationship surely made the daily lessons a little less trying. She also liked to believe that she raised the boy's self-esteem a couple of notches, because she now knew what it felt like to have your self-worth trampled on daily.

Oh, but how brief was the illusion that Matthew's perception of that steward's reaction was correct. Shortly after the boys' rest time, the afternoon tea gong sounded. With high spirits, Amanda cleaned the boys' and her face and hands from a small bowl and pitcher on the nightstand next to the bunk in her room. She chatted gaily at the prospects of meeting their fellow passengers.

The boys were awed at the fine dining room, with its gilded cornices and lavish display of sweets. At home they had always taken tea in the kitchen or the nursery, but never in the parlor or dining room with the adults. Amanda was able to seat them quickly, and had just seated herself next to them when a gruff baritone voice rang out.

"Get up. I am sure you are aware that *you* are not permitted to sit there." For a moment, Amanda was confused. She glanced around her, afraid that she had taken someone's chair.

"I'm sorry, I was not aware the seats were assigned," Amanda blurted out, a little put out by the impertinent tone of the voice. It was then, as she shifted to look into the speaker's eyes, that she recognized the disagreeable steward from that morning. Trying to hide her irritation by plastering a gracious smile on her lips, she studied his blotchy, weasellike face. His eyes were beady black slits filled with rage. Forcing herself to believe the man was objecting to the children, she tilted her head in a sympathetic, "I understand" way.

"I promise you, sir, the children will be on their best—"

The man's voice rose an octave, cutting her off with a harsh cracked shout. "The seats are not assigned, and it was not the children I was referring to." He lifted his chin, spread his legs shoulder width apart, and clasped his hands behind his back. His voice returned to its lower timbre as he continued to humiliate her. "You may stand behind the children's chairs or retire to the designated—'' This time, Amanda cut him off. Twisting her hand in the folds of her skirt, she fought to keep her voice even and controlled. She would not allow this crude little man to see that he had upset her.

"Sir, you are extremely rude, and I have no intention of leaving. Furthermore, I am not a servant to stand at attention behind these children. I am a highly educated and refined lady, and expect to be treated as such." With that, she scraped her chair across the polished wooden floor, scooting her knees fully beneath the table. She swallowed slowly, feeling her blood roil in anger, hurt, and humiliation. With her mouth in a firm, thin line, she stared straight ahead, dismissing the brazen bald man. Without looking, she knew that every eye in the room was upon her. In response, she lifted her chin a fraction of an inch higher. Turning slightly, she met Matthew's astonished, open-mouthed gaze. "Close your mouth, Matthew, it's not polite." Matthew's mouth closed shut with an audible snap.

The silence hung ponderously in the room. The tension was suffocating. Amanda felt the hostility of the stout man behind her burning through her shoulder blades, as if his eyes were hot pokers. Afraid that he might physically try to remove her, she wrapped her ankles around the legs of the chair.

Finding the silence unbearable, underlining the insult, Amanda shook out her white linen napkin with a flourish. Silently praying to God to give her strength, she recalled her aunt's words about courage and pride. With determination, she rattled and pulled her tea cup toward her, then carefully and loudly rearranged the silver. Gritting her teeth, she smiled pleasantly to all the frozen faces around her. Right then and there, she swore that she'd be damned before she let this sorry excuse for a man, or any other human being, intimidate her and force her to kowtow to them.

The following hour and a half were sheer hell. Everyone at the tables was served except for her. The one other black woman, who was standing behind her elderly white companion's chair, quickly excused herself after the outburst.

Amanda refused to give in, and instead smiled at the others, shrugging and acting as if it were a simple oversight. She then calmly reached over and took one of the boys' full cup of tea. Although the children had loaded it with sugar and rich cream, when she saw how quickly their cups were replaced, she found it hard to swallow the bitter brew. Biting the inside of her lip, she fought back the tears, counting the minutes until she could excuse herself with dignity and honor.

How she felt her spirits and courage plummet when she learned that the awful steward, Sam Jenkins, was only one of the many crew members who felt that as a *colored* woman, she was inferior. But it was Mr. Jenkins who personally saw to it that the rest of her trip was a nightmare. She even heard him mutter once, "I'll teach that uppity nigger to put on airs." She was ready to throw caution and propriety to the wind and slap him soundly, but at that moment, the same quiet mulatto from the dining room called out that her mistress was in need of help. The steward hurried across the deck to the stooped old white woman. The gentle young companion smiled briefly at Amanda and shook her head in a silent warning.

Reluctantly, Amanda let it go and hurried down to the privacy of her room. Leaning back against her locked door, she slid to the floor and felt her dreams and hopes come crashing down around her with her tears. In those moments of despair, she wondered what she had gotten herself into. She was terrified to think that she had traded a life of happiness and acceptance for one of heartless prejudice. As she buried her face in her knees, she wrapped her arms around them. For the first time that she could remember, she called on both God and her

African ancestors to guide and protect her in the many undoubtable battles ahead. That night, she closed her diary entry with the words, *"Please, dear God, let the men on this ship be a poor example of Americans."*

Three

For the next several days, Amanda chose to dine in her room. But always, without fail, she forced herself to return to the main dining room for tea. Day after day, she greeted Steward Jenkins with the utmost politeness. After a while, she even allowed herself to take a little delight in watching his pointed face turn a mottled red, his lips pinch in a twist of suppressed fury, and a thick, bulging artery throb in his forehead. She laughed now, as she recalled the little beads of sweat that dotted his bald pate. Oh, how she was tempted to pat that shiny dome. More than once, she lifted her hand toward that objective, pulling back just short of the desired destination with a deep, dramatic sigh. The man's eyes darted about him to the amused onlookers, seething with fury. Amanda would then hurriedly take her seat.

Day after day, she made sure that even if Sam Jenkins wasn't fully aware of her mischievous intent, there was no doubt left in his mind that she found him well beneath her. For some reason that Amanda was not able to grasp, Mr. Jenkins had not openly retaliated. Even now, she wondered if he were intimidated, not so much by her as by the apparent, although silent, support the other passengers gave her. There was also the ever-growing bevy of black crew members who found one excuse or another to enter the room at teatime. They all sneaked glimpses of her, their eyes shining with approval.

At first, Amanda resisted going to the designated dining room for those of *color*, just because the thought of the discrimination it implied made her blood boil. She was also afraid that it would undermine the stance she had taken. But by the fifth day of meals in a musty, cramped room, she grew tired of staring at four close walls and craved adult conversation.

Mr. and Mrs. Wall did not weather the motion of the ship very well and voluntarily kept to their rooms for the duration of the trip. The other English citizens, while not approving of the manner in which she was treated, did not raise a voice to object. They were either too intimidated by the white crew and the ship's bylaws, or they did not wish to appear too liberal. One young woman, in embarrassment, confessed one night in the darkened corridor outside her room that she found Amanda extremely admirable but hadn't said anything in her defense because—as she tried to so delicately put it—after all, many of the passengers, including herself and her sister, were going to make new homes in America. And surely Amanda understood that one must not *rock the boat*. Amanda turned without a word and closed her bedroom door in the woman's face. She had not understood then, and she did not understand now.

Later in the voyage, when the same timid woman tried to explain again, her overbearing, grossly overweight sister interrupted in a nasal voice, "You know, when in Rome, do as the Romans do." She then turned, flapping her ostentatious pink plumed fan toward her sister, her eyes fluttering coquettishly, and a smug smile creasing her painted lips.

Never at a loss for words, Amanda smiled back, saying, "I guess I must be patient and realize it takes a few ignorant sheep to follow the shepherd's lead." For a moment, the woman's brow wrinkled in confusion, the tip of her bulbous nose turning red with the twisted scrunch of her face. Then her eyes grew wide with the realization of the implication. Then, only two bright pink dots of rouge stood out on her ghastly white face. The woman sputtered for a moment, grabbed her younger sister's upper arm in a death grip, swirled in layers of pink frothy flounces, and marched away. Amanda was sure that had the boat been docked, the deck would have rattled with the weight of her outraged steps. Amanda bit her bottom lip now as she recalled the pressing urge to help that ample behind along with a swift kick from her shiny black boots. Again, she caught the eye of the lovely mulatto nurse companion. This time, the young woman shook her head, but also stifled a giggle with the back of her weathered, golden brown hand. Amanda hurried forward to talk with her, but suddenly the woman grew frightened and hurried off to wheel her charge and chair to some distant location.

That evening, a small note was slipped under her door. It was a personal invitation to join the other "distinguished people of color" in their own private dining room. Although the spelling of distinguished was atrocious, she was intrigued and pleased. After a few inquiries and a few smug answers, she found her way to a small boiler room behind the kitchen.

At first, she was shocked at the appalling contrast between the formal dining room and this small, shabby room. The room was uncomfortably hot, and the floor was dirty and stained with pitch. There was no furniture save a low table and a few raw benches. The other furniture was comprised of crates and packing boxes.

"Welcome to Jim Crow's dining hall," a large black man bellowed out to her as he rose from a vegetable crate turned on its end. The wooden slats creaked with relief as he straightened his long legs. The man towered well over six feet, and he seemed even larger with the low ceiling and the sheer brute size of his heavily muscled body. Even clothed, one could tell that there was not an ounce of excess fat on him. With a mischievous grin, the giant bowed low, one arm crossing his waist and the other hand pointing palm open, toward the seat he had just vacated. "Please take the seat of honor, most distinguished guest." Amanda smiled in return, feeling the heavy, oppressive loneliness of the last five days lift from her shoulders.

"Are you Jim Crow?" Amanda asked innocently. At first the man frowned, all mirth dissolving in his eyes. His thick black eyebrows drew together like threatening dark thunderclouds. Then his face relaxed, a sad smile spreading slowly over his generous lips. He studied Amanda for a few more seconds before he shook his close-cropped head.

"I shoulda known from yar funny accent, that y'all English. Honey, Jim Crow is a bad thing in the States. Don't never call nobody a Jim Crow. You see, back 'bout a dozen years or so ago, a white man named Tom Rice, well he kinda borrowed a poor nigger's song and dance routine. Dat Tom got hisself famous—rich, too—while'n that ol' nigger likely died starved in the alley. Oh, them whites thought Tom's show real funny and cute." Amanda flinched at the deep resentment and sarcasm punctuating that word *cute*.

"What happened? Was the poor black man Jim Crow?" she whispered, curious but afraid to stir more anger in this friendly giant. The tall man laughed a huge, reverberating guffaw.

"No'm, missy. See, when ol' Tom'd do his l'il show, he'd shout, 'wheel about, turn about, dance jest so; every time I wheel about, I shout, Jim Crow.' So'n like I says, the whites'd be laughin', but it hurt us Nigroes somethin' fierce. So now anytime us coloreds are treated bad and unjust like, we call it Jim Crow."

The other people in the room nodded. Amanda looked from one serious face to another, recognizing some as the ship crew who had sneaked in to watch her daily confrontations with the condesending ship steward. Others she hadn't seen before, but judging from their ragged and dirty clothing, they worked in parts of the ship she and the other passengers would never see or wish to see. One woman began to sniffle, saying into the back of her hand, "That's why we've got to stick together. That's why we are so proud of what you did to that swamp rat, Jenkins." Feeling slightly uncomfortable by this open display of emotion and praise from virtual strangers, Amanda wished to focus the attention elsewhere. She smiled and laughed.

"Now that you mention it, he does look rather like a rodent. Although I've never seen a swamp rat, I rather assume the description befits him most aptly." The large man who had originally greeted her grasped her hands and pulled her toward the seat he had offered earlier. The woman who had been sniffling rose to fill a plate of steaming stew for her.

Still holding one of her hands, her gentle but strong host smiled a beautiful smile, revealing startlingly white teeth.

"You sure do talk pretty. I'm Rollin, and that there is Melody, but I calls her Sweet Pea on account she can make a dish of peas, butter, bacon, and little onions that'd bring tears to your eyes."

The woman being discussed placed the plate of fragrant food in Amanda's hands, then good-naturedly swatted Rollin's behind. "That's about all you ever think about is food, ain't it?"

Rollin turned to run seductive, lazy eyes up Melody's ample figure. Licking his lower lip with a quick flick of his tongue, he responded, "Not likely."

The woman flushed darkly, her bronze skin turning a deep shade of coppery brown. "You ol' horn dog!" she shrieked in mock horror. Amanda blushed, but her shock and embarrassment was tinged with pleasure. She had never been around people who were so honest and open. It sent thrills of excitement and delicious danger through her blood.

Seeing her modest smile, Rollin said, "You sure is pretty, too." Amanda felt the blood creep higher into her cheeks. "Don't get me wrong, I's a happily married man, but I bet my big brother Jacob'd jest love to meet a brave little lady such as you."

Melody snorted in response, and Rollin turned toward her, a wicked grin on his face. Amanda's eyes went to the woman's ring finger and noted it was bare. Having noticed her gaze, Melody moved to Rollin's side, wrapping her plump arms about his hips.

"We are man and wife in the eyes of our Lord. You see, Rollin and I, we—" She choked a little, as if the words had been lodged in her throat. Amanda watched her Adam's apple bob up and down several times as Melody swallowed, took a deep breath, and continued. Amanda felt as if she were intruding on a private matter as the short woman locked her eyes with her husband's for support. "We were slaves. My mistress brought me North and set me free when she died, leavin' me about nine hundred dollars to make my way. Still, I had to work for four long, lonely years to save enough to . . . buy . . . my husband's freedom." Then she turned her bright, teary eyes to Amanda. "You see, in Louisiana, a man and a woman who are slaves can get married in a church, by a proper minister, but if the master or mistress don't say it's so, then it ain't."

Amanda watched Rollin's burly arm encircle his wife's shoulders, his massive hand squeezing the gingham arm beneath it. Melody smiled, then continued once again in a quavering voice. "Rollin was sold to a plantation in Georgia before our vows were but six months old. After Rollin left, my mistress's husband started getting ideas about him and me." At this point, Rollin's gentle face grew rigid with suppressed anger, his knuckles turning pale with the pressure he unwittingly placed on his wife's arm. Melody patted that hand, then left her fingers resting lightly on his. "My mistress weren't blind, and she was a God-fearing woman. She was good and brave and sought to save me. She knew she was dying and would soon be unable to protect me, so she took me to her sister's in Philadelphia."

For a brief moment, Melody paused, resting her upturned face on Rollin. Her eyes shone bright with love and pride as she turned and laid her hands on her husband's broad chest. He, in turn, reached down to stroke her round cheek, his eyes glistening with tears of adoration. Amanda's heart skipped a beat as she witnessed this raw, naked love. With a catch of her breath, she wondered if she would ever experience anything so wonderful. A small ripple of lonely vulnerability lapped at her inexperienced heart. Tears welled up in her eyes. She thought with sorrow and anger of how these beautiful people had suffered such tragedy. Yet still they could smile, laugh, love, and believe in a merciful God above. A single, silvery tear escaped from the corner of her eye and hung precariously on the thick shelf of her lower lashes. Feeling foolish, she swiped at it. The movement brought Melody's eyes to hers.

"Now, don't you fret." The woman fought hard to bring the earlier lightheartedness to her voice. "He's here now, never to be a slave again, bought and paid for, every inch of his glorious body." Her voice trembled with emotion. Amanda was not sure if it was from her pain and outrage at having to buy her husband or with the relief in knowing that the horror and constant threat of slavery, for them at least, was finished. Her handsome husband smiled down at his beloved wife, encouraging her attempt to put the past behind. In a stronger voice, she laughed and added, "Believe me, he weren't cheap. Near sixteen hundred dollars."

Without taking his eyes from Melody, Rollin spoke in a low

voice, husky with emotion, "And would you be want'n any less?"

The other people in the room—who had been relatively quiet, remembering their own stories of sorrow, or like Amanda, were stunned by the extent of the inhumanity of the southern states—now burst into uneasy, then boisterous laughter. The levity eased the oppressive tension that had been silently building. Once again the room regained its former warmth, but something inside of Amanda changed. She felt older, wiser, a little of her innocence gone, never to be retrieved.

Late that night, Amanda tossed restlessly in her narrow bunk. She hadn't been able to erase visions of the incredible cruelty her newfound friends had suffered. Fear and apprehension clutched her stomach. Again she wondered at the wisdom of leaving her sheltered life in London. She had experienced prejudice a few times in her young life in England, but it was nothing like the snubs she received on the ship or the inconceivable atrocities endured by the southern slave.

Now, as she stood on the dock, facing the bustling city of Philadelphia, she wondered how she would be treated there. Her spirits were low as she struggled to throw off her apprehensions.

Recalling how she had drawn strength and solace from looking at her crude sketch of her hero, Frederick Douglass, she fumbled for the dog-eared picture now. As she withdrew the small leather-bound Bible from her reticule, the pages practically fell open to the beginning of Exodus. Amanda had stuck the sketch there because she had come to regard Mr. Douglass as a Moses of sorts. Although his had been anything short of a spectacular childhood, he had been born a slave and had, like the great man of the Old Testament, become a great orator, a voice for his people, a man who might one day lead them from their oppression into a new land, a land of freedom.

As she studied the portrait, she smiled with pride at the sketch she had made from a photograph. She had been told many times that she was extremely talented, and a few of the Carringtons' friends had even offered to pay her for a portrait. She usually insisted that they sit for several short sessions before she would attempt a finished watercolor or ink drawing. But, unfortunately, she had never had the good fortune to meet Mr. Douglass in person. She sighed as she drew the picture closer. She sincerely doubted that even if she someday had the opportunity to meet him, he would sit for her to draw his picture.

"What you look'n at, Miss Manda?" a deep voice asked. She turned to smile with obvious pleasure into the handsome face of Rollin.

"To my friends, it's just Amanda, please." Rollin smiled a wide, toothy smile, nodding his head, mumbling something about his brother Jacob. Amanda couldn't help but smile more broadly at his engaging smile. "It's a sort of hero of mine. An American, Frederick Douglass. Surely you've heard of him?" Amanda queried.

The big man shifted from one foot to the other, for all the size of him looking like a schoolboy who had forgotten to study his lessons. "Can't quite say I has."

Without thinking, Amanda blurted out, "But he's been in all the papers, and he has written so much." Her voice trailed off as she saw her new friend's shoulders slump dejectedly. "Oh, I'm sorry. I'm so terribly sorry. I didn't mean to imply—" Rollin silenced her with a carefree wave of his hand.

"Its okay, miss, I mean, Amanda. You see, down South, a slave could get killed for trying to learns how to read. Or at least whupped purty good."

Amanda shuddered at the mental image that rose before her. Tears that had threatened all morning welled in her eyes. Instantly chagrined, Rollin took her hand in one of his. "Now, don't you go gettin' all soppy over me, mi—Amanda.'' Suddenly his eyes took on a mischievous twinkle. "I did learn to spell my name, though. The whole thing. Joshua Washington Coffey. You won't see this man sign'n no X for his name.'' His chest swelled with pride.

Amanda squeezed his hand in pleasure at the evident pride the man had in accomplishing this monumental achievement. She was afraid to ask what horrors he had possibly faced to master a task that she had, until now, taken for granted. As she smiled back at him, she struggled to submerge any anger at the sheer injustice and inequality of the whole thing. Instead, she asked, "Joshua? Where did Rollin come from, then?"

Melody suddenly appeared at his elbow. "Don't listen to any nonsense he may tell you about it being because Joshua in the Bible kept the chosen people *rollin'* into the promised land after Moses died. Because the truth of the matter is that before he met me, his eyes was *rollin'* over everything in a skirt, and then talkin sweet, and *rollin'* on!" Rollin laughed his loud, guffawing laugh and shrugged his huge shoulders in mock innocence.

Now Amanda laughed. Melody, who could no longer keep a straight face, broke into a silvery cascade of giggles. Suddenly, Amanda was overwhelmed with emotion, amazed at how close she had become with these people in one short week. On an impulse, she wrapped her arms around Melody and hugged her, tears streaming unchecked down her cheeks.

Melody immediately returned the embrace, patting her back in a wholly maternal fashion. "Now, now, you'll be all right. You're a good, strong woman. You have given us a lot of joy these past few days. Why, your stories of our native land, Africa, will be something we can pass on to our children. Even though we weren't from your parts, many of us didn't get a chance to grow up with our parents, or sit at our grandparents' knees to hear our heritage. So we'll just borrow yours.'' At these words, Amanda's tears started up anew.

Suddenly, Rollin slapped his thigh with a resounding crack. Amanda turned to him with teary eyes. "Why don't you come with us?" When this statement didn't seem to clear up the confusion in Amanda's eyes, Rollin continued. "We're going to New York on a . . . well, a sort of a holiday. The ship is being dry-docked for winter repairs, so we'll be goin' to the city to find work. Lots of folks are planning to head to Saint Louie in the spring to head out West. As a matter of fact, my brother Jacob and his—" A stern look and shake of Melody's head made him stop mid-sentence. "Oh Sweet Pea, she's a good woman. You said so yourself. Jacob could use a good woman for Penny on the way out West."

If Amanda had noticed the reluctance in Melody during this exchange, she ignored it as the offer Rollin was extending became clear.

"Oh, do you think your brother would take me with him? Do you know how far west he intends to go? Do you think his wife, Penny, would mind? I won't be any trouble."

"Gads, but I love that accent." Rollin laughed, ignoring the menacing glare his wife was giving him. "Penny ain't his wife. She's the cutest l'il five-year-old you's ever laid eyes on. Jacob's a little on the surly side, but then not every'n can be as friendly as me. As for the rest of those questions, we'll just have to go and see the man."

At the mention of a five-year-old, Amanda recalled her commitment to the Walls. She had just started to make some headway with Matthew. Her face fell as she relayed her promise to tutor the boys for a year before she headed west.

"Well," said Melody with a sigh of relief, "if you change your mind, come find us. Now, Rollin, let's go before someone starts asking questions." Amanda gave the woman a quizzical look, but the only response Melody gave was a smile before she toted her reluctant husband behind her.

Looking down, Amanda noticed she still held the drawing of Frederick Douglass in her hand. For the hundredth time, she studied his heavily lined face, the deep sorrow and burning passion in his dark eyes. As she recalled Rollin's words, she gained a whole new perception of this man's character. She hadn't fully realized the odds Mr. Douglass had overcome to become the eloquent speaker and writer he was today. What drove a man like that? Slipping the picture back into its place among the timeless tales of the hardships of the slaves of Egypt, she hugged the Bible to her chest.

"God bless you, Rollin and Melody. May the rest of your days be blessed, and may you find your promised land," she whispered. As she looked around at the crowded streets, so similar yet so different from London, she knew that she still had a long way to go to find hers.

"Is everything all right, Miss Smith?" a pale, wan Mrs. Wall inquired. Although her eyes reflected her relief in being able to finally disembark from the ship, her skin still had a slightly greenish pallor. Wistfully, Amanda drew her eyes away from the new friends she had so quickly made and now seemed to be as rapidly losing, possibly to never see again.

"Just fine, Mrs. Wall. But you look like you should be sitting down." The woman brushed her suggestion away with a wave of a limp hand. "I'll be just fine now that I have my feet on solid ground. *J'aime la terre, n'est-ce pas?*"

Amanda smiled, responding, "Yes, I love the land, too, but I am even more anxious to see the wild western lands of this country." A frown creased Mrs. Wall's pale brow. Amanda added quickly, "Don't be alarmed. I have every intention of fulfilling my promise to you and your family." The older woman stepped closer, the confined, musty smell of her ship cabin still clinging to her clothes.

"Miss Smith, if you would prefer to take your leave now,

it is perfectly understandable—well, if not understandable, at least acceptable. Mr. Wall and myself have heard of the terrible injustice you had to bear on the journey here. Had we known, perhaps we could have said something to the captain. But rest assured, we still intend to have a word with him. Anyway, the point is, we feel we have caused you enough trouble and don't wish to impose any more hardships on you. Although, why a woman of your education and obvious culture would voluntarily choose to go traipsing off into the unknown amongst all those terrifying Indians is beyond me.''

Amanda just smiled, knowing she could never be able to explain the need to see, to be a part of a new frontier, to maybe discover a little of her primitive past, to understand the wide open spaces of her ancestors, their love of the land. How did one explain that to a woman like Mrs. Wall?

"Oh dear, I do so go on. But what I mean is, you're young. You must do what you must do. I'm sure we could find a suitable governess here, although I'm not sure we could find one with your excellent qualifications and ability to deal with our *energetic* boys. But if you are sure you really want to go out there, I'm sure we'll manage, and you may leave with our dearest prayers and blessings.''

For a few moments, Amanda looked hard into her employer's eyes. The woman smiled and nodded, her head confirming that she meant what she said. Needing no more encouragement, Amanda raised her eyes to scan the crowd. Thank God for Rollin's height. She saw the top of his head moving down one of the alleyways leading from the pier. Grasping Mrs. Wall's hand, she squeezed it once, then lifted her skirts and took off running after the rapidly retreating figures of the Coffeys.

"Rollin! Melody!" Amanda gasped, as she twisted sideways to avoid a boy with a pushcart carrying fish. Afraid that they hadn't heard her, Amanda called once again, her voice cracking from the exertion as she attempted to catch up with them. This last cry reached the big man's ears. He whirled about, a look of concern and dismay on his broad face.

"What in tarnation?" he began before Melody turned and cried, "It's you!" All three stopped short in their tracks. The look of fear and distress on Melody's face sent a shiver of trepidation down Amanda's spine. She fumbled for words of explanation.

"You said—I mean, the Walls said—I guess what I'm trying to say is, does the offer still stand? The Walls have allowed me to go."

Rollin rushed forward, placing his large, callused hands on her shoulders before he smiled. "For sure it does."

Smiling with a hopeful curve of her lips, she gazed past him to meet the eyes of his wife. "Melody?" The woman's shoulders slumped in resignation as she nodded her head. Still not convinced, Amanda began, "If there is a problem, I guess I could go ask the Walls for my pos—" She got no further when Rollin cut her off.

"Of course not." Then he dropped his voice to a conspiratorial whisper. "Nothin' against you, Amanda. It's jes' that Melody is a little nervous 'bout too many people know'n 'bout Jacob an' Penny. See, Jacob an' his girl is on the run. We're to meet 'em tonight at the Minister Clay's house. He done help them this far. Melody and I gonna take Penny by train to New York, and Jacob's gonna continue on the underground." Amanda looked at Melody, who nodded in confirmation. Slowly, as if trying to fit the pieces together, she turned to Rollin.

"But I thought Negroes were free in the North."

Rollin shook his head sadly. "Slavery is agin' the law up here, but that only mean a person can't buy and keep a slave. See, lots of southerners, they come up here on vacation and try an' capture their runaways. The state kinda jes' looks the other way. But in New York, folks there feel much stronger 'bout it. And a slave's a lot safer.''

Melody interrupted now. ''But even there, an escaped slave's not entirely safe. There are slave hunters everywhere. They even place huge rewards on the return of a runaway. That's why Jacob's heading out West.'' Her voice dropped almost to a whisper when she added, ''That's why I had to have my Rollin's papers. I just couldn't go on day to day, afraid that someone might recognize him. Might capture him in the night. That I might wake up one morning to find him gone.'' Her eyes filled with tears, her chest heaving sporadically as she fought to suppress the memories and pain. ''I went through it once, and I'd die if I had to do it again.'' Amanda pulled free from Rollin's grasp and threw her arms around Melody again.

''You can trust me. I might even be able to help. Let me take Penny. No one would suspect an English black woman.'' Melody and Rollin looked at each other, their eyes speaking the language of two souls connected. They grinned, and Rollin laughed.

''Jacob's sure gonna find our Miss Amanda a true wonder, and if he don't, my mamma bore a bigger fool than I ever thought.'' Melody only shook her head.

Rollin then returned with Amanda to gather her trunks, grumbling good-naturedly about the English love for clothes. Amanda only laughed, intrigued now about his older brother and his daughter. She asked him to tell her all about them. He was only too happy to oblige.

Four

"Who the hell is she?" the disheveled black man said as he jabbed a finger at the air between himself and Amanda. Amanda had been totally unprepared for the sight that was before her. Rollin had painted a glowing picture of his older brother Jacob, but this man bore little if any resemblance to the proud, handsome man he had described. His face was streaked with dust and sweat, and he stank to the high heavens.

Completely ignoring his rude tone, Rollin introduced Amanda as if he were introducing royalty. "Jacob, this here is Miss Amanda Smith from London." He then turned to Amanda. "This here is my big brother Jacob." He left the word dangling, as if the name in itself were enough to inspire the awe he obviously felt.

Totally missing the great attraction in this man, Amanda turned to Melody for help. The woman merely smiled an "I tried to tell you" smile before asking, "Where's my niece? I want to see the child. Is she all right?"

Suddenly, the grubby man transformed before her eyes. His face lit up, his black eyes iridescent and entrancing. He smiled then, his teeth startlingly white.

"The little minx is sleep'n. She's been quite the champion. She didn't complain once the whole trip. When we rousted her out of her dreams night after night, she rubbed her sleepy eyes and smiled. Can you believe it, she smiled every damn time. She would have done Becca proud."

The way he said the name Becca, Amanda guessed she had been, or was, his wife somewhere. A small twinge of envy tugged at her heart. There was a lot about this man Jacob that was like his brother. For one, they were obviously devoted husbands. Unable to stop her curiosity, Amanda ventured to ask if Becca was coming, too.

As soon as the words were out, she instantly regretted them. The room fell deathly silent, and she could feel every pair of eyes on her.

In a deep, gruff voice devoid of emotion, Jacob spoke. "She's dead. Have you any more questions, your ladyship?" The bitterness in the last word was unmistakable, and Amanda wondered what she had done to merit such resentment. She lowered her eyes, feeling extremely embarrassed, and silently shook her head, when a small voice piped from the top of the stairs.

"Where's the lady? Is she gonna take us back?" Instantly Jacob was on his feet, taking the stairs two at a time, his six-foot frame engulfing the small girl he swept into his arms.

"No, baby, no one's going to take us back. No one's ever gonna hurt us again." The child smiled adoringly up into her father's eyes, and then rested her cheek against his broad chest. As he turned to bring her toward the chair he'd been sitting on, Amanda noticed the back of his dirty gray shirt was tattered and stained with blood. She gasped, then hastily clapped her hands over her mouth. Jacob turned to her, his eyes challenging her to say something.

"Oo, what a pretty lady. Is she the ship lady?" the child asked. For a moment, Jacob's forehead furrowed, his thick black brows becoming a deep V. Then his face lightened, and he laughed.

"Ladyship, honey. Although she did come on a ship with

Aunt Melody and Uncle Rollin.'' The small child slipped from his embrace and went over to feel Amanda's dark blue satin skirt. With no reservations at all, the girl dropped to her knees and scooted under the hem. Before Amanda could react, the child's head popped out.

"She's got on three petticoats, and one of em feels like real silk."

"Penny, get out of there this instant," Jacob growled, frustrated because he dared not retrieve her himself.

"That's all right. She didn't mean any harm," Amanda said, as she helped Penny to her feet. "I'm sure we are going to get along just fine. I love children, especially little girls." Amanda crouched on her heels, her eyes almost level with the child's bright, inquisitive ones. "I'm sure by the time we get to the end of the trail west, we will be the best of friends." Penny nodded vigorously, reaching out a small hand to stroke the fine lace collar around the snug neckline of Amanda's bodice.

Jacob nearly bolted out of his chair, startling Penny so she fell into Amanda. Amanda, in her precarious position, toppled over, pulling Penny into voluminous layers of her skirt and petticoats.

"Who says she's going west with me?" Jacob's eyes scanned the room angrily, finally settling on his younger brother. Rollin grinned sheepishly. Jacob growled and swung his livid glare back to Amanda, who was still sprawled out on the floor.

Between clenched teeth, he said in a very even voice that more than hinted at the restrained anger he struggled to leash, "I'm sorry, miss, but I can't be responsible for another liability. I've got a child to think of."

Cursing her petticoats, Amanda tried to rise with as much dignity as she could muster. "I fail to see how I could be a liability, sir. I assure you, I fully intend to pay for my passage."

Jacob slapped his forehead with the palm of his hand, as he laughed a mirthless sound. "For Christ's sake, woman, this is not some fancy carriage taking you on an afternoon clip through the park. We're talkin' some several thousand mile trek through some damn tough territory. I'll not be responsible for some—parcel of petticoats."

That did it! Amanda could feel her blood begin to boil. Who did this man think he was to talk to her like she was some errant child or idiot? "I am well aware of the risks, sir, and no one is responsible for my well-being but myself. From your brother's glowing recommendations and description of your character, I thought that perhaps we would be well-suited traveling partners. But now I see his gracious description extends only to your lovely daughter. I'm sorry to have troubled you. Good day, sir, and Godspeed." With that, she turned on her heel to collect her reticule and bonnet and headed to the door.

Five

Amanda, flushed with indignation, cooled quickly as she slammed the Clays' front door behind her, and the frigid night air slapped icy fingers across her face. Realizing immediately that her cloak, trunks, and virtually everything else she owned was in the house behind her, she miserably regretted her hasty exit. Chastising herself for her inclination toward the dramatic, she carefully considered her options. She could humbly return, begging apologies from her host, or she could send for her things later, and go. Go where?

Hugging her shivering arms to her chest, Amanda realized with a sickening feeling close to despair that she was a stranger in a new country, and although she spoke the language, she had found out all too unpleasantly that she was a black woman in a time and place where neither was regarded too highly. She fought back hot, angry tears as she felt her hopes of an exciting new life shatter around her.

Swallowing hard, she forced herself to be practical. Just as she was beginning to acknowledge that no matter the cost to her pride, she would have to be sensible and return to apologize in front of that despicable man, she was saved the humiliation by the onslaught of light and warmth spilling from the opening of the front door.

"Won't you please come back in?" the minister's wife

pleaded, as she glanced furtively up and down the dark empty street. When her eyes returned to Amanda's face, Amanda saw the fear and anxiety dwelling there. Nodding slightly, Amanda gratefully stepped past her into the blessed warmth of the small townhouse.

Madeline Clay's face instantly relaxed when she realized she wasn't going to have to make a scene in public, begging Amanda to return.

"Thank you," Mrs. Clay said softly, with deep sincerity. Amanda turned wide, questioning eyes toward the elder woman. Why was this woman thanking her when she, Amanda, should be the one begging forgiveness for her inexcusably rude behavior? Just as Amanda would have spoken, the minister's wife placed a silencing hand on her sleeve. "There are informers everywhere. Already there has been a reward posted for the return of Jacob and Penny. Penny is wanted alive and healthy, but Jacob—well, there are many who wouldn't think twice about turning them in and exposing my husband's position in harboring fugitive slaves."

Amanda stared incredulously at Mrs. Clay. It was a nightmare come to life. True, most of the information about slavery that she had been able to obtain from Mr. Carrington had been censored, but in her naïveté she had assumed she could fill in the gaps. Nothing in her innocent imagination had prepared her for the horrors that were slowly, dreadfully unfurling before her. Suddenly, she began to shake uncontrollably.

"Please come closer to the fire, dear. You are chilled." Mrs. Clay wrapped a solicitous arm around Amanda's waist and steered her toward the others. When Amanda would have drawn back, the older woman tightened her hold and whispered in a low, conspiratorial tone, "You will be of no help to us—or Penny—if you get ill."

As these few words sank in, Amanda allowed herself to be docilely led toward the hearth. She was unaware of the slight shake of Melody's head and the raised eyebrows and furrowed brow the minister cast at his wife. Jacob expressed his opinion less subtly. Leaning back in his chair with a loud grunt, Jacob folded his arms across his dirty, sweat-stained shirt. He opened his mouth to say something, when his tender back touched the chair rails behind him. With a loud curse he jumped from his chair, glowering angrily at Amanda.

Amanda felt miserably out of place and stood hopelessly unsure in the middle of the room, when Rollin spoke.

"Lordy Miss 'Manda you done give us a scare." Placing his large calloused hands on his wife's shoulders, he propelled her forward to Amanda. After giving her husband a disgusted backward glance, Melody moved to push a straight-backed chair close to the fire. Turning to Amanda, she motioned for her to sit.

"Don't never say as that I didn't warn ya. Jacob's got the manners of those beasts he tends."

Lifting her chin a fraction of an inch higher, Amanda turned her gaze to the silently brooding man she had tangled with earlier. Jacob's only response was a loud, angry snort. "See, he sounds jes' like one of those ponies, too," Melody continued, as she threw off the arm Rollin tried to lay across her shoulder.

Amanda could feel the heavy tension hanging in the sparse but elegantly decorated room. Suddenly, it all seemed so ludicrous. Here, these people around her were facing a matter of life or death, or more likely a fate worse than death, and she was making a fuss over a squabble with an obviously distressed man's rudeness. Amanda's lips spread into a warm, amused smile, her spirits rising as her naturally optimistic nature returned.

"Melody, I don't need any apology from Mr. Jacob Coffey. I just want to know how I can help." Turning slightly, she smiled briefly at Jacob. For a split second, she saw the anger on his face lessen. Amanda felt a thrill of satisfaction that her smile had not lost its charm and could touch even this bitter man. As if discerning her thoughts, Jacob's scowl deepened, and a muscle began methodically twitching beneath his beard. Taking a single threatening step forward, he glared at her.

"Good, Miss Smith, because you ain't getting one. And my name ain't Coffey." With that, Jacob strode to the bottom of the staircase in the entrance hall. Without turning around, Jacob uttered a sharp *"Good night"* and told Penny to follow him. He had nearly disappeared into the dark stairwell, when Penny moved quickly to curtsy before Amanda, and then scurry after her father. The group watched as Jacob paused and caught the child up in his arms. Her flannel nightgown rode up her calves as he hoisted her tiny legs around his waist. As father and daughter headed up the stairs, Penny peeped her head over Jacob's shoulder.

"Good night, beautiful ship lady. Please be here tomorrow." Penny's voice carried over the gathering in a loud stage whisper. Jacob paused momentarily. Turning to look at his daughter's profile, then shaking his head, he continued up the stairs.

Amanda stared after them in shocked disbelief. Seated where she was, she had a full view of Jacob's mangled back and the crimson gashes on little Penny's calves. The room suddenly seemed too warm. She tried to draw in a deep breath of air, but her corset refused more than a shallow gasp. She shivered involuntarily, and a high-pitched ringing began in her ears. Amanda closed her eyes, clutching her reticule tightly in her hands. She must not faint. She must fight for composure. Her mind whirled about her in confusion. Her attempts to placate Jacob had failed. If possible, his initial anger toward her had seemed to increase. What had she done? What had instilled in him such resentment toward her? As she tried to grasp something, anything to explain this, she recalled the last remark about his surname not being Coffey. Again she was confused. He was Jacob's brother, wasn't he? Surely a slave owner couldn't take away a man's last name! Amanda wrestled with these questions, but still the ringing in her ears continued. Now the insistent noise seemed to turn to screaming. Her imagination conjured up before her eyes the horrible beast or thing that had so brutally torn at father and child.

From a distance, Mrs. Clay's soft voice came to her. "Come on, dear. Let me take your bonnet and reticule. Perhaps I could get you a nice cup of tea." Amanda turned wide eyes of astonishment to her hostess. Hadn't that woman seen the tattered skin and cloth? How could she think of serving tea? Amanda turned her eyes to the others in the room. The portly white-haired minister's blue eyes were sympathetic. Rollin's and Melody's dark eyes carried the same horror and disgust as hers, but were touched with a sad acceptance or understanding. Turning back to Mrs. Clay, she grasped the older woman's hands. The woman sighed deeply. "Oh dear, there is so much to explain." Her gaze strayed to her husband, her kind gray eyes misty and sad. With a small shake of her head, the minister's wife turned her eyes back to Amanda, the haze all but gone, and in its place was a flicker of hope. "Perhaps, if you are willing, you could be an answer to a prayer. You will help, won't you?" With fierce determination Amanda rose, grasping the little woman's hands even tighter.

"Oh, yes, Mrs. Clay. No one has the right to hurt that poor little girl." Unable to stop them, bright tears pooled along the rim of her eyes. "She's only a child, a baby. I can't bear . . . What can I do?" The last words came out in a strangled whisper. Amanda had always had a soft spot for children, and she could barely stand to recall the sight of Penny's small plump legs gashed and torn.

"First, you can call me Madeline. May I call you Amanda?" Mrs. Clay responded. Amanda nodded vigorously, seating herself carefully back on the edge of the chair she had just vacated.

"Madeline, please tell me, what happened to Mr., er, Jacob's back, and to Penny's legs? Why isn't his name Coffey? And . . . why does he, he . . . hate me so much?" These last words had been hard to offer. Amanda had almost choked on them. She had been such a pet and darling of her aunt, the Carringtons, their close circle of friends. Now, in a few short weeks, she had brutally learned how sheltered she had been. Suddenly, the frightening reality of the decision she had made to come to America dawned on her. A menacing voice seemed to whisper, *"Go back home; you made a mistake."*

As if seeing her shrinking resolve, the minister stepped forward, his small, beefy hands resting lightly on the back of her chair. Twisting sideways, Amanda looked up expectantly at him.

The stout man cleared his throat and twisted the ends of his white bristly mustache. "I haven't known Jacob long, and I can't tell you much about his past." Here he paused, and moved over to where Rollin and Melody stood. "Perhaps Mr. and Mrs. Coffey could enlighten you on those subjects." Reaching out to Rollin, the minister clasped one of the large black man's hands in both of his small white ones. His voice became gentle, compassionate. "As for the wounds you witness, I will tell you of them if you really wish to hear." It was clear that the offered explanation was not so much for Amanda as for Rollin.

Melody clutched her husband's wide upper arm, as his shoulders slumped, and his dark, pained eyes reached out to Amanda. "Jacob don't hate nobody, Miss 'Manda. Hez jes' hurtin' real bad." The sorrow in the big man's voice was soft and poignant. It was obvious that no matter what face Jacob had shown to her, Rollin loved his brother deeply. Laying his free hand on Melody's supporting hands, Rollin looked deeply into the short man's eyes. "Tell me." After a long moment of silence, Rollin turned his head to look up the now empty staircase. "What dey do to him dis time?"

Without another word or movement, Amanda could feel the reserved sorrow and pain in her new friend shift and build, an angry temperance brewing beneath the surface. She knew Melody felt it, too, and her fingers pressed deeper into the fabric beneath her hand, causing deep creases in the sleeve of Rollin's shirt. Minister Clay, too, tightened his hold on the hand he held. They both braced themselves, as if preparing for a storm.

"Rollin? Rollin?" The minister demanded gently, as he tugged at Rollin's hand. "Jacob is a hundred percent better this evening than he was three days ago when he came here. We haven't removed his shirt yet because the cloth is embedded in the wounds. It would be too painful." These words did not seem to reach the large man. His eyes still searched restlessly in the dark stairwell for something. Defeated, the minister let go of Rollin's hand with a sigh. Slowly, he moved to a large wing back chair across from Amanda. Suddenly it seemed his body had grown old and tired. He eased himself into the chair, which all but swallowed him. His voice was ragged and worn. "Are you sure you want me to continue?" Amanda wasn't sure at all, but she held her peace and looked over at Jacob's brother. Rollin only nodded, his eyes still locked on a distant point. Because of the angle of the minister's chair, Amanda knew he could not see Rollin. After a moment's hesitation, she turned her attention to the minister and bobbed her head slightly. Lacing his short, pudgy fingers together, Mr. Clay rested them over the bulge of his stomach and began.

"It's a wonder he even made it at all. Someone in heaven is surely looking over him." Turning his bright blue eyes on Amanda, he directed his next statement to her. "You see,

Penny's master is a cruel, heartless man. He refused all offers from Jacob to purchase Penny's freedom. He said Jacob should pay for his loss of the child's mother, and if he didn't, he'd make Penny pay. So Jacob kidnapped her. When Penny's master, Rodney Whitingworth, discovered her missing, he set the hounds on them."

From somewhere deep within Rollin came a low moan and a croaking, strangled whisper. "No. No. Not dem dogs from hell." The strange, intangible strength emanating from Rollin crumbled as thick tears edged from the corners of his eyes. With his head bowed, he allowed Melody to lead him to a small settee facing the fire.

Leaning forward in his chair, the minister's voice became stronger, directed at Rollin. "Jacob's a strong man. He made it. He's alive. When the dogs came at him, he lifted Penny to his shoulders, out of harm's way. The beasts were only able to reach her legs. The wounds are only superficial; the tendons are all right. The damage isn't permanent." Rollin lifted his eyes, a look of thanks deep in their dark depths. Mr. Clay looked away, returning his gaze to Amanda. "Jacob didn't fare so well. He barely made it. When he arrived, we didn't think he would live. Some of it the slaves that had helped Jacob get on the property threw some kind of hot spice and pepper bombs at the dogs, blinding them temporarily. Some of it got into Jacob's open wounds." Grimacing at the pain this unlikely balm would have caused, the minister continued.

"Somehow, Jacob made it to the swamps. The hounds lost his scent. Jacob didn't remember much after this point, only sloshing around in the muck and slime. He was bitten several times by snakes. Thank the good Lord, none of them were lethal. Penny says she only remembers the alligators and screaming. She says it was then that the Queen of the Swamp took them to her house. She couldn't tell how long they stayed there. She said the kind queen told her not to worry, and made her wait outside while she dug the snake poison out of Jacob's leg. The next information we have is that Jacob and Penny arrived at one of the underground stations. Jacob's legs had been treated and wrapped in damp moss." His eyes met with Melody's. "We heard stories of this so called Queen of the Swamp before, but no one has ever been able to substantiate the rumors. Believe me, many have tried, especially those masters left empty-handed. But no matter, just thank the gracious Lord that whoever she is, she was there."

From somewhere upstairs, a man's deep cry of pain echoed through the dark hallway, followed by a muffled sob. The group below looked up the empty stairwell. Rollin moved a step in that direction; the minister shook his head.

"Leave him. He wanted only Cookie to tend his wounds." The silence hung threateningly, the group tensely anticipating the next anguished cries. Only the gentle sobbing persisted. The minister continued, as if he'd been uninterrupted.

"Fortunately for Jacob, the rest of the journey was pretty uneventful. But now it seems the hunt for him has heated up again, here in Philadelphia. After searching his property and the surrounding areas thoroughly, our sources say Whitingworth has become obsessed with hunting Jacob down. He has put a thousand dollar reward on his head—dead or alive." Another low, angry growl escaped Rollin's lips, causing Amanda to turn to the livid man.

"Jacob ain't no slave. He be a free man jes' like hez daddy. He done earned his freedom." Rollin rose to his feet. "Whitin'worth can't put no price on hez head!" Melody reached up to clutch her husband's massive arms, the muscles bunching and straining against the threadbare fabric of his sleeve. He brushed her hands aside. Melody's face was ashen with fear. She turned horrified eyes to the minister, imploring him to deny what he had said.

"They can't capture a free man." Melody's words were a

mere whisper of heartsick denial. Amanda knew, as if Melody had uttered the words herself, that if Whitingworth could hunt down Jacob, a free man, then what would prevent someone from coming after Rollin or herself. Mr. Clay turned sympathetic eyes to Melody.

"Yes, they can, dear. Whitingworth obtained a warrant for Jacob's arrest. He convinced the judge that Jacob had stolen his property and caused Penny's mother's death." Amanda gasped. Melody looked quickly at her, then back to the minister.

"But the other slaves, they know. They saw . . ."

The minister leaned forward to pat Melody's hand. "A slave may not testify for or against his master in slave states. His word just does not exist."

While Amanda stared at the minister with her mouth agape, finding it hard to believe what he had just said, Rollin's voice, deep with emotion, came slowly, trancelike, across the silence. "Poor Becca. Won't dat bastard ever let her soul rest?" Sinking down on the small settee, he lowered his face into his large, work-worn hands. His huge shoulders shook with silent sobs. Melody went to comfort him.

Amanda's eyes flickered wildly from one face to the other, looking for an explanation. The minister's face was a mirrored reflection of her own questions. Rollin's face remained buried. Both Mr. Clay's and Amanda's gazes rested on Melody. Melody shifted uncomfortably, and with a quick glance at Rollin, decided she would have to be the one to continue. Jostling her shoulders back and forth, she looked like a fighter preparing to face an intimidating opponent. Locking her fingers together, she studied them as they lay in her lap. Her audience waited in complete silence, only the gentle crackling and popping of the fire filling the room. Looking up, she sighed deeply.

"It ain't my story to tell." When no one responded, Melody fixed her eyes on a distant point above the mantel. "Rebecca and Jacob were childhood sweethearts. My husband says it just kinda happened, what with his name bein' Jacob and hers bein' Rebecca, an' the Bible an' all.'' Her hand fluttered loosely as if to help the point she was trying to make. "I don' know. I didn' know them then, but Rollin says they was together whenever time and circumstances allowed.'' Melody then laughed a sweet, wistful sound. "Rollin says Jacob would bring her wildflowers, and weave dandelions and black-eyed Susans in her hair, saying she was his queen.''

Slowly, Melody's eyes grew dark, clouding over with the memories of the past. "Then, jes' like always, someone's gotta go an' ruin it all. The missus, she wanted Jacob gone. Says he's the devil's spawn. The young master, he took him, tricked his folks, and bought Jacob. I don' know why they wouldn't let their son buy him, but his parents were right angry, and told their son not to come back no more. I met Missus Whitingworth one time, and she weren't quite right after that.'' Melody tapped her head for emphasis. "Rollin says the young master was good to Jacob, let him tend his prize horses. He says Jacob always had a way with animals and children. I ain't seen it, but if Rollin says it so, then it is.''

She turned to caress her husband's cheek. For a while she gazed with adoration at Rollin's hidden profile, as if she still couldn't believe he was there beside her. Amanda felt something hard and painful lodge in her throat. She wondered if her aunt had felt that way about her husband, or when in private if the Carringtons showed such emotion. She found it hard to believe. This public display of emotion was not a part of her strict Victorian world, but it filled her with a deep longing. She wanted to reach out and seize this feeling of protectiveness, this surge of emotion. No doubt it was painful, but it was genuine. It showed a bond of love that could withstand all. Melody then turned to her. Amanda smiled, tears welling up, as Melody's eyes locked with hers.

"Jacob was only thirteen. He swore to Rebecca he'd come back to her when he could, and that he'd marry her when he was a free man. Rollin said no one believed him, no one but his ma, Rollin, and Rebecca." One of Rollin's hands dropped from his face to wrap around the hand Melody had rested on his knee. Slowly, he turned her palm upward, lacing his fingers with hers. Now, as she spoke, she watched the pale silvery patches around Rollin's knuckles as he squeezed her hand over and over again.

"Jacob's new master was a good man. Unlike his father, he didn' believe blacks were inferior, born to be slaves. Because his father wouldn't sell Jacob or Jacob's mother to him, he had a friend obtain permission to buy Jacob from his ol' man. He allowed Jacob to work for others, and keep the money to buy his freedom and save for his future wife. Jacob was a fine horse trainer and blacksmith. By the time he was nineteen, he'd earned his freedom and was savin' to buy his mamma, Rollin, and Rebecca. Rollin was eight by then, I think." Suddenly Rollin's head came up, his eyes puffy and threaded with thin red lines.

"I was seven an' eleven months. He brought me a slingshot for my birthday. He was my hero. He'd come ridin' down dat lane, big as life. I'd run out to meet him, an' he'd swing me up front of him, on de biggest horse you'd ever seen. His hands be rough and pitch black from the iron he work, his arms and chest strong and smellin' like horse sweat and hay." Rollin closed his eyes, drawing in a deep breath through his nose, as if smelling the memory. A slow smile curved his lips at the sight behind his eyelids. "He'd muss what li'l hair I had, an' ask if I'd been watchin' out for hez women. Mama always smile when she see him. She'd be like a li'l girl dancing 'round dat horse tellin' him to get down so she could get her some hugs."

Rollin's eyes opened now, but they still seemed far away.

"He'd always bring her a present. I loved him for that. Mostly Mama was always sad, but not when Jacob'd tease her 'bout de present he brought her. He always slap hez forehead like he forgot or somethin', then he'd open his saddlebag and give her a jar o' rose water, a new kerchief. Oh, how she'd fuss and say he shouldn't, that he should save hez money, but de months between hez visits, I'd see her staring at dose presents, tears of sadness an' pride waiting inside de corners of her eyes, jes' waiting to spill over. Never did though, 'stead she'd hold me close and say some day wez all gonna be a family again and free. She told me Jacob gonna see to dat." Rollin now stood, shaking first one leg, then the other and began to pace.

"When I was twelve, he came one night without warning. It warn't safe for him to be dere after dark, but he was wild with excitement. Old Master Whitingworth had consented to allow him to marry Becca. A gentle smile spread across the large man's face as he remembered. "He swung me around three times and gave me a real harmonica. He said I could play at hez weddin' if I got good enough. Den he pulled out a stack o' bills and a bag o' coins the likes of I never seen afore. Momma said my eyes got big as a courtin' bullfrog's chest. Jacob grinned and said he gonna buy him a wife. Den he says he's gonna buy me and Mama next. Mama called all de folks in de shacks next to ours to come celebrate. Dat celebration was bigger den any white man's holiday." Rollin stopped now, his hands resting on the carved wood trim on the back of the velvet settee where Melody was still sitting. Amanda didn't dare move. Her eyes followed his movement with mesmerized horror. She felt she was watching a play, but with emotion too real to be mere theatrics. She knew something terrible was about to happen, and she squirmed uncomfortably in her chair.

Now Rollin's voice grew so soft, the words were almost lost. Amanda shifted, leaning her body forward, holding her breath. "It was den that I seed him cry. For de first time ever, he jes' broked down and cried dat night. Jacob who'd always been so strong. He jes' fell apart. He cried on my mama's knees like a loss child. I was so scared. I thought the dev'l was a comin'. I watched him from the shadows, scared to leave, and scared to stay. I jes watched while my mama rock dis big man, strokin' his curly hair, saying, 'God'll look out for hez own.' " Rollin clenched his teeth as his fingers dug into the maroon velvet beneath them.

Suddenly, violently, he smeared a single tear from the corner of his eye with the back of his hand. "Jacob pulled away from Mama when she says dat, and he cursed God and hez goodness. Says God's got no love for de slave. Said maybe dere ain't even a God. I was so scared. I waited for de wrath of God to strike him dead, like de preacher said. But I reckon he'd already done got hez punishment. Dat ol' bastard Whitingworth refused to sell Becca. He said Jacob could marry her or any of hez darkies, but he couldn't buy 'em. He said Jacob was strong and clever and would breed good stock." Rollin swallowed hard, anger mounting, flexing the columns of his throat. "Jacob said he tear de man's heart out o' his chest, jes' like he done to him. But that dev'l only laughed, saying if Jacob touched him, he sell his family south, and likely he'd never see 'em again. He told Jacob to go on and have his li'l ol' weddin', and make lots of li'l slaves. Den Jacob said dat man laugh Satan's own laugh, pure evil." Now Rollin let the tears run unchecked, rubbing abstractedly at the dark splotches they made on the velvet settee. After a long silence, he continued. The raw edge to his voice had faded to a sad tone of defeat.

"Becca said it didn' matter none to her, she still wanted to be hez wife. Dey was happy when dey could see each other. I mean happy considerin'. But Jacob always talked about runnin' away. He finally had Becca 'bout convinced, when she got a baby growin' inside her. She said their plans'd have to wait now, as it weren't safe. Jacob was near 'side hisself with grief. He knew de law say no matter de father a free man, de baby be same as de mother, a slave. He couldn' bear to think of hez child being born a slave.

"Jacob begged Becca not to tell anybody, but Becca, well, she always was a little airy an' flighty like. She be so happy, she was singin' and telling anyone who'd listen. She was proud as anything dat she gonna be a mama. She didn' see de danger. She jes' wouldn' believe it." Rollin came around the settee and fell to his knees before Amanda and Minister Clay.

Amanda was shocked by the sudden movement, and briefly pulled back, afraid he would touch her and make the horror even more real. She knew this grisly story was far from over. Then, quickly, she reached forward and grasped Rollin's hands. The pain he suffered for his brother was so real. She wanted to help him, to ease the memories. Taking her touch as a sign of understanding, Rollin turned pleading eyes to her.

"You know the ways of God. You bein' raised in a minister's house an' all. Becca, she really was a good woman, Miss 'Manda. Jacob loved her, she loved him. She was jes' kinda childlike. Her life was jes' as hard as anyone, but Becca believed in Jacob. She thought he could always protect her. She jes' fell apart when Whitingworth decided to sell her baby." A small, strangled cry of disbelief rose from Amanda's throat, and her eyes stung with tears. This was too awful to be true. Holding her hands tighter, Rollin continued, his eyes pleading with her to understand and say it was all right, whatever atrocity or sin Rebecca may have committed. Amanda moistened her dry lips with her tongue and nodded, encouraging Rollin to continue.

"Penny was 'bout six month old when de Whitingworths got a visit from a relative out of Virginia. Dat lady told de missus dat her daughter jes' had a baby girl 'bout five months ago, and she wanted to buy Becca's baby as a present for her new granddaughter. She thought it be so cute for them to grow up together.'' For the second time, Amanda heard the sharp sarcasm Rollin used on the word *cute*. "At first, Becca pleaded with de missus and Master Whitingworth. Den Jacob tried to buy Penny, offering twice what dem relatives was willin' to pay. But Jacob say dat ol' Whitingworth jes' laugh his evil laugh an' told him to go home and make more li'l babies.'' Rollin paused to take a deep gulp of air. He seemed unaware of Amanda's fingernails digging deep crescents on the backs of his hands. She wanted to tell him to stop, that she didn't want to hear the horrid ending, but she knew she'd never know peace until she did, so she bit her bottom lip and remained silent.

"Becca 'bout went crazy. She blamed Jacob, and hid de infant in de woods, not tellin' no one where she was. But dem hounds sniffed her out, and dey took Penny away. Den Becca did go mad. She screamed at poor Jacob, and tore at her hair and face. She refused to eat. Den she began to babble mindlessly for weeks. She'd rock endlessly on her cot, holdin' Penny's clothes to her breast. Den her milk dried up. De relatives gave Penny back, said dey didn't want no crazy woman's baby. But Whitingworth wouldn't give the babe back to poor Becca. Dey wouldn't even let her sees it. Next day she was found drown in the swamp." Rollin looked away from Amanda and spoke in a low voice. "She done sewed rocks in her clothes. She kilt herself." Suddenly his gaze riveted back to Amanda, his voice cracking with pain. "But I know God forgive her. I know she be an angel in heaven, guiding Jacob an' Penny to safety. Maybe she even sent you. After what dat sweet child suffered, God couldn't be so cruel as to deny her paradise with him." The last words rang out beseechingly, begging for confirmation, that although Rebecca had committed the unpardonable sin of taking her own life, God had understood and forgiven her.

Amanda felt hot, salty tears spill down her face as she heard herself say, "Of course he has. How could he not? She was a fine, brave woman, who bore a beautiful little daughter, whom I will help in any way I can." Amanda's eyes flickered to Minister Clay. His face showed disapproval of her remarks, but out of sympathy, he held his tongue. Clearing his throat, the minister awkwardly approached the kneeling man and clumsily patted his back.

"Here, here now. They are safe, and that is what matters right now." Amanda noticed how the short, white-haired minister avoided Rollin's pleading eyes. He refused to offer the hope that Amanda had. Looking down at Rollin's large hands still in hers, she thought about what he had said. Could her God be so cruel as to condemn to eternal damnation a woman who had suffered so much?

Some time during Rollin's emotional monologue, Madeline Clay had returned with a pot of steaming water, a crystal bowl with several tea leaves, and five bone china cups and saucers on a pretty, silver-plated tray. The delicate porcelain rattled loudly in the ensuing silence, as the minister's wife placed it on a low coffee table in front of the settee. In the distance behind her, Cookie, the Clay's housekeeper, could be seen walking haltingly down the oak staircase, holding a basin filled with dark, bloody water and pieces of stained linen. The black woman did not look up but proceeded down the hallway to the kitchen, a look of compassion and anger stretched tightly across her face.

"Rollin honey," Melody whispered, as she came up silently behind her husband. Her hand slid down the side of his neck, resting lightly on his slumped shoulders. "I'm sure Amanda understands. She said she'd help us. She's forgiven Jacob. She understands." Melody looked up, her eyes locking with

Amanda's. The reservations were still there, and a challenge that said "if you hurt or allow any of those I love to be hurt, you will answer to me." Amanda shivered, but held her gaze steady. She wasn't sure what she was getting herself into, but she would help these people. As a true Christian, she must.

Melody then bent to collect Rollin's hands from Amanda. Rollin gave one last look at Amanda and whispered, "God bless you." A small shiver of anxiety started at the base of Amanda's neck and radiated down her spine. This was no game she was offering to participate in. A child's freedom and a man's life hung in the balance.

As if divining her thoughts, Minister Clay spoke to her in a low, serious voice. "It is only fair to warn you, Miss Smith, what you are letting yourself in for. By helping Jacob and his daughter escape, you are aiding and abetting in the transfer of stolen property. It is a felony, and if you are discovered, you could face serious charges—hefty fines and imprisonment at best." He stopped for a moment, carefully considering his next words. After a moment's hesitation, he continued. "I must also warn you that because of your color, it is possible that you could be captured as a runaway slave and sent down South. True, you have your strong English accent to convince a court otherwise, but if you are taken in secret, you may never see a courtroom or justice." His kindly blue eyes had grown stern, unwavering. He had to know if she could be counted in their number. He had laid all his cards on the table. Now it was her call.

The silence hung ominously. Amanda could feel every eye upon her. She felt a heated flush creep up her neck, and she raised a hand to the large lace collar that now seemed too tight. Squaring her shoulders, Amanda knew her decision had already been made. If she refused to help now, she would never forgive herself. She would never be able to look in the mirror again. She would be worse than that timid mouse of a woman on the steamer who was afraid to stand by her convictions when it really mattered. No, come what may, she would do her best to see Penny to safety. She would make Jacob accept her.

"As I said earlier, I will do whatever I can to help Mr., ah, Jacob and his daughter." As Amanda uttered these words, she wondered again at the difference in Jacob's last name, but there was time. She was sure that before this adventure was over, she'd know a lot more about Jacob Coffey—or whoever he was.

Six

Lying in bed that night, she ran over the events of the evening in her mind. The Clays had few spare rooms, and a makeshift curtain had been hung between her and Melody and Rollin. She had the room's sole window, and they had the door. In the darkness she heard Rollin's deep, lumbering snores. She stifled a giggle when she heard a thud of hand against bedding, and Melody's angry whisper demanding her husband roll over. To relieve her mind of the horrible story she had heard earlier, she tried to imagine what it would be like to share a bed with a man. It was obvious that Rollin cherished and adored his wife. Amanda tried to imagine the young Jacob courting his bride. She tried to see past the gruff man she had met, to a man who was gentle with animals and children. She had caught a brief glimpse of his beautiful smile when he had talked of his daughter. She remembered his muscular frame as he strode angrily to the stairs. He was a big man. His tattered clothes had revealed the lean muscles beneath. She recalled now that he had moved with a grace that Rollin did not have. Both men were so different from the few men she had come in contact with in London. These men needed no padding in their clothes to fill out their chests and shoulders. She began to wonder what Rebecca had looked like. She was probably comely, as Penny was a beautiful little girl.

Amanda was suddenly startled by a wave of jealousy for the unfortunate dead woman. Never one to leave her thoughts and feelings unanalyzed, Amanda studied this strange emotion. After several moments, she decided it was the desire for a family, a child of her own, that had raised those ugly feelings. Placing her hand on her soft, flat belly, Amanda wondered what it would be like to have a child growing within her. A sweet, heavy yearning blossomed in her chest, a pain of wanting that which would probably never be. Closing her eyes, she tried to imagine that unborn child of her womb and knew she would love it with all her heart. She, too, might go crazy if someone tried to take it away. Suddenly, she sat upright, a cold sweat forming around her hairline and on the nape of her neck. Her mother, Monase. She had never once thought how her mother might have felt when she watched them take her infant daughter from her. Had she, too, cried, pleaded, and begged to have her child back? A deep sadness filled Amanda's heart. Into the darkness she whispered a silent prayer to God and her mother's God to bless her and offer her peace if her heart was aching for the daughter she thought was dead.

Early the next morning, Amanda pulled her writing box from one of her trunks. Dressing quickly by herself, she blessed her aunt for having the foresight to suggest she buy one of the new corsets that fastened down the front. Silently, she slipped past the sleeping figures of Rollin and Melody.

When she entered the morning room, she spotted Cookie, a large happy mulatto woman who had been the Clays' first passenger to their station on the underground railroad. They had been so pleased with their part that they had offered Cookie a job and an unconditional guarantee that if it came down to it, they would willingly pay her master his asking price if he came after her. It had been five years now, and she had earned enough to buy three of her children and send them to school. One was studying to be a minister under Mr. Clay's tutoring, and she had been told he was a frequent guest at the Clays' dinner table.

"Good mornin' Miss 'Manda. You shore is up early. Come in de kitchen and I'll make you some toast and hot tea. Or would you like some coffee? I believe I could find a little chicory." Amanda smiled at Cookie and wondered when the woman ever slept. As she followed the jolly housekeeper and cook into the kitchen, she was startled to see a clean-cut, attractive black man already sitting at the table. Assuming it was Cookie's son, Amanda walked over to extend a hand in greeting.

"How do you do. I'm Amanda Smith." She nearly dropped her writing box when the man lowered his cup, revealing a familiar face.

"I believe we've already met," Jacob drawled sarcastically and picked up his fork to eat a plate full of fried eggs and biscuits. Amanda was stunned for several minutes. This man barely bore any resemblance to the grungy, dirty man of last night. Forgetting her manners, she simply stared at the strikingly handsome creature before her. He had shaved his beard and mustache, revealing high, broad cheekbones and a sturdy, square jaw. His nose was slightly hooked before it flared out slightly above full, sensuous lips. When he looked up at her again, she noticed his dark brows nearly met over the darkest black eyes she had ever seen. Still, she did not speak, only boldly traversed his body with her eyes. Jacob was dressed in a clean white linen shirt, the button plackets straining over his broad chest. The shirt was obviously not his, and its snugness revealed muscles rippling with his every movement. He was a Greek statue in motion. She recalled her boredom in sketching the cold, gray statues in the London museums, and imagined Jacob in their place. Suddenly she blushed and looked away.

"Perhaps I will go sit in the morning room and write a letter to the Carringtons." Without waiting for a reply or looking back, she hurried off to the light, airy room alongside the parlor. Setting her box down, Amanda saw her hands were shaking. How could she have been so brazen? The years of training on a lady's proper behavior echoed through her head. As if to bring closer those who had helped mold her since birth, she took out a sheet of lavender scented paper and began to write. Within moments, the scratching of the quill and the floral scent eased her mind. Jacob had probably not even noticed. She would just have to remember to be more discreet in the future.

The letter had been a little difficult to word, as she didn't want to worry the Carringtons. Reading the letter over once more, she sprinkled it with blotting sand. As she leaned back in her chair to survey her handiwork, she felt a warm minty breath on her neck. She whirled around to find Jacob's face inches from her own.

"I never! Didn't anyone ever tell you it was rude to read another person's personal letters?" Jacob stood up straight, his hands deep in his pockets, a sprig of hothouse mint between his even, white teeth. With casual nonchalance, he removed the sprig and grinned.

"I can't read, so no." Shrugging, he strolled over to rifle through her writing box. Amanda was besieged with a mixture of emotions. Should she be offended at his presumptuous attitude in inspecting her property, or should she offer her apologies for possibly embarrassing him with her question. Before she could make up her mind, Jacob was flipping through her Bible and came across her drawing of Frederick Douglass.

"This your man?" Jacob asked, studying it closely. All thoughts of apology fled Amanda's mind as she snatched the picture from Jacob's hand, a now familiar anger returning.

"No, you . . . you overconfident, boorish cad. It is Frederick Douglass." When no light of recognition flickered across his face, she continued cruelly. "He is an eloquent speaker and writer. An escaped slave who taught himself to read and write." She pursed her lips tightly together, waiting for the sting of humiliation to reflect in Jacob's face.

She was disappointed when Jacob just shrugged and said, "Oh. Don't know him." Jacob then leaned his hip against the table and studied Amanda from head to toe. Amanda was miserably aware that her temper was rising. All her well-laid plans of last night to become a friend and confidante of this exasperating man were falling around her like shattered glass. Uncomfortable with his lingering eyes, Amanda folded her arms across her chest.

"Them yours?" Jacob asked carelessly.

"Pardon me?" Amanda demanded, her eyes burning a deep, claret red-brown.

"I asked if your breasts were for real." Standing up straight from the table, Jacob moved toward her. Amanda retreated a step or two, not sure if he meant to find out. "I've seen those fancy metal and padded, what do you call 'em, breast enhancers. Bet a man's real disappointed when he beds that woman."

Amanda's mouth dropped open in disbelief. Never in her life had she been addressed so crudely by a man! Gritting her teeth and letting a loud huff of air out of her nostrils, she swept by Jacob, holding her skirts away, as if the slightest touch would contaminate them.

"Well?" Jacob asked as he followed her to where she was hastily gathering her writing tools. This time, Amanda turned on him. He was standing a bare two inches from her.

"You are the rudest, most disgusting man I have ever—"

He cut her off, as he reached out to cup one of her breasts. Amanda pulled back in horror, the back of her thighs catching on the table behind her, causing her to fling her arms backward to brace herself and prevent her from falling flat on the table. His hand never left her breast.

"Feels pretty real to me, but you can never tell with those dang underthings you grand ol' ladies wear." Brazenly sliding his hand down her side, his eyes continued to study her. "Jes' seems to me that a skinny thing like you don't need all that binding and whalebone." As if to confirm his suspicions, he reached behind her with both hands and grasped her buttocks, pulling her to him. Before she could slap him, he released her, and strolled out of reach to the doorway. Stopping, he turned around. Placing the mint sprig back in his mouth, he shook his head. "Not much for a man to hold onto with you." Winking, he continued, "Close your mouth. You're catching flies."

He turned to go as Amanda lunged toward him, her teeth bared, twenty-three years of training falling away like useless trappings. Jacob turned around just in time, deftly catching her wrists, pulling them wide to her side so the momentum of her body sent her flying against the length of his hard, masculine one. "Still sure you want to go out West with me, darlin'?" he drawled.

Amanda could feel her heart beating rapidly against her ribs, while humiliation and indignation flooded her senses. She would not allow this man to intimidate her. She hopelessly searched his black eyes for a spark of tenderness, compassion. Instead, she saw disgust, resentment, and something dangerous. Plucking up what little remained of her courage, Amanda breathed deeply, and in a controlled, ladylike voice, spoke. "Why is it that you don't like me?"

Jacob pulled her arms down past his hips, so she leaned in closer to his body. There was no mistaking the hard shaft of manhood she felt press into her belly. "Oh, I like you jes' fine like this." He responded in a husky voice. Amanda flushed heatedly and had to look away. Jacob laughed a bitter laugh and released her. "I don't imagine your high and mighty wants to find out how much, so why don't you jes' get up on your high horse and ride back to your safe little life in England.'' He turned then and left, humming.

Amanda felt spent and strangely weak. She had never been that intimate with a man before, and it had done some strange things to her body. She could not truthfully say she enjoyed it; she had really been too angry to analyze it at the time. But now that the antagonist was gone, she could evaluate the feelings Jacob's words and actions had stirred in her. Breathing deeply to steady herself, she began to have misgivings about her promise to help the fugitives. Perhaps Jacob was right, and she was all bravado with no backbone. Maybe she wasn't up to this. Should she turn tail and go home? Suddenly, her angry, hurt pride came to her rescue. Damn that man if she was going to allow him to intimidate her or to make her doubt her strength! She was going to help Penny and go out West with or without Jacob's blessing. She'd just have to be a little more careful around Mr.—*that man*—in the future.

Seven

Jacob continued humming a cheerful tune until he was sure he was out of hearing of Miss Amanda Smith or anyone else who might have been within earshot of their encounter.

Grabbing a hat off a hook by the kitchen door and winking mischievously at the flour-covered Cookie, he strolled out into the dead, winter garden. The closing of the heavy oak door sent a gust of air that blew the light dusting of snow off the brick walk. Abruptly, Jacob stopped humming. The garden was silent, except for an occasional breath of frozen air as it rattled through the few tenacious dead leaves still clinging to the dormant trees. Pulling his hat low over his eyes, lest one of the neighbors gaze out of their window and recognize him from the reward posters, he moved into a shadowy corner of the small, enclosed yard. Damn that woman, Jacob thought, as he crouched to angrily pull at a handful of withered yellow grass that poked through the new snow. He had only meant to scare her, rattle her a little, send her packing. He had meant to have the upper hand, and if she had started to cry, so be it. He'd be unmoved. Damn that woman! His neatly laid plan had backfired. She had gotten to him, and the painful throbbing between his legs was evidence of that. He had called her skinny, accused her of falsifying her womanly curves, when all along he had known, seen that his accusations were untrue.

His mind flitted back to the early morning hours when he had gone in search of Penny. He had known that she had probably gone to seek out Miss Smith, but he had hoped he was wrong. He had soundlessly searched the sleeping house thoroughly before he forced himself to check the room where his brother and Melody slept. He had cursed noiselessly in the dark when he saw no third lump in their bed. As he reluctantly moved toward the curtain dividing the room, he saw the small mound that was unmistakably his daughter on the end of the Englishwoman's bed, silhouetted by the moonlight coming through the window.

Holding his breath, Jacob had crept around the curtain, praying that no loose floorboard would creak and betray him. At the time, he had wondered how he would explain himself if he were caught. Saying he had come to retrieve his wandering child seemed barely reason for a half-dressed man to enter the sleeping chambers of a proper young lady. For a moment he hesitated, wondering if he should wake Melody and ask her to get Penny. That thought was immediately banished when Miss Smith inadvertently turned in her sleep, the blanket falling gently to her side, revealing a fine, semitransparent chemise haloed in moonlight. The dark richness of her skin was clearly defined beneath the fabric, and he was able to make out the deliciously shapely hills and valleys of her young body. He moved closer, his breath stirring a row of tendrils at her temple. He froze, sure she'd awaken. When she remained sleeping, he boldly reached out to touch the curls he had disturbed. As his fingers felt the springy softness, she turned her face, trapping his fingertips beneath her satiny cheek. He pulled back his hand as if he'd been seared by flame. With his heart beating like a trapped rabbit, he scooped up his sleeping daughter in a single swoop and silently escaped the room.

It was not until Penny had been securely tucked into her

little cot that Jacob breathed easy. He knelt for a long time beside Penny. He loved her so much, and would give her the world if he could. He reached out to pull her thumb from her soft, pliant lower lip where it rested. She had not awakened, but the subconscious interruption of her sleep had brought on the thumb sucking again. This sweet daughter of his wanted a mama so badly. Although she had never known her own, she missed her terribly. She spoke of her often in terms of an angel in layers of lace. He had known immediately when he saw Amanda Smith that Penny would be drawn to her. Grudgingly, Jacob had to admit that even with his prejudice against her from the start, Miss Smith was beautiful. Dressed in her elegant woman's clothing with her impressive poise and grace, she did look like one of the pictures of angels in the Whitingworth chapel. Except she was black; so like him, but so different—so beyond his experience.

Shaking off the memory, Jacob rose. Frustrated and angry, Jacob wrung the innocent pieces of grass between his hands. Suddenly, his ire returned in full force. What his brother Rollin had found so inspiring about the Englishwoman, he found annoying and promising of trouble. Miss Amanda Smith had no idea what she was up against in this country. She thought and acted white, and he knew that would not be tolerated here. For all her self-confidence and poise, he saw her for what she was—a naive, gullible, unsuspecting child—and he was not going to be duped into being her protector.

A sharp pain ripped at his chest when he recalled another child-woman who had looked to him for protection. Breathing the crisp morning air deeply, he felt the never-ending waves of guilt and regret washing over him. Leaning his back against the cold brick wall behind him, he closed his eyes as the old despair crept back. God, he had tried. What could he have done differently? His mind raced over the well-worn track in his brain. The arguments, the pleas, the groveling. But nothing had swayed that cruel-hearted devil, Whitingworth. Then it was too late. Maybe if he had stayed with Rebecca, had made Rollin follow her every move . . . but no, there was no hope. She was already gone long before she took her own life. He should have told her before she became his wife. He should have shared the secret that had almost shattered him when he first found out. But there was nothing he could do now.

A blinding rage welled up inside him. His fingers scraped along the rough surface of the wall as they clenched into iron fists. He had saved their child. He would take Penny as far away from that southern hell as he could. He would not be seduced into playing nursemaid for some helpless woman who might, no matter her intentions, impede their escape. Maybe out West he'd find and marry some capable Indian squaw. She could raise Penny. Hell, he was a quarter Seminole Indian himself. It would be a fine match. He knew Indian women were self-sufficient, obedient. You wouldn't find any self-respecting Indian woman insulting and lunging at a man.

As Jacob tried to imagine this fictitious future bride, Amanda's face and body kept appearing in a buckskin dress. With disgust, he threw the thoroughly strangled blades of grass away in an angry motion. The frigid wind lifted them, throwing them back into his face. Damn that woman! Damn her! It was all her fault. Jacob wrapped his arms around his coatless, shivering chest and stomped off toward the kitchen. The frozen outside had done little to cool him off. His blood was still boiling.

Having made her decision to persevere, Amanda began to pace, to release the unladylike anger coiled tightly inside her. Her long, elegant fingers clenched and twisted in the smooth gray satin skirt of her morning dress. On her third pass by the partially shuttered windows, she paused; a movement outside had caught her eye. Peering between the slats, she almost laughed outright, as she saw the brown grass fly into her antagonist's face. Covering her mouth to stifle the laughter bubbling up in her throat, she was caught by surprise when a little voice squeaked out a cheerful "Good morning."

Amanda's heart skidded to a halt against her ribs, then pounded frantically against them.

"Good Lord, Penny, you nearly frightened me to death."

Instantly the little girl's eyes flooded with tears. "I'm so sorry, Miss Smith, I didn' means to." The sincere, plaintive little voice tugged painfully at Amanda's still erratic heart. She stooped down and brushed the tears away with her thumbs. The child quickly caught one of Amanda's hands and ran them lovingly over her face, smearing the silvery tear droplets across her cheek. "Oh, you have the softest hands. Daddy's and Nanna's are oh so rough." With this explanation offered, Penny turned Amanda's hand palm up. "You ain't got no bumps or blisters at all."

Unable to stop herself, Amanda instantly replied, "Don't." Feeling she'd been chastised, the little girl dropped her hand and apologized again.

"No, no, sweetheart," Amanda began, instantly regretting her ingrained need to correct the child's English. "What I mean is you should use the word don't instead of ain't." Penny looked baffled for a minute, then a bright smile lit up her whole face. "You gonna teach me to talk pretty like yous do?"

Amanda returned her smile with no criticism at all this time. "I will if you want me to."

The little girl began to dance up and down with excitement. "Oh, Miss Smith, yous is the most wonderful thing I ever did see." Amanda smiled, feeling her loneliness ebb away slightly with this warm outpouring of affection.

"Why don't you call me just Amanda."

Penny pursed her lips and wrinkled her brow, looking remarkably like her father, Amanda thought. "Think it'd be all right if'n I call you *Miss* Amanda? My daddy would like that much better. Sayin' I shouldn't get too familiar."

Amanda smiled again. "All right then, and I shall call you Miss Penny." Penny seemed thrilled. Tugging Amanda by the hand she had earlier released, Penny pulled her over to the table. Amanda laughed. "Perhaps I will even call you by the formal form of your name, would you like that?"

Penny stopped, her eyes wide. "I ain't . . . don't got no other name. It's just Penny, on account of my daddy said I was as bright as a new penny when I was born, and was worth more than all the pennies in the world. My momma thought that was clever and named me Penny. My daddy even gave me a penny." She reached around her neck and pulled out a tarnished coin threaded on a thin strip of leather. It was large, with the regal face of Lady Liberty's profile embossed upon it. Holding the copper object in her palm, Amanda turned it over. On the other side was the wreath of laurel and the bold words "one cent," surrounded by slightly smaller words, "United States of America." Flipping the coin over again, she studied it.

"Eighteen forty-five," Amanda murmured to herself as she ran her finger lightly over the raised numbers. She gazed down at the solemn face of the little girl standing so near. She recalled Jacob's proud and tender smile when he had talked about his daughter last night. Now she envisioned him as an exuberant new father, holding his baby gently, tears of pride and joy in his eyes, gazing with love and adoration at his young wife. A bittersweet yearning wrapped its painful tentacles around her heart. She was filled with sorrow for the family that was lost, and her family that would probably never be. For all her words of independence, Amanda secretly wished for the warmth of a family of her own. Releasing the coin, she chastised herself. The likelihood of finding a suitable match in America, much less the West, was slim at best. A grim smile of determination stretched across her lips. She would have to be content with her lot in life.

"You're much prettier, Miss Amanda, when you smile real big and show all them pretty white teeth." The little face broke into a grin. Amanda's mouth twitched until she relented and bestowed one of her best smiles on this entrancing child.

"In England, the name Penny is short for Penelope. Would you like to hear about the origination of the name?" Penny's eyes shown brightly, and she nodded vigorously. She hadn't a clue what the word *origination* meant, but anything this wonderful woman had to say would undoubtedly be exciting. Penny intertwined her fingers with Amanda's. Maybe, just maybe, if she was real good and told Miss Amanda how brave and strong her daddy was, then maybe they'd fall in love and get married, and she could have a real mama. She looked up into Amanda's smiling face and sighed. Just maybe things would be better, her daddy would smile more and be happy. Just maybe she'd have a baby brother or sister to take care of and boss around. A shiver of excitement coursed through her little body. She shut her eyes briefly and thanked the good Lord and her angel mama for sending Miss Amanda to them.

Penny sat quietly with her hand tucked tightly between her knees. She shifted ever so slightly on the low needlepoint footstool at Amanda's feet.

"Penelope was a beautiful maiden who lived a long time ago, in a faraway land called Greece."

Penny could barely contain her curiosity. After all, this was about her name. "Was she colored like us?"

Amanda cocked her head and contemplated the question carefully. Penny was delighted to have such thought given to her question. Miss Amanda must have considered it a good one.

"Well, Penny, it was long ago, so I couldn't say for sure,

but considering Greece is in the Mediterranean, I would have to say that although she wouldn't have been as dark as you or me, she was rather brown." Penny nodded solemnly. Amanda smiled and continued.

"Penelope was married to a very brave captain named Ulysses. Every time he would go out to sea, she would kiss him and wish him a safe journey and a swift and speedy return. On one such voyage, he didn't return. Month after month Penelope would stand on the cliffs watching for her brave and handsome husband. Other sailors said he had died in a battle. Still others said the lovely sea sirens of the ocean had lured him to his death on the rocky shores of the many islands. But Penelope continued to wait. As the years passed, her father insisted she remarry."

Penny shook her head vigorously, her mouth rounded in a silent "no."

"Yes," Amanda responded to the unspoken word. "She had many suitors who begged her to marry them. She refused, saying she wouldn't marry any of them. When her father became angry and insisted she choose or he would choose for her, she consented on one condition."

Penny leaned forward, her eyes wide with anticipation. This story was much better then the stories her Nanna had told her about Brer Rabbit and Brer Bear.

Amanda lowered her voice in a conspiratorial whisper. "She said she would not marry until she had woven a shroud for her father-in-law. Her father thought this was fair. So Penelope began to weave a beautiful tapestry befitting of her dearest husband. Day after day her father and potential suitors saw the intensity with which she wove and the steady progress she made. What they did not see was that night after night, when everyone had gone to sleep, Penelope ripped out the careful patterns she had made that day." Amanda sat back, letting the top of her back touch the chair rungs, her eyes never leaving Penny's face.

"That can't be all," the child demanded.

Amanda chuckled softly and patted the girl's soft frizz of curls. "After several years, Ulysses came back. Penelope never gave up hope that her husband would return."

Penny smiled smugly, happy with the ending. She clasped her hands together before her face and looked past Amanda.

"Daddy, I want to be called Penelope from now on. It is my truly formal name." Amanda was surprised and uncomfortable. She straightened her shoulders and sat up straight, twisting slightly in her chair to see her unannounced visitor. Jacob pushed away from the door frame he'd been leaning on and walked into the room.

"It was, I was just . . ." Amanda floundered. This man unnerved her, and the dark expression he wore on his face bore no goodwill.

"Your name is Penny. That's all. Got it?"

Penny pushed out a generous bottom lip and sulked. "Penelope is prettier," the disappointed child remarked. Jacob ignored her and spoke to Amanda.

"You read that in some book?" Amanda nodded and was about to speak, when Jacob turned away. "See that reading done you a lot of good. Gets you full of nonsense. It ain't life."

"Don't," Penny piped in, with a grin of satisfaction. Jacob whirled around.

"What?" he responded in a deceptively soft voice. The little girl retreated a step, then stood her ground.

"You ain't, I mean, don't use ain't. It ain't, I mean, don't be proper." Her face twisted in confusion at the garble her words made. She looked to Amanda for help. Amanda could barely repress a grin at the situation.

"What she means to say Mr., uh, what do I call you?"

Jacob glared at her before he turned back to his daughter. "Jacob'll do fine," the angry man muttered.

Amanda sighed and moved forward. "What she meant, Mr. Jacob, was that *ain't* isn't a proper word. You see, *ain't* is slang that is used in the place of many words like *won't, don't, isn't*—"

Jacob cut her off before she could say more. "You learn that in your books, too?" The question was tinged with sarcasm.

Amanda nodded.

"Well, it seems to me that *ain't* is a whole sight better than havin' to remember a whole mess o' words. More economical, you might say." A triumphant grin crossed his face when Amanda had no response. The tense muscles in his back loosened, and he purposely spoke to his daughter using a strong emphasis on her name. "*Penny,* come upstairs. We got to get ready. *We* are leaving in the mornin'." He then turned to Amanda, the smug smile still on his lips. "And you, Miss Smith, *ain't* comin'."

As he strode out the room, Amanda balled her fists at her side and called after him loudly. "The word is *aren't,* and I certainly *am!*"

Amanda knew better than to demand an explanation from Jacob. Taking Penny's hand in hers, she gave it a squeeze. Although she knew it was improper for her to encourage the little girl to go against her father's wishes, Amanda just couldn't resist the temptation to have one up on Jacob.

"Penny, you can be Miss Penelope when it is just the two of us." The little girl's eyes sparkled a clear, rich brown. Amanda resisted an urge to kiss her small, upturned nose. Instead she gave Penny a gentle push toward the stairs. "Go along now and see what your father needs. It will be our little secret. I promise."

As Amanda watched the child disappear up the stairs, she

went in search of the Clays or the Coffeys. A thrill of excitement and anxiety skittered down her spine. It appeared the time to begin the perilous journey west had arrived. She was anxious to learn her part.

Eight

Amanda felt her frustration mounting when she discovered that neither Rollin and Melody nor the minister and his wife were at home. They had gone to Sunday morning services and would probably not return until late that evening.

As Amanda plopped down in one of the chairs around the kitchen table, she knew her complaints to Cookie sounded spoiled and whiny. Cookie only shrugged her bulky shoulders and continued to roll out the pie dough.

"Well, Miss 'Manda, seein' as yous is Methodis', and de Minister an' his Missus is Baptis', it don' surprise me none dat dey didn' 'vite yous." With quick, skilled hands, Cookie flipped the flattened dough into two large pie plates and deftly cut around the edges with a sharp knife. Amanda watched in fascination, wishing she had spent more time in the kitchen and could cook something—anything.

"What about Mr. Jacob and Penny?" Amanda asked, her voice becoming less petulant but still with a hint of stubbornness that she had been slighted.

"Well, dey is in hidin'. 'Sides, Mr. Jacob say he ain't believe in no God, least one he cares to pray to. He say God got no time for the black man. Says he shore ain't no lovin' father if'n he allows his children to be slaves. The good minister tries to tell him 'bout Job an all, but dat man jes' don' listen."

Cookie paused for a moment and crossed herself, leaving a white patch of flour on her dark forehead. With a duck of her head, she smiled with embarrassment. "Ol' habits is hard to stop. My ol' master down in Louisiana be a Roman Catholic. Lord, how he'd make us ol' niggers kneel for hours say'n amen and crossin' ourselves while'n he says de rosary." Amanda nodded, and continued to watch the old cook's nimble fingers dance around the edge of the pie plate, fluting the crust's rim.

"Would you teach me how to do that?" Amanda asked suddenly.

Cookie stopped short. "Ta say de rosary?" the older woman asked in astonishment.

Amanda laughed, her sullen mood of a few moments ago gone. With amusement twinkling in her eyes, she jabbed her finger at the finished pie before Cookie. Cookie looked down, then up at Amanda, and joined in the laughter.

"Shore, honey." She said between loud, horsey snorts. "But don' you know hows to cook?" Amanda shook her head remorsefully. "Landsake chile, you ain't never gonna catch no man dat way."

Amanda immediately opened her mouth to dispel this woman's belief that she was out to find a husband but then decided against it. No doubt from the way she had gawked at Jacob in front of her this morning, she wouldn't believe it. Besides, if she did, she might not teach her these wonderful culinary skills. Amanda had learned last night, when she had followed Melody into the kitchen and been introduced to Cookie, that the woman's name wasn't really Cookie at all. She had learned that many women slaves in the South who were given the great responsibility of cooking for a household were named Cookie. When Amanda had started to call the woman her given name of Sarah, Cookie had laughed and said it had been so long since she'd heard that name that it didn't even seem like it belonged to her anymore. She said it was all right now to call her Cookie, and that she was proud of her talents in the kitchen. As Amanda remembered the delicious meat pie and buttered yams she had hungrily devoured last night at supper, she could see why.

Hours later, covered from head to toe with flour, Amanda was beaming with pride and satisfaction. Small rivulets of perspiration streaked the flour smudged on Amanda's forehead as she stood, hands on her hips, surveying the three pies and six loaves of bread she'd made.

"Lordy, Miss 'Manda, you 'bout white as a ghost." Rollin's booming voice startled her momentarily, as she had been so engrossed in cooking that she hadn't heard him and Melody enter the warm kitchen. "But it shore do smell good. Why, yous gonna be givin' ol' Sweet Pea here some competition 'fore you know it."

Amanda rewarded his compliment with one of her dazzling smiles. "I figured if I'm going to be striking out on my own out West, I'd better learn how to cook."

At these words, Melody exchanged a "see how you're gonna handle this one" look with her husband. Hastily, Amanda wiped her hands and face on a towel and slipped her apron over her head. Moving around the wide wooden table, Amanda asked the question she had been waiting all day to ask.

"Jacob says we are to leave in the morning. Is that the plan?"

Without answering, Rollin gently took her elbow and ushered her up the back stairs to the room they shared. No words were spoken as she trailed behind the large man up the narrow flight of stairs. The repetitive squeak of the floorboards told her Melody was not far behind. When they had reached the room, Rollin pulled the lone chair forward to face his bed. Melody silently closed the door, but remained standing. Rollin motioned to the chair and Amanda sat on the edge, her back straight and tense with anticipation. Sinking down in the soft feather bed, Rollin rubbed his powerful hands up and down his newly pressed gray trousers. Amanda was clearly confused at the need for secrecy here in the Clays' home, and Rollin could see that.

"You can't be too careful," he began.

"But surely Cookie can be trusted!" Amanda blurted out, suddenly sick at the possibility that she couldn't and that Amanda had inadvertently let something slip in their hours in the kitchen together.

"Most certainly she can, but de less she knows, de less it can hurt her. See, if someone come askin' questions, or if'n Cookie is detained, say at de market or on her way home from services, dey can have some pretty persuasive ways of convincin' a body to tell all dat dey know." Amanda shivered and tried to block visions of possible methods of persuasion from her mind.

Melody's voice came soft and urgent from her post. "Cookie is also a fugitive. Although it's been years, she is not beyond recapture." Rollin nodded in confirmation. Amanda's heart skipped a beat at the danger that was implied. She struggled with a rising feeling of panic. She would not betray her fears. Covering one hand with the other, she drove her thumbnail into the tender skin of her palm. The sharp, biting sting caused her to sit up straighter, to quell the shaking that had threatened to weaken her resolve.

"Jacob's leavin' for Saint Louie in de mornin'. You and Miss Penny is going to New York day after next on the evenin' train."

"Does Penny know?" Amanda interrupted. She doubted the child would take well to the idea of being separated from her father, or the father from his daughter. Hesistantly, she added,

"And Jacob, he agrees?" Rollin looked to Melody, who turned away.

"Some friends of de minister an' his wife lives in Saint Louie, an dey gonna pass Jacob off as'n a roustabout, a slave that de master leases out to do odd jobs 'round the levee. That way he can save a li'l money and learn whose de safe steamboats for yous all to take down de Missouri to Independence." Then the large man paused, his strong fingers clenching the starched smoothness of the cloth covering his thighs. "Penny don't know, and Jacob hez got no choice, but he knows it's for the best." Rollin looked away from Amanda's penetrating eyes. He did not want her to guess at the battle with Jacob that had ensued over this plan. His brother's final acquiescence had been reluctantly given.

Amanda didn't have to see Rollin's eyes to know that Jacob had been less than enthusiastic at the idea of being seperated from his daughter, much less knowing her safety was being placed in the hands of a woman he knew little of and cared for even less. With grim determination, Amanda turned her mind to more practical matters, things that she could control. She did a quick calculation of her funds. The trip to New York was an expense she hadn't expected. "How much will the ticket to New York be? And how long will we be staying there?"

Rollin smiled, looking over to where Melody stood in the long, late afternoon shadows filtering in through the curtain blocking Amanda's side of the room. Melody stepped forward, a smile of apology on her face. Amanda looked from one to the other. It was all written there. Melody doubted her still. What had she expected Amanda to do? To balk, to change her mind just because of the money? Rollin's grin had the smug satisfaction of "I told you so. I knew the girl had pluck."

"Don't you worry none about money," Melody responded softly. At the minister's church he takes up a second collection for the poor and needy of his flock. Though it ain't right out and said, that money funds the underground. Abolitionist and good Christian folk help out with places to stay."

Amanda nodded, swallowing with relief. "So we all will depart on Tuesday evening?" Amanda smiled, trying to make her voice light, but it cracked with the fear roiling in her stomach. Again, the couple looked at each other. Melody looked back at her first.

"No. Just you and Penny leave Tuesday. Rollin and I will leave Thursday." Before Amanda could blurt out a protest, Melody silenced her with her outstretched palm. "It has to be that way. Whitingworth knows Rollin is Jacob's brother and Penny's uncle. He also knows me. If he is up North personally or has sent one of his overseers or a local slave catcher, they could track Jacob and Penny in a minute. Many people in town have seen us. There could be trouble for the minister and his wife. We thought it safest if you went alone with Penny. You dress and act the fine lady, and with your accent, it'd be believable that you and you daughter was visitin' from England." Taking a quick gulp of air, Melody continued her argument. "I promise you, you'll be met at the station. We can't give you names now, but they will know you." Her hands clasped Amanda's. "Trust us. For Jacob's an' Penny's sake, jes' do what we say an' trust us."

Amanda swallowed her misgivings bravely and nodded. She would trust them.

Nine

Since the morning Penny had awakened to find her daddy gone, she had clung to Amanda like a shadow. Amanda allowed her to sleep curled on the end of her bed, and the little girl sucked her thumb constantly. The adults of the house tiptoed around her, since the slightest upset could send the child into wails of terror and grief. No explanation that her daddy was all right and would be with them soon soothed her. The minister and his wife, and Rollin and Melody began to have grave concerns about the impending trip to New York. They had counted on Penny's stoic nature to see her through. She had been so brave through the horrors of the first leg of the journey from slavery. She needed to act the part of a privileged English child on holiday. Only Amanda was calm. Although she quaked with fear and misgivings on the inside, she allowed none of it to show. In order for Penny to believe it could and must be done, she, Amanda, must show the child she expected her to pull through like a champ. Any words to the contrary she would squash with a haughty, "Shush, what nonsense." By Tuesday afternoon, it seemed to be taking some effect. Although Penny wasn't her bright, chipper self, she was no longer wailing like an infant. She was sullen, sucking her thumb with one hand and holding onto Amanda's skirt with the other. For the whole day, she held onto Amanda as if she were her last hope in the world. Every time Amanda looked down, she would find herself swallowed up by those large pools of pain and betrayal. Amanda said nothing, but she would smile and pull the child closer to her.

"I don't know, dear, it's an awful chance. If Penny starts her wailing and draws attention to herself and someone looks too closely, well . . ."

Amanda was sick of the doubt. The train was leaving in less than three hours, and these words of foreboding made her uneasy. Sweeping into the parlor with Penny at her side, Amanda glared at the speaker.

"Madeline, really! I appreciate your concern, but I have the utmost confidence that Penny will be wonderful." As if to seal her words, she wrapped one arm around the ever-present Penny. "Right, sweetheart?"

The little girl only stared back, her thumb moving rapidly in and out of her mouth.

As if she had responded, Amanda looked back at the four adults in the room. "See, I told you so. Now, Miss Penelope and I must finish our packing."

A small smile peeked out on either side of Penny's thumb. For a brief second her eyes shone as she followed Amanda out of the room.

The evening sky was a deep violet tinged with crimson as the carriage they had hired pulled into the station. Amanda turned to pull the dark wool cloak tighter around Penny's shoulders and to straighten the navy bonnet upon her head. Penny smiled up at her as she continued to stroke the soft fur muff in her hands. Amanda smiled back. It had been a brief moment of pure inspiration when she had remembered the mink muff Elizabeth Carrington had given her on her twenty-first birthday. Amanda had been concerned about the thumb sucking, especially with the white gloves the child would have to wear. Quickly, Amanda pulled the snug white gloves onto

Penny's rough little hands. Even at five, they had seen their share of fieldwork and lye soap.

"Don't forget to leave the gloves on at all times. You may keep both hands in the muff, and stroke it along your cheek if you wish, but a proper lady always keeps her hands covered."

Penny smiled at Amanda's use of the words *proper lady,* and sat up straighter.

"Good girl, Penelope." Amanda smiled. "And remember, I'm Mother."

Just then, the carriage door opened, letting in a swirl of cold, night air. Amanda shivered, but icy rivulets of perspiration ran beneath the stays of her corset. They had sent her on her own, and now it was up to her to get them to New York.

The station was fairly empty as the cab driver helped Amanda and Penny down from the carriage. Amanda paid him after he had loaded her trunks on the loading dock, and she walked to the clerk behind a small, barred window to purchase their tickets.

"Two first-class tickets, please," Amanda requested politely. The little man didn't look up as he began to print out two pale yellow slips. Amanda glanced back quickly at Penny, whom she had left sitting on a polished wooden bench by their luggage. Penny sat contentedly, rubbing the cherished muff against her face over and over again. Amanda smiled and turned back to the clerk. The man wrote slowly, precisely, as if he had all the time in the world, not fifteen minutes before departure. Amanda's eyes scanned the small enclosure. It was crowded with papers and pencils, ledger books and quills. In the far corner was a small, black safe with a notice board above it. One large poster in particular caught her attention. The word "REWARD" screamed out at her. The skin beneath her collar began to grow clammy. She gasped shortly when she read the words "father and daughter." The little man glanced up at her. Amanda quickly tried to compose her face.

"Damn, you're a darkie! Can't have no niggers in first class. You done fool me with that there English accent of yours." With a none too pleasant string of words, the man proceeded to rip up the tickets he had so laboriously printed. Still muttering, he grabbed two pale pink slips and began to make out the information again.

"Excuse me, sir." Amanda began, anger scorching her cheeks. "I fail to see . . ."

The little man lifted bloodshot gray eyes to her. His mouth was set in a grim line of determination, challenging her. She remembered the weasellike face of the steward, Jenkins. Although this man's face was round and bulbous, the eyes were the same. She breathed deeply, prepared to give him a piece of her mind, when she recalled Minister Clay's parting words.

"And whatever you do, don't bring any undue attention to you or Penny. Fade into the background. Try to be unnoticed." Swallowing her battered pride, Amanda muttered an apology for any inconvenience she may have caused him. The man grunted in return and went back to his work. Amanda batted back the stinging tears of humiliation that threatened to fall. This would be the hardest part, to accept the role of submission. She glanced back at Penny. The child had curled up on the hard bench and was fast asleep. Amanda smiled a weak, watery smile. It was worth it. Anything to deliver this sweet, trusting child to safety.

Amanda's stomach growled loudly in protest as she looked with dismay at the disgusting car she and Penny had been shown. Her spirits sank as she pulled the child closer to her. In the mad rush and confusion to arrive at the station in enough time, she had forgotten their supper box. Now, what lay before them was a long trip in a close, cramped car with hard wooden benches and a few narrow windows that were just above Amanda's head when she was standing. Fortunately, a few of the windows had been cracked, and a little of the refreshing cool air outside dispelled the rancid smell of cigar smoke, rotting food, and unemptied chamber pots. Moving slowly toward an empty bench, Amanda kicked aside some loose trash. She carefully stepped around a large glob of expectorant. Pulling two scented handkerchiefs from her sleeve, she handed one to Penny. Watching Amanda carefully, Penny lifted it to her nose and sniffed. She smiled as the sweet rose water muted the pungent stench around them.

Amanda had just seated herself and was smoothing out her skirt when a loud squawk from behind her caused her to jump to her feet. She whirled around to stare at a filthy young white man holding a live chicken. Amanda was shocked at the sight of a live bird, and her mouth hung open in dismay. The youth laughed heartily.

"Ah, pardon Miss Molly. She be a wee bit scared right now." He laughed again, giving Amanda a mischievous wink. Holding out the scrawny chicken for Amanda to have a better look, he laughed again as she backed away. "Now, don't ye be worryin' your pretty little head none. She's a fine lass. Seems she's already takin' a shine to ye." He pulled the chicken back to rest it against his worn overcoat that appeared several sizes too small on his gangly body. With a soft, soothing voice, he spoke some strange words to the flustered animal. Instantly the animal calmed down.

Pulling Penny up, Amanda moved away from the man to sit in seats across the aisle from him. For a long time the man continued to study them. Amanda shifted uncomfortably under his scrutiny, then ignored him. There was no mistaking his thick Irish brogue, and she was English enough to know that the Irish were an uncouth, rougish lot. She wanted nothing to do with him.

Penny nestled comfortably against her side and promptly fell asleep. Amanda's head began to roll and nod, then her stomach rumbled loudly. She had missed dinner. She couldn't remember the last time she had missed a meal, and her body was in protest.

"Here, lass. Share in me bread, and quiet that rumblin'," the tall lad whispered loudly, as he bent across the aisle to hand her a chunk of a sweet-smelling bread. Amanda was mortified at his audacity to acknowledge the noises emanating from her stomach.

Lifting her nose slightly and sniffing loudly, she refused. "Thank you all the same, but I couldn't."

The man sat back briefly, his twinkling green eyes still. A frown rippled his forehead. Shrugging, he thrust the food toward her again. "Ye caught me by surprise there. I sure wasn' expectin' ye to be no English. Da would have me by the seat o' my pants if'n he was to know I was sharin' with a queen's man, or woman." He continued to study Amanda from beneath long, coal-black eyelashes.

When Amanda's stomach growled even louder, he smiled knowingly. Grudgingly, she accepted the offering. It was delicious. When she broke it in half, obviously to save some for Penny, the man shook his head.

"Me aunt packed plenty." Miss Molly's owner jerked his head toward a large canvas bag at his side. Turning his dark curly head to the sleeping Penny, he smiled gently. "She be a pretty wee lass. Who's is she?"

Amanda stiffened at the question, then forced herself to relax. "Thank you. She's my daughter. We are here on holiday from London." The last words died on her lips, as the young man shook his head sadly.

"That tale's full o' holes, it 'tis. That wee thing don' look a think like ye." Looking back up at Amanda, his mouth twitched in amusement. "Perhaps her Da is an Injun?"

Amanda looked quickly at Penny's sleeping visage, then

remembered herself. "Yes he is, does. My husband has American Indian blood."

The impish smile remained on the lad's face. "Hm, white blood, too, I'd say."

Amanda shook her head in a series of startled shakes. She opened her mouth, then closed it, her head still shaking.

"She's sure as I'm sittin' here not English. I heard her talkin' to that wee furry thing back at the station. Sounded southern as you please."

Amanda's mind began to race frantically as she gazed at the fur muff in Penny's lap. She had told Penny not to talk on the journey, and now this man knew. She glanced back at the Irishman, her eyes imploring.

Just then, the door behind her banged open. Two well-dressed gentlemen walked into the dark car. One man had a stack of reward posters in one gloved hand, a black silver-tipped walking stick in his other. He turned to his partner.

"Believe me, Jeremy, they always think they're safe when they hit the North. Dang fools'll hop right on the first train headin' to New York. Ya see ya gotta catch em 'fore they get there."

The shorter man grinned gleefully and held out his hand for half the posters. "Give me my share, and I'll start at the other end. And please, let's hurry. The stench is enough to set a man retching." This man was obviously from the North and had a flat nasal twang to his words.

Amanda felt her stomach pitch back and forth; the sweet bread of a few minutes ago turned sour and leaden. Pulling Penny's bonnet lower over her face, Amanda said a quick, silent prayer. *Please, dear God, don't let these men be looking for Penny.* Out of the corner of her eye, she saw the southern man rest his gloved hand on the back of her seat. The small hairs on the nape of her neck rose, sending prickles of fear and foreboding down her spine. She heard the rustle of the papers in his hand as he pivoted to look at her. Clenching her teeth together, she smiled politely.

"Good day, sir. Is there something I might help you with?"

The man was taken aback. He had clearly not expected such a cultured English voice to come from her. Regaining his composure, he narrowed his eyes suspiciously. "Where's your man, girlie?" he hissed.

Slowly but surely, anger seeped over the raging panic that lurked in her mind. Maintaining her composure, she ignored his insolent tone and answered, "I'm traveling alone on holiday with my little daughter." Amanda smiled graciously.

The man laughed, a loud honking noise. "Jeremy, come here! You gotta see this. I got myself a cultured darky."

Amanda felt outrage burning up her neck and cheek. Over and over, she repeated to herself that she must stay calm for Penny's sake. An angry retort stung the tip of her tongue. As the northern man sauntered up the aisle, he spat at the Irishman's feet.

"We got plenty of em' up here." Without taking his eyes from Miss Molly's owner, he sneered at the boy. "Hey, you, what you doing back here with the coloreds?" Her interrogator turned to look at the Irishman across from her.

"Well, sir, accordin' to the Know-Nothings, as the station master so pleasantly put it, 'The black man may be black on the outside, but the Irish are black on the inside' " Leaning back against his wooden backrest, the young man cocked his head and smiled. "No matter to me. Saved me a bob or two."

The man who had addressed him spat again. This time his saliva hit the Irishman's worn boot. "Damn Mick. Wish you and all the other foreigners would go back from where you came." He turned a glare at Amanda. He stopped as he squinted at Penny's face. "Stuart?" the short, stocky man began. Amanda felt her palm go slick with perspiration. The man had recognized Penny. She looked over to the Irishman, pleading for help. He must have seen it, too, for in the next second, he tossed Miss Molly at the man's legs.

The chicken squawked in protest, flapping its wings in fright, shedding feathers everywhere. The man backed up the aisle, one hand thrown in front of his face. The chicken began to relieve itself all over his pants leg.

"Blasted beast, catch him, Stuart!"

The man named Stuart laughed and backed up toward the door. "Get your stinking fowl away from me, you trouble-makin' Mick."

The chicken, agitated by the man's loud voice, squawked and fluttered nervously, the foul-smelling excrement becoming unbearable.

"Let's get out of here, Jeremy. None here today." The gloved man brushed a stray feather off his sleeve and pushed on the door.

"But what about the little girl?" his companion asked as he, too, edged to the door, the now angry chicken pecking unmercifully at his leg, dodging the few kicks directed at her.

Stuart's voice was muffled now, as he headed into the noisy passageway between cars. "The little girl we're looking for is with her father or aunt and uncle. Not an uppity English nigger." Jeremy turned to kick one last time at the frantic chicken. He missed. Frustrated, he swung his fist at the Irishman, landing with a solid thud against his eye socket. The dark-haired lad raised his fist. A gloved hand reached through the narrow opening of the door and hauled Jeremy out before the heavy door swung shut and the Irish lad could reach him. Amanda's breath came out in a loud gush, and she began to shiver. Penny, wide-eyed, rubbed the remaining sleep from her eyes.

"I owe you," Amanda began as the Irishman rose, fingering his swelling eye, to collect his chicken.

"T'was nothin'," began the man, as he smoothed Miss

Molly's feathers. "Although my da might have somethin' to say 'bout the shiner I'm sure to be gettin'." He winked, then grimaced in pain.

"He'll be angry that you were fighting?" Amanda asked sympathetically.

"Nay," answered the young man with a quirky smile. "He'll be mad that I did na' get me punch in." He laughed at the dismayed expression on Amanda's face. He doffed his cap. "Me ma always said her boys is hopeless clods. Here I did na' even introduce myself proper. I'm Kevin Patrick McCarthy, at your service, ma'am."

Amanda smiled at the ludicrous picture before her. With trousers that barely reached his shins, Mr. McCarthy stood bowing before her with a battered fisherman's cap in one hand and an agitated chicken named Miss Molly in the other. The stress and tension had been too much, and now this. Amanda burst into genuine peals of laughter.

"I'm Miss Amanda Smith, and this is my daughter Penelope." The words were barely out, when she had to clap her slender gloved hands over her mouth to stop the definitely unladylike snorts of laughter that threatened to follow.

Mr. McCarthy proved to be a quite enjoyable companion, dispelling many of the unfounded prejudices against the Irish under which she had been raised. Kevin, too, had a slight softening of the heart toward the English, at least this one, and was thrilled when he found out she could read.

"Would ye be mindin' readin' a wee letter from me sister Margaret? See, she's workin' in a fine house in Saint Louis and is learnin' her letters from the grand lady she works for." Without waiting for an answer, Kevin pulled a wrinkled linen envelope from his breast pocket. "She went with me older brother Seamus 'bout four years ago. He's a pathfinder and trapper, don't ye know. He's been out to Injun country. First white man in some parts. Says the Oregon Territory is green as Ireland, but with rich, black, fertile soil. He says the trees grow so tall, ye can't much see the sky for the branches. Someday I'm gonna get me some land out there." Kevin closed his eyes to savor his dream.

Amanda fought the desire to tell him that she, too, was going to head out West, not someday, but soon. She gnawed on her bottom lip, knowing she could say nothing. She might endanger Jacob and Penny.

"Tell me Mr. McCarthy—"

"Kevin please, Miss Smith. It don't seem right being called a mister. I aren't used to it."

Amanda smiled and nodded. "All right. Kevin, if I were to, say, go to Saint Louis while I was on holiday, would you consider writing a letter of introduction to your sister for me?"

Kevin smiled, then chuckled inwardly, as if at a private joke. "I'd be pleased to do so, but ye'd be the one writtin' it."

Amanda nodded and ducked her head. How silly of her! Obviously, if he couldn't read, he couldn't write. She smiled sheepishly, and held out her hand for the rumpled letter he held.

The letter was difficult to read. The writing was awkward and the spelling atrocious, but Amanda plowed through it. Thankfully, it wasn't long. As she refolded the letter, Kevin sighed. "Ain't she grand? Tis her learnin' that lets us folks back here know what Seamus is about."

"Your brother certainly sounds courageous," Amanda encouraged. "Does he often visit Saint Louis?"

Kevin eyed her suspiciously, as he spoke. "Nay, but he does get 'round to Independence, Missouri, a lot. See, that's where the wagon trains heading out West leave from. With the findin' of gold in the Californias, lots of folks are heading out to find their fortunes." Sitting back and stroking Miss Molly's shiny beak, he continued. "Not for me, though. I wager a man's fortune to be with ownin' land." Turning his one swollen eye and one twinkling green eye back to Amanda, he grinned. "Would you be wantin' a letter of introduction to me brother, now?"

Amanda laughed and fidgeted with her reticule strings. "Maybe . . . just maybe." She tried to sound nonchalant, but she knew it wouldn't hurt to be prepared. There was still no guarantee that Jacob would take her out West with him, and she'd need some insurance and protection.

When Kevin continued to study her, she fought to find a new topic of conversation. "Mr.—Kevin, I mean, tell me who the Know-Nothings are. I've never heard of them."

Kevin sighed deeply, taking his eyes from her to stare at the ceiling. "It's funny. Thought we'd find a land o' golden opportunities when we got off the boat. For months on that filthy, stinkin' ship we talked about the land of freedom." Now he turned, a wry smile crossing his lips. He repeated the word *freedom*. "The land of equal opportunity. The black man's a slave in the South, and the black man and foreigner is barely tolerated up North. How's that for equality for all?"

It took Amanda slightly by surprise to hear the bitterness in one so young. Kevin's face grew serious, his twinkling eyes still pools of brooding anger. "They're called the Know-Nothings because when asked about a beating or fire, they claim to know nothing at all. They especially hate us Catholics; say we're after getting the Pope to rule the United States. My sister Mary was pulled from her convent one night, where she was a novice. They stripped her bare and searched her for . . ." His voice broke, and tears threatened to fall. His voice quavered as he drew it in slowly. "They said the good sisters was breeding papist bastards to take over the country." Turning his head away, he fought for composure. Amanda laid a comforting hand on his shoulder. Penny clung to her tightly, eyes wide with fear. When Kevin turned back, he smiled at the child. "Don't worry, wee one. They don't have much to do with black folks. Actually, some of them claim to be abolitionist." Penny nodded slowly, but retained her grip on Amanda.

After this revelation, Amanda and her companion grew silent, both lost in their thoughts. With no windows to look out, Amanda pulled out her Bible and began to read in the book of Job.

The train stopped with a lurch, and the Bible lying loosely in Amanda's sleeping hands, went skidding across the filthy floor. With a cry of dismay, she rose to get it. Kevin reached it first and handed it to her. His eye was no longer red, but had turned a mottled shade of violet, and his cheerful smile had returned.

"Last stop, New York!" Turning to the bag beside him, he gave Amanda a wrapped parcel. From the sweet scent that emanated from the package, she knew it was some of the bread she had eaten earlier.

"Thank you," she said, as she nodded to first the Bible, then the bread.

Kevin smiled, his face growing solemn. "Someone meeting ye at the station? New York isn't the safest of places for a couple of young lasses to be wanderin' about at this time of night."

Amanda nodded, and taking Penny's hand, rose to exit the door that had been propped open. Kevin hopped down and offered his hand. Amanda was grateful for the assistance, as there was no conductor or step down to assist the passengers in their car.

As Kevin doffed his hat and scurried off into the dark recesses of the station, she suddenly felt very afraid and lost. Tightening her grip on Penny's hand, she scanned the few faces on the platform. No one seemed to recognize her or come forward. She swallowed hard, but icy fingers of dread seemed to tighten about her chest. They had said to trust them, that someone would meet them. Biting the inside of her cheek, she tried to remain calm for Penny's sake. She had not even been given a name. Squaring her shoulders, she started off toward the mound of luggage being unloaded. Pushing her fear from her mind, she pointed out her things to a bag boy. Looking around again, she spotted the two rude white men who had entered their car looking for runaways. Her heart stopped. She felt faint, and gripped Penny's hand tighter. The child looked up to her with solemn, trusting eyes. She had to do something. She was supposedly safe in New York, but she wasn't taking any chances.

Hailing a carriage, she ordered the man to load the luggage as she tipped the boy. Taking one last look at the thinning crowd milling about, she allowed herself and Penny to be lifted into the cab. After a moment's hesitation, she asked the driver to suggest a place to stay. She told him that she and her daughter had delayed their visit, and would be returning to Liverpool in a fortnight. The driver seemed satisfied with her story and explained that not many hotels accepted colored clients. He did know of a boardinghouse in the tenth district run by an abolitionist. Looking again at Amanda's fine clothes and numerous trunks, he apologized that it wasn't in the best of neighborhoods, but was reserved for the Negroes and the Irish. Amanda smiled resignedly, and told him to take them there.

The landlord was most gracious, and hastily had them installed in some tiny but clean rooms. Amanda had just tucked Penny into bed and entered the small sitting room to get her toiletry case, when she heard a soft, urgent knock on the door. Again, Amanda's heart began to pound. She didn't know a soul in New York. Who would be coming to call at this hour? Who even knew where she was staying? Moving toward the door, she laid her cheek against the smooth, painted surface.

"Who's there?" she whispered loudly.

"Kevin McCarthy," a familiar voice replied. Opening the door a crack, Amanda slipped out, so as not to wake the sleeping girl. With incredible control, she refrained from throwing her arms around the boy's neck with relief.

"Oh, Kevin, how pleasant of you to call! How did you find us here?" The lad smiled a wide, wicked grin.

"The truth be told, I was worried about ye an' the wee lass. I saw those two gents a lookin' after ye, and thought it bore no good. Limey, the hack driver, knows me father. They share a few pints now and then. I asked, and he told me."

A frown wrinkled Amanda's forehead. She wasn't pleased with the driver's obvious indiscretion.

"Well, I was thinkin' it wasn't right, given the circumstances an' all, that there wasn' a soul to meet ye. So I asked 'round the pub a little. It's just down the street. I hear it told that Senator Clay sent a bill before the gov'ment today, askin' for a compromise. Seems most likely he's gonna get it, too. Most of the gov'ment's scared the Union is gonna split. Slave owners are a might angry over no slavery in the new territories and their slaves runnin' away. They say a man's got his right to his property, and that the Yanks are preventin' them from getting their people back."

Amanda shook her head in confusion, and after glancing quickly up and down the deserted hall, she beckoned Kevin to come inside. He hesitated, knowing that it was unseemly for a young man to be entering an unchaperoned lady's room at this hour of the night.

"Come on in, before someone sees you. I know it isn't right, but, well, it isn't safe to talk in public," Amanda whispered, as she turned to enter the room.

Kevin nodded, seeing her reasoning, and followed her, closing the door softly behind him. Nervously, he stood by the door, ready to bolt. "See, Miss Smith." He had taken to using her formal name, as if to make up for the inpropriety of their situation. Amanda ignored it, and stood by the shuttered window. "Although the Missouri Compromise isn't a law yet, folk say it's a matter of time. The bill calls for stiff punishments for those aiding or concealing fugitive slaves." Amanda didn't answer, but wrung her hands. The answer was becoming clear. The people who were to have met her and Penny had gotten scared.

"Then you'd better go now, Mr. McCarthy," Amanda said softly. She had to think, and she didn't want to get this generous boy in trouble.

Kevin stuck out his chin obstinately. "Where are you gonna go, Miss Smith?"

Amanda looked up at him and cocked her head to one side, frowning. "I don't see that it is any of your affair, Mr. McCarthy," she responded politely.

Kevin ignored this and moved a step toward her. "Ye should go take the girl back to England. I saw the reward poster. That's her, isn't it?" His last words were more a statement than a question, and Amanda didn't answer. "Her da could be dead, but if he comes looking, I'll be sure to let him know where you've gone. He can find ye there." Amanda thought over the words. She thought of Penny deprived of both mother and father. Then she thought of Jacob waiting in peril for her to deliver his daughter so he could head out West and offer her the family life she had never known.

"No," Amanda stated flatly. When Kevin took another step closer, she retreated. "I can't. I promised her father. He's waiting."

Kevin turned back to the door, his hand on the brass knob. He stood silently for several minutes, his shoulders rising and falling slowly with his deep breaths. "Ye are going to Saint Louis, aren't ye?" That question as well lay unanswered. Kevin continued as if she had admitted to the plan. "My brother Seamus will be in Independence, Missouri, come spring. I'm going with ye.''

Amanda's gasp forced him to turn around. She was visibly shaken. He smiled a lopsided grin, almost a smirk. "Surprised I guessed so much?" Amanda shook her head, her hand still at her silent mouth. "It weren't verra hard, Miss Amanda. Ye got that look like me. When I tol' ye about the West, your eyes sparkled the way I suppose mine do. Ye best be heading to the Northwest, because the law says all territories north of the Mason-Dixie line, and west of the Rocky Mountains is free soil.''

Amanda moved to a low slipper chair by the bedroom door. She sank down, her skirts billowing out around her, then falling to a silken pool of copper brown around her. She had never been one to bite her nails, but she did so now. Kevin stood awkwardly at the door, his cap in his hands, turning it around and around before his hips.

"I can't go until Friday," Amanda whispered, her soft voice strained and tired. When Kevin didn't answer, she looked up to him. "I'm to meet someone on Thursday night's train."

Kevin nodded. "I'll be back Friday. I guess I'd better let me ma and da know me plans." With a mischievous wink, he slipped silently out the door. Amanda rose and went to the window. Pulling down on one of the slats, she peered out into the street below. It was dark. Only one of the street lamps was lit. She saw Kevin saunter down from the boardinghouse steps. He placed his hat on his head; tucking his hands in his pockets, he headed toward the only lit building down the street. She watched as the door to the pub opened, the light and noise spilling out into the icy street. Kevin stopped, faced her window, and doffed his hat. She couldn't make out his face from the distance, but she was sure he was smiling. She let go of the slat and stood for several moments facing the shuttered window. She had to think. Kevin was so young, but he was white, and he was male.

After a sleepless night, Amanda decided the best course of action was to follow the original plan, until she could talk with Rollin and Melody. She assumed their train would be the same one she and Penny had taken, and would arrive at the same time on Thursday evening. In the meantime, she and Penny would continue to be the mother and daughter on holiday.

"Penelope, listen carefully. I don't want you to talk, except to say 'Mother,' and 'yes sir,' and 'no sir,' and 'thank you.' But you are only to say those things if I tell you that you must." After several hours of practice, Penny's accent on those few words was passable as an English child. Calling on all her courage, Amanda left the boardinghouse with her daughter in tow. Picking their way carefully along the boardwalk, Amanda was disgusted by the few drunks lying sprawled before the now silent pubs. Thankful for the cold, which made the mud streets solid, she stepped down and around the men. A florid policeman stood nearby. In a loud voice, Amanda pointed out the sin of alcohol to her supposed daughter. Penny nodded with wide eyes, saying nothing. The policeman tipped his hat. Amanda approached him and asked if he could hail a cab for her, and could he recommend an eating establishment and a dress shop? The policeman shifted uncomfortably from foot to foot and said he could not. His accent was a heavy Scotch-Irish brogue, and he flushed under Amanda's scrutiny. His breath smelled of liquor, and she was sure he was afraid of a tongue-lashing on his vices. Just then, an empty carriage clopped by, and the uncomfortable officer waved it down.

After taking them to a small bakery, the driver dropped them off at a large mercantile store. Looking about her, Amanda was disappointed. She had expected America, especially a big city like New York, to be grander. It was busy, crowded, and dirty like London, but the buildings were so much smaller and cruder than those at home. Although a few buildings spoke of some wealth and refinement, these didn't quite measure up to the fine old architecture of London.

Penny, on the other hand, was flabbergasted. She had never been outside of the small Georgia plantation on which she had been born. All her travel since then had been limited to secrecy and enshrouded by night. In broad daylight, New York seemed massive and frightening. She moved closer to Amanda's heavy, fur-lined cloak. Sensing the child's fear, Amanda bent down to whisper encouragement in her ear.

"Don't worry, darling. Stay close to me so you don't get lost. What do you say, we go look at a doll for you? A souvenir of the States." These last words she said loud enough, so that any passerby could hear.

Penny looked up with total astonishment. Did Miss Amanda mean that she was to have a real doll of her own? Not just a stick with a cloth pinned around it, but a doll with arms and legs? She was bursting to ask her questions, when she remembered her promise. Squeezing Amanda's hand tightly, she nearly skipped into the store.

Penny stopped short. Never in her wildest dreams had she envisioned such a spectacle as that which lay before her! There were shelves and shelves of every imaginable goods. There were bolts and bolts of jewel-colored silks and satins. Wheels and wheels of lace and ribbon. On the shelves were glass and china jars and vases, and over near the window was the most wonderful array of toys in the world. The plantation where she had grown up had no white children, so Penny had never seen a toy, save for those that were depicted in the background of the painting of the young Master Whitingworth when he was a boy. When Miss Amanda tugged her over to that part of the store, she was afraid to touch them. Amanda had no such qualms. She bent to pick up a small doll on a rocking horse to look at the tag. A small, white, mealy mouthed lady scooted swiftly out from behind her counter and scurried over to Amanda and Penny.

"May I help you, miss?" the woman asked in a haughty voice. She was caught off guard when Amanda turned around and said, "Yes" in her most authoritative voice.

Penny stifled a giggle as she saw the woman give Amanda a once-over glance, then shrink. The woman had obviously underestimated Amanda's position and wealth. In an attempt to cover her ill manners, the woman smiled a pitiful smile that looked rusty and unused.

"Oh, you're English. What can I help you and your lovely—sister with?"

Amanda smiled a cold, arrogant smile, enjoying the woman's obvious discomfort. It served her right for every other less fortunate Negro who had browsed on the premises.

"This is my daughter, Penelope, and we have come to purchase a doll for her as a souvenir." Amanda turned back to the array of wooden and papier-mâché dolls. "These won't do."

Penny's heart sank. These dolls were all wonderful, and any one of them would have been perfect.

"I was looking for a porcelain doll, with teeth and real hair."

The clerk's face lit up. "Oh, I believe we have just what you are looking for. We keep them high up, so they don't get broken by careless children." The woman turned to head toward a small stepladder. "Now, would you be wanting a baby doll, or a fashion doll?" Without waiting for an answer, the woman had a black boxboy of twelve or thirteen climb up the ladder and bring down several boxes. Staggering beneath their weight, the boy thankfully rested them on the counter. He smiled brightly at Amanda, obviously enjoying watching his employer squirm beneath a black woman's demands. One by one, Amanda had the woman pull out the beautiful, angelic creations. There were blonds, brunettes, redheads, boys, girls, and bonneted babies. In the last box, the woman pulled out several smaller wax and leather dolls. In the bottom of the box was a small, thirteen-inch Negress doll. Penny released a small cry of joy. The woman pulled the doll out of the tissue. She was papier-mâché with a molded wax face. The face was ethnically correct, with tightly curled hair. Her dress fell softly off her shoulders, revealing a painted gold cross on a chain, and a pair of gold earrings. The woman reluctantly handed the doll to Amanda. It was not one of the more expensive ones. Amanda turned to hand the doll to Penny. Penny held it gently, running a shy finger over the billowing sleeves and over the smooth, black wooden limbs. Unable to contain himself any longer, the helpful boxboy stepped closer to Penny.

"She's got a black leather body, and real petticoats and bloomers." Suddenly embarrassed by his confession that he had looked at a doll's underclothing and body, he flushed and hurried off, saying he might be needed in the back. The clerk glared after him before she turned an apologetic smile to Amanda.

"It is so hard to find good nigger help." The woman froze, her face draining of color when she realized what she had just said. Her mouth moved, but no words came out.

"Boys will be boys. They are the *same* the world over," Amanda retorted icily. She then turned to the entranced Penny. Penny's head was bent low over the doll, and was counting the number of petticoats. "Penelope, is that the doll you want? Or would you like to look some more?"

The woman shifted uneasily behind the counter. This was all she had to show. Penny looked up at Amanda as if she had gone crazy. Why would she want any of those other dolls, when she could have this doll? Who cared if the others could blink their eyes, or had teeth and hair? This was the most beautiful doll in the world, and she was going to name her Rebecca.

Amanda smiled a knowing smile and asked the price. The woman hedged and looked put out. She had been expecting a big sale. The porcelain dolls before her were worth up to one hundred dollars. The clerk pulled out a list from a small drawer near the register. She pursed her thin lips and ran a finger along the list of words. Amanda moved down the counter to study the list upside down. With a long, graceful finger she pointed to a figure at the bottom of the page. A red line had been drawn through it, and by its side was written the amount of two ninety-five. The woman studied it a bit longer. "That must be a mistake. I'll have to check with my husband."

Amanda opened her reticule and waited while the woman disappeared behind a curtained door. In a few minutes, a booming, deep voice sounded from behind the closure.

"Let her have it. Christ, it's been sittin' in my inventory for months. I'd be givin' it away if you don't sell it to her. Now go. I've got work to do, woman."

The crimson-faced woman appeared from behind the burgundy curtain. She ran her hands along the length of her dark skirt and smiled nervously at Amanda. Glancing back over her shoulder, she cleared her throat.

"Miss, I will be happy . . ."

Before she could continue, Amanda handed the woman three crisp dollar bills. She had no intention of dickering with this woman. The woman stared for a few minutes at the bills lying on the counter. When she raised her eyes, a shrewd, calculating look flickered through them. Amanda clicked her money purse closed with a determined finality.

"That will be all, thank you. Come along, Penelope, we've other shopping to do." With that, she marched out of the shop. Penny followed, her eyes never leaving her precious Rebecca.

* * *

Amanda stretched out on her bed while Penny played happily on the floor. She was pouring tea into a thimble for Rebecca while she sipped from her own real cup. Amanda closed her eyes, letting her cup of tea grow cold. Today had been quite an ordeal, and she didn't know if she was up to another day of it tomorrow. Glancing down at the little girl happily chatting with her doll, Amanda knew she would, and must. Tomorrow, Rollin and Melody would arrive. She would discuss things with them. Surely, they would have some answers. Sitting up, she crossed over to the small table under the mirror. Picking up a small piece of paper, she unfolded it carefully. The note had been left under her door when they had arrived this afternoon. The scrawl was awkward and unpracticed, but the words were simple: "Porick's 9 tonight." Folding the torn sheet up carefully, she placed it in her Bible. She knew Porick's was the pub down the street, and she had no doubt that Kevin had sent the note. What she didn't know was why Kevin had to see her tonight and who had written the note for him. One more person, one more risk.

Later that evening, Amanda pulled the door closed and prayed Penny wouldn't awaken while she was gone. The child smiled blissfully in her sleep, Rebecca in her arms, but still, the nightmares might come. They didn't come as frequently nor were they as terrifying as before, but they were still enough to wake the child and leave her trembling and frightened. With these worries, Amanda sneaked out the kitchen door of the boardinghouse and hurried down the street. She'd just tell Kevin to be brief.

Out of the darkness, a hand grabbed her arm, while another slapped over her mouth. Amanda struggled, to no avail. A harsh laugh behind her made her squint into the darkness, trying to see her abductor. It was the dark, swarthy man from the train. She tried to scream, but the man jabbed his thumb upward between her ribs, cutting off her air.

"I think I'll just take you far enough down South that no one will know where to look for you. Those southern gents would pay a pretty price for a pretty one such as you." When Amanda tried to struggle again, he pressed her hard against him. "I wouldn't try anything, if I were you. It would be a shame to mar the merchandise." He stroked one rough thumb over her cheek. Amanda's heart pounded unmercifully against her chest, her breath coming in short pants, made all the more difficult by the man's hands on her mouth and ribs. The man leaned forward, his heavy breath rasping in her ear.

"Promise not to scream, and I'll let you breathe a little easier." He licked the rim of her ear. "Um, I might have to sample the goods first myself."

Amanda drew back in disgusted horror. The stocky man tightened his hold, his arms crushing her ribs. Small splotches of black danced before her eyes; her head was pounding. She couldn't faint; she had to keep her head. She had to figure out how to escape. Amanda nodded her head, promising not to scream. The man's grip on her loosened. He turned her toward him. Although he was only a few inches taller than her, his shoulders spread a half a foot past hers. This man was small but strong. He pulled her close against him. She felt his solid manhood press against her, but unlike Jacob, this did nothing to excite her. It only repulsed her. As Amanda struggled to calm herself, she took mental notes. She realized his breath was tainted with brandy. His words were slightly slurred as he nibbled her neck and ear.

"Hell, those stupid bastards down South would sell their own kin. Met a man in Kentucky once who said he did." Her capturer laughed with genuine amusement that sounded sadistic and terrifying. "The man actually stained and tanned his own flesh and blood dark as niggers. Sold 'em. Yes he did." Again, a drunken, sinister laugh filled the dark alleyway. "Um, but you taste sweet, better than them whores by the pier. You ain't bad for a darkie."

Amanda remained frozen, while the man loosened his hold altogether and allowed his hands to roam freely over her body. Amanda forced her mind to concentrate on her surroundings. The man was drunk, but how drunk? If she were to escape, where could she go? Could she outrun him? The man was fumbling with her skirts, and she was thankful for all the "damned underthings" as Jacob had called them. The man was definitely intoxicated and was cursing under his breath as the petticoats kept slipping from his fingers. *One, two, three!* Amanda drew in a deep breath, then raised her knee with all the power she had in her body. The man crumpled to the ground, cradling his groin in pain. Drawing her foot back, she landed a swift kick to the man's temple. She closed her eyes and grimaced when she heard the soft thud. Looking down into the still face of her attacker, she prayed she hadn't killed him, only given herself enough time to escape.

Tearing her eyes away, she hesitated. Had Kevin really sent her the note? He couldn't write. But he could have had someone write it. If he hadn't written the note, and this man had, then perhaps—oh, dear God, not Penny! Amanda fled down the street and raced up the stairs to the boardinghouse. The light was on inside as she tore down the hall to her room. She fumbled for the key, her heart in her throat. The door was unlocked. She burst through the door, not sure what she would do if Penny was gone, or if the southern companion of the man who had just attacked her was there. A scream was rising in her throat, when it died to a whimper of thanks.

Amanda fell to her knees, tears streaming down her face. Penny sat asleep in Kevin's lap as he rocked her in an armless rocking chair. Rising, Kevin put Penny back in bed and closed the bedroom door. He hurried over to Amanda, deep concern etched in his face.

"I was worried, when ye did na show tonight. I was afraid something happened. Then the child started to cry out." He raised Amanda to her feet, his eyes taking in her disheveled hair and the ripped seam connecting her bodice to her skirt. His voice grew quiet. "What happened? Did he find ye then? Are you all right?"

Amanda began to tremble, the tears slipping down her cheeks again. Kevin pulled her to his chest. Awkwardly he began patting her back. "There, there, wee one, don't ye cry." Amanda drew in a sob, then choked on a little laugh. Kevin held her away, confusion in his emerald eyes.

"Wee one?" Amanda choked out as sobs mingled with laughter.

Kevin smiled back and shrugged. "Well ye are a mite smaller than me."

Amanda rubbed her eyes and laughed softly, while the tears continued to squeeze past the barrier. "Kevin, what are you, fifteen, sixteen?" She pulled her hands down and looked at him, a trembling smile on her lips.

He understood. He had seen his sister Mary like this after, after—she, too, had had to laugh, asking ludicrous questions, so she wouldn't break down. He crossed his arms and drew himself up to his full height of five foot eleven inches. "I'm seventeen. Be eighteen in a few more months. I'm a full-grown man."

Amanda smiled, wiping the tears away with the slightly soiled handkerchief he handed her. The crisis had passed. She was all right. Her natural resilience was returning.

"Kevin, those men know where I am." She relayed to him the story of what the northern man on the train had said and done. Kevin whistled a low, quiet whistle. His eyes shone with admiration.

"Serves the varmint right. I'll be bettin' he has his pocket picked clean by now. His boots, too, most likely. That's what

I wanted to warn ye about. He'd been asking around. But yar right. If he's still alive, he'll be angry as a leprechaun bereft of his pot o' gold. Leave yar things and come with me now. I'll tell the landlord to hold it 'til we can send for it. Ye and the lass can stay with me family for now, but we can na wait for Friday.''

Amanda knew he was right, but her heart sank at the thought of not being able to see Rollin and Melody, to let them know she and Penny were all right.

Ten

"Damn it lass, it's not safe! If they go and take ye, who'll be lookin' after the wee one?" Kevin's father's voice boomed through the apartment as his beefy fists slammed down on the table. Maureen, his diminutive wife, cringed each time the wooden planks rattled from the blow. Kevin stood with his arm around his mother, an amused, quizzical look in his eyes. Amanda didn't flinch. Kevin had told her his father was all bark, no bite. Also, in the last two days, she had witnessed his gentle, loving manner to both his wife and the four remaining children at home.

At first Sean Francis McCarthy had been furious to find two unwelcome colored guests in his house and one of them English, to boot. He had gone on about the friction between the blacks and the Irish in the tenth district. Jobs for both were few and far between, setting one against the other. His heavy, florid face had nearly glowed as he shook his tall son's shoulders. What would the patrons at his pub think? Him giving shelter to a black woman and child, when there were plenty of their own kind that needed help.

Kevin had stood silently while his father had raged, only speaking when his father finally collapsed with his head in his hands at the table he now vigorously thumped. In his charming, perceptive way, the young man had reached his father's heart with the threat imposed on Mrs. Smith and her daughter. Grudgingly at first, the man had opened his home to them. And now Amanda knew from his paternal protective outrage that more than just his home had been opened to them.

"Mr. McCarthy, sir, I must go to the train to see these people. Besides, it will give me a chance to practice my disguise," Amanda explained calmly.

The large man ran a hand through his thinning gray hair in exasperation. "Are ye sure ye haven't any Irish blood in ye? Yar as stubborn as the best of 'em."

Amanda smiled inwardly. He was giving way. Sinking down in his chair, Mr. McCarthy grinned at her. "Imagine what me ol' buddies down at Porick's will say when I tell 'em a fine, cultured Englishwoman called me sir." Now Amanda allowed her smile to show. She had won. Kevin shook his head ruefully.

"I don't think its a verra good idea meself, but anyone who can beat the master McCarthy in stubbornness deserves a chance."

A mock frown creased his father's brow. "Go on ye, now. Let's see this here disguise. And mind ye now, if I can see through it, you're gonna have to convince me all over."

Maureen rolled her eyes and led Amanda into the small partitioned-off kitchen. "Ye of little faith," the woman laughed, and the men groaned.

With great care, Mrs. McCarthy unwound the braid at the nape of Amanda's neck. The thick rope dropped to the small of her back. Taking a large pair of sewing shears, the woman paused.

"Are ye sure ye want to be doing this, now?" Amanda nodded, not trusting her voice. She tried not to envision her long, coal-black hair gone. What had she come to? She closed her eyes as she heard the crisp scatchy noise of the blade cutting her hair. Then, with an almost noiseless thunk, the plait

FREEDOM'S SONG

fell to the floor. It was done; it had to be done. She had sworn before God to do her Christian duty to help Penny. What was the sacrifice of vanity to the protection of an innocent child? Amanda felt a strange lightness to her head as she twisted her neck back and forth.

"Stay still, so I can be evenin' it out." Amanda stopped her movement as Maureen trimmed the back of her hair in a even line at the nape of her neck. When she'd finished, both women were silent for a moment. "My boy's really going, isn't he?" Mrs. McCarthy asked as she brushed away the stray clippings of hair on Amanda's collar. Amanda nodded, and turned to face the woman who had given her refuge the previous night.

"Yes, he is," she said with underlying sympathy, as she slipped out of her clothes and into the ones Kevin had provided.

"All my children are going. First Seamus, then Margaret, Mary—now Kevin. Back in the homeland, the children stayed. They farmed together. They took care of their parents in old age. The grandmothers took care of the wee bairns. Now . . ." Maureen's voice broke with the age-old anguish of a mother for her chicks leaving the nest. Amanda wrapped an arm around the dainty woman and thought of her Aunty Daba. Arm in arm, they returned to the main room.

"Well, I'll be an Orangeman damned in hell!" Kevin cried, as he slapped his knee. He rose from the long table and circled around Amanda several times. "Ye look better in me clothes than I do meself." Mr. Sean McCarthy just sat there with his mouth gaping.

"Shut your mouth, man, or the banshees will come an' steal your soul." Maureen laughed at her husband. The tears of a moment ago were gone, an amused grin spread across her weary face. Life was hard, and she had learned that there wasn't much time or use for tears. She smiled at her stunned husband. She had learned to enjoy life day by day, moment by moment. At this moment, she was thoroughly enjoying her part in putting that look on her husband's face.

"Sure'n begor'n. I'd not believe ye'd be a lass if I did na know it for the truth." The large man stood up, wiped his eyes, as if to get a different perspective. Amanda threw back her head and laughed, a deep guttural sound.

"Sir, I be most grateful for yous compliment," Amanda replied in her best imitation of Rollin. The big man laughed, twisted his finger in his ear, and shook his head.

"Go on now, ye scamps," he laughed again, the booming sound shaking the room. Penny and the McCarthy's youngest, Kathleen, peered from behind the curtain that divided the sleeping quarters from the rest of the apartment. Penny's eyes grew round and watery.

"Oh, Miss Amanda! What did they do to you? Where's your pretty hair and clothes and—breast?" The little girl cried. This last remark sent father and son into a bout of hilarious laughter.

"Oh, yes, Miss Amanda, do tell where ye did hid those pretty breasts," Kevin asked with a devilish grin. Amanda ducked her head, and his mother swatted his shoulder.

"Behave yourself, young ruffian." Kevin winked at the flushed Amanda and hugged his mother. She looked up at him with adoring eyes.

"It will be all right, Penny," Amanda replied squatting down near the child. She smiled at the freedom of movement she had without her corset and petticoats. The tight linen binding across her chest ached a little, but she would get used to it.

"But Daddy will never love you as a boy," the poor girl whimpered, not at all amused by the joking going on around her. Grabbing the long braid coiled in Mrs. McCarthy's hand, she tried to place it back on top of Amanda's head. Tears streamed down her face as she saw her dreams falling away like Miss Amanda's shorn hair.

"Penny, your daddy doesn't have to love me, honey," Amanda said, as she pulled the weeping girl into her arms. Penny pulled back, poking Amanda's bound breast with a jabbing finger.

"You ain't soft no more, and my daddy won't wanna hug and kiss ya and make little babies." Amanda's face drained of color and then flushed darkly. Sean and Kevin slapped the table with glee. Mrs. McCarthy stifled a giggle and attempted to glare at the men.

"Penny, your father and I aren't married and don't even plan to get married," Amanda said, trying to keep her voice calm. Wryly, she thought to herself, he doesn't even like me. But then her mind switched back to the time when he had held her close, his desire pressing deep into her pliant skin. *"I like you jes' fine . . . like this."* Amanda shivered at the strange, uneasy feeling the memory gave her. She turned her attention back to the present. "Now, be good while I go and see your uncle and aunt." Amanda rose, not letting her eyes meet Kevin's. The unnerving memories she had tried to shake would not go away, and she didn't want to let the all too perceptive Kevin see them in her eyes.

Staying out of the main throng of people milling about the station, Amanda and Kevin sat swinging their legs from the top of a half stone wall that divided the platform from the ticket offices.

"Ye got something going with Penny's father?" Kevin asked nonchalantly, but by now, Amanda knew him better than to guess that this was an offhanded question.

"No, but I believe it is none of your affair," Amanda replied, fixing him with a stern frown. She thought she and Kevin had an unspoken pact not to discuss any aspect of her relationship with Penny. She had told him the less he knew, the better.

Kevin ignored her warning. Staring straight ahead, he continued. "Wish ye did?" he asked, his legs swinging a little faster now. Amanda tightened her lips and stared hard at his profile. She could remind him again that it was none of his business, but then he would go putting his suspicions together and, as always, come up with something quite uncomfortably near the truth, whatever that might be. It wasn't something she was prepared to think about right now. Suddenly, she smiled. She'd just have to outfox him.

"Why, are you interested?" she asked smugly. Kevin turned to her with a serious look on his face. Amanda pulled back. She wasn't prepared for his solemn expression. It made her uneasy.

"Ye are the smartest and bravest lass I ever met. I know I'm young, but out West Seamus says men even marry Injun squaws. No one cares much out there."

Amanda laughed nervously. "Is that a proposal, Kevin?"

Kevin studied her face for a long time, searching, then he dropped his eyes, and began swinging his feet again. "Nay, just an observation." Bracing his hands on the wall, he jumped down and turned to offer her some assistance. She brushed his hand away.

"Remember, I'm a boy," she whispered under her breath. As suddenly as the serious Kevin had appeared, he disappeared, and the old teasing lad appeared.

"I'll try, but I know where ye hid your pretty breasts," he cracked.

Amanda reached out to swat him, and lost her balance. With a crash, she fell hard upon her rear end.

"Clumsy!" Kevin shot at her with a grin as he strode away.

Amanda scrambled to her feet, wincing at the unlikely bruise she'd have. Fortunately, no one would see it. She hurried to catch up with Kevin. The evening train had arrived.

Cursing her disguise as a station boy, she placed the last of the trunks on the wagon. A gentleman dressed in gray kid gloves and a splendid beaver hat tossed her a nickel. She gave a little bow and looked about for Kevin. She spotted him over by a slight, auburn-haired white man of about thirty. The man was standing nervously by the colored car, checking his watch every ten seconds. Kevin beckoned to her with a slight movement of his head. Amanda smoothed her sweaty palms along the length of her trousers. It felt strange to feel the warmth of her skin beneath the fabric. She headed over toward the jumpy young man. Just as she came within fifteen feet of the colored car door, her friends, the southern gentleman, and his bandaged and bruised companion hopped down. She froze in her tracks, ready to run. They turned toward her. Out of the corner of her eye, she saw Kevin move about twelve feet behind her. The men were angry. They were arguing. The northern man was sure that the man and woman on the train fit the description Mr. Whitingworth had given them of the aunt and uncle of his slave, but where was the little brat and her bastard father?

Upon hearing the name Whitingworth, Amanda felt sick. These men stood between her and the Coffeys. She saw Rollin get down from the car and help his wife alight on the platform. The nervous man looked visibly relieved. He then led them to the stairs going up to the main street. Amanda glanced their way. Within minutes they would be gone, lost in the crowds of New York. She lowered her head and looked out from under her cap at the two men. The one who had accosted her seemed to be staring right at her. His eyes narrowed suspiciously. Her heart began to race, the blood pounding in her ears. Like the fox cornered by the frothing hound, her feet would not move. She was frozen where she stood. Suddenly, a shrill whistle came from behind her. The suspicious look on the northern slave catcher's face turned into one of murderous intent. The men came barreling toward her. She managed to retreat a step or two. As she squeezed her eyes shut, the men brushed past her, one on either side. Dazed, Amanda turned to see them round the corner after Kevin. Then they were out of sight. Amanda continued to stare, then her mind focused. Kevin was long gone. He knew the back alleys and had friends everywhere. She would be of little help to him now if she tried to follow. Silently blessing him and praying for his safety, she took off up the steep stairs after Penny's relatives.

Breathless, she arrived, just as Rollin was climbing up on the box with the driver.

"Sir, sir!" Amanda cried, trying desperately to maintain a gruff southern voice. Tucking his cloak tightly around him, Rollin ignored or did not hear her. He nodded to the driver to go. The driver raised the reins.

"Mr. Coffey, sir!" Amanda shouted. She feared her words were lost in a strong icy wind whipping at her back. Rollin stayed the driver's arm with a hand and looked down at Amanda. His face was puzzled as he lowered himself to the boardwalk.

"Boy?" Rollin asked, as he drew nearer. When he was almost toe to toe with Amanda, she whispered his niece's name. Rollin pulled back as if slapped. Then he grew angry, his large hands grasping each of Amanda's upper arms. He shook her fiercely, his face taut with anguish. "What do you know? Tell me! Tell me!"

Amanda felt dizzy from the motion and placed her hands on his chest to steady herself. Rollin stopped. Looking more closely at Amanda, he gasped. "Miss 'Manda?" Relief flooded his weary face. Then he looked around. Concern creased his brow. "Where's Penny?" Amanda pulled away from him and glanced around. No one had heard, except perhaps the driver.

"Rollin, not here. Treat me like a boy. Take me with you in the carriage," Amanda whispered. Rollin nodded, straightened his shoulders, and climbed back on top of the carriage.

"Boy, climb on back and I'll sees what kina work I can git for you."

Amanda didn't hesitate, and with some difficulty climbed onto a low step on the back of the hack. The carriage started with a jolt, the wheel spraying her with a mixture of freezing water and mud. As she sought to wipe the goop from her eyes, the horse veered into the street. She abandoned her efforts and hung on for dear life.

Amanda was exhausted after the rough ride, but was insistent on helping Rollin carry the trunks inside in order to keep up pretenses. As soon as the front door closed and the driver rode away, Rollin changed from a domineering employer to the gentle man she knew.

"Are you all right, Miss 'Manda?" Rollin asked, as he chafed her cold hands between his large warm ones. Melody stood, shocked, as she ran her eyes over and over the disguised Amanda Smith. Suddenly, she burst out laughing. The laughter was strained, the kind brought on by the release of pent-up stress and tension. Rollin looked angrily at his wife. Their host looked confused. Amanda looked from one face to the other, then joined Melody in her laughter. She welcomed the long overdue release. The women hugged, and continued to laugh. Rollin moved closer to the smaller man. They looked at each other, then at the crazed women before them.

"Ahem," the slight man cleared his throat. Amanda looked at him, then burst into a new peal of laughter. The man frowned and looked to Rollin. Rollin stamped his foot three times. Melody smiled at him, wiping tears from her eyes. She tried to speak, but then turned to kiss Amanda's cheek. They threw their arms around each other and started to cry. Rollin looked worried, then confused. If he hadn't been so desperate for information about Penny, he would have thrown up his hands in disgust. In those few minutes, a strong lasting friendship was bonded between Melody and Amanda. There would never be any doubts again.

"Tell us, Amanda, is Penny safe? Must we go to her now?" The words came out in a soft, urgent rush from Melody's mouth.

"She is safe for now," Amanda replied, her eyes on Melody.

Melody caressed her short hair, then her cheek, knowing what Amanda had sacrificed. Turning to the men, she smiled. "Penny is safe. Amanda needs rest. She can tell us more at supper." With that, Melody led Amanda up the stairs to a small room where her and Rollin's belongings had been placed. Rollin and his friend, Frederick Rauling, stood stupefied at the bottom of the stairs.

After washing herself and donning a clean shirt and pair of trousers courtesy of their hosts, Amanda felt much better. She relayed the whole story to the Coffeys and Mr. Rauling. When she had told them how no one had been there to meet her at the station, Frederick rose in anger. In frustration, he told the Coffeys about the proposed bill that would place stiff penalties on anyone helping an escaped slave. In the silence that followed, Amanda confided to them Kevin's and her plan. In a fortnight she would go as Kevin's manservant. Penny would be Amanda's little sister. Kevin, unable to read or write, would keep his right arm in a sling, and request any required signature be waived. From now until departure, Amanda would work with him on his diction and accent. Mr. Rauling leaned forward on the table, excitement quivering in his voice.

"I could help there. Send the boy to me. I'll dress him, have him groomed. By God, I'll teach him what he has to know."

Amanda nodded with pleasure. Rollin sat quietly during the

whole exchange, his massive arms folded across his chest. Scraping his chair back, he rose.

"No, Miss 'Manda, I can't let ya. It's too risky. I'm gonna take her myself." Rollin glowered at the people at the table, challenging any of them to argue. Amanda looked to Mr. Raulings, who looked to Melody. Melody looked at her husband, her face stern.

"No, you ain't." Turning to Amanda, she smiled. "Don't you go doubting Amanda, now. I was wrong before." Laying her hand on top of Amanda's, she leaned forward to kiss her forehead. "Go, my brave sister, and may God go with you."

The words embraced Amanda with a warm closeness. No matter what the future held, she had been right in offering her help. She graced the table with one of her most bedazzling smiles.

"Ah, damn," Rollin muttered, and that was the end of the conversation.

"Oh, my Lord," Amanda whispered, as she looked at her bruised and battered friend. Immediately she was on her knees by the bed. "Oh, Kevin!" she wailed, as she ran her gaze over his face. Kevin chuckled weakly.

"Should have seen the other fellow." He wheezed painfully. "It's only a few ribs." Glancing down at the sling on his right arm, he smiled ruefully. "Dislocated the collarbone, too. The doctor says I'll be in a sling for weeks. No need to go off pretendin', now. Thank the Lord for wee blessins, eh?" His green eyes twinkled in amusement under swollen purple lids.

Amanda would have swatted him for his insolence, if he hadn't already been in such discomfort. Stroking the black, tangled mass of curls on top of his head, she sighed. "Thank you. Can I do anything for you?"

Kevin shook his head. "Ye found them, then?" he asked, his eyes bright with curiosity.

Amanda nodded, then hesitated before she asked the question she knew she had to ask. "Can you, are you still willing to follow through with our plan? I'll understand if . . ."

Kevin sat up straight in his bed, wincing with the pain. "Of course I'll be goin'. Damn their black souls to hell." He stopped, peering up at Amanda from beneath his puffy lids. "Sorry 'bout the black part an all." Studying her with a mischievous glint in his eyes, he spoke slowly. "Ye aren't really black, but more of a sweet maple syrup brown, I'd say."

Amanda flushed uneasily at his husky, intimate tone. Kevin eased himself back on his pillows carefully, watching her discomfort with poorly hidden pleasure. Chuckling softly so as not rattle his ribs, he winked. "Got ye now, didn' I?"

Amanda laughed, hesitated, and them placed a gentle, sisterly kiss on his battered forehead. Kevin pressed back against his pillow, the back of his good hand against his eyes. "Ah, now I've surely heard the fairies sing," Kevin murmured as he closed his eyes in mock ecstasy.

Taking his hand, Amanda laughed and told him of her meeting.

Eleven

The two weeks flew by, and Amanda and Penny had begun to feel as though they were part of the family. At first, the cramped, shabby, apartment had made Amanda feel uncomfortable, and she had longed to see Melody and Rollin again. But they had made it quite clear that it would be dangerous, possibly leading the slave catchers to Penny, if they were to meet again. She would miss them. The final farewell had been filled with prayers and tears, so much sorrow, so much loss, yet so much hope. The Coffeys would remain in New York until their ship was repaired, then they would return to Philadelphia. Melody's eyes and soft voice, telling her she was as dear as a sister, echoed in her heart and mind.

As she lay on the straw mattress at night, she wondered why she had given up the luxuries and ease of her life in England. Her hands were becoming coarse, and her normally well-cared-for nails were jagged and unsightly. Since her arrival, she had become thinner, and with her short, tufted hair, she felt she had become downright ugly. But the McCarthys' warm, welcoming ways had lessened the pain, and she began to actually enjoy the intimacies of their family life. Still, something deep inside her was anxious to continue her journey. New York City was not pretty. It was cold and dismal, and in many ways, it was worse than London. Her old dream had not died, and she longed to see the wide open plains of the West. And though she tried to deny it, there existed a certain excitement at seeing Jacob again.

"Another two weeks." Amanda collapsed onto the small bench in Sean's office. The Coffeys and Frederick Rauling had felt that another two weeks was needed to hone Kevin's skills. She could see the soundness in their decision, but didn't want to delay any longer. Although she occasionally went out in disguise, most of her time was spent in Sean's tiny office or in the cramped apartment. She was beginning to feel restless.

Rising from the bench, Amanda took her leave and headed up the small, rickety outside backstairs to the McCarthy's home. The sun was shining weakly through a gray sky. Pausing, Amanda sat down on the fourth stair from the top. Cupping her chin in her hands, she leaned forward on her elbows and gazed down the back alley to the bustling street beyond. How could she possibly stay here for another two weeks? By the time they reached Saint Louis, it would be mid to late March. She wondered if Jacob knew about the delay.

She was surprised at the warm feelings thoughts of Jacob evoked in her mind. Frowning, she wondered why, after the unacceptably rude way he had treated her, after the way he had talked to her and touched her, she didn't react with disgust at his memory. A strange quiver ran through her stomach at the memory, and she felt her breath come faster. This time, she didn't stop herself as her mind conjured up that moment again. His eyes had burned with a deep, unreadable emotion that had taken her breath away. No one had ever looked at her like that before. The heat from his hand had seared through the bodice of her dress as if there were nothing between it and her naked flesh. Amanda felt her nipples strain against the linen binding. Why was this happening? She turned her head abstractedly toward the building beside her. She caught her reflection in the dirty pane of glass in front of her face. Before her was a bony, ragged looking boy. Penny was right. Her father would never . . . She stood up angrily. What did it matter what Mr. High and Mighty Jacob—who wouldn't even tell her his last name—liked? She was only helping him for Penny's sake. He, and any other man for that matter, could go to hell!

By the time the next two weeks were up, the sleet and snow had turned to rain. It rained continually, and Amanda ventured out only so far as to purchase a daily newspaper. Once home, Amanda would scour the paper, reading it cover to cover to relieve her boredom. Often the McCarthy family would gather around the table as she read the news aloud.

"The Mississippi River is rising at an alarming rate," Amanda read, her voice laced with concern. "It says that the water is is expected to fill the floodplains by early spring." She looked up at Sean. "Do you think we'll have any difficulty getting there?"

The older man shook his head noncommittally. Leaning back in his chair, he pulled out a gold pocket watch that never left his side. It had been the only thing of value that he had taken with him from Ireland, and it had been in the family for three generations, a wager from a land overseer who couldn't hold his liquor.

"Seems to me Kevin should be gettin' here by now," Sean said, as he slipped the treasured piece back in his pocket. As if on cue, there was a solid knock on the door. The small group around the table froze. It was late, and they weren't expecting anyone other than Kevin, and he'd never knock. The sound came again, followed by a loud "Ahem."

"Now, who the devil could that be?" Sean scowled, as he nodded to Maureen to answer the door. Nervously, the little woman rose. Smoothing her hands down her coarse brown skirt, she moved to the door.

"It's late. What ye be wantin' at this hour of the night?"

When a muffled voice answered, she cracked the door an inch. The door burst open, and a dandy young gentleman entered. Maureen, still holding the door, gaped at the barely recognizable young man before her. His hair was immaculately groomed in the latest style, and a thick black mustache curled attractively at the corners of his mouth. He was dressed in a fine pair of very tight fawn-colored trousers and an elaborately embroidered waistcoat. Over this he wore a black frock coat with a pearl pin in his cravat and a heavy black velvet collared overcoat. He carried a silver-topped walking stick and silk top hat in his hand.

"Evening, ladies and gentlemen. I'm so sorry to be disturbing you at this hour." Removing a small pair of gold-rimmed bifocals, the young man revealed yellowish brown faded bruises on his eyelids. When no one answered or moved to welcome him, Kevin raised his arms, and turned around for inspection. Then, as he finished the last rotation, he did a little jig.

"Jesus, Mary, and Joseph!" his father exclaimed, as he rose slowly from his chair. Maureen closed the door gently, never taking her eyes from the spectacle before her.

"A fine pair we make!" Amanda cried in a deep voice. Clasping her hands together, her spirits rose. It had been worth the wait. Kevin was magnificent.

The train ride to Cincinnati was without incident, and Kevin played his part marvelously, much to Amanda's chagrin. Kevin not only allowed her to carry the bags but to scrape his shoes of mud as well. Once on a stopover, a white man in Kevin's car had brushed up against her, saying that if she were smart, she'd be rid of this overbearing brute before they hit Missouri. Amanda had suppressed a smile and said that she had her little sister to think of, but thanked him for his concern and assured him that Kevin was not all that bad, and that she was paid well.

When they arrived in Cincinnati, the town was teeming with pigs. The noisy animals were snorting loudly as they were driven through the muddy streets. Porkopolis is what she had heard one man call the new Ohio town, and now she could believe it. Although it was clear that Cincinnati was a booming city on the rise, it was a far cry from the sophistication of New York, and an even farther one from London.

"I'll check into a hotel and make sure ye and Penny are secure before I venture out to obtain our passage on a riverboat," Kevin whispered, letting his precise diction slip. Amanda nodded.

"Yes'm sir," she said quite loudly, with a quick frown at her supposed employer. They had come this far without incident, and she didn't want to make any mistakes now. Wading her way through the thick mud and the fine drizzle that seemed to fall endlessly from the sky, she felt cold and weary to the bone. She was barely able to hold on when she climbed on back of the carriage that would take them to their hotel.

"Sir, all guests must sign the register. It is the rule." The hotel clerk turned the large lined book to face Kevin. Amanda placed her hands on Penny's small shoulders. The girl remained admirably quiet.

"Good sir, I would if I could, but as you can surely see, I can't," Kevin responded, concealing any anxiety he must surely be feeling as he patted his slinged right arm. The clerk looked miffed, then turned the book around with a loud huff of air.

"Well, we don't allow any colored folk to have rooms here," the small man said, looking pointedly at Amanda, "although there is a women's and a men's lodging out back. But the girl can't stay with her brother."

Amanda could feel Penny stiffen under her hands, then begin to shake.

"Pardon me, sir. My employer here is in need of my assistance. He can't manage by hisself. I hafta watch out for him," Amanda blurted out in a strained, but respectful tone.

The clerk again looked agitated, then after looking nervously around, leaned forward and whispered, "All right, but the girl can't stay, and once you're in the room, boy, you stay there. I don't want to see you wandering around making a nuisance of yourself." The small, tight-lipped young man stared directly at Amanda. Amanda lowered her head and nodded. "Good, then it's settled," the clerk grunted and turned to hand Kevin a large gold key.

And settled it was, as Kevin and Amanda hastily crammed the belongings of one trunk into the other and had Penny climb inside the empty one. For a few extra coins, the coach driver was more than happy to carry the trunk upstairs while Amanda watched the horses.

That evening Kevin ordered a very large supper delivered to his room, and together they laughed over the unsuspecting clerk.

"I guess I'd better be going down to the dock," Kevin said, as he swung his great overcoat over his shoulders. Amanda nodded as she wrote down the boat information. In the lobby, Kevin had secured a schedule of departing steamboats. Folding the slip of paper into the pocket of his pants, he repeated the information aloud. "Don't ye worry none. I'll be back in a flash," Kevin whispered to the definitely worried Amanda.

"Kevin, please hurry. I'll pray for you." Amanda replied. Although they were on free soil, she had heard the talk on the train, and Kentucky, a slave state, was right across the river. She didn't want to be separated from Kevin.

As Amanda paced the floor in the small room, Penny curled into a little ball and fell asleep. Lifting her gently, Amanda placed her on the solitary bed. Instinctively, Amanda began to pace again, jumping at every little creak outside the door.

"This is utterly ridiculous," she scoffed to herself. "Kevin is fine." Looking around, she sought for something to occupy her time. Taking out a paper and pen, she sketched the sleeping child. Looking at the peaceful, relaxed lines of Penny's face, Amanda was overwhelmed with a strong, protective love. Putting the pen down, she crawled in bed beside the little sleep-warmed body and pulled her close to nestle in the curve of her stomach. Penny sighed, and snuggled in deeper. Amanda's chest pulled tight with the leashed desire to hug the child tighter. She hadn't planned it, but Jacob's daughter had wormed her way into her heart. She must convince the man to let her travel with him, if for no other reason than for Penny. She couldn't bear to think he'd refuse, and she'd never see the child again. With these thoughts, she drifted off to a restless slumber.

Twelve

Jacob joined in with the other roustabouts on the Mississippi dock. The deep, sorrowful song reverberated along the line of sweat-drenched black men. A large man named Luke led the tale of toil and hardship. Jacob didn't even stop singing when the words told of Jesus coming to lead them to the promised land. The singing made the work go faster, and helped him to take his mind off his daughter.

Another time, he would have scoffed at his fellow black man's pitiful belief that some white man's God would come save him from his obvious chosen. Sure, he heard the argument over and over that God tests those he loves, that they must believe in Jesus in order to earn their way into the heavenly kingdom. Well, it just didn't sit well with him. Why did the black man have to work a thousand times harder and suffer so much more, so that he could pass through that proverbial needle's eye with the white man who didn't know the true meaning of the word *suffer?*

Jacob threw down the heavy cask of beeswax that he'd been loading. A sharp voice barked at him to watch it. Jacob nodded, playing the submissive role he so despised. Although it was only April and the weather was still cool, the sweat rolled off his body in a steady stream. Straightening to wipe the salty sting from the creases around his eyes, he squinted up the river. The young couple he had been staying with had received word that his daughter would be arriving on the steamboat *Allisia* sometime in April. There had been no other information, and he had been distraught and frustrated. Early last week he had been able to secure a position on the riverfront, and day after day he waited patiently for a steamboat with the letter *A* across its bow.

His supposed owners, the Wikets, had written the name for him on a small slip of paper, which was stuffed deep into the pocket of his trousers. But he knew that all he'd have to remember was the single letter *A*, and then he could ask. Every night, when he collapsed in exhaustion on his mattress, he stared at that piece of paper, willing the letters to be emblazened on his brain forever.

"Hey, you, boy, get a move on. The water's rising fast." Jacob turned to face a yellow-toothed beanpole of a white man. The man looked worriedly at the muddy, swirling water. Jacob bent to heave another hogshead of tobacco. The man was right; with the steady onslaught of rain since March, the mighty Mississippi was growing rapidly. Last night, John Wiket had read to him from the paper that the water was rising a foot every twenty-four hours.

Jacob squeezed his eyes shut and tried to envision Penny. If the rain didn't stop soon, all hell would break loose. Barges and steamboats alike would be blocked from coming to Saint Louis. *Please let her arrive soon, and safely.* To anyone who might have heard these unspoken words, they would have sworn Jacob was praying, but Jacob had no faith in anyone other than himself. It was going to be his sheer grit and determination that led his daughter and him to the promised land—the West.

A long, deep whistle blast rolled down the river. It was followed by two more short blasts and finally another ear-shattering long blast as the dingy yellow steamboat, *Allisia*, sent dark brown slops of water over the dock. Jacob looked up, unbelieving, at the large green letters splattered with mud. The other roustabouts paused only momentarily in their work and then continued, their songs uninterrupted.

Jacob let his eyes wander hopefully over the large graceful *A* at the beginning of the ship's name. Carefully, he counted the other letters. There were seven in all. His heart leapt with excitement.

"Excuse me, sir!" Jacob shouted to the job overseer over the din of commotion as the large steamboat began to lower wooden ramps. The skinny man looked up, a scowl across his face. "What's the name of that boat?"

The deep creases radiating from the corners of the white man's eyes deepened, as he studied Jacob. Jacob's heart pounded loudly against his chest. "She's the *Allisia.*" The man moved closer, a menacing look flickering across his eyes. "But don't you be gettin' any idears. Your master done and promised you for a day's work. If you bolt an' tries to git work offa that boat afore you're done with mine, I tell Mr. Wiket, and no doubt he'll send ya on down to B. M. Lynch at the slave pen on Fifth and Myrtle."

Jacob shook his head, letting his eyes grow wide with mock fear. It wouldn't do any good to let this nasty man get any ideas.

"Good, now. Git back to work, boy," the greasy man said, as he spat a large wad of tobacco into the swirling, muddy water by Jacob's feet. Jacob bent to his task, never taking his eyes off the yellow steamboat's ramp. He heard the overseer move away, and Jacob swore that once he'd crossed the Rockies, he'd never let another man call him boy again. Now he'd just have to find Penny.

Suddenly, the *Allisia* burst into flames, steam and black billowing clouds of smoke engulfing the shore. Jacob didn't hear the voices screaming after him as he sprinted for the riverboat. A low hissing was followed by another explosion and a large cracking noise, as the hull of the ship gave way, emptying livestock and screaming people into the muddy water.

"Stay back!" a uniformed man shouted from the levee. "It's a boiler fire, and the other ones could blow at any minute. Stay back."

Jacob ran past him, defying his words. He had to get to Penny. *Dear God please, please don't let her die.*

Kevin had come down to the lower deck looking for Amanda and Penny. As he squinted into the dark hold, he felt guilty for the obviously luxurious conditions he had been enjoying on the upper decks. Cursing, then apologizing, he stepped over the bodies huddled together under burlap sacks. The air was cold, dank, and it reeked of animals, unwashed bodies, sickness, and rotting food. He felt his supper of braised leg of lamb roil threateningly in his stomach. He stopped by an upturned barrel, where a young mother was trying to nurse a listless infant. He looked away, embarrassed, when a young man rose up before him.

"What are ye lookin' for down here with the likes of us, sir?"

Kevin stepped back in surprise. The young Irish lad couldn't have been older than he was. Again, Kevin was stung by the world of difference that fine clothes and a little money could give you.

"I'm looking for my manservant."

The boy eyed him a little longer, but didn't move. Kevin moved to step around him, but the lad moved with him. "For some coppers I might make it a bit easier on ye."

Kevin fumbled in his coat pocket, found and retrieved two coins.

Placing them between his teeth, the boy grinned. "Annie, I'll be right back," the boy threw at the discouraged woman, now weeping over the baby. He then beckoned Kevin to follow him into the dank, cavernous room.

Amanda squatted on the hay-covered floor, Penny between her knees. She pulled a thin burlap cloth tighter around the child. Penny coughed weakly and pressed a feverish forehead against Amanda's knee.

"Not much longer, sweetheart," Amanda assured her, as she stroked the soft curls beneath her hand. The trip had been longer than anticipated, and their food and water had run low. Twice Amanda had tried to go upstairs to reach Kevin, and twice she had been turned away. The child moved restlessly beneath her hand, and Amanda worried again for the girl's health. For the last few days, she had watched the sickly pallor of some of the lower deck's occupants, and she worried that some of them carried the dreaded sickness, cholera. In the darkness she could hear weeping, retching, and the smell of vomit, blood, and body waste.

"My God!" Kevin started, as he gazed down at the shadowy couple. Gently he lifted Amanda by one hand. Penny whimpered meekly. Without a second thought, Kevin swept the sick girl into his arms. "Why didn't ye tell me?" he whispered angrily. The young boy who had been his guide looked on with amazement. Amanda scowled crossly at him, ignoring Kevin's question. After a moment, the lad left, slipping his hand into his trousers to jingle the two coins that lay there.

"Don't you think I tried?" Amanda demanded angrily. Kevin sighed in apology, his eyes dark with unspoken emotions.

"I'm sure ye did. But come now. We've got to get ye out of here. I was playin' a bit of cards with the first clerk, and he had a bit too much." Amanda followed him, waiting for him to say more. "He's gotta be doing the books, don't ye see, and he hasn't a head for numbers right now. I told him I could help him in exchange for a meal and comfortable passage upstairs.'' Amanda felt her eyes fill with tears. Kevin hadn't forgotten about them. Her voice was gruff with emotion as she told him not to forget his accent. Kevin smiled and turned to her. In the dark of the stairwell, he kissed her. She couldn't see his eyes, but she heard the emotion in his voice. "I'll always look out for ye, if ye'll let me."

Amanda looked away, unnerved yet comforted by the sincerity in his voice.

Settled in the first clerk's quarters, Amanda ticked off the rows of tiny numbers as she stuffed another hot buttered roll in her mouth. She had never been so hungry. Their host lay sprawled out, drunk, on the thick floral carpet that covered the floor. Kevin sat in a small chair by the bed, spooning steaming chicken broth into Penny's mouth. Amanda paused as she watched the handsome boy coax Penny into swallowing one more spoonful. Kevin was really sweet, and she didn't doubt he thought he felt something for her. But he was so young, so different. She simply didn't feel that way about him.

Her eyes traveled to Penny. In a few short hours, she was looking better already. Penny pouted, then graced Kevin with a deep, dimpled smile. Amanda's heart skipped a beat. She looked so much like her father. She recalled the handsome man in the Clay's warm kitchen. She remembered his warm minty breath on her neck in the morning room. She remembered his strong callused fingers on her. She jerked her head back as if she'd been slapped. Where did these loose, evil thoughts come from? She turned back to the ledger before her, hearing the warning whistles of landing. Here in the upper floors the sound was much louder, causing her to start. She had to get these numbers added before they docked. Suddenly, the room shuddered around her. The stool tipped back, and she found herself on top of the passed-out first clerk. The cabin rattled again, followed by an immense boom. She scrambled to the bed, where Penny sat huddled in Kevin's lap. Wrapping her arms around the two, she closed her eyes and whispered a fervent prayer. A loud crack was followed by screams and wailing. A thin plume of black smoke curled under the door. Kevin pulled her to her feet and burst out of the cabin door. With Penny in his arms, he screamed at Amanda to follow him.

Covering her mouth with her hand, she plunged into the dark, smoke-filled corridor. The floor shook beneath her, and she stumbled. Bracing her hand against the wall, she heard Penny cry out for her doll. Reaching the outer railing, she saw the pandemonium below her. Tall, orange flames licked at the side of the boat, while the water beneath it sizzled. The muddy, swirling Mississippi sucked at the pigs and cows struggling in its icy hold. A hysterical woman's high-pitched scream pierced the din, and Amanda saw a charred infant and man roll off the deck into the water.

"Jump!" Kevin demanded. Amanda looked at Kevin, but his words made no sense. Thrusting Penny into her arms, he again ordered her to jump. Amanda clung to Penny and backed away from him. Penny sobbed out Rebecca's name. The boat shuddered again, a loud hissing sound seeping unrelentingly through the din. Angrily, Kevin grabbed Amanda's arm, and pushed her off the deck. She felt herself falling. Her instincts were to throw her arms wide, but she clung to the small life in her arms.

A loud explosion rocked the boat and catapulted them clear of the flames. Amanda felt the breath knocked from her as she hit the icy water and it pulled her downward. Still holding Penny with one arm, she struggled to rise, glad she had no heavy skirts and petticoats to hamper her. Again, the water rose over her head, Penny clutched frantically at her clothes. A large, jagged plank of wood came barreling down on them. Amanda kicked, her shoes coming off as her feet touched thick, oozy mud. If she could just get her footing, she could clear herself of the—

"Daddy!" Penny screamed, as the plank slammed into the back of Amanda's head. A bright burst of light exploded around Amanda, as the pain speared through her whole body. Then all was black, the icy waters of oblivion dragging her down to their muddy depths.

Throwing the unconscious boy over one shoulder, Jacob hugged his precious daughter to his chest. Stuggling with every ounce of his strength, he fought the debris and water pushing him downriver.

Suddenly, Luke, the man he'd been working with, was by his side. With ease, Luke removed the dead weight from his shoulder. Together, the men plowed toward the shore. The greasy, yellow-toothed beanpole of a man was screaming at them from down on the dock. Both men ignored him until they reached the cobblestone street away from the noise.

"Dis your kin?" Luke asked as he gently laid Amanda on a bale of hemp. Jacob nodded, as he rocked Penny back and forth.

"This is my daughter. I don't know who the boy is. He saved my daughter." Tears streamed down his face as he buried it in Penny's wet curls.

"You best git dem dry 'fore dey freeze," the large man remarked. His voice was deep and rich with the loose structure of a southern plantation field hand. Jacob thought of Rollin and wondered if he and Melody were on that same boat. "I gotta go back now," Luke stated. Jacob nodded and debated whether or not to go back down to the fire.

"Penny. Penny, honey," Jacob asked gently, as he peeled the little girl away from him. She stared up at him with big soulful eyes. "Did Rollin come with you?" he asked.

The girl shook her head, her eyes filled with tears. "No.

Just Miss Amanda and Mr. McCarthy and Rebecca." At the name of his departed wife, Jacob's heart twisted with guilt and pain.

"Rebecca?" her father asked.

The little girl nodded, fresh tears streaming down her face. "Mr. McCarthy went back for her, my bootiful doll Miss Amanda gave me." The child collapsed against his mud spattered shirt and sobbed.

Jacob looked back down the hill at the remains of the *Allisia*. Mr. McCarthy, whoever he was, was most likely beyond recognition by now. Miss Amanda. He grimaced to think of her beautiful body and face a charred or bloated mess. Scanning the crowd, he saw no well-dressed Negress among them. The child in his arms shuddered and coughed softly. With eyes filled with concern, Jacob touched the girl's burning forhead. Turning to his right, he glanced down at the still boy beside him. His face was turned away, and a dark red trickle showed through his damp hair. He would have to get all of them back to the Wikets' house. Reaching beneath the waistband of his trousers, Jacob pulled out a rolled-up linen handkerchief. Coins jingled as they fell to the bale on which he sat. Calling out to a small, dirty waif, he beckoned to the child with the shiny coins.

Jacob sighed with relief when the small urchin boy returned with the dry clothes. They weren't new by any means, and the dress was probably ten sizes too big for Penny, but they were dry. Between bribing the warehouse manager to allow him shelter and buying the clothes, he only had a few half pennies left with which to buy food. He turned to the little boy and asked him to buy some hot soup. Pulling the leather thong from around Penny's neck, he promised it as a reward. The child scurried off.

Stripping the now sleeping Penny of her wet clothes, he carefully dressed her. She murmured but didn't waken. She was rightfully exhausted. Covering her with some empty burlap bags, he settled her down on a bale of hemp. Satisfied, he turned to the young boy. Again, he wondered who the boy was. He sure was a skinny thing, Jacob thought, as he ran his eyes along the boy's back. He had laid him down on his stomach so he could get a better look at the crack in his skull. He wondered if the boy had gotten a serious concussion. As he knelt beside him, he saw the wide linen binding beneath his shirt. Jacob felt a wave of protective anger wash through him. Had this child been an escaped slave, too, beaten or wounded perhaps? Gently, Jacob fingered the matted mass of bloody, sticky hair. Although the wound was still tacky to the touch, the bleeding had stopped and was crusting over. The boy moaned beneath his hand. Gently Jacob turned him to his side and pulled the soaked shirt over his head. Grabbing the end of the linen binding tucked in the back of the wrap, he loosened it. Instantly, the front binding beneath his finger pushed out, filling with warm, soft flesh. Jacob pulled his hand back in surprise, and the young woman groaned as she slipped to her back. Jacob gaped in disbelief as he saw the swell of breasts rising above the bindings.

"Mister?" a small voice called from behind him. Jacob hastily threw the shirt over the feminine body. He turned, taking the soup and rolls from the boy, and handing him his daughter's necklace. The urchin scampered off happily. Jacob stared off into the darkness after the retreating child, afraid to turn around. Another groan finally forced him to look at his daughter's rescuer. Bending low over her face, he recognized the beautifully shaped bones of Miss Amanda Smith. Now he groaned. How could he have not recognized her? He allowed his eyes to travel down the rest of her, and he felt his body respond. He backed away, then realized that he owed his daughter's life to her. Judging from her cropped hair and male clothing, she had sacrificed a lot. The least he could do was to dress her in dry clothes to prevent hypothermia. He prayed that was enough, and that he wouldn't have to strip her and warm her up with his body heat. His manhood jumped at the thought. He scowled at his body's betrayal of his nobler thoughts.

Since his wife's death, he had slept with only one other woman. That night had left him feeling empty and in no great hurry to search for more. Instead, he worked himself into exhaustion every night so his body craved nothing but sleep. Now, as he hesitantly removed the rest of Amanda's clothing, he told himself not to look. His fingers fumbled with the buttons to her breeches, as his manhood pulsed painfully against his own. His fingertips burned as they brushed across her smooth, supple skin, and he closed his eyes, swallowing hard, as he remembered her in the moonlight in Philadelphia. Over and over again he told himself that nothing between them could ever be. They were of different worlds. She was a proper young lady, and he owed her his daughter's life. Still, the desire burned.

Unable to resist any longer, Jacob opened his eyes and gazed down at her naked body. In the faded light of the warehouse, her body shimmered in muted and dark shadows. His mouth felt dry as his eyes traveled over the dusky globes of her breasts to the dark, erect nipples. Unconsciously, his hand hovered over the firm peaks. His fingers twitched slightly, itching to caress them. Fighting his desire, he followed the smooth, hollow expanse of her belly, bracketed by curving hipbones, to the dark nest of curls between her legs. Amanda moaned and shifted, her right leg jerking and then falling until she lay spread-eagled before him. Jacob felt small beads of perspiration form on his upper lip and forehead. Desperately, he licked his dry lips, willing his heartbeat to slow down. He couldn't stand it any longer. He must touch this woman. A small voice pierced the stillness.

"Daddy, is Miss Amanda all right?" The sweet voice brought Jacob back to his senses and he realized what he had been dying to do. Quickly, roughly, he pulled the dry trousers over Amanda's slim legs. He cursed her and himself every time his knuckles grazed her satin skin, and he felt the fire burning through his groin.

"Go back to sleep, honey. She's jes' fine." Jacob turned and smiled at his daughter, glad that from her vantage point she could see nothing.

"Daddy?" The little voice asked softly.

"Yes, honey?" Jacob responded, coming to her side.

"Miss Amanda's still a girl, and still has her nice soft breasts. She jes' hid 'em."

Jacob choked before he answered. "I know, honey. You just go back to sleep." Oh, God, did he know, and now he'd have to watch her sleep, knowing she was within reach but totally out of his grasp. Suddenly he was struck with an uncomfortable thought. He'd have to explain that he'd undressed and dressed her. How would she react? He looked at her as she lay so motionless before him. A rising fear clutched at his heart. What if she never awakened? Could life be so cruel as to lay the responsibility of another innocent on his already overburdened shoulders? He sank his head into his hands and groaned.

"Daddy." Then silence. Jacob waited. "Don't worry, her hair will grow back. Then you can hug and kiss her and make babies." The little girl smiled, curled up on her side, and went to sleep. But sleep was the farthest thing from Jacob's mind.

Thirteen

Amanda was bathed in sweat as she relived the nightmare over and over in her dreams. Her voice rang harshly in her ears as she screamed for Kevin. She struggled to open her eyes and saw concerned white faces looming above her. The back of her head pounded, sending sickening waves of pain and nausea throughout her body. She coughed, and the pain got worse, threatening to split her skull. She closed her eyes, trying to retrieve blissful oblivion, but the host of voices around her wouldn't let her.

"Miss Smith, Miss Smith," a soft voice called, as it reached into the dark, shadowy recesses of her consciousness. Amanda tried to push it away, but it turned into a gruff, insistent male voice.

"Miss Smith. Miss Amanda Smith, can you hear me?"

Amanda groaned, unable to form the words to tell them to leave her alone. Where was Kevin? He said he'd protect her. Why didn't he make these people go away?

"Miss Amanda." A small familiar voice broke through the thick, fuzzy clouds enveloping her brain. It was Penny. She was all right. Amanda fought her way back to the surface of the drowsy warm water of unconsciousness. She opened her eyes and was assaulted by the bright light of the room. She shut her eyes as tears began to nettle her eyelids. Again, the small, pleading voice, the warm little hands. Gritting her teeth, Amanda opened her eyes again. This time the curtains had been drawn, and the room was bathed in a gentle, flickering glow. A gray-haired old man looked deeply into her eyes. When she tried to turn away to search for Penny, he held her jaw.

"You've had quite a shock and a blow to your head. Stay still, young lady." The man's gruff demands hinted that he was in command, a doctor. Amanda remained still, but her eyes still searched, looking for the owner of that sweet, familiar little voice.

"Where am I?"

The hands released her, and she turned to see Penny and Jacob standing at the end of her bed. Penny struggled to come to her, but her father held her shoulders firm. His eyes met hers. They held concern.

"You're in Saint Louis. The Wikets, John and Mary, are our hosts." Jacob turned his head slightly, nodding at a middle-aged man standing just behind his left shoulder. The man smiled, nodding his head in greeting.

"Welcome to our home. We are so glad you are..." He paused, blushed slightly, and glanced at the doctor. Amanda followed his eyes back to the gray-headed man hovering above her. He looked away, sticking his hands in the large, black leather case by his side. "You were very fortunate, young lady. Fortunate that Jacob was there, and fortunate to have jumped ship." His words crashed through her still foggy brain. The ship... Amanda glanced about her desperately.

"Where is Kevin? Where is Kevin McCarthy?" Amanda managed to ask, as she tried to sit up. Two hands pushed her back down onto the smooth, white pillow. Thankfully, she obeyed, as she felt her head throb and every muscle in her body ache. As Amanda looked around the room, she saw the faces look away. Her eyes grew wide, desperate. Penny broke away and came to her, the sweet little hands cupping her cheeks.

"He's gone to heaven with Mama. He brought my doll Rebecca, so Mama won't be so lonely without me anymore." Amanda felt her lungs collapse in her chest, as she struggled to unleash the painful sobs burning in her bosom. Not Kevin! Not her champion, her sweet, darling Kevin. She closed her eyes and felt the room swirl around her. She saw his face, wreathed in horrid black smoke, telling her to jump. He'd gone back for a stupid doll. She ground her teeth and hated the tears rolling down her face. He left her. Damn him! He'd promised to protect her. A huge, racking sob escaped her tight lips. She was going to miss him. How could God take him away? He was so good, so young. He had promised. The pain and the sorrow drained her, and she silently slipped away into a troubled sleep.

Later that night, Amanda awoke to find the room dark and empty. Gingerly rising on one elbow, she was startled to see Jacob sleeping in a chair at the foot of her bed. The moonlight trickled through sheer curtains, dappling the polished wood floor with pools of silver. The right side of Jacob's face was oulined in a haunting, bluish cast. She studied the rough lines of his face. Even when he slept, he looked hard and dangerous. Nonetheless, he was beautiful. The lunar light shimmered a rainbow of colors across his high cheekbones, his thick black lashes casting long, mysterious shadows beneath his eyes. Lifting herself up a little higher, she let her gaze wander down the length of him. As his body lay limp and relaxed across the wooden chair, he maintained an easy grace. His arms were folded across his broad chest, the sleeves rolled back to expose muscular forearms. Why was he here? she wondered, as she searched the room for Penny. Then she remembered Kevin and caught a sob at the back of her throat. Jacob startled awake. His eyes were red from lack of sleep, and he massaged them with strong fingers as he struggled to awaken fully.

"You okay?" he asked as he moved his chair closer to the bedside. He took her hand in his, and absentmindedly rubbed his rough thumb over hers. She snatched back her hand and began to cry. Jacob shifted uncomfortably in his chair and glanced at the doorway.

"No," Amanda snuffled as if reading his thoughts. "I don't need anyone. I just want to be alone with my grief." Jacob rose and turned to the door. He stopped and turned back.

"This Kevin—Mr. McCarthy. He was . . . you two was real close?" His question hung in the air.

Amanda knew what he was asking but couldn't explain what she and Kevin had. If she'd had a brother, perhaps she'd have known, but now all she could think of was that he was gone. "Very close." She answered, silent tears dropping onto the top sheet beneath her hands. She was so lost in her grief she didn't question the inappropriateness of his presence in her bedchamber.

Jacob stood there, his thumb caressing his forefinger, like it had done to her hand a moment ago. Suddenly, Amanda wanted him to sit back down, to take her hand again, to comfort her while she cried. She was so alone. Jacob studied her in silence, then slowly, as if drawn by an unidentifiable force, he sat back down. His fingertips rested on the edge of the bed.

"Wanna talk about it?" he asked, his voice quivering like he wasn't sure he wanted to hear about it. Amanda nodded and sniffed. She placed a tentative finger on his hand. In response, it turned, lying curled beneath her fingers. Slowly, he drew her hand into his.

"We met him on the train. The train to Philadelphia. He rescued us from the slave catchers," Amanda began in a halting whisper. His hand tightened slightly, then his thumb began to stroke her palm. Amanda closed her eyes as the small movement crept through her body, making her feel safe and cared for. "He took us to his home. His family was Irish."

Jacob withdrew his hand and stood up. Amanda's eyes flew open. What had she said? Jacob turned his face from her, the muscles working hard in his throat as his Adam's apple pumped up and down.

"He was a white man?" Jacob asked, his voice a rough, ragged whisper.

Amanda nodded, knowing he'd seen her, although he didn't turn to her.

"It ain't right. It don't breed nothing but pain and trouble." His voice hissed out in an angry sizzle.

Amanda twisted her face in confusion. Jacob ran his hands through his hair, then around the perimeter of his jaw. His eyes looked haunted, bitter, dangerous. Their eyes met and locked. He seemed to draw the very being of her through those portals. She looked deeper into those murky depths and saw loathing: sheer, unadulterated hatred. Then the windows snapped closed, and Jacob turned and left.

Fourteen

Amanda was relieved to awaken from her fitful sleep. She was not surprised to find the warm little body of Penny curled up beside her. She smiled at the precious, sleeping visage, so like her father's, yet softer, less bitter. Turning her head, she winced at the throbbing pain at the base of her skull. Slowly, she recalled the vivid nightmares, the smoke, the screaming, Kevin. She blinked back the tears. Jacob, Penny's father had saved her after the wood had hit her and everything had gone black. Carefully, she turned to the empty chair at her bedside. Had he really been sitting there holding her hand last night or had that, too, been part of her dreams? He had been so gentle, so caring. Then she remembered the anger, the bitterness that had separated them—something about Kevin.

The little girl beside her stirred, then stretched. Her tiny hands curled into fists as she raised them over her head, her mouth stretching wide to reveal small, even white teeth and a pink tongue. Amanda laughed softly.

"You look like my old cat Solomon when you do that."

Penny smiled back, blinking the sleep from her eyes.

"Is you better, Miss Amanda?" the child asked hopefully, kneeling in an upright position. Then, without waiting for an answer, she continued, "Do you miss Solomon lots? Daddy says yous gonna go back to Inland to see 'em?" Penny tugged nervously at the small ringlets that danced upon her shoulders as she shifted her bottom from one heel to the other.

Amanda frowned, feeling her ire rise. Here she had saved this man's daughter, and his only thanks was to try to send her back to England. She opened her mouth, then closed it again. Sinking deeper into her pillow, she shut her eyes. The realization hit home: Jacob still wasn't going to take her out West with them. With Kevin gone, her other option was closed. Maybe she should go back home, home where it was safe—and dull. A silent tear slid from beneath her closed eyelids. Perhaps her injuries were worse than she suspected. Perhaps she wasn't up to traveling yet, and she knew all too well now that Jacob had to get Penny away. Here in Missouri they were in more peril than ever. Missouri was a slave state.

Soft fingers broke into her miserable reverie, touching her damp cheek.

"Don't cry, Miss 'Manda. Daddy says we gotta be brave, 'cause if we don't have our courage and pride, we ain't, don't got nothin'." The serious words so sweetly spoken made Amanda smile and open her eyes.

"You're right, Miss Penelope." Amanda scooted herself to an almost sitting position. "We must not forget our courage and pride. I most certainly am not going back to England."

Penny squealed with delight, throwing her arms around Amanda's neck. "You'll come with me and Daddy then?" The little girl asked, her bright liquid brown eyes inches from Amanda's. Before Amanda could answer, a brief knock sounded on the door, then it swung open.

"Thought I'd find you in here." Jacob's familiar gruff voice rolled into the room. The sound created a strange mixture of angry rebellion and sweet anticipation to swirl through Amanda's being. When her eyes met his, the rebellion was swiftly replaced with fearful excitement. Jacob stood, one hand on the door. There was no denying the burning desire in his eyes as they raked her from head to foot, then rested scorchingly on her chest.

Immediately Amanda's hands sought the source of this inferno and gasped when she found that the large shirt she had been sleeping in had slipped off one shoulder, and its missing buttons gaped between her unbound breasts.

He couldn't move. Memories of her naked body danced unmercifully through his brain. Last night he had felt protective, then hurt and angry. At that time there had been no lust to torment him. Now, with her tears gone and in her seductive disarray, he felt his knees go weak. If he had known what awaited him, he would never have entered. Amanda should have never allowed him to enter. But the door had been open, almost an invitation. It wasn't his fault. He swallowed hard, a tightness clawing at his throat. With embarrassment, he heard his voice crack slightly.

"The door was open," he blurted out and started to turn. His daughter pulled away from Amanda, running toward him, dragging the top sheet and quilt with her. Amanda gasped and Jacob tried to look away, but he was unable to, as the tumbling linens exposed her long, shapely bare legs. Her nightshirt barely reached the middle of her thighs, and her sudden reach to cover herself only hiked it dangerously higher.

"Go git dressed, Penny." Jacob barked at his little daughter, his eyes never leaving the sight before him. Penny frowned, then obeyed, dancing gaily through the open door.

Amanda lay there in shock, struggling to retrieve the fallen bedding. Her eyes were wide with horror and humiliation, and she looked like she might cry. Jacob stepped forward to help her, hesitated, and turned to leave. Unable to make the full pivot, his eyes stayed riveted on her, refusing to separate from this wanton display of naked female flesh. As Amanda squirmed and twisted, trying to cover herself, the nightshirt rose even higher, exposing more smooth skin. For a moment, the heavy quilt lingered over her thighs, then slid back to a puddle of calico on the floor. In desperation, Amanda pulled her legs up beneath her shirt, and hugged them to her chest. Incredibly, the four remaining buttons on her shirt strained, then popped. She watched helplessly as one rolled off the side of the bed and skittered across the floor, stopping at Jacob's feet.

Tearing his eyes from the newly exposed skin, Jacob followed the tiny white button as it whirled across the floor. Slowly, he bent and retrieved it. Moistening his dry lips with his tongue, he rubbed the small bone piece between his finger and thumb. Amanda sat frozen, her ineffectual attempts to cover herself suspended, as she watched his callused fingers caress the small button. Fearfully, she raised her gaze to his face. His eyes had grown dark and deathly still. If possible, their earlier display of desire flamed brighter. With embarrassment, she felt her nipples tighten, and the crux between her thighs become damp in response. She was mortified by the passionate heat swirling through her veins, parching her throat, causing her to tremble. When she tried to speak, her voice came out a husky, raw sob.

"Get out! Please get out." The words seem to release Jacob from his frozen stance. He paused, then deliberately moved slowly toward her, his outstretched hand fondling the button. Drawing back with a sharp intake of breath, Amanda felt her heart pounding savagely against her ribcage. Jacob placed one hand on either side of her. She could feel his hot breath wafting down the wide, gaping neckline of her shirt. Slowly, he grinned. With great care, he placed the button precariously on her kneecap. Moistening his lips, he blew a gentle puff of air, just enough to send the button sliding down to rest on the deep crease where her breasts pressed up tightly against her thighs. For a moment, they both stared at the button, so white against her rich chestnut skin. Then, abruptly, Jacob straightened and turned away. She saw the back of his shoulders rise and fall with a deep intake of breath.

"My guess is that you'll be needin' a new shirt." His voice betrayed nothing. Then, without turning back, he took two long, purposeful strides out of the room.

Outside in the hall, Jacob inhaled lungsful of air, his heart pounding with the fury of stampeding horses' hooves. How dare she taunt him. He hated the feelings of wanting and desire that welled up inside him. He didn't want to want her. He didn't want to need her. As his breathing came more slowly, he closed his eyes. He was a man, a man who had gone a long time without a woman. These feelings were natural. She was a beautiful woman. He squeezed his eyes together more tightly as a slow ache began constricting his chest. What of last night? Had those feelings of jealousy and overpowering anger been natural, too? When he had held her hand and seen her sorrow, he had wanted to protect her, to wrap her in his strong arms and hold her safe. He had wanted to ease her grief, to make her smile at him the way she smiled at his daughter. The ache grew stronger, more binding, and he drew in a ragged breath. No, those feelings were not natural, those feelings were dangerous.

Amanda trembled with small exquisite shivers of relief, regret, fear, and what she disgustedly realized was lust. As the strange and heady sensation began to ebb, she felt the first stir of anger. Jacob was trying to intimidate her once again. Placing her feet on the cold wood floor, she marched over to the door and slammed it shut. For a moment, she leaned back against it with her eyes closed. The dull throb in her head returned in full force, making her feel weak.

"*Courage and pride*," she whispered to herself. Her eyes roamed the room as she desperately looked for something, anything, to steady herself, to wash away these evil feelings of anger and desire. They fell upon a leather Bible on a one-drawer table in the corner of the room. Amanda walked over to the small Bible. Tears of relief slid down her face as she opened it with shaking hands. Although it was her host's Roman Catholic Bible, not her familiar King James Bible that had been lost in the *Alisia*'s fire, the words were similar. Always before, when she had been troubled or in doubt, she had turned to the Lord's word as Minister Carrington had taught her. Lately, she had been so caught up in this perilous adventure that she had forgotten the refuge it offered. Now, dressed only in a scant torn shirt, she felt unclean and guilty as she touched the smooth pages beneath her fingers. Falling to her knees, she closed her eyes and prayed for the Lord's forgiveness. She begged him to cleanse her mind of her evil thoughts of lust.

As she buried her tearstained face in her hands, she also prayed for the repose of Kevin's soul. Recalling his young, shining eyes, she wondered how she could have ever questioned God's will. How could she have doubted his wisdom? The Lord had called Kevin to be with Him, and she knew that she should be filled with joy that now he was happy with God in heaven, truly in the promised land.

A timid knock at the door had Amanda scurrying for the protection of her bedclothes. A small flicker of excited anticipation shimmied up her spine as she breathlessly bid the caller to enter.

"Miss Smith?" a tall, pale blond woman inquired as she peered around the door. Amanda felt her heart sink with disappointment that it was not Jacob, then chastised herself angrily for being so hypocritical and weak.

"Please come in," Amanda answered in a meek whisper. The woman entered with several dresses draped over her elbows, carrying a tray of food.

"I thought you might be hungry," the woman stated, looking sharply at the gaping neck hole of Amanda's shirt. "Mr. Jacob said you might be in need of, uh, proper clothing." These last words burned Amanda's cheeks with humiliation, forcing her to lower her eyes. What exactly had Jacob told them?

"I'm much obliged," Amanda murmured more to her fist that clenched the gaping shirt around her neck than to the woman before her. The blond smiled, placing her offerings on the small dresser by the window. She turned, smoothing a hand along her stiff blue skirt.

"My husband and I are going to high Mass. Jacob informs me that he isn't of a religious bent." The woman cast her eye on the opened Bible. "He has informed me that you are of the Methodist persuasion." She then picked up the Bible, turned, and handed it to Amanda. "I know not of your religion. I was raised Catholic. But, perhaps for your safety as well as the others," the woman paused, a deep rose staining her cheeks, "my husband feels it would be best if you didn't venture outside the house just yet." The woman's eyes implored Amanda to understand. Helpless to do otherwise, Amanda nodded. She thought about her aunt and the Carringtons holding their heads high as they headed for Saint John's in London. Now, here she was, hiding, unable to worship openly, seeking refuge from the temptations Jacob presented.

She wanted to scream, *"I'm a free woman! I'm not being hunted!"* but she knew that someone could have seen her with Penny or Jacob. Their safety was still too tenuous. No matter what Jacob said, Penny needed her help. The woman smiled, patting Amanda's clenched fist.

"Bless you for understanding. For the little girl's sake, I'm glad one of you has placed your faith in the Lord."

Amanda smiled at the woman as she ran a hand along the smooth leather cover of the Bible.

"Jacob has suffered much. I'm sure he will find the good

Lord with time." Suddenly, Amanda felt a warm ray of purpose engulf her. That was it. God was testing her. Jacob needed her, too. She would help him find faith in God again. Her mind began to race. Like the Carringtons before her, she could spread the word. She could be a missionary. She remembered reading about a group of Indians that had come all the way from the Oregon Territory to Saint Louis seeking religious leaders to teach them about their God. Jacob and Penny could be her first converts. If Jacob wouldn't help her get to Oregon, her church would.

Fairly beaming at the woman before her, Amanda asked for her assistance.

"I understand your concern, but I must get in touch with the Methodist leaders here in Saint Louis. I wish to enlist in their missionary needs out West." The woman greeted her smile with an equally brilliant one, promising that she would do whatever she could.

"You are so brave, Miss Smith. That I would have so much courage." The woman sighed as she pulled several petticoats out of a chifferobe in the corner and laid them on the bed. *Yes,* Amanda thought, as she turned to allow the woman to tighten the laces at the back of the corset she wrapped around her, *I have both courage and pride. I'm going to show you the way, Mr. Jacob.* She sucked in deeply as the corset bit into the skin at her waist. She had forgotten how confining and uncomfortable these things could be.

"Damn blasted woman," Jacob muttered beneath his breath. She'd be the death of him. One minute she was a tempting demon, the next a Bible spouting prissy minister's daughter. He turned away in anger as he heard Amanda's serious voice telling his daughter the Lord's Ten Commandments.

"How do you covet a wife?" the little girl asked innocently.

A wicked grin tugged at Jacob's mouth as he turned back. This could be interesting. After two weeks of continuous Biblical quotations, this was one answer he'd like to hear from the lovely Miss Smith. Amanda coughed uneasily, and then opened her mouth to speak. Jacob entered the parlor and leaned insolently in the doorway. Amanda's eyes met his. Her mouth formed a silent pink O. Jacob's gaze dropped to those sweet, tender lips. He watched in amusement as deep color flushed her cheeks and her small tongue flicked the perimeter of that small, pink circle. He ran his tongue, in turn, slowly over his lips, his eyes remaining on her mouth, waiting for some pious explanation to fall from them. No words came, and Amanda began to nibble nervously on her full bottom lip. Following Amanda's uneasy gaze, Penny turned around to face her father.

"Daddy, Miss Amanda's teaching me the Bible. She says she'll even teach me to read some. Says courage and pride isn't enough. Gotta have faith, too." The excitement was barely contained in the little girl's voice, as she turned back eagerly to Amanda. "What does it mean? You know, the part 'bout not coveting your neighbor's wife?" Amanda's color darkened even more. Jacob moved into the room, seating himself next to Amanda on the tiny settee, his knee brushing up against the side of her thigh. She jerked as if she had been stung, and her knees swung away from his touch. Jacob moved closer.

Amanda rose, fidgeting with the now closed Bible. Jacob leaned back, his hands behind his head, as he stretched one long leg after the other out before him, blocking her passage between the low chair where Penny was perched and the sofa on which he lounged. He was thoroughly enjoying Amanda's discomfort.

"Yes, Miss Smith, tell us what you know about coveting."

This was not working out at all like she had planned. Her

attempt to enlighten both father and daughter was proving to be more difficult than she had anticipated. Foolishly, Amanda now realized, she had expected to have both of them begging her to teach them the surest route to heaven by now. It had always seemed so easy for her to believe wholeheartedly in the Methodist faith that she had thought anyone with a lick of sense would embrace it fully once they had been given the knowledge. But it simply wasn't so. As much as she would have liked to believe Jacob was a simpleton, she knew that he wasn't. With a sinking heart, she began to doubt her strength in her faith. Maybe it wasn't strong enough, and that was where the fault lay.

At first she had seen their delayed departure for Independence, Missouri, as a sign from God, as a gift of more time for her conversion attempts. But the days had turned into two long weeks. It was now late April. Sunday's paper had said the Mississippi River was rising at the alarming rate of a foot every twenty-four hours. The Missouri River had been temporarily closed to steamboat travel. After determining that the overland trip to Independence, the launching point for the wagon trains heading west, was too dangerous to take due to its being heavy slave territory, the Missouri River had seemed the only somewhat safe possibility. So Amanda, Jacob, and Penny were forced to wait.

At first, Jacob had stayed clear of Amanda, unwilling to even meet her eye. Day after day he would seek work on the riverfront as a roustabout, and night after night he would exhaustedly crawl to his quarters in the back of the house. The only time Amanda had seen him was at suppertime, and she never missed the opportunity to tell him of the true way in the light of the Lord. He had grumbled and tried to ignore her, but he hadn't cast any more lustful looks her way. There had been a time when she had felt smug in her belief that Jacob was beginning to see the ways of righteousness, and she was sure faith would not be far behind.

But that had all changed when the Mississippi River had flooded to the point where the barges had been prevented from landing. There was no longer any work on the docks. Jacob had searched the city, but a new outbreak of cholera was paralyzing Saint Louis. Unknowns were feared, especially slaves and the lower class, who were believed to spread the dreaded disease. As the days passed, the number of dead grew at an alarming rate. Now Jacob was idle; no work was to be found. Their hostess, Mrs. Wikets, was out daily, helping the Sisters of the Visitation clothe and feed the newly orphaned and widowed. It left Jacob with precious little to do, and no one to talk to save his daughter or Amanda. Amanda had pressed harder, thinking this would be a perfect opportunity to teach him and his daughter more of the Bible. Although he never came to sit with them, she knew he was listening. So, in her enthusiasm for her first converts, she had read loudly to Penny from the Bible.

Now, she stood pacing the small space allotted to her in the parlor. Frustrated and uneasy, she saw the wicked and lustful side of Jacob had returned. Suddenly, she stopped. Carefully, she worded her definition.

"Well, Penny, to covet something or someone is to want very badly something that isn't yours or that you can't have." Amanda sighed heavily, hoping this explanation was sufficiently clear. The little girl sat thoughtfully, chewing on her bottom lip. A deep scowl crossed her normally smooth forehead. Then her eyes grew round and bright with understanding. Amanda grinned triumphantly at Jacob. He would get no compromising words from her.

"So my Daddy aren't sinnin' if he wants you to stay with us, 'cause you don't belong to nobody, and he can have you if he wants. Right?" Penny cried with excitement.

Amanda's look of triumph rapidly dissolved into horrified

shock. "What?" Amanda nearly screeched, as she whirled around to face her student. Jacob, too, had jumped to his feet behind her, and had nearly knocked Amanda off hers. As she tottered, he caught her by wrapping his arm around her waist. His big hand sprawled across her midriff. Amanda caught her breath as the cursed familiar feeling of excitement and desire sliced through her. Trying to move away from his body, which was so close to hers, she nearly tripped again. Her skirt and petticoats had wrapped in an unbalancing swirl around her legs. Jacob's other hand pressed to her back as he gently turned her, her skirts unwinding, her gaze meeting with the dark triangle of chest at the neck of his shirt. His warmth and musky male scent overwhelmed her as she fought the urge to sag into that great wall of masculinity. He must have felt something, too, for his hand tightened at her back, pulling her toward him. She felt herself falling forward. Instinctively, she braced her hands against his chest. She could feel the rapid pulse of his heart beating beneath her hand, could hear his ragged breathing.

"You should kiss her, Daddy." Penny's little voice chirped from behind her. "You said it's okay to kiss someone you like. You like her, don't you?" The child's voice had risen with a hint of concern. The memory of Jacob saying, *"I like you jes fine—like this"* rang over and over in Amanda's ears. Jacob's lips were so close to hers that she could feel his warm, unsteady breath on her mouth. Swallowing hard, she moistened her lips. She must pull away. This was embarrassing. This was not what she wanted. But another voice whispered deep in her heart that this was exactly what she wanted. Oh, God, he was going to kiss her! Her lips parted slightly as she dared to look up into his hungry ebony eyes. They were darker than the darkest night, without pupil or iris, just black, unfathomable depths, devouring her with their fiery desire.

Somewhere along the line, his teasing had turned to something dangerously more.

A little push from behind caused her to fall forward, closing the distance between her heated body and his. Jacob's soft lips covered hers. His warm breath slid seductively over the dampened surface of her mouth. Then he began to move his lips slowly, pulling gently at her bottom lip. She sighed as his tongue flickered along the inner rim of her upper lip. She gasped at the exciting small intrusion, and felt his arms tighten around her, pulling her closer. She felt her breasts crush up against the hard wall of his chest, his hand curve around her buttocks, pulling her hips against his solid thighs. His kiss deepened, stealing her breath. She was drowning in evil, wicked, carnal desire, and she hated herself for not wanting to be saved.

"Daddy, let her breathe." Penny's voice came to her as if through a dense fog. Amanda tried to push the words and the speaker away from her consciousness. She didn't want this glorious feeling to end. But slowly the words sank in. She pulled back in horror. Confused, she raised her hand to slap Jacob's face. His eyes met hers. She let the hand fall with her eyes. She was as much to blame as he was, or more. She knew what she had done was wrong and willful, but she had let the devil tempt her. In her weakness, she had given in to him. With tears in her eyes, she fled the parlor to the security of her room. As her feet touched the first landing on the wide staircase, she heard Jacob's deep and steady voice responding to a muffled question from his daughter.

"I'm sure she liked it, honey. She just don't know it yet." *Of all the stupid arrogance,* Amanda thought as she slammed her bedroom door. Then she started to cry harder. He was wrong. She knew all too well she liked it, and it was wrong, terribly wrong to feel that way and to desperately want more.

Fifteen

Now it was Amanda who avoided Jacob. She didn't trust herself, and she certainly didn't trust him. If he had set out to undermine her determination, he was succeeding. She had no intention of letting him see this or of giving him another chance to shake her weak resolve. Even Penny got bored sitting in Amanda's room, listening to her mumble prayers and read the Bible. After a few unsuccessful attempts to drag her back downstairs, the child gave up in favor of piggyback rides and make-believe games with her father.

The Wikets were rarely home, as the number of fatalities from the cholera outbreak rose to the gruesome tally of one hundred twenty-six. The muddy, rain-swept streets were filled with dismal grief and keening. Amanda kept to her room, praying for the numerous dead and dying, trying to convince herself that this was how she could be of the most service. Jacob and Penny were only two of so many. Their salvation could wait. Looking out her window day after day at the numerous black hearses clopping down the liquid streets, Amanda felt fear seize her heart and yearned to be free of this dying city. For the first time in her life, a cloud of ominous depression settled around her, making her doubt herself, God's will, and her decision to come to this forsaken country. She was even considering going back home to England, to admit failure, to return to her safe, dull old life.

One dreary, rainy afternoon in mid-May, she listlessly gazed out her bedroom window. She could hear the muted chatter below. Suddenly, a tightly wrapped figure emerged from a black hack carrying a large, battered trunk. The figure darted for the front stoop. Rousing herself out of her lethargy, Amanda pressed her nose against the glass to get a better look. In the distance, the door knocker sounded loudly. The hushed voices downstairs rose to a higher pitch of excitement. After a quarter of an hour, sounds returned to normal, and Amanda watched as the all-encompassing dark cape of the messenger dashed toward the waiting vehicle. The steady drizzle made it difficult to decipher the name on its side, and all Amanda could read were the last two words, "*at law.*"

"Miss Smith?" Mrs. Wiket's amiable voice inquired through Amanda's closed door. Amanda considered not answering, feigning sleep, but dredging up her sense of propriety, she decided against it. Instead, she rose and opened the door.

Mrs. Wiket stood before her, looking tired and ragged. Guilt washed over Amanda as she realized how little she, Amanda, had really helped by hiding in her room while this woman was working herself into the grave for the unfortunate of the city. Amanda's lips twisted in a wry, depreciating smile as she reflected on Mrs. Wiket's earlier belief that Amanda was the one with courage.

Before she could say anything, Jacob came down the hall lugging the large, battered trunk that she had seen through the window.

"This came for you, or rather, for Master McCarthy," the blond woman said softly, while looking sympathetically into Amanda's eyes. "They have just now sorted out..." Her voice drifted off wearily, as she waved a frail hand in the direction of the charred and beaten piece of luggage. Mrs.

Wiket smiled as Jacob hunkered down to set the chest on the floor. "Jacob can help you. I really must finish seeing to the washing and mending of the good sister's hospital's linens. There is so much blood. So much need." With that, the older woman turned and walked toward the stairs. Amanda had seen little of her hostess, but enough to know that she had changed dramatically. Suddenly feeling ashamed and effused with the first bit of energy in a week, Amanda started to go after her. Jacob's hand on her shoulder stayed her.

For a moment, she paused. In wonder, she turned to gaze up at the handsome man behind her.

"Leave her be. She's got her work to do, and you got yours." Jacob's voice was flat, almost forced, as he stared after Mrs. Wicket's retreating figure. A strange chill washed over Amanda and she shivered. In the short time she had known Jacob, she had seen him display many emotions, all of them passionate, but never this icy, cold indifference. She opened her mouth to speak, but instead she pushed past him to the waiting trunk. She didn't know what to say, so she squatted and opened the lid.

Raising her hand to her mouth, all thoughts of anything but the few remnants of Kevin, her past life, and all their carefully laid plans vanished. Biting down hard on her bottom lip, she tasted the salty metallic tang of her blood. Large, silent tears trickled down her cheeks, beneath her fingertips. Falling forward, she landed on her knees, gripping the trunk's edge. Slowly, she lifted her few prized, now charred books. For a moment, she placed a loving hand on her beloved Zebra skin that had wrapped her as an infant. Then she saw her black Bible. Carefully, she opened the brown, brittle pages. A small slip of paper fell out. It fluttered to the ground beside her, blank side up. She covered her eyes and began to weep. She heard Jacob stoop and lift the scrap. His voice was deep, questioning.

"This important?" She heard the paper rattle, as he turned it over. It was the note Kevin had given her telling him to meet her at Porick's pub. She shook her head. After a while, she looked through bleary eyes at the remaining items still in the trunk. She sifted past several dresses and a satin, rose-colored bonnet. Suddenly, her hand stopped, as it unburied a parcel wrapped in brown paper. A small note was pinned to the twine knotted in the front.

> Items found on the deceased, Mr. Kevin McCarthy
> Given address: 1869 Eighteenth Street,
> Saint Louis, Missouri
> Passenger *Allisia*, April 1849

With trembling hands, Amanda struggled with the double knot. It didn't budge. She began to tug frantically at it. Suddenly, she felt all her bottled frustration, anger, and helplessness at the injustice of it all focused on that knot. Throwing back her head, a ragged sob of agony stole from her lips. Immediately, Jacob squatted down beside her. He deftly sliced through the twine with a small hunting knife. Amanda turned to him, her face streaked with tears.

"I wanted to do it. It was mine to open. Why did you? It was . . ." She closed her eyes in pain, her face twisting, resisting, then giving way to open sobbing. Jacob knelt beside her, gathering her into his arms.

"Shhh. It'll be all right." One big hand stroked her from shoulder to elbow, over and over. He continued to talk in a low, soothing voice. Amanda didn't resist him. Vaguely, she imagined this was how he talked to children and horses. For the first time since England, she felt safe. She knew it was just an illusion, but for now she needed it. It felt so good to lean on someone else.

As her crying subsided, she rested peacefully, her cheek against Jacob's chest. Strangely, she didn't feel embarrassed or angry, she just felt drained. Feeling the weight of his cheek against the top of her head, she shifted, and he slightly tightened his arms around her. She stilled, as she felt his warmth surround her. For a moment, her grief drained from her heart, and was replaced with a sensation of contentment and love. She shook her head. That was crazy; she must be imagining things, wanting too much. He was only being considerate. It was she who was beginning to want more. Slowly, reluctantly, she pulled away from the security of his embrace. Without looking at him, she began to unwrap the brown package. Inside was Penny's doll. Her head faceless, a melted mass of wax. Amanda turned and handed it to Jacob.

"This is Penny's Rebecca," she whispered brokenly.

Jacob hesitated before taking it, and Amanda remembered Penny's story of how Kevin had taken it to heaven to keep her mother company. Looking up, she gazed into Jacob's eyes. They were kind, concerned, unsure. Gently, she retrieved the doll, placing it beneath the bonnet in the trunk. It was better to let the child think it was in heaven.

Looking back in her lap, she lifted a small tissue-wrapped package. Carefully peeling back the paper, she found Sean McCarthy's gold watch. It was his only possession of any real monetary value, and he had given it to his last son. Now that son was gone. She felt the uncontrollable tears begin to well up again, when Jacob's gentle voice dragged her from her memory.

"That's a fine piece of metalwork." His callused fingertip stroked the engraved surface. "A family heirloom?" he asked.

Amanda shook her head; her vision blurred.

"No, it was Kevin's father's. He gave it to him." Almost before the words were out, Jacob snatched back his finger as if the gold surface were a glowing iron. Amanda looked at him, the unspoken question in her eyes. This time Jacob did not look away. His face was set in a grim, hard way. She could see his teeth grinding slowly back and forth.

"I don't set no stock in blacks mixing with whites," he growled. It sounded familiar, and slowly Amanda recalled Jacob's words when first she had told him about Kevin.

"But surely you don't believe all white people are bad?" She asked incredulously.

"No. There's some bad white folk, and some that does good, jes' like there some black folk that are good, and some that do bad. I jes' don't think they should mix." With this explanation given, Jacob wiped his hands down his thighs and rose. Amanda was sure he was going to leave, but instead he moved over to the dressing table and leaned forward on his palms to gaze into the mirror at his reflection. Amanda followed, setting the watch she held on the lid of the trunk, and stood behind him.

After a moment, Jacob continued his conversation with both his and her reflection. In an odd way, Amanda thought, it was like he was trying to convince both of them of what he said.

"There are white folk that help those held in slavery escape. But they owe us that much. I figure most do it to ease their conscience of what their supposed Christian brethren's been doing to us Negroes for so long."

Amanda watched his eyes fade from hurt to anger to bitterness to sorrow as he spoke. She would have never guessed that those ebony eyes could have taken on so many hues.

Jacob continued, undaunted that she didn't respond. "I know I need their help now, and I'm not above using them, like they been using us for centuries. But after that, there ain't no more. I don't believe there can be true friendships, or—more." At this point, he turned around, straightening to his full height, his eyes accusing.

Amanda stepped back, feeling the full impact of his meaning. Her first thought was to tell him there wasn't any *more* to her relationship with Mr. McCarthy, but there was. Not in the sense he meant, but she had loved Kevin. She'd loved him for what he'd done and was willing to do. She'd loved him for who he was. She loved her foster Aunt and Uncle Carrington. She knew these people loved her, too, not because of some ancient guilt, or to use her, but for who she was. She stepped forward, determined.

"You are wrong, Jacob, so very wrong."

Jacob reared back his head in exasperation. Amanda reached up, grasping his face between her hands, bringing his gaze back to hers.

"Jacob, some cruel people have hurt you and those you love, but don't let it destroy you, make you unable to see past the color of a person's skin. Be better than that. I know you are." She knew she was pleading, but suddenly she desperately wanted him to understand. Jacob tore his face away from her hands, snorting angrily.

"You innocent! I don't know why I expected you to understand. You don't know what it's like to be told you're nothing—no, less than nothing, a piece of property, dependent on the whim of the white man." Now he leaned close to her, his voice coming shallow and ragged. "I can never forgive the white man for what he has done to me, what he has taken from us." The burning passion and despair that burned so brilliantly in Jacob's eyes was almost more than she could bear. Her voice came softly, strong but gentle.

"No one can really take anything from you unless you give it to them, just as no one can really give you anything unless you are willing to receive it." Amanda raised a hand to caress Jacob's tormented brow, thought better of it, and folded her hands demurely before her. Jacob leaned back against the dresser, shaking his head from side to side.

"I wish I could believe you. Rollin told me the stories you told him on the trip to America, the stories of Africa, your heritage. I don't even know mine. All I know is my great-

great-great-great-grandmother was one of the first slaves sent to this country in the sixteen hundreds. She was packed so tight on a slave ship that the rafters rubbed her pregnant belly raw. She didn't make it. The poor little baby did, unfortunately. I don't know who her husband was. My heritage died with her in the hold of that ship. Sure, her blood got passed on, but it was diluted, most likely, time and time again." Now his eyes locked with Amanda's, challenging her to pity him, to dispute him. "So what am I now? You may be some king's granddaughter or such, but I'm a bastard, pure and simple, and I have the white man to thank for that."

The sheer hatred and animosity in his words spewed out like poison, making Amanda frightened. There was a dangerous power in this kind of rage. Her mind raced for the correct response. Should she plead some more? Should she cry for him? Part of her wanted to turn away, to say it was his problem, his burden to bear. But she knew she couldn't. One day it would be Penny's, and countless others'. She suddenly realized with crystal clarity that she wanted this man to experience love again, to learn how to love, to love her, to love himself. She needed to offer Jacob hope and faith. Faith in mankind. She tried to imagine what her wise Aunt Daba would do. Suddenly, with grim determination, she marched up to Jacob, grabbed his hand, and rapped him firmly across the knuckles.

"Shame on you for doubting yourself, your heritage! Our African ancestors were a strong, proud people, and I'm sure they would not respect a man who wallows in self-pity. The world can change, and you have a responsibility to change it. But violence and fear never succeed in the long run. You may not see it in your lifetime, or even your children's, but allow your great-great-great-grandchild the ability to be glad his bast,—er, illegitimate grandfather survived." If Amanda could have seen herself at that moment, she would have been startled to see how much she looked like that wise aunt she was trying to emulate.

Jacob was stunned at the force of her conviction and shaken by her words. Preachers, his mother, his brother, and many others had told him to accept his fate from God, to wait for the afterlife, the ever elusive promised land. That had done nothing but turn him from God. Now this mystery of a woman was turning the tables, making chinks in his impregnable fortress. He didn't know if he liked it, or if he could or wanted to change his way of thinking. He'd carried his hatred and resentment so long that it was comfortable in an odd way, like an old pair of shoes.

Frustrated and a little bit panicky, Jacob sifted through Amanda's argument for a weakness, a fault. She had said no one can take anything from you unless you give it to them. That was it. He turned on her with a new, feral intensity.

"No one can take anything from anyone? Yeah, well you try telling that to my dead wife Rebecca." Feeling vindicated, Jacob kicked the trunk lid closed as he walked from the room. The gold watch slid to the floor, the crystal shattering, but remaining intact.

Sixteen

That night, a ravishing fire broke out along the Saint Louis riverfront. A steamboat named the *White Cloud* burst into flames. Within moments, the blaze leapt to the *Edward Bates*. As smoke filled the horizon, a sharp, northeasterly wind blew the inferno toward the shore. One boat after another fell victim to the flames. Fire bells clanged wildly and frantically through the ominous night. Twenty-three boats blazed brilliantly, reflecting off the swollen Mississippi River.

Jacob and Mr. Wiket raced toward the wharf with all the other able men of the city. The wind continued to drive the heat of the flames inland. Helplessly, they watched the fire wrap greedy fingers around the freight lining the wharf near Locust Street. The river inferno had become a holocaust on land.

Stripped to their waists, the men worked side by side, watching their city burn. To Jacob, it seemed hopeless, as building after building burned to the ground. Regardless of their efforts, the fire advanced. Block after block of Saint Louis homes and businesses succumbed to the blaze.

Suddenly, out of the brilliant, incandescent sky, came the explosion of a thousand cannons.

"Oh, dear God, it's the arsenal! The fire has reached the kegs of gunpowder." John Wiket's face grew pale, colored only by the flickering flames reflected off his fair skin.

"Then we better move farther inland, Mister Wiket!" Jacob shouted above the hysterical pandemonium. John Wiket stood rooted, unable to move, his eyes wide and unblinking. Jacob grasped his shoulder, but the smaller man only stumbled back a few steps, then headed straight toward the explosion. Jacob watched in shocked disbelief. "You's crazy." He muttered under his breath. Angrily, he folded his arms across his sweat-drenched chest. He'd be damned if he'd follow that fool. He didn't owe him or any man that much, to go following him to hell's own doorstep. He watched as John Wiket's figure dodged the falling debris, heading toward the anguished screams of men in pain. Guilt washed over Jacob and he fought it back angrily. "Damn Christians! They have to take on the responsibilities of the world." Mr. Wiket was almost out of sight, just a wavering mirage in the heat of the flames, when suddenly he lurched and fell forward. Jacob waited. John didn't get up. "Damn! Damn!" Jacob screamed into the deafening din. "Damn that fool of a white man!" Jacob's feet flew across the burning street toward the fallen body.

"Can you hear me?" Jacob gasped against the acrid smoke filling his lungs and nostrils. John Wiket did not respond. With a strength borne of anger, not fear, Jacob lifted the limp man onto his shoulders. Struggling against the weight and the stifling heat, he moved away from the flames.

"Help me! Please!" a deep, pained voice cried out to Jacob as he passed a burning building. Breathing heavily, Jacob paused to see a large, bearded white man trapped beneath a massive wooden beam. From this angle, he could see that the man's ankle was trapped, and that although no flames had reached the man yet, it was only a matter of time.

Jacob turned his face away. He wasn't responsible. Perhaps he owed something to Mr. Wiket, but he certainly didn't owe anything to that stranger. For all he knew, the man could be a slave trader, or worse, a slave catcher. When the large man didn't cry out again, Jacob looked back. Maybe the man had worked his own way free. Jacob's gaze was met by clear, sky-blue eyes. The bearded man just looked at him, not begging, not angry, but waiting. Sweat trickled down his tan brow and his mouth was a tight line of pain, but still he didn't call out to Jacob, only waited with a silent pride. Jacob hesitated, his respect growing for this man who would not beg. Irritated with himself, he knew he couldn't just walk by.

"Can't you see I've already got my hands full?" Jacob glared accusingly at the silent man. Still the man said nothing, his piercing gaze unflinching. Looking around him, Jacob found a semi-safe spot beneath a brick overhand and laid John Wiket down. Shaking his head, he could not believe he was risking his neck not just for one white man, but for two. And the second one he didn't know from Adam.

As Jacob approached the heavy beam, the man said nothing, just followed him with those unwavering eyes.

"When I says to move, move." Jacob shouted viciously. Somehow he knew this was all the pious Miss Amanda's fault. Something in her sweet, innocent words had obviously struck a chord with him, but he'd be damned if he'd ever let her know.

The fallen oak beam was massive and difficult to move. The flames were growing nearer, and Jacob's palms were slick with sweat. Glancing around, he picked up a smaller wooden bracket. Wedging it under the large rafter, he leaned on it with all his weight. The timber shifted, and Jacob ordered the man to move. Just then the brace snapped, and the beam crashed down within inches of the man's damaged ankle. Another flaming rafter came after it. Hobbling, the big man just escaped. In silence, he helped Jacob place the still unconscious Mr. Wiket on his shoulders. Together, the three of them headed toward the dark, cooler streets farther away from the river.

"Thanks," the wounded man finally said. "The name's McCarthy." He extended a deeply tanned hand. The buckskin fringe from his coat sleeve slid over his arm to swing gently beneath it. Shifting Mr. Wiket's weight, Jacob studied the man, thinking he was wearing the strangest outfit he'd ever seen. Before this, Jacob had taken little notice of the man's appearance, but now that the man stood erect, towering a good three inches above Jacob's own six-foot frame, he took in his whole mien. The man's coat was covered with intricate beadwork, as were the sides of his pants. Jacob had heard about Indians in the West wearing similar clothes, but he doubted an Indian would have such blue eyes. Scanning the man's face, he noted it was still possible that he had some Indian blood. Although his eyes were an unsettling blue, his face was deeply tanned and his hair was a sleek blue-black. Then the name hit him. McCarthy. The man was Irish. The same name as that dead man who'd been on the boat with Amanda and his daughter. He didn't take the offered hand, and Mr. McCarthy let his own drop. For a moment, they stood there. Then Jacob turned and walked toward the house on Eighteenth Street. Seamus McCarthy watched him go.

The following morning's paper was filled with the grueling details. The fire had destroyed four hundred buildings, twenty-three steamboats, and over fifteen city blocks. Appraisers had totaled the losses to the staggering amount of a shocking six million dollars. These headlines were followed by an even more horrifying story: the cholera epidemic had gone from bad to worse. The illness was wiping out more than fifty-seven lives a day, and no end was in sight.

The four adults at the table looked morosely at their plates. John Wiket had recovered and sipped thoughtfully at his tea, reading and rereading the news aloud, as if he didn't believe it.

"I think the time has come for you to move on," he finally said, as he laid the paper down and looked at Jacob. "The city is in a panic, and many will be leaving. The steamboats on the Missouri are being allowed to travel again, and they will be packed. If anyone is still trying, it will be almost impossible to single you and the child out." Jacob only nodded, his eyes weary and bloodshot.

Amanda listened, hearing the reference to both Jacob and Penny, but not to herself. She felt the uneasy rise of panic in her stomach. "And what of me?" she asked in an unsteady voice. Before anyone could answer, she turned to Jacob. "Please, just let me go with you as far as Independence. From there I'm sure I can find my own way."

Jacob turned to her, silently brooding. She gripped the fine white linen tablecloth beneath her fingers. He had to say yes. She had to buy at least a little more time. The Methodist missionary commission had not contacted her yet, and she could not very well go alone. It wasn't safe. Besides, they needed her. Never had she been so sure that *both* Jacob and Penny needed her, and she needed them. She closed her eyes while the silence continued, waiting for the damning denial.

"All right. But just to Independence," Jacob responded gruffly.

Amanda opened her eyes with a dazzling smile. "You won't be sorry!" she cried.

"But I already am," Jacob muttered as he pushed back his chair from the table. What had gotten into him lately? First he was risking his neck for strangers, then breaking his promise to be free of Amanda Smith. She was beginning to mean too much to him and Penny. As much as she had annoyed him with her Bible talk, he had found himself looking forward to her cheerful enthusiasm, no matter how misplaced it might be. But it was getting dangerous. He had found himself attracted to more than just her optimism, and it was all too obvious from her passionate response to his one kiss that she was, too.

As he paced the floor in his small room, he tried to rationalize his behavior. He liked Amanda, she liked him. Penny liked Amanda, she liked her. He could offer the woman a passage westward, and she could watch over Penny. He could provide protection, and she could provide . . . He stopped, remembering her lovely young body, his burning lust, and he slammed his fist into his palm. It would never do. He could offer her nothing. Hell, even if he'd wanted to, he couldn't even offer her his name.

Jacob stopped pacing, shocked by the direction his thoughts had taken. Sure, he wanted to make love to Amanda, but since when did that equate to wanting to spend the rest of your life with someone? Hell, they couldn't even see eye to eye on most things. They were from entirely different backgrounds. He laughed a mirthless sound. If they were to tie the knot, he figured it wouldn't last past the honeymoon. No, it was better to be done with her, before he did something they'd both regret.

Independence, Missouri, was little more than a main street. But in the spring of 1849, it was a bustling one. People anxious to set out for the western territories, find new fertile land, get away from the dreaded cholera sweeping the country, and make a better life, crowded the overburdened town. Rumors were beginning to trickle in that gold had been found in California. Farmers and adventurers were trading in their homesteads for a wagon, a plow for a sturdy pack mule with some picks and shovels. The blacksmiths' forges burned late into the night, and the muggy, mosquito infested nights were filled with the clanging of hammers and anvils making wagon wheels and horseshoes.

Jacob helped Amanda drag her fire blackened trunk onto the wharf. Penny danced excitedly behind, singing a little ditty she'd made up about Indians and ranges. He eyed Amanda suspiciously, knowing that she was the one who had undoubtedly supplied the child with the underlying story for the song. He was caught short by the sparkle of excitement in her eyes. She turned to him, flashing a dazzling smile. It was so magnificent that it actually hurt somewhere deep in his chest. God, she was beautiful—so innocent, so trusting. For a moment his resolution to be free of her weakened. His arms ached to wrap themselves around her, to soak in her goodness and joy. Her face shone with the hope and happiness he was craving. He turned away. Leaving her behind was best. He struggled to resurrect some of his earlier indignation. She did think this was going to be a carriage ride in the park. He felt a hand on his arm.

"Look, Jacob. There's an office for wagon train information and membership. Do you think we could get into a train leaving this week?" Without waiting for an answer, Amanda had opened up her reticule, and was waving a wad of bills before his face. "Here. I can contribute two hundred dollars toward the purchase of a wagon and horses, or perhaps oxen. They do look a little sturdier. Besides, I heard one man on the steamboat say that they are better for farming. What do you think?" She gazed up at him, breathless, her eyes a liquid amber.

Jacob felt his chest constrict, making it difficult to breathe. Hadn't she heard a word he had said before they left Saint Louis? This was it. He'd done his part. Now she was on her own. "Put that money away, you little fool," Jacob snapped irritably, as he crammed her fist and the money back into her reticule. "You want every bit of conniving trash to know what you're worth?"

Amanda looked shocked, then repentant, as she followed Jacob's order. "I'm sorry. I was just so excited. I just can't believe I am finally so close to my dream." Her eyes swept the noisy hubbub around her, then twinkled up at him. Dare she tell him that he now was a part of her dream? "I promise to be much more careful in the future. Your word is my command." She grinned as she saluted him. Jacob glared back at her.

"I don't care what you do in the future, because . . ."

He was cut off by a deep, throaty laugh from behind him. Jacob whirled about, and had to throw his head back to gaze up at the tall, familiar man on a bay gelding.

"McCarthy?" Jacob asked in surprise.

"One and the same," the man laughed, as he swung down from his horse. "Ma'am," he said to Amanda, doffing his wide-brimmed hat. Amanda just stared back, incredulous. Seamus McCarthy laughed again. Turning back to Jacob, he said, "I wouldn't be so quick to refuse an offer like the one the little lady just gave ye."

"Ye?" Amanda asked, still in a daze.

"Ye," said Seamus, turning back to Amanda. He stopped, as he caught the look of confused recognition on her face. He stepped closer. Amanda hurled herself into his arms.

"You're Kevin's brother, aren't you?" she sobbed into the soft, supple hide of his coat. Amanda didn't see Jacob turn away in disgust, or feel the awkward way in which Seamus patted her back.

"I do have a brother named Kevin. But he's back in New York. He's just a wee lad. I haven't seen him for near on five years or more." As he spoke, Seamus's brogue grew heavier, as if the memories washed away the new, blander accent he had acquired.

Disentangling himself from Amanda's embrace, Seamus moved back toward his horse. Women were a mystery to him, and he'd just as soon keep it that way. Amanda followed him, shuffling through her reticule with one hand.

"Wait, Seamus, I mean Mr. McCarthy. I didn't mean to be so presumptuous, it's just that I feel like I know you. Kevin and your family talked so much about you. I have something of his, or your father's, for you. He gave it to Kevin before Kevin passed a—" She broke off in mid-sentence, realizing what she had been about to say. She had come to terms with Kevin's death, but this man, his brother, didn't even know.

Seamus froze, his light blue eyes growing dark and wary as they shifted from her face to the hand that held a small white tissue bundle.

"Before he what?" Seamus demanded slowly, his eyes cold and icy like an Arctic wind. Amanda moved forward, taking his hand and placing the heavy parcel in it. Seamus looked down at it, unmoving. Amanda folded back the paper to expose the cracked crystal glittering in the afternoon sun.

"There was an explosion. The steamboat we were on caught fire." Amanda felt a tug on the hand that held his wrist as Seamus slumped against his horse.

"He was just a lad," Seamus said quietly, dazed. His eyes were the soft, hazy blue of summer morning. "He should have stayed with his ma." Suddenly the haze broke, and his eyes were once again a hard, icy blue. "What was he doing with ye on a steamboat?" Seamus demanded. He straightened, grabbing both of Amanda's wrists, letting the watch fall unheeded to the ground. "Why are ye here and my baby brother ain't?" His voice cracked with a savage fury.

Penny, who had been silently standing by, let out a little yelp. Jacob turned back to witness McCarthy's fearsome hold on a frightened Amanda.

"Let her go!" Jacob growled, as he approached the big

man. Seamus instantly stepped back, staring down at his hands. A crowd had gathered, and a murmur ran through the crowd to get the sheriff. A slave was about to hit his master.

It was Seamus who reacted first. He bent to retrieve the watch, then turned to the crowd.

"It is nothing. Go about yer business."

The onlookers seemed disappointed that this was all the excitement they were going to get to see. Seamus turned back to Amanda and apologized. Jacob squinted one dark, dangerous black eye at him before he grabbed Penny's hand.

"Don't expect me to go thankin' you for savin' the day just now," Jacob sneered at Seamus. "I don't owe you nothin'."

Seamus only stared at him for a moment with a blank stare. Then a slow smile spread across his face. "Quite to the contrary, sir. It is I who owe ye for saving me life."

Jacob scowled, and told him to forget it. Amanda watched him leave, not knowing if she should follow or stay. Seamus touched her gently on the shoulder. She turned.

"I'm sorry about what—it's just that—would you tell me?" the large man struggled for words. Amanda nodded. It was the least she could do. Besides, she wanted to know how he knew Jacob.

Seventeen

Several hours later, Amanda sat across from Seamus with a half-eaten piece of pie and a steaming cup of tea. Not once since Seamus's original outburst of grief had he shown any emotion in his intense azure eyes. He had listened without comment as she told him everything. Twice she had been near tears, but he had sat stoically. She was glad he had reacted earlier, or she would have thought Seamus McCarthy a cold man, undeserving of a brother like Kevin.

Studying him now, she was continually accosted by the resemblance, yet difference, between the brothers. They both had their father's tall frame, but Kevin had been thin and small-boned like his mother. Both brothers had the same raven hair, but one's eyes had been emerald, alive with the joy of life, and the other's were a cold, distant sapphire, wary and reserved.

Seamus asked no questions, and when Amanda finally had nothing left to tell, the silence hung uncomfortably between them.

"You've met Jacob before, I take it?" Amanda hedged, as she brought her teacup to her lips.

"Is that his name?" Seamus shrugged noncommittally.

Amanda sipped slowly, thoughtfully. Seamus was not as

open as his brother, but something warned her that he was every bit as perceptive.

"Why do you owe him?" Amanda asked, refusing to parry any longer.

Seamus sat back in his chair, one hand stroking his full beard. "Can't say as it's any of your business."

Amanda nearly choked on her next draft of the hot liquid, as she sputtered out a laugh. "Kevin would have loved to hear you put me in my place." Amanda laughed again. "Kevin was always asking me questions that were none of his business, and I let him know."

As Seamus watched Amanda bubble with laughter, he fought back a smile. "I would guess my little brother was quite taken with ye."

Amanda's smile softened, becoming wistful. "You're right. At least he thought he was. He promised to take care of me if I'd let him. I guess that's what he thought he was doing." Amanda looked away, then felt Seamus's rough hand cover hers. She looked at him through watery eyes. His lips broke into a sympathetic smile.

Jacob nearly choked on his irritation. The brother Kevin wasn't even cold in the grave, and already she was holding hands with the other one. He recalled the few times he had touched her. He scowled. Each and every time she had fought it, and now here she was in broad daylight, carrying on with this strange white man, laughing and tossing her head for all the world to see. Well, McCarthy could have her. He was finished with her. Still, Jacob didn't move from his spot outside the canteen window. Just then, a very wide woman moved in front of the glass, blocking his view. Jacob cursed beneath his breath. He was sure, just sure Amanda was doing something she shouldn't with that big oaf of an Irishman. Who did he think he was in that getup, anyway? An Indian? Denying the growing jealousy he felt, he turned to his daughter.

"Penny, go in there an ask Miss Smith . . ." He paused, not at all sure of what she should ask. The little girl stood patiently waiting. Jacob scowled and stomped off the boardwalk, stepping right into a mud puddle. "Don't jes' stand there, girl," Jacob demanded, as he shook off his mud-splattered boot. "We ain't got all day. Follow me." Penny sighed and followed her father across the street, careful to avoid the mud puddle. Ever since her father had kissed Miss Amanda, things had gotten worse, not better. She wished Nanna were around to talk to, but Jacob didn't even like Penny to mention her grandmother's name. He always said, *"She made her bed, now let her lie in it."* Penny sighed again. She just wanted him happy, and she had been so sure Miss Amanda could have been the one to make that dream come true.

Amanda watched the two proceed across the street. Jacob had been watching. Her spirit soared. Maybe, just maybe he was beginning to feel something, too. Turning her attention back to Seamus, she saw he was grinning. Heated fingers of color splayed across her cheeks. Was she so obvious?

Jacob grumbled again as he ran down the list the man at the outfitting store had given him. He couldn't read a damn thing, and he wasn't about to let this good-for-nothing, snooty little shopkeeper know. Slowly, he ran his finger down the rows of squiggly lines, then across to the numbers that he recognized.

"You sure you got all this here in stock?" Jacob asked with feigned authority. The man behind the counter nodded. "It sure seems that there's an awful lot more then jes' a man and his daughter need," Jacob muttered.

"Believe me, it is a most thorough list. Samuel Parker swears by it, and Mr. Fremont and one of his foremost scouts, Bos McCarthy, says it's a sure fool who don't have it all," the balding little clerk said defensively. He turned away to smile at a female customer entering the store.

Jacob wanted to scream. He was sick of the name McCarthy. And no doubt the Irishman with Amanda was none other than Bos himself. He hadn't liked the clerk's gleam of admiration when he said the name.

Suddenly he stopped. McCarthy had said he owed him. Maybe Jacob would just see if he needed all this, and what it would run him. With all his planning, he hadn't counted on this. Sure, he could add up a few simple charges for shoeing a horse, replacing a wheel. But there had to be close to fifty items on this list, and each price had a lot of zeros behind it. He thought about the thick stack of bills rolled in his pants waistband. It was all the money he had saved to buy his wife, his daughter, and his mother. He hadn't needed any of it. It was close to twenty-two hundred dollars.

The clerk went to attend the woman who'd entered the shop. Jacob didn't notice their heads bent low, whispering over some bolt of calico. He was still trying to figure out how he was going to handle this dilemma.

"You got your papers, boy?" the clerk called out suddenly to Jacob, as he puffed out his chest and strolled toward him. Jacob's head whipped up at the term *boy*. Anger burned in his eyes, turning them to smoldering black coals. The fat little man retreated a few steps, and slipped behind the counter. "Well, have you got any papers?" the man attempted again, only this time with a little less bravado.

"I don't think that is really necessary, do you, Willaby?" Seamus asked, as he ducked his head to enter the doorway. Jacob turned his anger toward the tall man.

"We were just doing a simple business transaction," Jacob began, turning to glower at the clerk cringing behind the counter.

Seamus raised a single black eyebrow, shrugged, and

stepped back to let Amanda move around him.

"Yeah, sure, that's what we were doing. He was just asking if he needed everything on the paper, and how much, and all." The pudgy man's jowls trembled slightly, as he spoke the lie.

"Really?" said Amanda, as she sidled up to Jacob and primly plucked the slip of paper from his hands. "Let's see. Five barrels of flour at $2.95 each." She went on until she had recited the entire list. Then she ran a gloved finger down the right-hand column of numbers. "Sir, there seems to be a problem with your computations here." The clerk turned bright red at her implied accusation. When no one moved, Amanda proceeded to the counter where she showed the man the discrepancy. "It would seem you have totaled the amount of four hundred and ninety-five dollars for wagon, oxen, and supplies, when in truth the total should be four hundred and thirty-five dollars." When the little man didn't respond, but only nervously twisted his hands in his apron pocket, Amanda continued. "Do you see that I am right? Or perhaps you could show me where the extra sixty dollars lies?" When she looked up, she saw that the man was no longer looking at her, but past her at Seamus McCarthy.

"A simple mistake, I assure you, Bos," the little man began, as he bent to retrieve a new list from under the counter. "Ah, here it is. It seems I have given the gentleman the wrong list." He giggled nervously. "I saw my error last night, and I made up a new one." The clerk shifted guiltily from one well-polished boot to the other, as he held out the new list.

Seamus calmly strode across the room, taking the new list from the man's quivering fingers, and handing it to Amanda without looking at it. As he took the old list from her, he spoke in an even, flat voice, "Miss Smith, please be so kind as to check the accuracy of this list." In the silence that followed, Seamus quietly and precisely ripped the old list into sixteen small pieces, letting them flutter to the sawdust floor. "It would be a shame, Willaby, if some of the good folk of this town were to find out you was cheating anybody." Moving a step closer, Seamus continued in the same even tone. "Perhaps I should check with the folks in my train before we depart on the morrow?" Though the words were spoken without malice, the threat was obvious.

The clerk began to tremble violently as dark, half-moon stains appeared beneath his armpits. "Ah, I don't think that is necessary, Bos, ah, Mr. McCarthy," the pitiful little man replied, turning first to Amanda, then to Jacob. "For your inconvenience, let me offer you a discount of, say, ten percent?" The man looked hopefully up at Seamus. Seamus scowled. The man stuttered. "May—may—maybe twenty percent would be better?"

"Lovely," said Amanda as she smiled at Seamus, then turned to Jacob. "I'll just calculate it out for you Jacob, so you don't get . . ."

She didn't get to finish her sentence before Jacob stomped out of the store. Bewildered, she stared after him, then back at Seamus. Seamus struggled to suppress a smile and slid his hand over his face. He nodded to the storekeeper, and left. Amanda followed.

"And what, pray tell, was that all about?" demanded Amanda, as she walked up alone to Jacob. He ignored her as he continued to inspect the horses in the livery behind the store. "I was just trying to help us," Amanda began, when Jacob turned on her with fire in his eyes.

"Us? Us?" he charged. "What us? It ain't or aren't or don't, or whatever fancy word you need to understand, *us*. I said to Independence. We're here. We're done." He turned back to the horse before him so he wouldn't have to look at the hurt in her eyes.

"But Jacob, I—you—you need me!" she cried in a broken

whisper. "Can't you see that now?" She gestured back toward the store.

Jacob moved away from her, leaving her behind the fence while he wandered through the herd. "No," he called out to her, "you're wrong there. I don't need you or anyone 'cept for Penny, and you most certainly don't need me. I made it this far on my own. I can do the rest with my eyes closed." He closed his eyes to demonstrate. A sleek black mare nuzzled his head, and he stroked the white star on her nose.

Frustrated, Amanda climbed up the split fence, leaning far into the corral.

"Jacob, don't be a stupid fool. I can read, I can write, I can add and subtract. These hands," she cried out in frustration, as he turned his back on her, "they can help you." Helplessly, she waited. She was desperate now. She knew she was pushing too far, but she could not stop herself. She half climbed, half fell into the pen and walked up to his back. "Jacob, Whitingworth may still follow. I'm not being hunted. If not for yourself, then for your daughter's sake."

Jacob turned around slowly. His eyes were lethally still, like a snake before it strikes. He moved toward her, and she backed up into the flank of a large brown horse. Jacob closed in on her. She held up her hands before her. He encircled one wrist with his long fingers. Slowly he peeled off her glove, turning her palm up to face him. With studied preciseness, he began stroking the sensitive middle with his forefinger, his eyes never leaving hers. The sensation was exhilarating, his eyes were frightening.

"Your hands? What can they do for me?" Jacob drawled, his eyes hard, but his voice silky, sensually lazy.

Amanda felt the heated blood rush to her face. Oh, God, not this again. Jacob's finger had progressed to her wrist, and was drawing pleasurable circles there. Amanda shut her eyes, trying to block out the sensation. She would not let him weaken her again. He would not. She snapped her hand away. "You evil, wicked, lustful . . ." she spat at him, as she hurried to the safety of the split rail fence.

Jacob's cruel laugh floated over the restless nickering of the animals. "You're not going to stay and save my putrid soul? I thought I needed you." Again the bitter, heartless laugh. She didn't dare turn around. "But then, perhaps Bos McCarthy needs some savin', too."

Amanda stopped in her tracks, her skirts held high, bunched in each hand, as she paused in the muddy corral. She whirled around, but was too late. Jacob had gone back to inspecting the animals. His face was hidden. She was incredulous. Had she heard jealousy in his voice? He was jealous of another man. This time it had nothing to do with black against white, she was sure of it. This time it was man against man. She grinned vindictively. There was hope. Cruel as it may seem, she would use it. It was a start.

Amanda let a wide smile of victory spread across her face as she sloshed heedlessly through the remaining muddy distance. "Very well then, Jacob. Have it your way. I'm going with you, and you can't stop me. If I have to, I'll get Seamus McCarthy to escort me. Then see how you like that," she whispered to herself. Just then, she saw the Bos's tall figure riding by on his bay.

"Mr. McCarthy! Seamus McCarthy!" Amanda called loudly. The horse slowed down, the rider turned her way.

Hidden by a horse, Jacob watched. Suddenly drops of blood dripped to the mud between his feet. Damn that woman, he thought, as he brought his injured thumb to his mouth. It was her fault that he had cut his thumb with the blade he'd been using to dig out the dirt in the horse's hoofs. He might have enjoyed the store clerk's bringing down if it had been anyone other than that McCarthy fellow forcing him to. Then, to have that blasted Miss Smith act as if he needed to be looked after.

Well, it was just too much for a man with any pride to swallow. His eyes scanned the surroundings for his daughter. He found her sitting on the store porch, staring forlornly after Miss Smith as she scurried after that McCarthy man. He felt a familiar sick despair tighten his gut, as he watched his child's sad face. What was that woman doing to them? Before, they had needed no one, save each other. Placing his knife back in the band beneath his shirt, he headed toward his daughter. It would be that way again, once they were free of that bewitching woman.

Jacob knelt on the wooden step beside his daughter and draped an arm tenderly around her waist, drawing her close. He laid his cheek on the soft frizz of curls on the top of her head. Once they were gone, they'd forget all about her. Deep in his mind a voice laughed, *Sure, sure you will.*

Eighteen

"They ain't gonna be on our train," a thin, coatless man named Jed Turner cried as he clenched and unclenched his fists at his side. " 'Sides, Oregon don't 'low no niggers there. Neither slave nor free."

"He's right, Bos. No colored are allowed to even cross into the territory. The citizens of the area voted no over and over to slavery, but they also don't want the competition of cheap black labor," an older man named Dr. John Winslow remarked.

Seamus ran a large hand through his unruly sable curls as he listened to the doctor. Dr. Winslow was a shrewd man with a good reputation as an animal and people doctor. The party needed him on the trip, and he didn't want to have him change his mind about coming.

"Hell, Mr. McCarthy, we're already gettin' a late start. You yourself said we should have left 'bout the first of May if we wanted to get past the mountains 'fore it snowed. Let someone else worry 'bout them darkies," Jed whined.

Seamus had about had it with the sniveling little man from Mississippi. He knew from the moment he had set eyes on Jed and Opal Turner that they would be trouble. Normally, he stayed out of all aspects of a wagon party's doings. They paid him to lead the way, and that was all he'd do. He made it a point to never get involved with any of them. It was easier that way. The only thing he demanded was that they follow his every order with no argument.

Narrowing his eyes to icy slits, he stared at the complaining man. Without taking his eyes from him, he addressed the doctor. "The man and his family can deal with the Oregon laws when they get there. Right now, I think it is a good idea to have a skilled blacksmith along." As he repeated the information Miss Smith had offered him this afternoon, he hoped it was true.

The doctor steepled his fingers and flexed them thoughtfully. He had given his word that his party would follow Seamus McCarthy's dictate to the letter, but he, Johnathan Winslow, was responsible for governing the people in the wagon train. Having a black man, his wife, and daughter along was going to prove to be a thorn. Most of the people in the party, including himself, didn't really care one way or the other. But a few like the Turners would be dead set against it.

"Is this an issue we can vote on, Mr. McCarthy?" the doctor asked hopefully.

Without hesitation, the Bos answered no.

"I see," Dr. Winslow answered, slightly relieved that the decision had been lifted from his shoulders.

Turner turned an angry shade of purple and stomped off into the starless night. Johnathan Winslow and Seamus McCarthy watched him leave. Turner had been elected as second in command and was a vindictive man.

Staring into the darkness, Doc Winslow spoke sadly. "Jed Turner isn't a man to take lightly."

From his side, Seamus responded quietly, "And neither am I."

At these words the doctor smiled and rubbed a hand over his weary eyes. "Of that I am sure. I guess I best be getting off to bed. Sunrise comes early."

"Five forty-five" Seamus responded, and turned toward the small fire outside his hide tent.

That night's sleep did not come easy to Seamus McCarthy. Although the night was cool, he restlessly threw off his striped Hudson Bay wool blanket. For the past twelve years, life had been simple, uncomplicated. At thirty-two, he had seen more of the western United States than most white men. He spoke six Indian languages well, a smattering of three others, and enough French to carry on business transactions with the Canadian traders. For more than a decade, he had been happy to sleep under the stars, eat what was available, and converse only when he wanted to. His large size had been an advantage, gaining respect and fear among men and admiration from women. His lack of greed and nonthreatening ways had endeared him to many tribes. Even a willing squaw to warm his bed had not been too difficult to find. Once or twice he had taken up with a white whore in one or another of the larger towns, especially in California, but all in all, he preferred to remain a loner. Now he had taken on the responsibility of not one but three people, two of them female.

Reaching for his buckskin coat, he crawled out of his tent. The sky had cleared, and the stars were shining brightly. It was a good sign, Seamus thought, as he walked down toward the river. Several steamboats stood moored off the dock, silent and gleaming in the moonlight. Unable to keep the thought of his younger brother locked away, he pulled the broken watch from his pocket. In the still night, the crickets chirped, the water rushed by, and in the distance was the unceasing clang of the blacksmiths.

He had lied when he told the leaders of the party that Miss Smith was Jacob's wife. He had felt that the more religious and priggish of the group would find that more acceptable.

Less complications. Now, as he watched the lunar light glint off the watch case in his hand, turning it from gold to silver, he thought about Miss Amanda Smith. He wondered how much she had meant to his brother, and how much Kevin had meant to her. He smiled as he tried to imagine his baby brother's interest in any female more than just someone to tease. The smile died in his eyes, as he remembered his brother had nearly been a man. Almost at the age he was when he had left home.

His sister Maggie had written him about Kevin's antics, how he got into so much trouble one time that he had been sent to stay with their uncle in Philadelphia for a time until the Know-Nothings had cooled down. As Seamus's thoughts turned to his sister Mary, he shooed them away. He had enough to think about without letting memories of her bring him to tears.

Kevin had been a scrapper. Seamus was—had been—proud of him. Proud of Maggie, too. He hadn't been planning to lead a train this spring. That was why he'd gone to Saint Louis to see pretty Maggie. She obviously hadn't known about Kevin or she would have told him. He wished now that she had. She was learning to write, and she could have written to tell Ma and Da. He closed his hand around the cool metal, caressing its smooth heaviness. His ma had always said, *"No one said life is fair, but it is every man's responsibility to see that it is as close as it can be."* Well, life certainly hadn't been fair to his little brother or his parents. He tried to imagine his gentle mother's face when she heard the news. He knew his father would be strong—on the outside. He opened his fingers from around the watch. He'd have to send them a letter. They deserved that much. Slipping the watch back in his pocket, he looked over his shoulder at the glowing fires of the town. Maybe Miss Smith could write the letter for him. He'd seen today that she could read and add faster than anyone he'd ever known. She was a smart little lass, pretty to boot, and Jacob was a fool if he couldn't see that. Seamus chuckled as he remembered the scene in the store today. Jacob had been so angry, and sweet little Miss Smith had no idea what she'd done wrong. The woman had a lot going for her, but she sure didn't understand much about men and their pride. As a matter of fact, he thought, as he remembered her pitiful act of coyness when she'd asked him to escort her out West, she didn't know much about anything when it came to men. She'd batted her long black eyelashes so outrageously that he'd laughed and asked her if there was something in her eye. She had been so outraged that her pretty gold eyes had turned to liquid fire. He was surprised at a stirring in his loins at the recollection of her glittering, passionate features. He wondered if perhaps his baby brother had experienced this passion expressed in a different nature. He smiled tenderly as he turned back to the river.

"Don't worry, little brother. I'll look out for her for you." His whispered words were drowned in the muted sounds of the night as he chuckled to himself. It had been quite a day. His simple life was becoming too complicated. He was glad they were setting out in the morning. He stretched his arms out over his head. The confinement of cities and towns got to be too much for a man of his nature after a while. No doubt half the party would hightail it back to the safety of civilization by the time they reached the Platte River. They always did. But not him. The farther from the hustle and bustle, the better he liked it. Heading back to his quarters, he wondered what Miss Smith's reaction would be. As he snuggled down under his blankets, he felt a stab of disappointment, as he figured with her citified ways, she'd be one of the first to call it quits. Hell, the woman obviously wore not only a corset, but enough petticoats to make covering for a dozen wagons. No, she probably would be swooning before the river. Pleading for someone to take her back.

* * *

"You what?" Jacob demanded in a low growl. Seamus's countenance didn't change an iota.

"I said you and your wife and daughter will be joining our party, with you as the party's blacksmith."

"I don't remember asking you for your damn help," Jacob growled louder. Penny trembled in the dark recesses of the wagon they had purchased yesterday. The sun wasn't even up yet, and this big man with the scary blue eyes was making her daddy mad. Penny closed her eyes tightly and wished Miss Amanda were with her.

"Jacob," Seamus began, as he started to harness the oxen Jacob had purchased, "this is the last wagon train leaving this spring. Any that leave after this most likely won't make it. I owe you. It's that simple." Seamus moved on to another two oxen hobbled on the side. He studied Jacob's handiwork. "Miss Smith's right, you do some good iron work."

"What's Miss Smith got to do with this?" Jacob demanded angrily, as he, too, helped hitch the oxen. Seamus paused, his bright blue eyes mischievous.

"I told you, she's going as your wife."

Jacob could barely contain the strangled cry that rose through his throat, and would surely have awakened the whole camp. Clamping his teeth shut tightly, he only glared at the man he'd saved, wishing to hell that he'd left him where he'd been lying in that fire.

"And what does Miss Smith think of all this?" Jacob finally managed to choke out.

Now Seamus broke into a merry grin. "She don't know yet. I'm leaving that to you to do." Turning, Seamus ran a hand along the flank of a sorrel horse. "Hm, seems you have an eye for *horse*flesh, too."

"Who says I'm going with you?" Jacob nearly screamed, still struggling to keep his voice down. He didn't like being told what to do, and he didn't like the way this arrogant bastard equated Amanda with some bit of horseflesh.

Looking straight at Jacob, all traces of humor erased from his face, Seamus responded quietly and evenly. "I do." With that, he turned on his heel and walked off. Jacob felt the fragile leash on his anger and resentment breaking, as he snapped the leather reins between his hands.

If he looked at it rationally, it made sense. He needed to be with a party, and it needed to be this one if he was to go this year. It also made sense that he needed someone to watch over Penny. He wasn't deaf or blind. He had seen the hostile looks and comments some of the party had flashed his way. There wouldn't be much help from them. If he stayed, the storekeeper would cause trouble the minute Bos McCarthy left. And as much as he hated to admit it, he didn't like the idea of leaving Amanda here on her own, either. But, damn, how he hated having someone else dictate the rules.

Grumbling, he walked toward the wagon, telling himself that McCarthy wasn't bossing him around, he was just trying to even out a debt he owed him, and this was the way it had to be. "Penny, get out of—oh, you're awake," Jacob whispered softly, as he peered into the dark wagon. The sun was beginning to crest over the trees in the east, and a bugle call could be heard distinctly through the dewy morning. The wagon train was getting ready to head out. "Honey, go get Miss Smith. Tell her to get down here in five minutes, or we are leaving without her." Penny scrambled down from the buckboard without question. This was too good to be true, and she wasn't going to ruin it by wasting time and giving her daddy a chance to change his mind.

"Miss Amanda, yous gotta get up. We is leavin' now. Daddy says five minutes is all you got. Please, Miss Amanda, git up," Penny pleaded, as she knocked on the window on the ground floor of the shack of a boardinghouse off the main street. She was frantic. The proprietor, a yellow-toothed, dirty old woman, had refused to let her enter, saying it was an ungodly hour of the morning, and she wouldn't have a little brat ordering her around. Penny's heart beat desperately as she pounded harder on the glass. Finally, the window slid open.

"What's wrong?" Amanda asked with concern, as she rubbed the sleep from her eyes. When Penny repeated word for word what had happened, and what her father had said, Amanda's face turned ashen. "Five minutes? I couldn't possibly."

"Oh, but you must!" cried Penny, as she hoisted herself up on the sill. "I'll help you. Jes' tell me what to do."

In a little over seven minutes, Amanda was packed and struggling to fasten her corset down the front.

"I wouldn't bother with that," a male voice floated through the open window. In her rush, she had forgotten to draw the curtains. Now she stood in her petticoats and chemise facing all too interested blue eyes. Quickly turning her back to Seamus McCarthy, she hissed at Penny to draw the curtains.

"What are you doing spying on me, Mr. McCarthy?" Amanda demanded angrily.

Seamus's deep chuckle carried through the thin muslin curtains as he stood watching the curvaceous silhouette profiled through the cloth. "I wasn't spying," he responded innocently. "I was just checking to see that you knew it was time to leave. After all that pretty pleading you did to come with me, I'd hate to see you get left behind." As he spoke the words, he meant them, and again he wondered how much of her feminine attributes his little brother had been privy to.

Suddenly the curtains snapped back, and a fully dressed Miss Smith leaned out the window. "And just what is that supposed to mean, Mr. McCarthy?" Amanda glowered down at him. For the first, and probably the last time, she would have the advantage of looking down on him.

Seamus simply laughed, a genuinely hearty laugh. "I see you are taking this arrangement as well as Jacob. Fire and gunpowder. Well suited, I'd say." With that he turned and walked back to the rising dust of the readying wagon train.

"I won't have this insolent behavior, sir!" Amanda shouted after him.

He cut her off, as he glanced back over his shoulder. "Enough Miss, uh, Mrs. Smith. Get used to it. Privacy is extremely hard to come by on the prairies. Three more minutes and counting, Mrs. Smith. You haven't much time." He laughed again good naturedly and continued toward the compound.

Jacob stared in utter amazement at Miss Smith and his daughter straggling down the hill, dragging that battered, charred trunk behind them. His heart started beating in an irregular pattern as he saw her flash a smile and wave at him. Damn it, if he didn't want to wave back. This irrepressible surge of happiness angered him. Hadn't he worked this out already, that he and Amanda were better off without each other? Frustration overwhelmed him as he felt his control slipping.

"There ain't room for that!" Jacob yelled up to them, his finger pointing at the offending piece of luggage.

Amanda was breathless when she arrived. Dropping the trunk, she placed a hand tightly to her side, taking great gulps of air. "Yes," she said, gasping for breath, "there is." With these words finally out, she collapsed on the black chest, panting loudly.

While Jacob would have argued more, he was interrupted by the jangle of spurs. Turning around, he saw McCarthy on his big bay behind him. The man's eyes were laughingly on Amanda.

"Didn't take my advice about the corset. You should strip yourself of that and your petticoats, too."

Jacob turned back to see Amanda flushing darkly. No, it wasn't possible. What did this man know of Miss Smith's underclothing? Jacob gritted his teeth in anger. What had Miss Smith offered this man in exchange for her passage? No doubt it was more than what she had offered him: her ability to read and write. Oh no, most likely her hands had done more for Bos McCarthy than that. When Amanda said nothing, only lowering her eyes in embarrassment, Jacob knew he was right. He wanted to lash out and pull the man down from the horse, too. Training his dark eyes on Amanda, he controlled these urges, and in a soft deadly voice, he spoke. "I'll ask you not to speak to *my wife* like that ever again."

When Seamus laughed in response, it took all of Jacob's willpower not to turn around. He heard the sound of Seamus's horse as he rode off. Amanda stared open-mouthed at Jacob, shocked bewilderment in her eyes. Jacob smiled a slow, wicked smile. He'd get his share, too. He hated her for being less than he had thought. She had destroyed the little flicker of good he had seen.

Amanda saw it all in those frightening black eyes. She rose, backing away, dragging her chest with her. When he advanced toward her, she released the trunk and fled, with Penny's beseeching voice floating after her to come back.

Nineteen

The rising sun in the east cast pink and orange shadows over the western sky, stretching out like long, thin fingers before the wagon train. The Winslow-Turner party was in high spirits. Their train was small compared to the ones that had left earlier that spring. It was made up of only forty-two wagons. But they were optimistic. With a seasoned pilot, a gifted doctor, and more men than women, they felt they'd make the trip with few major problems.

Jacob received a few disapproving stares, but he ignored them for the most part. Right now, his mind was occupied with the woman he had left behind. He really hadn't meant to leave her, but she had run off, and in all the confusion, he had been unable to find her.

As the sun rose higher in the sky, Penny's wimpering subsided into sniffles as she fell into a deep slumber. Jacob glanced over his shoulder at her figure curled up in the back of the wagon. The child had been horrified that Jacob was going to leave Miss Smith. Jacob ran the back of his hand over his eyes before he turned them back to the oxen before him. Over and over he tried to convince himself it was for the best.

"Where's the little woman?" Seamus called, as he trotted up next to Jacob's wagon. He smiled companionably, as he craned his neck to peer into the dark recesses of the wagon.

"Changed her mind. She's not here!" Jacob snapped.

Seamus's eyes whipped around to bore into Jacob's profile. "What?" Seamus asked in a stern, even tone.

Jacob didn't turn, but continued to gaze at the lush green trees before him. "I told ya. The woman changed her mind." Having said all he intended to say on the matter, Jacob arched his shoulders before they returned to the bored slump of a few minutes ago. Seamus continued to study him in frosty silence.

After a few moments of this uncomfortable silence, Jacob couldn't resist the urge to see how the news had affected this man. "What's it to ya?" Jacob asked in a slow drawl. He forced his face to remain impassive, unaffected.

"You're a fool, man. That's what ye are," Seamus said in a soft, emotionless whisper that could barely be heard above the rattle of wheels and oxen hooves. With these eight words spoken, Seamus kicked his horse into a gallop as he headed for the front of the line.

Some nerve that man has, Jacob thought, as he watched Seamus disappear down the line. I don't need him, and I don't need some young lady who needs baby-sitting, or more likely who isn't a lady at all.

As he thought these last words, he felt guilty. Maybe he had read too much into Seamus's words about her underthings. Maybe he had come on too strong. But, damn it, the woman confused him. She mixed up everything. Things had been simple with Rebecca. They had always known they wanted to be together. He had wanted to protect her, give her everything he could. The bitter pain and guilt returned. He brushed them away angrily as he tightened his grip on the reins lying lax in his hands.

No, his feelings for Amanda were different, more complicated. She didn't need him. She didn't need his protection. Instead, it was she who wanted to help and protect him. But it was more than that. She did things to him that he thought had long since died. He wanted her so badly that it was a physical ache. But it was more than her body. It was her spirit, her enthusiasm for life and people. Everything she believed, she believed with a passion. She had hope. She trusted in the future. He had long ago squelched those hopes in himself. At first, when the young Master Whitingworth had managed to buy him and then just gave him his freedom, he had begun to hope. When the younger Whitingworth had continued to house and feed him for free and allowed him to keep his wages, Jacob had believed in the future. He had almost begun to have faith in a just God. Then it had fallen apart. It had all been a cruel joke, with himself as the pawn. First his mother, then his wife. He felt the surge of hatred swelling in his chest. They had tried to destroy his daughter, too, but he, Jacob, alone, had saved her. He needed no one. It was better this way. He would have only caused Amanda sorrow. He could not be responsible for another. McCarthy was wrong. He was not a fool. Amanda was better off in Independence, safe from the likes of both of them.

Only at the last moment had a young newlywed couple agreed to carry Amanda's trunk for a fee of twenty dollars. Now, as the morning sun reached the pinnacle of its ascent, Amanda saw the wisdom of Seamus McCarthy's words and wished she had abided by them. Her lungs ached so badly from the constrictions of her corset that she felt they should have surely burst by now. Her petticoats were hot and cumbersome. They had only traveled about seven miles at best, and those miles had been in the relative shade of trees. She didn't even want to think about what it would be like in the middle of August in the desert somewhere.

Looking down, she noticed that the hem of her gray muslin dress was severely grass stained. Mrs. Carrington would surely have a tizzy if she knew. She had frequently warned young Amanda that a lady's feet should rarely touch the ground, and only when standing at church or when properly placed on a thick carpet. She smiled as she gazed out at the continuous rolling hills of vibrant green. In a manner of speaking, this was truly a lush carpet.

A sharp cry of excitement reached her ears. Suddenly, the young groom, William Foster, jumped clear of his wagon. His wife Sarah was crying.

"Don't cry now, Sarah," the young man pleaded as he struggled to untie the brown mare he had tethered to the back of the wagon. "All the men are going. We're only going a little ways out to hunt some food for dinner. I'll be back before you know it. You'll do fine, and I'm sure there aren't any Indians out there yet." At these last words, he looked down sheepishly, unable to meet his new bride's eyes, because he knew them to be a lie. The young woman just continued to blubber that she couldn't do it on her own. For a few more minutes, the man continued to try to convince her until he turned his eyes on Amanda. With little hope, he said, "Miss Smith will be here. She could help."

The petite little woman wiped her green eyes and stared down at Amanda. "But she's just a woman, too. Oh, Billy." The new Mrs. Foster began to weep again.

Amanda could see Mr. Foster was anxious to be off, and the chance to ride for awhile looked extremely tempting. "Only a woman?" Amanda cried in amusement. "We will just show any Indian that tries to mess with us to beware of only women." Billy Foster looked much relieved, and even offered Amanda a step up onto the buckboard. With more bravado then she felt, she took the reins from the trembling pale fingers and patted the young woman's knee. At first Sarah jumped, pulling herself as far away from Amanda as possible, then smiled a weak apology, or at least Amanda chose to take it as such. Young Billy let out a war hoop and was off to join the other horses disappearing over the crest of the hill.

The two women rode in silence for a long time, until Sarah broke the silence with a stilted little voice. "I've never known anyone who was so dark before."

Amanda looked at her as if she had said she had never seen rain before. "Where are you from?"

"I grew up in a small village in Maine," Sarah began, as she stared intently at the bonnet strings she was fiddling with. Suddenly, she looked up, her watery green eyes becoming wide. "It isn't that I've never seen a Negro person before. There are a few there, and since I married Billy, I've seen quite a few." She paused as she lowered her pale, silvery eyelashes over those pools of innocence. "Well, it's just that I never met or talked to one before. My mother grew up in Charleston, South Carolina, and, well, she said I wasn't to speak to any. She said that you are only to be told what to do, and you don't have much brains to think for yourself." Now a deep crimson blush spread over the young girl's cheeks.

Amanda sat silently, her back stiff, anger riding the muscles in her shoulders and neck. "And what do you think?" Amanda asked in a controlled, emotionless voice.

Mrs. Foster looked up, then away at the trees up the slope from the river they were following. "Bill, Mr. Foster, says that what my mother says is pure nonsense, just southern garbage." Sarah's bottom lip began to quiver. "My mama doesn't approve of Billy." Her voice had slipped to the wounded tone of a spoiled child. "We ran away and eloped. I'm only fifteen, and Mother forbade my father to give his permission." Now her eyes skipped to Amanda's stern, patient profile. "I think you are the nicest woman to come help me when we treated you so uncharitably, practically forcing you to beg." The young woman smiled when she saw Amanda smile. Tentatively she reached out a hand to place it on Amanda's sleeve. "Could, would you be my friend?" She sucked in her breath and waited.

Amanda turned to the girl beside her, suddenly feeling very old. "Sure we can." Silently she added, *"I can use all the friends I can get right now."*

As the sun touched the tops of the western tree line, turning its leaves into a golden crown, the men came back victorious. Several deer carcasses, rabbits, and quail hung from a few packhorses. Amanda was beginning to regret taking over the reins. The hard wooden seat on which she sat had no give, and her rear end was sore and bruised. Now she was thankful for the layers of petticoats. Tomorrow, she promised herself, she would walk with no corset and only one petticoat.

Sarah Foster had lost all her inhibitions, and chattered on cheerfully about how her husband was going to start an apple orchard, and that he had been told the soil in Oregon was as rich as in the East, but more plentiful and very inexpensive.

Amanda followed the wagons in front of her as they began to circle in the ring Bos McCarthy had drawn in the dirt. An hour or two before they had arrived, Seamus McCarthy had chosen a site, drawn a circle, and was helping to direct the wagons to their proper positions for the night. It was amazing that every last wagon fit without so much as a single gaping foot. As he grasped the yoke of the lead oxen, his blue eyes met hers. Although his lips didn't move, she saw his eyes smile.

"I thought I'd choose my own traveling companions," Amanda quipped, as he moved closer, one hand dragging along the flanks of the oxen. Now he really smiled, deep white lines radiating out from the tanned, weathered skin around his eyes.

"Is that so?" he challenged, as he held out his hand for Amanda to step down.

"Yes," she laughed. "And you were right about the unnecessary clothing."

Now Seamus gave a genuine hoot of amusement as he slapped his thigh. With the laughter still lingering in his eyes, he studied the small wisp of a girl still seated on the buckboard.

"Mrs. Foster?" Seamus asked as he extended a hand to help her down. The young woman giggled and let him lift her down. When her feet touched the ground, she fluttered her eyelashes delicately at the pilot. Seamus raised one raven eyebrow, and turned to Amanda. Amanda blushed, as she recalled her own inadequate attempt at such a coy action.

"You are a newlywed, are you not?" Seamus asked, as he glanced around for her husband and saw the young man hurrying toward them.

Sarah nodded and blushed prettily.

"Then I shall ask that Miss Smith join me for dinner, and leave you two to your honeymoon," Seamus said with a gallant bow to Amanda.

Sarah looked disappointed, then blushed again. As they were walking away, Amanda smiled up at the big man beside her. "You aren't very subtle, are you? Poor girl." Suddenly she laughed again. "You know, you are a lot like your brother."

Seamus laughed in turn. "And is that good or bad?" he asked lightly, looking at her upturned face.

"Both, I suppose," Amanda responded as they neared his tent, where a spit sat above a glowing fire, a rabbit and quail brown and bubbly. "I only hope your culinary skills are better than his or mine. I'm famished."

Seamus pulled his saddle closer, indicating she should sit back against it. As she situated herself, spreading out her stained and hopelessly ruined skirt, he squatted by the fire, turning the meat slowly.

"I've been told this is one of the few things I do well," he said with a wink. Again, Amanda laughed.

"Modest, aren't we?" she said as she stretched out her hands at her side and looked at her host. "What, pray tell, are the other things?" she asked stifling a chuckle.

Seamus did not look at her but continued to turn the spit, studying the meat. In the silence, the fire crackled and the fat sizzled and popped as it hit the flames. "Everything I do well, I do with slow attention to detail. I leave no spot unattended. I'm not much of a talker, but more of a doer." As he talked, his voice became low and seductive, but still his eyes never left the spit. "I take care to prepare thoroughly, so that everything is perfect." Now he turned to her, his face golden and shadowed from the fire and the growing darkness. He smiled slowly as he broke off a crisp limb from the spit and extended it to her. "No one ever goes away from my door with their hunger unsatisfied."

Although Amanda knew that they were talking about food, something in his tone made her feel uncomfortable. Did all men speak with such *other meanings implied* in their words, or was it since she had been tempted by Jacob that she was seeing and hearing things with another set of senses? Hesitantly, she took the offered roasted leg from Seamus and was startled when his warm fingers brushed hers. He pulled off another limb for himself, then settled down next to her. Biting into the succulent meat, the savory juices rolled down her chin. Embarrassed, she looked at Seamus. His eyes were dark, unreadable, as he sat watching her. Nervously, she swiped at the moisture on her chin. Gently, he reached out, wiped the dribble, and brought it to his mouth.

Putting down the half-eaten leg, Amanda struggled to rise.

"I'd better be going off to sleep now," she said in a strained, nervous voice.

"Oh?" Seamus asked, as he made no move to stop her. "And where will you sleep tonight?" His question caught her off guard, as she realized she couldn't very likely go back and bunk with a newly married couple. She had been so hurried that she hadn't thought about her gear. Everything she'd need was in Jacob's wagon. She looked at the man in the semi-darkness, and thought about Jacob. Neither choice seemed safe at the moment. "Stay for a while." He held up her half-eaten meal. "Didn't I say I don't allow anyone to go away hungry? Especially such delightful company."

Seamus must have seen the unease in her face, because he relented in his suggestive teasing. The mischievous glint in his eyes softened, and his face became solemn.

"Miss Smith, I am your friend. I will not hurt ye, or allow anyone else to, for that matter. Ye meant something to me brother Kevin, and on his memory, I promise to look out for ye." Seamus hadn't moved, but still held the roasted rabbit leg out to her. Amanda was touched by the deep sincerity she heard in his voice, noting with affection how his Irish brogue had grown stronger, reminding her of Kevin. With a forlorn little smile, she recalled that Jacob had made no such promise.

It was probably just as well that she stay clear of Jacob. The man had made it clear that he wanted no part of her. The knowledge stung, twisting painfully in her chest. Jacob was a complex man who had been deeply hurt and trusted very few. Yet, in the short time she had known him, she had been able to see past the gruff exterior he presented to the world. He had shown her glimpses of the gentle, caring man he could be. How she wished at that moment it was Jacob offering to look out for her. Spreading her fingers wide, she pressed them against her torn and stained skirt. Her decision made, she re-seated herself, gracing Seamus with a quiet, thankful smile.

For a long while they sat in companionable silence, eating the remaining meal. Amanda turned to look off in the distance at the vivid fires of the wagon party, their sparks shooting high into the dark night. The wagons' canvas coverings glowed iridescent orange and yellow, as mothers and fathers entered with their lanterns to put their children to bed. Outside, around the fires, could be heard laughter, singing, and a feeling of cheerful camaraderie. Someone pulled out a fiddle, and the sweet, cheerful strains of music drifted happily over the calm night.

Briefly, Amanda wondered if Jacob was around one of those fires, singing, laughing. A feeling of loneliness, of not belonging, descended on her weary shoulders. They sagged, as if heavy with the load. Fighting off the feeling, she leaned her head back to drink in the beauty of the clear night sky.

The sky was a rich, deep, velvety blue, with more stars than Amanda had ever seen at one time. Drawing in a deep breath, she searched the night sky for the North Star, the Big and Little Dipper. Since her first introduction to Greek mythology as a young girl, she had loved the stories of the ancient legends that traipsed across the glittering heavens.

Suddenly she cried out with delight, "There's Gemini, the twins!" When Seamus didn't respond, she reached out her hand, pointing to the stars. "See, there is Pollux. She's the brightest. The somewhat fainter star over there is Castor." Briefly, she turned to look at Seamus, then lifted her face to the sky again. Closing her eyes, a small wistful smile played at the corners of her mouth. "I've always felt they were my guardian angels. I know it sounds silly, but I feel it is a good omen when I can see them." She opened her eyes now, and looked sheepishly at the man beside her. "Ever since I first read about the myths behind the stars, I've grown . . . I don't know . . . hopeful, that somehow . . . well, it's just that somewhere out there I have a twin brother, and he lives a life that is so strange and foreign to me now that it is almost as if he lives in another world." A sudden weak chuckle that quickly turned into a deep sigh escaped her lips. "I don't even know if he is alive anymore. I never even knew him."

She could feel Seamus's eyes studying her. She felt her cheeks grow warm. He must think her some blithering idiot. She turned to him, her face apologetic. Lifting her shoulders in an abashed shrug, she laughed lightly. "I don't know, I just feel better when I can see the twins." For a moment, she turned back to the sky, her eyes a honeyed gold and her skin awash in the milky blue glow of the moon.

Amanda was afraid to look back at Seamus again. What had possessed her to tell him of the foolish dream that she had kept to herself all these years? She hadn't even confided this superstitious hope to her Aunt Sondaba, and now here she was telling it to an almost complete stranger.

It was just that tonight, watching the other families and couples celebrating, dreaming, and hoping for a bright future together, she had been made painfully aware of how alone she really was. There was no one with which to share her dreams, hopes, future. She didn't even have a place to sleep tonight. As these thoughts flowed through her mind, she felt the tears of self-pity burning the backs of her eyelids. She struggled to contain them, unwilling to allow Seamus to believe she was any more of a whimpering foolish female than he most likely already did. Pressing her clasped hands tightly against her lips, she heard Seamus's soft, low voice.

"It ain't so strange to believe there's things not of this world. I believe in ghosts, or spirits," Seamus laughed, as he took off his dusty, wide-brimmed hat, laying it on his thigh, and looked up to the heavens. "Guess you know we Irish folk are a superstitious lot, believing in wee people who play among the forests. I personally don't put much stock in these mischief-making fairies, but I sometimes feel I can hear the banshees wail when the cold winds blow through the mountain passes. They're female spirits that come to mourn the imminent death of someone close." He paused, all laughter gone from his face. "I heard them wailing nigh on a month ago."

For a moment, their eyes locked, each thinking of Kevin and aware of the dangerous vulnerability they had allowed the other to see. Carefully, Amanda considered Seamus's words. Growing up in the Carringtons' house, she had heard often enough about the weak-minded Irish believing in leprechauns and other foolery. Minister Carrington had said it was due in part to all the whiskey and ale they consumed. Until now, she had never considered her tenet in the stars as anything like the Irish beliefs.

She and her Aunt Sondaba had laughed along with the Carringtons and their friends about the Irish stories of a pot of gold at the end of a rainbow. Yet her aunt had believed that snakes were ancestors who could tell of the future. Was it all the same? Stars, banshees, snakes? She steepled her forefingers against her lips, moving them slowly back and forth.

Once life had seemed so simple. The first twenty-two years of her life had seemed so black and white. There was truth and nontruth, right and wrong. Now she sat here beneath the same sky seeing a whole new set of stars, and it was all becoming jumbled.

Slowly, Seamus reached out a large, callused hand and placed his thumb in the crease between her brows. Gently, he smoothed the skin in a small circular motion.

"Why the frown?" he asked, his voice genuinely concerned. Amanda smiled and shrugged. How could she explain how her life, which had once seemed so certain and directed, was unraveling slowly into confusion and presenting somewhat frightening new discoveries?

"I don't know. I guess I was pondering your question. Where I plan to spend the night. I guess I will have to smooth my battered pride and ask Mr., er, Jacob for my bedding," Amanda partially lied.

Seamus opened his mouth to say something, then let it close without uttering a word. Instead, he lowered his hand and rose to kick up some dirt over the fire. The keen smell of smoldering wood filled her nostrils, and she blinked her eyes and coughed. Seamus didn't look at her when he spoke in a low, gravely voice.

"Well, good night then, Miss Smith. It will be an early morning, so I best be turnin' in, too." He scuffed up another layer of dirt with the worn toe of his boot, then suddenly turned to her. "Remember what I said to ye. I promised me brother, too." The large man shrugged, the fringe on his jacket swaying with the motion. Amanda smiled up at him as she held her hand out for him to help her rise. Just like his brother, his brogue grew thicker when he allowed emotion to dictate his words.

You're a loner, Seamus McCarthy, but I can tell you're true to your word like your brother before you, of that I am sure. You will be a good friend to have, and I have no doubt I'll need your friendship. As Amanda thought these words, she felt the slight tremor in Seamus's hand as he helped her to her feet. Suddenly, she felt a jolt of panic race through her hand. She searched his eyes. *Please, dear God, don't let Seamus McCarthy allow another type of feeling to come between us.* She thought of Kevin's shy kiss on the steamboat. No, there would be nothing shy about this man. As their hands stayed clasped together, both thinking their own thoughts, a harsh voice from behind her hissed through the stillness.

"See you changed your mind about comin', Miss Smith," Jacob spat, as he threw a roll of blankets at her feet. Amanda whirled toward him, snatching her hand guiltily from Seamus's. His voice had set her skittish heart beating at a frantic pace. She searched the dark shadows of his black eyes and was shocked, pained, and elated to see the hurt and angry jealousy there. For all his denials, was it possible he really did care? Why she cared, after the way he had treated her, she couldn't fathom. But the cold, hard truth was that she did, and the tightness in her chest attested to it.

Jacob moved a step closer, squinting his eyes to study her face more intently. "Here's your gear. You planning to spend the night here?" he asked, his once sensuous, full lips a tight grim line, masking his emotions. Amanda swallowed hard, fighting back the urge to touch his arm, to reassure him. The threat of tears from a few moments earlier sprang back, unbidden, to burn her eyes. She swallowed again, wanting to ask him if what she hoped was true, that he cared. But she was afraid of his answer, afraid to be rejected, afraid she had been mistaken. Instead, she spoke softly, her voice a mere whisper.

"I was just now considering my options. Have you any suggestions?"

Jacob stared at her for a few moments, his eyes relaxing from their slitted squint, but still wary. He hadn't expected this. Hell, he hadn't expected anything. He hadn't expected to ever see her again, and the relief and joy that had flooded over him when he had seen her familiar willowy figure walking behind Mr. McCarthy earlier had nearly caused him to run over and hug her, kiss her soundly, and beg for her forgiveness for his callous behavior.

He had fretted over her safety and well-being for the last twelve hours. Twice he had considered turning around. He had visions of that lowly shopkeeper turning her over to some slave traders, saying she was a runaway. Over and over in his mind, he heard her soft laughter, her excitement at reaching Independence, even her hurt at being told he would take her no farther. Yes, especially her hurt.

Penny had made matters worse. When she wasn't crying over the loss of her new friends, Mr. Kevin and Miss Amanda, she was retelling the stories of how kind Miss Amanda had been on the trip to Saint Louis, how generous and brave she had been. Silently, he had allowed her to remind him of his selfish, foolish conduct.

His joy at seeing Miss Smith there with the wagon train was short-lived. He had not gone over to her at first because he was afraid of her reaction. The last time their eyes had met, she had been frightened of him. But, as in the past, he knew how quickly that fear could turn to rage and indignation. This time, he knew she had the right to be angry with him. Although a little pushy, she had only meant well with her plans, and she hadn't asked too much, really.

For nearly two hours he sat in the silent darkness of his wagon, watching Amanda and that damn McCarthy eat, talk, laugh, and touch. Her back had been to him, but he had been able to see McCarthy's body language. The man wanted her. The thought gnawed at his gut, making him sick to realize that he wasn't the only one.

He cursed McCarthy, knowing the man probably wouldn't give her a second look in the morning. Men like McCarthy didn't settle down. Even if he did, it would be one of his own kind, a white woman—he hoped. The thought that he could be wrong made him desperate. When he saw McCarthy put out the fire and Amanda extend her hand to him, he panicked. He couldn't let her do it. She couldn't really mean to stay the night with the man. Before he had given any thought to what he would do or say when he got over to them, he went.

Now he stood there like a fool, not knowing what to answer to her simple question. He looked up at the tall, solid man behind her and saw Seamus pull the brim of his hat down low over eyes twinkling with laughter. He would not, could not, let another man, especially this man, hear the things he really wanted to say to Amanda. Instead, Jacob squared his shoulders.

"Yeah, you started this cockamamie story about being with me and Penny, and you can finish it. You can sleep in the wagon with her. I'll sleep under it." The words had barely left Jacob's lips when he realized he'd just opened himself to rejection. Well, fine. Let her tell him to get lost. At least it would be out in the open, and he could stop this guessing and wondering. But deep inside, he knew it wasn't fine, and he couldn't stand the humiliation on top of the hurt if she were to do it right under McCarthy's nose. He whirled on his boot heel and marched back to his wagon, leaving Amanda to decide for herself. But just in case she decided to come, he arranged his blankets under the wagon bed.

A few minutes later, he smiled as the wagon above him creaked with the weight of a body climbing up the back. In the morning they'd talk about it. Hell, he'd have all day to straighten out the mess he'd made. Twelve hours side by side. For the first time, he thought, that didn't sound half bad. Now he'd just have to figure out exactly what it was he was going to say.

Jacob hadn't slept well. His mind twisted and turned with phrases and ways of explaining, of letting Amanda Smith know how things stood, or how he wanted them to stand. For once, he wished he were an eloquent man, but around most women he had always been tongue-tied and uneasy. Now, this knowledge taunted him mercilessly, even in his sleep.

In the early gray hours before dawn, he finally drifted off into a restive sleep. He was startled and confused when the morning bugle sounded the start of a new day. Rising, he bumped his head on the underside of the wagon, making his already throbbing head worse.

"Get up, you two," Jacob growled through the canvas wagon cover as he dipped a ladle full of water out of the barrel at the back of the wagon. The heap of blankets inside moved, and he saw Penny's little outstretched fist reach high into the dark interior. Grunting, he moved on to unhobble the oxen and his horse. "Put coffee on, and some breakfast," he called over his shoulder. He smiled. It was going to be all right having a woman around to take care of such matters. Even if Amanda Smith couldn't cook much, she'd learn. But for now, coffee and a little pan bread would be fine. Surely she could manage that.

Twenty minutes later, Jacob returned to find a tearful Penny sitting next to a box of broken flints and a cold fire.

"What in God's tarnation?" Jacob roared, as he stared in disbelief at the scene before him. His daughter began to cry harder.

"I tried . . . you said to . . . I couldn't." The last few words dissolved into a fresh onslaught of tears.

"Shush now, darling," Jacob crooned, gathering the distraught child in his arms. "Shush. I didn't mean for you. Where is Miss Smith?" At the beloved name, the little girl stopped weeping, her eyes growing wide in disbelief.

"You left her, Daddy, back at the town."

Jacob looked down at his daughter, then up at the wagon. Releasing his child, he strode to the wagon. Pulling himself up on the open back, he climbed over the barrels and boxes to the mound of striped wool blankets. She was not there. Still unable to believe it, Jacob pulled the blankets aside, strewing them carelessly everywhere.

Walking to the front of the wagon and standing on the buckboard seat, he scanned the circle of wagons. In less than three minutes, he located her. Amanda Smith sat side by side with a pale wisp of a blond girl, sipping coffee and eating the fresh hot pan bread he had anticipated. He clenched his teeth, the jaw muscles working rapidly under the black stubble of a day's growth of beard. Fine. Let her sleep here, eat there. No, it was not fine. He jumped down from the wagon and headed toward the fire where Miss Smith sat, when a small voice called out to him.

"Daddy? I'm awfully hungry. What can I eat?"

Jacob paused, his anger giving way to parental responsibility. He squinted at the faint pink streak along the eastern horizon and knew that there wasn't much time before the bugle would blow again, signaling it was time to move. He and Penny had to eat. They'd never last until dinner.

Dinner. That was it! He'd talked to her then. His mind raced over all the things he had thought to say last night, and he realized he had never come up with a successful way to tell her what he wanted to say. Turning, he kicked hard at a clump of grass beneath his boot. No matter. There was plenty of time to think of something before then.

Amanda's heart nearly collided with her ribcage when she saw Jacob jump down from his wagon and come toward her. She was fervently hoping that he was coming to ask her to ride with him and Penny, and desperately afraid that he would ask that very question. When he stopped and returned to his wagon, she felt her hopes fall leadenly to the pit of her stomach. She watched him go to Penny, wrap his strong arms around her, and after seating her on the back of the wagon, start a morning fire. She barely heard the words that Sarah Foster spoke, as she longed to be a part of that little family.

"Did you hear me, Amanda?" Sarah asked crossly. "I said I'm gonna have a baby." When Amanda finally turned a wide-eyed stare at her young companion, Sarah's eyes fell to her tiny hands that pleated and smoothed her skirt. "This is the third time I've missed my woman time, and I'm starting to feel a pinch when I fasten the buttons at my breast and waist. I didn't say nothing before, because I wasn't real sure, but now I am." Sarah didn't see the fast calculations in Amanda's head, as she figured the child's conception and birth date. She didn't say anything about the child's obviously having been conceived well before the Fosters' elopement. Sarah had related to her yesterday that it had only been six weeks earlier. But she did ask about the due date.

"Sarah, are you saying the child growing in your womb is already three months old?" Amanda asked cautiously. Sarah nodded, her face dejected. Amanda continued, trying to keep her voice matter-of-fact. "Then there is a good possibility you'll give birth somewhere between here and Willamette." Sarah's face became ashen, her features fell slack, and her pale bottom lip began to tremble. Like Amanda, she had been raised in a family and society where women were pampered and treated like eggshells when they were with child. Now this young girl, almost a child herself, glanced about her at the open wilderness before them. As the golden sun rose over the trees from where they had just come, spreading honeyed shafts of morning over the dew-glittered hills before them, Sarah saw none of its beauty and promise, only the fear of the unknown, and the fear of being so far from home and civilization, and being with child.

"I can't do it, Amanda!" Sarah suddenly shrieked. "You must help me convince Billy to turn around." Her cold, small fingers gripped Amanda's sleeve as her large hazel eyes pooled with tears. Any suggestion of joy and anticipation had been wiped clean from her face, leaving it blanched and terrified.

Amanda patted the clawlike fingers gripping her arm, torn between helping her new friend and possibly losing her traveling companions.

"I . . ." Amanda started, but was interrupted by Sarah's husband, who had come up behind them.

"Convince me to do what?" the young man asked, thunderstruck. His young face was red with exertion and rage. "Why in God's name would I want to turn around?" William

Foster asked, his voice demanding. Sarah began to weep and moved closer to Amanda, burying her face in her shoulder. William's angry glare turned to Amanda.

"What's this all about? What nonsense you been putting in my woman's head?" he charged. "I knew you'd be trouble when I found out that your husband's on this trip, and you ain't even riding with him."

Amanda felt her ire rise with his unjust accusation, and his callous response to his wife's obvious distress. "This has nothing to do with me, Mr. Foster," Amanda snapped, her glare meeting his. "Your wife is with child, and understandably so, is frightened." With this said, she turned to console the sniffling woman, expecting William's anger to soften and be replaced with joy and concern. His next words broke over her like a unexpected douse of icy water.

"Great, just great. You've really gotten us in trouble this time, Sarah!" William exclaimed with acrid sarcasm. He pushed Amanda to the side and grabbed his wife by her arm, pulling her to her feet. His face was inflamed with fury. "It won't work, damn it. We're going, you got it? I'm sick of your whining and tears. You're my wife. I'm stuck with you, and you'll damn well do as I say." He shoved her back to the crate she had been sitting on, and ran a hand through his sandy brown hair. Sarah stumbled, her right thigh grazing the crate's corner as she fell in a heap onto the ground. Amanda rose immediately to the fallen woman, squatting down beside her.

"Leave her," Sarah's husband demanded. "She's gonna have to learn to fend for herself from now on." When Sarah let out a devastated sob, William Foster got angrier. "Stop your sniffling, woman, and pack up." With that, he tossed the rest of his coffee into the fire, grabbed the saddle off the back of the wagon, and stalked off.

Amanda was shocked at the transformation in the young man. She had assumed the couple to be young newlyweds blissfully in love. So much so, that they had eloped to avoid their parents' objections to the marriage. In a soft, low voice, Amanda urged Sarah to her feet. With one arm wrapped around the shaken girl's waist, she brushed the dirt-stained tear tracks from her cheek.

"He . . . he . . . does . . . doesn't love me," Sarah sputtered out, as fresh tears rolled down her wan cheeks.

"Shush now," Amanda began, trying to quiet the girl. Others in the camp had turned to watch Mr. Foster's outburst, but now they all turned back to their chores as if nothing had happened. The sun was rising rapidly. Soon it would be seven, and time to move out. Helping Sarah into the back of the wagon, Amanda told her to lie down awhile, while she drove.

"I'm sure your husband was just taken by surprise and will come—" Amanda stopped herself before she said more. She didn't know William Foster, and had no idea what the man's next move would be. She wouldn't offer false hope. Sarah shook her head sadly, looking very young and vulnerable.

"No, he won't come around. Billy worked for my father. His own father's orchard was really leased from ours. He tried to court me, but my mother wouldn't hear of it. Said he was beneath us. My father didn't mind, saying it was a passing thing, and he would turn a blind eye when he'd see us stroll through the apple trees." As the young woman spoke, her face grew soft and reminiscent, the mention of her father wistful, full of love. "But when he spoke of marriage, my father forbade him to see me again. Said he'd probably let things go too far. That night we slipped out, and Billy made love to me under the apple blossoms. Afterwards, he told me that now my parents would have to let me marry him. But my parents only threatened to send me away, and my father told him if he ever set foot on the property again, that he would deny his father's renewal on his lease. After Billy left, my father cried, and my mother locked me in my room. I thought it so unfair, and when Billy came to my window, I went with him. His older brother was a priest, and offered to marry us the next day. I slept with Billy again that night, and thought I was the luckiest girl alive.'' When she said this, her eyes filled with tears again.

In the distance a bugle blew, then wagons creaked, harnesses jingled, and muffled voices of anticipation filled the crisp morning air. Amanda saw the fear in the young woman's eyes, as she reached out her trembling fingers and laid them on Amanda's sleeve.

"I don't want to stay back here alone." Sarah peered out from behind the coarse canvas covering the wagon, glancing around, then over her shoulder to the driving box that could be seen through the opening at the other end. Leaning her head closer to Amanda, she whispered pleadingly, "Please, let me ride up front with you, or walk with you. Just don't leave me."

Amanda felt true sympathy for the young woman as she saw the sheer terror in her eyes. She paused, aware that perhaps she shouldn't allow her to become too attached. Sarah might become too dependent on her. After all, she was married to William Foster, for better or for worse, and she was his wife until death parted them. As she gazed down at Sarah's pale, thin fingers now gripping her arm, she felt the woman's desperation. Amanda nodded and turned her face away. Marriage could be as much of a bondage as slavery. The laws gave women few rights. A husband was even able to abuse his wife, and she had little or no recourse. To leave her spouse and return home to her parents caused her to be an outcast, a leper among society. And if there were children—the pain of knowing that after this trip she might never see Penny again she knew was nothing compared to that of a mother's choosing to leave her children behind, especially if the father were a beast. If it was the woman who left, the law would undoubtedly sever her ties with her children. Besides, where would she ever find the money or the means to return home?

Amanda scanned the wagons rumbling by her, forming a single line. She searched for Jacob and Penny, recalling his offer last night to continue their farce as man and wife. Again, she couldn't help the flare of hope and excitement that blazed in her chest, but almost immediately, it was tempered by the cold dash of reality of a husband's absolute control over his wife. She could not deny the surliness and torrid temper she had witnessed in Jacob.

Amanda was surprised by the direction her thoughts had taken. When had her desire to help Jacob as a good Christian changed to her thinking of him as a potential husband? Lifting her hands up to help Sarah descend from the high wagon, she studied the helpless woman. Amanda wondered if the girl had ever been strong. Had Sarah been blinded by her physical attraction to her husband, and not seen the warning signs of a possibly brutal man?

With a sudden, sickening realization, Amanda knew that she wasn't willing to take that chance. She knew it wasn't fair to classify all men together. Her guardian, John Carrington, had been a fine example of a man and husband. Rollin, Jacob's brother, obviously adored his wife. She had even witnessed how Jacob could be caring and tender to his daughter, and even toward her, but she couldn't overlook the fact that she had also been a victim of his wrath and his stubborn will.

Tightening her lips into a firm line, she tried not to cry. It was best not to let anything more develop between herself and Jacob. She had already grown too fond of Penny. If she could not give them her Christian charity without losing her heart, it was best to stay clear of them.

"It looks as if Mr. Foster has decided to ride today," Amanda remarked, as Sarah's small feet touched the ground. "So I guess that if we don't want to be the tail end of the train today and eat everyone else's dust, we'd better get a move on it," Amanda continued, trying to keep her eyes on the petite woman before her. But her eyes kept roving to the passing wagons, searching.

Stop it! Do you hear me, stop it! she screamed to herself. *Look at this woman before you. Do you want to be a helpless victim like her? Or like your Aunt Sondaba? Stay true to your original plan. Remember your words to Elizabeth Carrington. You don't want to be some man's slave, cooking and cleaning up after him.*

Amanda tried to bring back the earlier dream of a little house in a town, lined with books, paintings, and beautiful things. Maybe a schoolhouse or an office, where she would do her accounting work. But always the vision was her, by herself, in quiet solitude. Time to paint, read, work in a garden. She closed her eyes briefly, trying to remember it, to block out the vision of bleak holidays, lonely nights; a lifetime of solitude.

"Why, Aunty Daba? Why did you have to die?" Amanda cried in a choked whisper.

"Did you say something to me?" Sarah asked, as she hurried to catch up with Amanda's determined stride. "What's wrong?" the young woman cried, as she caught Amanda by the arm and pulled her around to face her. Embarrassed, Amanda swiped at a solitary plump tear that rolled down her face, showing a glistening streak of bronzed skin through a thin film of dust.

"Nothing, Sarah. Nothing at all," Amanda responded, as she turned to continue toward the front of the wagon, where the oxen waited patiently.

"You're crying for me?" Sarah cried with a mixture of joy and disbelief, then wrapped her arms around Amanda, resting her cheek upon her breast. "You are truly the most caring and considerate woman I've ever met. You were crying for me."

Amanda patted the young woman's shoulder gently, struggling to prevent any more of her tears from falling.

"You're right," Amanda said softly, as she tenderly unwrapped Sarah's arms from around her waist. "I was moved to tears by your plight, and that of many other women."

Sarah looked up and their eyes met. Together, hand in hand, they found their way to the driver's seat. One fair, and one dark, but women with the same fears and hopes for a brighter tomorrow in their hearts.

Twenty

By eleven o'clock in the morning, the lush vegetation had tapered off to small shrubs and flatter land. There was no relief now from the blazing sun, and the cool morning air had dissipated hours ago. Children crawled into the backs of the wagons seeking relief from the heat, and women pulled their sunbonnets farther forward over their faces.

As Seamus McCarthy twisted in his saddle to look back at the steady flow of wagons, he chuckled at the sight. Wagon after wagon looked the same. Although the people in the party were as different as flowers in a field, from this distance they all looked the same. Wouldn't Opal and Jed Turner love to hear that. Seamus had walked up behind Opal earlier that morning to talk to her husband about resting and grazing points when he heard her degrading remarks.

"I won't be doing this work every day, Jed Turner. This is nigger's work. Speaking of niggers, have you seen the way that Smith woman has been carrying on with that Mrs. Foster? It just ain't right. And it is that pilot McCarthy's fault. In sight of everyone, he takes that tramp to his fire for dinner, treating her if she were a real lady. And her husband just stands by."

Jed Turner, who saw Seamus approach, tried to warn off his wife with a slashing motion of his hand, but she either didn't understand or more likely chose to ignore it. Seamus stood there as long as it had taken him to swallow his rage at her words and present the distant, emotionless demeanor for which he was known.

He had worked for years to curb his innate Irish temper, so much like his father's. He found that displays of temper gained him nothing, and appearing removed and indifferent gained him much more respect and authority. It had almost become a natural instinct for him now. He hadn't cared about what others said or thought about him for a long time, as long as it didn't get in the way of his getting what he wanted done. Now he felt that rusty old outrage of his youth rising, tightening his chest, making it ache, making him want to beat something or someone with his iron fists. Clenching his teeth, he tried to think of soothing things: the cold, snowy mountains, the hawk lazily circling the azure sky.

When he was barely twenty, an Old Nez Percé chief had taught him to lose his anger in nature. That to keep it inside would eat a man alive, and to unleash it on another was dishonorable. He thought of the wise old man now and stroked the sash of blue crystal beads sewn onto a strip of deer hide he always had looped around his shoulder.

Blue was the most prized of colors for the Nez Percé and most other tribes out West. The beads were worth many beaver pelts, and Long Feather had given them to him, to always remind him to bury his red anger in the cool blue of nature.

With relief, Seamus felt the familiar calm stealing over him, and he walked into the circle of the Turner camp.

"Lady?" Seamus said, his blue eyes intently fixed on the dilated gray ones of Opal Turner. Opal blushed an unbecoming crimson, making the spiderlike capillaries around her thin nose stand out in relief. Then, regaining her bearings, she threw back her shoulders, thrusting forward her ample bosom encased in a dusty cranberry and cream calico dress.

Seamus felt the calm of a few moments ago ebbing away

as he struggled to keep his tone civil.

"Lady, Mrs. Turner?" Seamus repeated sarcastically. "I'm not sure you'd know one to see one." He almost regretted the words the moment they were out. He saw Jed Turner stiffen, his nostrils flare, as he moved next to his wife. There would be hell to pay for those few moments of satisfaction, Seamus thought. The two men stared at each other until Jed broke the silence.

"I thought you said that Amanda girl was Jacob's woman." Jed's eyes narrowed to sneering slits as he challenged the big man before him. When Seamus didn't answer, he continued, "Then what are you doing entertaining the *lady* at your campfire late at night?" There was no mistaking the vehement asperity in the wiry man's words. Opal beamed up at her husband, her eyes shining bright with obvious relish at the possibility of taking Bos McCarthy down a notch or two.

If they were expecting Seamus to blush or show any signs of discomfort, they were sadly disappointed. Seamus only smiled a knowing smile that barely curled his lips and fell far short of warming his eyes. Pausing for a moment to show that their snide words had no impact on him, Seamus doffed his hat to Mrs. Turner.

"Ma'am, sir, I don't see as how that is any of your business." Replacing his hat, he turned and strolled casually toward Dr. Winslow's wagon. He didn't need to turn around to see the hatred and anger burning in the Turners' eyes. It was fairly boring a hole through the clothes on his back.

Now he twitched his shoulder uncomfortably, as if he could still feel the heat there. He wasn't afraid of the Turners' revenge for himself, but more for Miss Smith and Jacob's little girl. He had no right to inflame the resentment toward them that was already smoldering. Dr. Winslow had told him as much this morning when Seamus had told the doctor about the exchange.

Seamus scanned the serpentine line of white canvas tops winding their way up the rise. Maybe he'd just check up on Miss Smith and the little girl. Jacob could take care of himself. But God, if that man wasn't as dumb as a brick, and as stubborn. It was so obvious how Miss Smith felt about him, and it was no mystery that if Jacob would stop being so pigheaded, he'd see he felt the same way.

Seamus sighed as he spurred his mount down the gradual incline. It sure would make his life a whole lot easier if Jacob and Amanda were to hook up by the time they reached the Oregon Territory.

Last night, after Amanda had left, he began to think about her chances on her own once she arrived in Willamette, Oregon. They weren't very good. He liked her, not just because of his brother, but because she was bright, kind, and appreciated nature and life's mysteries like he did. She didn't seem to mind the discomforts of the road so far. She also had been able to laugh at herself and admit he was right about her undergarments, and she hadn't held any resentment at his earlier intrusion on her privacy. Yes, he liked her—maybe a little too much. He spurred his horse on faster. Maybe he'd just have to help Jacob see the light a little sooner. The sooner the better for all concerned.

"Yo, Jacob!" Seamus hollered, as he approached the swaying wagon on which Jacob was perched alone. Seamus slowed his horse to a trot as he turned and moved up alongside the buckboard. "Where's your women?" Seamus asked, as he tipped the brim of his hat back with his thumb, a smirk on his face.

"Penny's in the back," Jacob said, without looking at Seamus. They rode for a moment in silence, Seamus waiting, and Jacob ignoring him.

"And Miss Smith?" Seamus finally asked, aware that the information wouldn't be voluntarily given. Jacob only shrugged and kept his eyes on the sloped backs of the oxen ahead of him. Seamus pulled the brim of his hat lower over his eyes and studied the flat terrain around him. The grass was a golden green, but would be yellow as straw by mid-June. The trees were all but gone. It made the rippling fields seem endless.

"I was hoping you could come with us today to hunt for prairie chicken for noon dinner, but if there's no one to drive..." Seamus let his voice trail off as he watched Jacob's black eyes shift to his face, looking for the world like a small boy told he couldn't go hunting with the men.

"You know I ain't got a gun, nohow," Jacob spat angrily. Seamus had not been there when the shopkeeper had denied Jacob the firearm. The man had informed Jacob that in the state of Missouri it was against the law to sell a gun to a black man. His pride had not let him ask McCarthy to buy one for him, and there was no other white man who would have. He knew Seamus McCarthy didn't know about the exchange, but he was angry that he wouldn't be able to go, even if he had someone to drive.

"Well, that ain't a problem," Seamus shrugged, as he twisted in his saddle to unhook one of two long rifles from his pack. He weighed the heavy gun in one hand, then tossed it to Jacob. Jacob nearly dropped the reins to grasp the precious rifle. For a moment, he ran one finger along the hot, shiny surface of the barrel. Then, quickly, he set it down. Seamus tossed a bullet casing onto the seat next to Jacob.

"You'll need that to make the balls. I hope you bought gunpowder?" When Jacob didn't answer, Seamus continued. "Well, no matter. You can barter some for blacksmithing. Another day or two of this rough road and crossing the Platte, someone is bound to need your help with a thrown shoe or loose wheel rail. Then I'll teach you to make the bullets and use the gun, and we can call it even." Without waiting for a reply, Seamus kicked his heels into his horse's flanks and rode off.

As the hot air whipped through his hair, Seamus felt the brief reprieve of cooling perspiration. It felt good. He felt good. He had settled a score and at least provided some protection for the little girl. Now to see about Miss Smith.

Amanda and Sarah sat side by side on the hard, ungiving seat of the Fosters' wagon. Each rut jolted them, rattling their teeth and bones. Perspiration made their bodices cling to their bodies, which they had wisely deprived of corsets and all but one petticoat. Amanda drove while Sarah talked and fanned them with the stiff brim of an extra bonnet.

Throughout the morning, Amanda had learned how Sarah's father had arrived at the Foster farm to bring her home and had wept openly when they had led him to the bed chamber where she and Billy lay together. Amanda had felt uncomfortable at learning these intimate details about her new friend, but had remained silent, letting the girl speak.

Sarah's father had signed the papers allowing her, an underage girl, to wed. Sarah told how her father had consented to sign the papers only after he had been given a few moments of privacy with her. First he had held her, rocking her in his arms as if she were still his little baby. Then he had told her that William was a money-hungry gold digger, and that if she married him, she would inherit nothing from him, and no child of theirs would be received or acknowledged. Sarah told how she had been outraged at the time, telling her father it wouldn't matter to Billy because he loved her for who she was, not how much she was worth. Her father had cried some more, and had given her some money that she should save in case she might need it someday. He left before the ceremony, and she hadn't seen him since.

Amanda asked her what had happened to the money, and

Sarah waved at the wagon and gear around her, smiling a wry, sad smile. They traveled along in silence, each in their own thoughts, until Sarah told Amanda about last night.

"Last night," Sarah turned her face away, a slight rose blush tinting her already heat-infused cheeks, "Billy wasn't very gentle."

Amanda shifted uncomfortably on the seat, keeping her gaze in front of her.

"I cried and asked him if he really loved me. He was kind, told me everything would be better once we got to Willamette. He said that would give my father enough time to come around, and he could go down to San Francisco and wire for some money. That's when I told him that my father disinherited me." Sarah turned pleading eyes to Amanda. "I really didn't think it would matter." Casting her eyes down at the wilted bonnet twisted in her hands, Sarah continued. "But it did. Billy called me awful things. He said I had tricked him into marrying me. He said that I'd ruined everything. I told him I wanted to go home, and he laughed. Not a nice laugh, but a cruel, heartless one. He said that now that I wasn't worth anything, I have to earn my keep." Now a steady flow of tears coursed down Sarah's pink cheeks. "Oh, Amanda, I don't know how to do anything. Billy's right. I'm completely useless." The young woman let the unused bonnet flutter to the floor and buried her face in her hands. Her shoulders shook violently without a sound.

"You're tired. Go lie down in the back for a while," Amanda said softly. Without a word, Sarah rose and climbed through the opening, over the trunks and crates, to the small nest of blankets. Amanda was glad for the solitude. It gave her time to think, and to see this wild, open land that she was passing.

A warm spring breeze stirred, making golden waves in the long, coarse grasses around them. A few trees bowed gracefully over the swollen river they followed. The air was muggy, filled with the smell of a new vegetation growing along the rich, brown banks.

She watched the shadow of a large bird, possibly a hawk, circle over the rippling field. Looking up, she saw it hover for a few lingering moments, then dive in a graceful descent on some hapless prey.

Turning her gaze, she watched the rushing water sliding smoothly over stones and fallen branches. The water was pristine and unpolluted, shimmering in the morning sun. She closed her eyes momentarily, letting the reins go slack in her hands. The oxen plodded on, following the wagon ahead of them. Amanda inhaled deeply, letting the fresh smells of damp earth, warm air, and wide open space fill her nostrils.

This was what she'd come for. This was the smell of true freedom. Nowhere were there tall, dismal, gray buildings crowding the streets. No murky, gray, polluted waters filled her senses with rot and decay. The London of her childhood had been swept away with an artist's broad brush, filling the landscape with a rainbow of color. As if to complete the spectrum of color, a beautiful iridescent-headed pheasant with splashes of red flew up from the high grass a few feet to her right. Amanda let out a gasp of appreciation.

"Should have shot it." A male voice spoke from her side. She turned abruptly to see Seamus riding on his horse beside her. He smiled, nodding his head out toward the small dot of a bird. "That's a male ring-necked pheasant, good eating. But there ain't too many of them 'round here. Mostly grouse and prairie chicken."

"Good morning, Mr. McCarthy," Amanda acknowledged, looking back to the spot where the beautiful bird had now vanished. "He is much too pretty to eat. I'd rather paint him."

Seamus laughed. A warm, genuine smile softened the hard edges of his face, making him look younger, more friendly,

Amanda thought. She couldn't help smiling in return. It felt good to smile, after the grim memories of this morning. She wondered what kind of man Seamus McCarthy really was. Would he, too, turn off the charm once a woman said, "I do"?

"How do you know the bird was male?" Amanda flushed slightly, as she added, "Surely you weren't close enough to check."

Seamus cocked his sun bronzed head at her and burst out laughing. "Don't think I could rightly tell if I was to look—on a bird, that is. But it's the males that wear the fancy plumage. Strutting their stuff for the plain brown females." When Amanda opened her eyes in surprise, he laughed again and continued. "Unlike us confused humans, most animals have the male wearing the fine spots and colors."

Now it was Amanda's turn to laugh. "I just can't imagine you, Mr. McCarthy, wearing satin gowns, petticoats, and corsets." She giggled again, as she imagined him wearing such things. Seamus gave her a mock frown, then ran his gaze over her figure.

"I see you've taken my advice and given up on them, as well. You look a whole sight better, and more comfortable, too."

Amanda's earlier flush deepened, as she was all to aware of how snugly the muslin covered her body, with no stays or padding, and clinging now with perspiration. She quickly changed the subject to the weather, but Seamus's eyes kept wandering to her soft, curvy figure.

She's too good for that ol' sourpuss, Jacob, Seamus thought, as he rode happily alongside, chatting with Miss Smith. She proved to be a witty and entertaining conversationalist, and he took his leave with regret when he had to round up the hunting crew for the afternoon meal.

*   *   *

After McCarthy gave Jacob the rifle and rode away from his wagon, Jacob noticed that the trail boss slowed and stayed about seven wagons back. Leaning as far to the side as was safe and not overly noticeable, Jacob strove to see who was driving the wagon where McCarthy lingered.

Try as he might, Jacob couldn't see past the wagons behind him, and he could only make out the solitary figure of the pilot astride his horse at the wagon's side.

Gazing down occasionally at the shiny rifle at his feet, Jacob longed to hold it in his hands. He looked over his shoulder into the back of the wagon and saw that Penny had fallen asleep. For a moment or two, he watched her sleeping face. He would never grow tired of it if he lived to be a hundred. When he looked up, he caught a glimpse of Amanda. For a brief moment, as the wagons rounded a curve in the river, he could see Amanda laughing and smiling at McCarthy, who was riding by her wagon's side.

Any charitable feelings of good will that Jacob had felt toward the man who had given him his gun were gone, replaced by sheer, unadulterated jealousy. Jacob thought of all the things he was going to tell Miss Smith at the noon stop, and they all seemed inadequate. Turning again, he tried to see Amanda, but the six wagons between them blocked his view. He felt his heart sink. Maybe she had agreed to eat with McCarthy again. He couldn't talk to her in front of him.

He tried to conjure up the memory of the kiss they'd shared in the Wikets' parlor. He began to question what he had been so sure of before. She had responded, hadn't she? He recalled that he had been the one to initiate it. Had he forced her? Imagined her returning passion? He was a straightforward man. He had planned to tell Amanda that he had changed his mind and that she could ride with him and Penny. He was going to tell her he couldn't promise anything once they arrived, but that something might be arranged. He had been egotistical enough to hope she would jump at the chance. He looked back again, just in time to see McCarthy ride off, touching the brim of his hat to the hidden figure on the wagon, his Amanda. He felt the sting of disappointment jab at his gut as he watched a group of other men join McCarthy and head off to a distant cluster of trees.

Jacob yanked hard on the reins in irritation. One head ox bellowed a loud roar of protest, and continued plodding forward.

"Damn ox could drive themselves," he muttered under his breath. He pushed back his new felt hat from his forehead, and rubbed at the band of sweat that had gathered there. It didn't matter what he said to Amanda. Hell, he couldn't even offer her a decent meal. McCarthy would no doubt come back with some meat, and all he and Penny had were some dried beef and cold biscuits.

During the brief break at dinner, Jacob avoided the others, and he and Penny walked down to the stream to cool their feet. He sat back on the bank, resting his weight on his elbows and forearms, watching his daughter frolic in the refreshing water. He tried to be thankful for the sight before him and the new taste of freedom, but now he wanted more, and he knew from experience that to want more was to set yourself up for heartbreak.

He didn't see the amber eyes watching him and Penny, wishing she could join them, but afraid to for fear she might lose her freedom or be unwelcome.

The days and nights took on the same form and pattern. Even the terrain barely changed. The sun rose hot and grew hotter. The trees became fewer and the meat supply more difficult to find. Amanda continued to ride or walk with Sarah during the day, dine with Seamus in the evening, crawl late at night into Jacob's wagon alongside Penny, and be gone before dawn. Jacob never questioned her; he was just glad to know she slept in the wagon above him and not in McCarthy's tent. Several times he approached her, but each time she was with that skinny little Mrs. Foster or McCarthy. In the end, he'd only ask her how she was faring, and was it what she'd expected, and other unimportant questions. He just couldn't face the possibility of her rejecting him in front of anyone else.

True to his word, Seamus taught Jacob how to make the metal balls in the iron cast he'd given him and to properly load and fire the rifle. As much as Jacob hated to admit it, he grew to admire the tall Irishman, and he listened carefully to his instructions on tracking, hunting, and cleaning the kill. Several times Penny tagged along, until Mrs. Winslow, the doctor's wife, offered to watch her. The woman even offered to spell Jacob sporadically so he could go and hunt with the rest of the young men. Jacob's spirits began to rise. When he managed to hit and kill something, he would invite Amanda to dine with him: a real meal.

It was on one of these occasions that Jacob returned to find his daughter, Mrs. Winslow, Miss Smith, and Mrs. Foster sitting in a circle near his wagon, snipping at small pieces of material and sewing them together into quilts. They all looked up and greeted him, then went right on with their sewing, chatting happily.

Quietly, Jacob went about the business of placing his skinned rabbit and prairie chicken on a spit. He listened to the happy chatter and laughter. He liked it. He hadn't realized how much he missed the company. Looking over his broad shoulder, he saw his little girl flitting from woman to woman like a social butterfly. Guilt washed over him. She missed it, too. He had saved her from bondage, but stripped her of the only maternal and family figure she had ever known, his mother.

For the first time in months, he let the image of his mother drift before his eyes, her black Seminole eyes so like his, but softer, kinder. Her beautiful copper brown skin and smooth black hair. She looked more Indian than Negro, but her skin was darker, and her lips fuller. Her mother, his grandmother, had been a prized beauty from the Caribbean Isles, where she had been born a slave then sold to a plantation owner in Georgia. He recalled the beautiful love story his mother had told him about her father, an Indian brave from deep in the Swanee land, and her beautiful mother, the bait in a trap set by the white authorities to catch him.

As a young boy, he had loved that story, imagining himself brave and daring like his grandfather. His mother told him it was only love that mattered, and that it could overcome anything. He had believed her, and let love dictate his heart and mind. He had believed if he loved Rebecca enough that they could overcome all. When he had asked as a child who his father was, his mother had stared off into space dreamily, and said only, "a man I love very much."

Jacob vaguely recalled a large, kind slave who had lived with them for a while. He had been only five or six at the time. He remembered the man was good and gentle, but his mother only cried, saying she could not love him. Then had come Rollin, his half brother. At first his mother had been sad, then happy when Rollin arrived. Of course, he hadn't been Rollin then, he had been only Joshua Washington Coffey, such a big name for such a small boy. For two years they had been a happy family; his mother, if not happy, was content.

Then Rollin's father was gone, sold in the New Year's auction. Jacob had been about eight, and was cleaning the stables when they took him away. He never got to say good-bye to the only father he had ever known. It was when he found out that night that he swore to be the father Rollin would never know and to find a way to free them all so that they would never be separated again. Over and over, Jacob would tell this to his family until his mother began to believe him. That was when young Master Worthington started to come and see him. The man would mysteriously appear at the stables or in the field. He talked kindly to Jacob, giving him small trinkets and coins. Jacob was always wary, but he grew to like the man.

Then Master Worthington offered to take him away from slavery, to give him his freedom. Jacob felt his eyelids prickle with unshed tears. The memories, the shattered hopes, weakening his resolve.

"Oh, dear, it has grown so late. We've been so busy with our quilting that we hadn't even thought that our husbands would be returning with dinner as well," Mrs Winslow stated, as she gathered up her shears and quilting squares. "Tomorrow, ladies?" she inquired to a return of resounding yeses from the others. Penny looked about herself helplessly, as she saw the women prepare to leave.

Jacob rose slowly, wiping his dirty hands on his still dirtier pants legs. Adjusting the brim of his hat several times, he walked over to the group of women. Careful not to look at Amanda, he nodded his thanks to Mrs. Winslow. She patted his arm and complimented him on the fine looking rabbit and bird he had caught. He smiled self-consciously, pleased by the praise, especially within Amanda's hearing.

"Are you dining with Mr. McCarthy again?" Sarah Foster asked Amanda as they turned to leave.

"I . . ." Amanda began, when Jacob cleared his throat and interrupted her.

"If ya got a moment, Miss Smith, I'd like to talk to you."

Amanda paused, turning wide eyes of astonishment to Jacob. "Of course, Mr. Jacob."

The departing ladies paused as well. Jacob shuffled his feet uncomfortably, wishing the women would leave, but they didn't.

Word had spread through the camp that Amanda and Jacob

were not married, but that the situation was, to say the least, a little unusual. That was all the information that anyone had been able to ascertain, and it had caused the bored wagon party's tongues to waggle, and the queen of gossip herself, Mrs. Opal Turner, to insinuate some pretty raunchy possibilities. Now that perhaps a little light was to be shed on the mystery, even the proper Mrs. Winslow was loathe to leave.

When the silence continued, Amanda prodded Jacob gently, aware of his unease.

"About what did you wish to speak with me?"

Jacob glanced up at her face, turned quickly to the women around her, then down at his hat, which had found its way into his hands. It had been easy to tease and intimidate Miss Smith when she had been nothing more than a burden for him to bear. It had been easy to talk to her when he had been angry or she had been weak and defenseless. It had even been easy not to talk at all, but to kiss and hold her in his arms. But all that ease fled him now as he stood before her, wanting to ask her to stay for dinner, and wanting more than anything for her to agree.

At one time he had wanted nothing more than to have her, to sink into her warm, soft body. Now he just wanted her company. Not that he didn't still have lustful thoughts of her slender body sleeping every night in the wagon bed above him, but that need wasn't as strong as the need to just be with her.

Suddenly, he realized these thoughts frightened him, and he placed the hat back on his head, glancing over his shoulder at the cooking meat.

"It was nothing. I just . . ." Jacob didn't finish his sentence, but moved over to turn the spit.

Amanda felt disappointment and relief settle her heart to a slower pace. She turned to leave with the other women, as Jacob presented his back to the company. As the women moved around and separated to go to their individual wagons, Amanda lingered behind. She watched Sarah go slowly, dawdling, unwilling to return to her husband. She saw the robust Mrs. Winslow fairly skip into her husband's outstretched arms. As her new friends faded off to their evening rituals, Amanda turned back to the wagon she had just left. Threads of doubt, curiosity, and hope swirled and tangled their skeins through her mind. She stared for a moment at the faded red wood of Jacob's wagon, then let her eyes travel the sun-bleached bow of the canvas cover. She closed her eyes and imagined the small family on the other side: the happy child, the shy Jacob she had witnessed just now. She wondered if she were to take just a few steps more, to round that corner, if Jacob would tell her what he had wanted to say earlier. She imagined him asking her to stay with them.

She took a few steps closer, when she heard Seamus McCarthy's unmistakable voice call out her name. She opened her eyes and turned to see the bearded man coming her way. She glanced once over her shoulder regretfully, then turned a smile toward Seamus, leaving the wagon and dream behind.

"The pheasant is nearly done. I was afraid someone else might have gotten to ya before I could." Seamus looked up quickly at the wagon behind her, his eyes bright with mischief. Amanda laughed and let him link his arm with hers. Together they strolled to his somewhat distant camp. She nudged him with her elbow when he nodded and tipped his hat at Opal Turner, who promptly stuck her nose in the air and turned away.

Once out of hearing distance, Amanda let her laughter ring out as Seamus mimicked the terrible lady's expression.

Twenty-one

Opal Turner was beginning to feel that she had been slighted once too often. She had been the sweetheart of her town in Wakefield, Kentucky, a respected and sought-after woman. She had founded and headed the First Baptist Woman's Committee, and had been the cousin of the sheriff. In Wakefield, she had been a woman to reckon with.

When Jed had first hooked up with the beginnings of a wagon party heading out West, she had campaigned and persuaded the others to elect him as one of their leaders. She had never had a doubt that she would play as important a role in the West as she had back home, but this time, the important man would be more than a cousin, he would be her husband. Through him she would once again be indispensible.

Now, this Negro woman was causing no end of problems. The pilot, Bos McCarthy, was setting a poor example by treating the woman like she was just as good, or better than anyone else. He was giving the little tramp respect far above what she deserved. Why, she had so bewitched Mr. McCarthy that he was insulting her, Jed Turner's wife, for pointing it out to him and every other decent person exactly what she was. She really didn't expect such an uncouth man as Seamus McCarthy to turn down a woman practically throwing herself at him, but he was a good-looking man, and it irked Opal that he hadn't so much as looked twice at her but preferred that black baggage. Opal spread her long fingers before her, then curled them in disgust as she saw the fine white skin had turned red and raw, sprinkled with freckles. She hated this wagon train, the Oregon Territory. She had been a much sought-after woman when she had married Jed, and he was making her old before her time.

Pursing her lips, she squinted off into the rapidly growing darkness. For a moment, she watched the silhouette of the couple by the pilot's fire. She felt anger burning in her bosom, clenching her stomach, making her physically ill.

She could not turn back the hands of time, so she would make the best of the here and now. Amanda Smith would not ruin that for her.

At first, Opal Turner had carefully spread gossip of Amanda's strange sleeping and eating arrangement among the womenfolk of the wagon train. Already bored and craving some diversion, many of the women had joined in with the speculation and thrilled at the prospect of a real scandal.

Opal Turner had thrived on the power and attention it had given her. But then that Black witch had deceived the doctor's wife. Now Mrs. Winslow was not only taking care of the black man's brat, but sharing company with Amanda, raising the women's esteem for that Black tramp.

Slowly, one by one, many of the other women of the group had seen the group of women quilting outside Jacob's wagon every evening. They had hesitantly, then boldly asked to join in, not minding that Amanda sat among them as an equal.

But not Opal, she had remained aloof, unwilling to compromise her superiority. She had been certain that the others would change their minds, see their mistake.

She had seethed in red-hot fury when Amanda had opened her trunk, pulling out several fine dresses, the likes that Opal had once worn, but only dreamed of owning now. Then

Amanda had offered them up for quilt squares. Opal blinked her eyes rapidly, the corner of her lip twitching with rage. How could that woman not only have the audacity to own such fine things, but to offer them up with a laugh, saying that they would do her little good in the wilds of Oregon.

Opal gnashed her teeth as the other women became blinded by the little hussy's conniving ways. The women no longer listened to Opal's malicious gossip. More than one had told her Miss Smith really was a nice woman, and extremely intelligent, too. This had almost sent Opal over the edge, as she herself had never been formally educated. Her papa had assured her that it was unladylike, that it only filled women's heads with nonsense and dangerous notions. Opal was sure that those books in Miss Smith's trunk were nothing more than scandalous depravity.

The others might be fooled, but she wasn't. The woman was no better than the savage, devil-worshiping slaves she had heard moaning and chanting in their little shacks behind her father's house. Those people had no respect or knowledge for the sanctity of marriage and commitment, Opal believed, and it was obvious Amanda Smith shared that belief as well.

Opal squared her shoulders. She would not be daunted. It was her resposibility to shield the children and God-fearing folk of this wagon train from this woman's sluttish behavior.

Everyone had fallen into the easy belief that no one had seen Amanda actually enter Mr. McCarthy's tent. Therefore, they had just excused it as a simple friendship between the two.

Opal smoothed back the stray auburn hairs that escaped from the low bun at the nape of her neck, a sinister smile forming along her mouth. Let Amanda Smith dazzle these simple folk with her knowledge and worldly goods, but Mrs. Jed Turner, wife of the second captain, would not allow any jezebel to go unpunished under her husband's command. If she couldn't expose the woman for what she was, then she'd punish her through someone else.

Opal's smile grew more malicious as she turned to gaze at Jacob's wagon. There was something suspicious in her target's relationship with Jacob and the little girl. She really had no problem with the man. He kept a proper distance, didn't assume to join in with the other white folk. But she hadn't been blind to the longing and hurt looks in his eyes whenever Miss Smith went off with Mr. McCarthy. She had also witnessed a similar fondness in Amanda's eyes when she had watched Jacob. Why, if it was possible for a colored person to have feelings of love, Opal might have believed the two were in love. But that wasn't conceivable. Nonetheless, there was something there, and perhaps she could use it. She'd just bide her time.

She didn't have to wait long. Two days after Opal had pledged to find a way to punish Amanda Smith, she got just the sort of information she needed. Jed had just found out that Jacob and his daughter were wanted by the law.

"Are you sure? Tell me everything, exactly. Leave nothing out," Opal whispered in the darkness of the wagon, as she lay next to her husband.

"Aw, come on, Opal. I already told you twice. There ain't no more. I'm bone tired, and I need to get some sleep," Jed grumbled, as he shifted to his side, facing away from her. Opal moved closer, fitting her body along the contours of his back.

"But ain't it dangerous? I mean a fugitive could turn dangerous if threatened. Did he kill anyone? Sometimes they do, you know. My papa once told me about some slave uprising, and they just massacred the poor, unsuspecting white folk." Opal began stroking the soft skin behind Jed's ear. He moaned, and turned to wrap his arms around her.

"Do you know what you do to me when you do that?" Jed

asked in a husky voice. Opal tried not to shrink away at the foul smell of whiskey on his breath. She knew he and Seamus and Dr. Winslow had been drinking, and that it was thanks to the alcohol that Jed had gotten this tidbit of information. It probably was the only reason she was privy to it. She wriggled in Jed's grasp as he placed loud, wet, sucking kisses on her neck, and his dirty fingers tugged at her white flannel nightgown.

"Jed, Jed." She stayed his hand that had begun to yank at the small buttons down her chest. "Miss Smith. Is she involved? Did she help them escape? Is she wanted, too?" Jed paused in his noisy kissing, and she could hear his labored breathing in the darkness. She held her breath so as not to miss a word and so she wouldn't smell his rancid breath.

"Can't we talk about this later?" Jed whined and began fumbling with the small buttons again. Opal moved away, her body becoming stiff and unyielding. Jed knew he could take her, and she couldn't stop him, but it was a hell of a lot more fun when she participated.

In the darkness, he smiled at the memory of their wedding night some five years ago. At first he had been shocked at the skilled response in his young *virgin* wife. He had been angry, demanding an explanation, talking about annulment. Then Opal had shown him the possible pleasures that he had never dreamed of before, and that she could be a useful wife in more ways than one.

It was true. Jed had been surprised that Opal's father had allowed a young upstart like himself to marry his precious daughter. Although Opal's father was not a wealthy plantation owner, he was a very well-to-do farmer, and he wanted only the best for his daughter.

Jed was only the third son of a cotton merchant, and had only dreamed of even courting the likes of Opal. He had precious little to offer any woman, much less one in Opal's class.

He had watched the young Opal parade through the small town of Wakefield, shopping with the neighboring plantation owners' daughters, and never looking his way.

She had been all lace and innocence; then she had disappeared. Visiting an aunt in Boston. The stay had extended to a year and a half. When she returned, she was changed. How, exactly, it was hard to say, but she no longer was the frivolous girl of before. She became involved with the church, chairing its charities. Jed had told her at one church bazaar that he admired her dedication. The next thing he knew, he was asking her father for her hand, and the old man was readily agreeing. Her father had even suggested he seek his fortune out West and offered him the money to undertake the trip.

At the time, Jed hadn't realized that Opal had set the trap, and he had taken the bait. It had seemed too preposterous to even think that was possible back then. He hadn't even questioned Opal's father's sudden desire to see his precious daughter go thousands of miles away, out West to a wild, rough, unsettled land, probably never to see her or any potential grandchildren again.

No, Jed had been blind to it all until his wedding night, when he discovered his wife was not a virgin, but a robust and accomplished lover. After his intial shock had worn off, she had told him of the man she had met in Boston. He had seduced her, and she found she adored the physical act, was addicted to it. She became pregnant. She had begged the man to marry her, and he had refused, then disappeared. In the next few weeks, she refused to eat, became weak, and miscarried the baby in her second month.

Her father was furious and refused her request to come home. Finally, after a year of praying and being the model of repentance, he allowed her to return, but the father/daughter relationship was changed forever.

Jed had pitied her, and secretly was thankful for her unabashed ways. At Opal's request, they stayed in Wakefield. Outwardly, she was the pillar of the community, admired by all. Her secret stayed buried from the public, and Jed reaped its benefits in private.

Over the years, Opal learned to curb her appetite, to use its power over Jed, rewarding or depriving to gain her way. But all in all, Jed held the ultimate weapon. He knew the shame she had buried, almost denied, and when he wanted to head out to the Oregon Territory, she had no choice.

Now, as he felt her rapidly withdrawing from him, he felt the whiskey helping to heat up his blood. He wanted her tonight, and he wanted her participation.

"Opal, honey, I don't know any more. Doc just said Jacob was wanted for stealing his daughter from some Georgia plantation owner, and that Seamus was set on seeing them to Oregon." In the silence that followed, Jed could feel Opal thawing. She inched closer, her bare toe touching his, running up and down his foot. In the darkness, he smiled. She was playing the game. He rummaged his foggy mind for more. "I think he said something about a reward." Opal's hands pulled his shirt from his trousers, her cool hands running up and down his chest, circling the perimeter of skin beneath his waistband. He groaned. "I think Miss Smith helped the girl get to Saint Louis." Opal began unbuttoning his pants. He felt her hot breath fan the exposed skin. He felt himself pop free of the material.

"You'll help me, won't you—expose them, protect our, your party?" Her voice was husky, muffled against his skin. Jed groaned again, unable to think, unable to do much else but nod vigorously, his voice strained and desperate as he answered yes over and over.

Twenty-two

Seamus slowed his horse, then paused. He was like a statue, his profile frozen and intent. His horse was obviously used to such sudden stillness and remained as immobile as his master. Jacob followed suit, taking his cue from Seamus. For all that he disliked and sometimes even hated the man, he admired his abilities in the wild, and took the opportunity to learn from him.

Before the men and horses were even visible, Seamus had turned to face the direction in which they came, and he whispered to Jacob to ready his gun. Jacob had moved slowly, loading his new rifle, seldom taking his eyes away from the direction in which Seamus gazed. Suddenly, three trappers and an Indian in a turquoise calico shirt seemed to appear out of nowhere.

Jacob blinked twice and fought down the terrible urge to break and run. The men were coming fast, and Jacob was afraid they wouldn't stop. His horse, feeling his unease, shifted restlessly, pulling on its bit in a jerky manner.

Seamus raised his arms and made some strange sort of signs with his fingers, and motions of his hands. The white men stopped, but the Indian let out a whoop of joy, gesticulating wildly himself, and proceeding forward at an accelerated rate.

Jacob drew in a deep breath, willing himself to stay calm.

He knew little about the Indians in the West, and what he did know was not good. He felt small trickles of sweat run down his temples and under his nose. The blood in his head was pounding with a sickening ferocity, and his scalp tingled beneath his hat. He had heard that western Indians liked to scalp their victims, and so did some fur traders. He felt it increasingly harder to swallow, as the Indian grew closer and closer, revealing a silver ring threaded through his nose.

"Boston, Bos, my friend!" the Indian called out, his hands signing wildly. Jacob glanced nervously toward Seamus. He relaxed only slightly when he saw the Irishman smile. For all he knew, the Indian had just offered to deprive them of their horses. He remembered all too well that Seamus had told him that one must always remain polite with the Indians. That they did not see stealing a white man's horse the same way the white man's society did. Jacob wished he had asked if that held true for a black man, too.

When the Indian pulled up closer to them, he stopped to stare at Jacob. The bronzed man ran his eyes up and down Jacob's body, pausing over and over again at his face. He then turned to Seamus, gesticulating and speaking rapidly. Jacob heard the word *York,* and froze. First the brave had said *Boston,* now *York*. Did he know something about Jacob's escape? Jacob felt the reins slip beneath his slick palms, but he didn't dare move them. He waited a century, it seemed, for Seamus to react.

Seamus threw back his head and laughed. The Indian scowled, and the trappers began moving forward.

"Flying Hawk wants to know if you are the legendary York of the Lewis and Clark expedition." Seamus laughed again, and signed back to Flying Hawk. Flying Hawk moved closer to Jacob, pulling his hat from his head. Jacob jerked away, his eyes wide and frightened. He didn't know any Lewis or York. He should have known better than to trust Seamus. Seamus had probably agreed to allow this Indian to have Jacob's scalp. The Indian murmured something, then ran his long copper fingers across Jacob's hair.

That was it. He wasn't waiting around for more. Jacob kicked his heel into his horse's side, making the animal step backward and then turn. Before he had gotten ten yards away, he was surrounded by the three grungy trappers who had been with the Indian. One had a rifle trained at the base of his skull. Jacob pulled to a stop.

"And who might you be, boy?" the small, freckle-faced man with the gun asked in a distorted, but clearly southern drawl. "Don't remember McCarthy being one for havin' a nigger afore. Hows 'bout you fellas?" the man asked his companions, then spit a wad of tobacco into the tall grass alongside his horse.

Suddenly, Jacob feared the Indian a lot less than these foul-smelling men around him. They smelled of unwashed bodies and rotting animal carcasses. The stench was becoming overpowering, and Jacob felt a wave of nausea wash over him. Could he make a run for it? Would Seamus stand behind him if he told these men to go to hell? He thought of Penny, and then he thought of Amanda, of all that he hadn't told her. Silently, he vowed that if he escaped this unharmed, he'd tell Amanda he—

Seamus's angry voice interrupted his thoughts. "Put that rifle down. This here is Jacob, Jacob Smith, and he ain't nobody's boy." Seamus pushed at the squat redheaded man's rifle barrel so hard as he rode up to the group, that the gun nearly fell out of the man's hand. Flying Hawk and his mount pulled up between Jacob and the other two trappers, a clear sign that if it came down to it he would side with Seamus. Jacob felt a little of the apprehension fall from his shoulders, but he knew it wasn't over yet.

Three against three. The trappers eyed Seamus, Flying

Hawk, and Jacob; then the redheaded man laughed, and the others followed suit.

"Ain't you gonna 'vite us for supper, McCarthy? Sure you got a train here somewheres. Though must say it's mighty late to be starting. Snow'll be in the mountains 'fore you even see the pass," the freckled redhead stated. When Seamus didn't respond, the other men who had been quiet up until now spoke up. A hairy, swarthy trapper spoke first, sounding anxious to break the uneasy silence.

"Come on, McCarthy. We can tell yous all the news. We just come from where yous going, and we know."

The third man, a thin yellow-toothed, leather-skinned man, spoke next. "Have a heart, Mick. We ain't had more than each other for company, and our own dag cooking for nigh on three months. You got pretty womenfolk there? Any available?" He winked lewdy at Seamus.

"Come on, then, but stay away from the women," Seamus said reluctantly, turning to Flying Hawk. "You will be my guest at my fire?"

Flying Hawk nodded, and then pointed a finger at Jacob. "York son, too." Seamus laughed and nodded.

"Why don't you and Penny eat at my camp tonight? I'm sure Miss Smith will be thrilled to meet a real Indian."

Amanda was more than thrilled, and she scarely took her eyes off Flying Hawk all evening. She allowed him to touch her hair and skin. Jacob watched with envy, and was only slightly relieved to see that Seamus, too, was a little covetous. Flying Hawk taught Amanda how to say a few words of his Cayuse language and to sign. Seamus translated some ancient Indian stories that Flying Hawk told, as well as some information about their religion, medicines, and homelands.

Penny was as delighted as Amanda, and couldn't have been happier as she snuggled up against her side.

"Daughter?" Flying Hawk said, as he motioned to Penny. Amanda laughed softly as she wrapped an arm around Penny's shoulder, drawing her closer.

"I wish she were," Amanda responded, then felt her face grow warm as she realized the implication that might be derived from that. She kept her eyes on Flying Hawk, but was dying to look at Jacob.

"You. York son." Flying Hawk paused, struggling for the words, meshing his fingers together. Frustrated, he turned to Seamus. "Boston, you tell me word." He again made a blatantly obvious sign with his hands. Amanda giggled nervously.

"Why does he call you Boston, Seamus, and who is York son?" Penny asked curiously.

"That's where I got my nickname, Bos," Seamus said, translating to Flying Hawk. "See, the first white men the northwestern Indians ever saw were from Boston. They continued to call all white men Bostons. I stayed with the Nez Percé and Cayuse for a while, and it sort of stuck." Remembering, Seamus smiled fondly at the young brave.

Impatient for an answer to her whole question, Penny prompted Seamus. "And York son?"

Seamus laughed and looked at Jacob, sitting across from him. "Back about forty-six years ago, two pathfinders named Lewis and Clark were hired by the United States government to explore the West. They did, too, but they brought a black man named York with them. York was a big, strong man like your daddy, and the Indians thought him magical." Seamus paused, and turned a teasing smile on Jacob. "Seems they even wanted him to, er," he glanced around at his avid listeners, then had the decency to blush before he meshed his fingers together, "with the women of their tribe."

Penny meshed her own fingers, studied them, looked puzzled, then shook her head. Amanda looked away, her cheeks

flushing darkly, and Jacob looked interested.
 The rest of the evening passed rapidly, and the small group around Seamus's fire didn't notice what had become of the other three guests.

Twenty-three

Jed Turner looked on uneasily as his wife hooked an arm through two of the visiting trappers' arms. He watched her flutter her long, sable eyelashes flirtatiously at the gregarious red-haired, freckled one named Dean Garrett. She sighed dramatically when he told her he had spent a large part of his youth in Kentucky. Mr. Garrett watched with appreciation the slim white hand she placed on her generous bosom for effect.

Jed knew she was up to her scheming ways, a spider luring her prey into her inescapable web.

"Well, gentlemen, my husband and I would be honored to have you dine with us. Our fare is meager, but as the good Lord said, 'When I was hungry, you gave me to eat.'"

Jed cringed at her pious act, and watched in disgust as the men took the bait, their eyes shining down on her like she was some selfless angel. After five years of marriage, Jed knew her to be the most selfish person he had ever known. Usually, it served him well, so he let her be, but this time, something made him uncomfortable. Besides all their other unpleasant odors, these men smelled of trouble.

As a matter of fact, these trappers were so rank that Jed moved farther from the fire to avoid the stench. He marveled that his wife didn't even flinch when standing so near them. That was not a good sign. Opal was planning something. He had had plenty of opportunities to see her implacable determination before, and he knew it would take close to a miracle to turn her from her course. Silently, he cursed himself for letting his tongue slip the other night. He had partaken of just a bit too much of Doc Winslow's fine Scotch whiskey. He hoped that Opal's scheming had nothing to do with Jacob or Amanda, but with an icy chill of certainty, he knew that it did.

There would be hell to pay if Opal caused any harm to those people. For some reason, Bos McCarthy and Doc Winslow had taken a shine to them and the little girl. If they found out he'd been the one who'd started it, he'd probably loose his commission as captain and might even be run out of the wagon party.

Damn, his wife could really be a problem at times. He really didn't mind the fellow, Jacob. The man had proved more than once that he was an able blacksmith, and hell, everyone knew there would be plenty more need of his skills before the trip was over. The woman wasn't bad, either. She kept McCarthy out of his hair and in good sorts. Why did Opal have to get so bent out of shape over the black woman anyway?

Jed glanced over at his wife, who was in an animated conversation with Garrett. He'd been so lost in his troublesome thoughts that he hadn't paid much attention to their conversation. But his wife's next words made him gasp in disbelief, and once again curse his taste for whiskey.

"You don't say. You mean Jacob just took off at the sight of you gentlemen?" Opal paused dramatically, shivering and folding her arms under her breasts, pushing upward, to show them to their advantage. The effect was not lost on any of their guests. "Well!" she continued, leaning in closer toward the men and whispering in a conspiratorial whisper. "He is on the run, you know." She glanced around her as if checking for eavesdroppers, fixing wide, frightened eyes on her listeners. "He's wanted by the law. He's a runaway, and so is his woman. I hear there is a hefty reward for their return. Dead or alive."

This time, Jed choked on his coffee, burning his lips and chin as the hot liquid came squirting out. Never had he mentioned either the size of the reward or conditions on their return. As a matter of fact, he hadn't really said much about Amanda's part in all of this at all, or at least he didn't remember. Jed sank his head in his hands and groaned.

Opal turned to where her husband sat and glared at his outburst, her eyes an icy challenge. But her voice was all sweet with sugary southern concern. "Darlin', are you all right? Perhaps you should go lie down a spell in the wagon. Alone." She put just the right amount of emphasis on the word *alone* that Jed knew the word could mean sleep alone for a very, very long time, if he interfered.

Jed mumbled that he was fine, and he sat sullenly, listening, as Opal led the men to believe that it had all been their idea to kidnap Jacob, Amanda, and Penny, and take them back East with them. He watched with sinking hopes as the men rubbed their hands greedily at the thought of the reward.

"You mustn't let Mr. McCarthy or Doc Winslow know of your clever plan," Opal warned. "You see, I believe they are abolitionists at heart, and would deprive a man of his freedom to choose whether he keeps slaves or not." Opal turned to smile triumphantly at her husband, and Jed smiled weakly in return. For the first time in his life, it struck him as odd to hear the words *freedom* and *slave* used together, but not in contention with one another.

The following morning, the sky was gray, filled with ominous black rolling clouds. In the distance, thunder rumbled, and the oxen bellowed pitifully.

"Looks like we are in for a big one," Seamus remarked, as he dismounted from his horse alongside Amanda and Sarah, as they packed away the morning dishes in the box fastened to the rear of the wagon.

"I know, but it won't be for long," Amanda replied, then quickly added, "It will clear up by late afternoon, and it will be hot and muggy for the next day or two." Both Sarah and Seamus said nothing, but stared at her in disbelief. Amanda flushed and smiled sheepishly. "I was blessed with the gift to foresee the weather." When neither Seamus or Sarah responded, Amanda shrugged, and went back to her work. "Wait, you'll see," was all she said. Seamus laughed and shook his head.

"I hope you're right, 'cause if this storm is a drencher, we'll be lucky to make a mile or two today."

Amanda frowned up at him. "I'm afraid it will be just that. A complete and thorough soaker." Sarah, who had still said nothing, just stared at Amanda when she said this. Seamus's good-natured grin faded to a scowl, and he shifted uncomfortably from one foot to the other. He looked up at the sky, then back down to Amanda's serious face. She wasn't kidding, and he didn't quite know what to make of it.

Fifteen minutes later, the rain started. It came down in an avalanche. The sheets of rain bounced off the hard ground in great sprays of water. Wagoners pulled the drawstrings on either ends of their canvas covers tight, and riders, drivers, and walkers pulled their hats lower or wrapped themselves in oilcloth.

As the train trudged forward, the ground beneath them turned to a field of mud. Oxen sank down to their knees and stubbornly refused to move. Opal Turner sat in the back of her wagon, cursing the weather and the temporary hold on her well-laid plans.

An hour later, the wagon party halted, unwilling and unable to move forward. Families scrambled into their wagons, and those who didn't fit struggled to set up tents. But as the torrential rains continued, even the quick makeshift ditches that had been dug around the tents collapsed, and water seeped beneath the canvas and thoroughly soaked the inhabitants.

In one of these tents, Flying Hawk sat silently listening to the three trappers, who had hired him as their guide, talk about their plans. Foolishly, the three men had supposed that since Flying Hawk spoke little English, he understood little as well. They talked openly about their plans to kidnap Jacob and his woman and child when the rain stopped and it got dark. One of them would offer to do the night watch while the other two would bind and gag Jacob, Amanda, and Penny. If Jacob struggled, they'd just kill him, or at least maim him. Together, they laughed. Mrs. Turner had said the authorities wanted him dead or alive. Their talk then turned to the gracious Opal Turner, and her *gracious* body.

After a while, Flying Hawk grunted and crawled from the tent. The trappers laughed at him, saying even the greatest call of nature wouldn't make them budge from the tent. Garrett called him a crazy savage, and laughed as he retied the tent flaps.

Flying Hawk struggled through the still torrential downpour. He had to find McCarthy so he could warn his friend. York son—Jacob was a good man, and Amanda-bird was beautiful. He pushed harder against the blinding rain.

By late afternoon, the rain had subsided, leaving everyone and everything thoroughly drenched. As the day slipped into dusk, the sky darkened only slightly. The fires were weak and smoky, as all the kindling had been caught in the deluge.

Jed, who had refused to stay in the wagon with his wife, sloshed through the mud angrily as he wrung his hat in his hands. He knew now that the rain had stopped, trouble would start, and he wanted to be as far from camp as possible. He wanted no part in Opal's designs. If he were away from camp, he could claim ignorance. He scanned the flat gray horizon and noticed a small outcrop of rocks. They would provide enough shelter if it started to rain again. Hell, he was thoroughly drenched already. How could a little more hurt? As he walked through the knee-high grass, he passed a few wooden markers. The first said, *"Here lies Jessica May 1847–1849."* He walked on a few more feet and found an empty shallow grave, a few rocks and bones scattered around it. The wooden cross had been covered by a few of the larger stones, which presumably had covered the now empty grave from possible predators. Moving the stone, Jed squinted in the fading light at the chisled words, *"My dear baby, born 1849."* The words were simple and pitiful, and Jed felt sorrow tug at his heart. He and Opal had no children, and due to her miscarriage, probably never would. He thought of all the cheerful little rosy faces back at the camp, and then of the little brown one. He shook his head, wondering at this new sentimentality. He tucked the dry wooden cross under his arm, and continued toward the rocks. The baby was dead and gone, and the marker could start a nice fire.

The hours cramped in the back of the wagon with Penny and all their supplies made Jacob's long limbs ache, and the close quarters make him crave the open air. He had spent far too much time in confined spaces, hiding.

By the time the rain had stopped, Penny, too, was glad to be free of the wagon's narrow quarters. She half ran, half waded to the Winslows' wagon. Mrs. Winslow nodded to Jacob that it was all right, and he smiled back gratefully.

In the distance, he could hear the haunting howling of coyotes or possibly wolves. He scrutinized the horizon for any sign of the woeful animals, and caught sight of the flickering fire in the distance. Grabbing his gun, he headed cautiously toward the illumination.

When Jacob neared the small camp, he heard a strange whimpering sound, then a low guttural growl. Several large boulders blocked his view, and he loaded his rifle silently before creeping up on the rock's damp, cold surface.

As Jacob slithered across the top of the highest surface, he saw a trio of shaggy wolves cornering something in the crux of the rocks just below him. For a moment, he hesitated, then slid closer on his belly. Right below him was a man crouched in the corner of the rocks, shirtless, bootless, and rifleless. Looking quickly around the camp, Jacob saw that the latter had been propped up as a kind of clothes line for the shirt, and every time the man tried to move toward the rifle, the wolves growled and moved closer.

The wolves were hideous creatures, with their yellow slitted eyes, and their bared dingy teeth. According to McCarthy, there weren't many wolves this low down, but it had been a hard winter, and from the looks of the mangy beasts, they were hungry. Well, so was he, and wolf couldn't be any worse than hard biscuits and jerky. Raising his rifle slowly, he aimed, said a prayer, and fired.

The blast jolted his shoulder, bruising his jaw, which had leaned against the butt of the gun. One animal whimpered and fell, a large gaping hole in the white fur of its chest. The other two paused and stared with confusion at their fallen conterpart.

Jacob remembered that McCarthy had said wolves travel in packs and were very loyal to their fellow pack members, that they rarely departed each other in times of need. Jacob loaded again quickly.

Obviously, Jed Turner was unaware of the allegiance in these animals, because at that moment, he sprang for his rifle. In a split second, the other two wolves lunged at him, their mouths drooling, and vicious snarls rising from their throats. A shot from Jacob's rifle sliced off the right side of one of the animals' heads. Jed screamed in terror and pain as the last wolf sank its teeth into his bare shoulder. Hastily, Jacob loaded again, but his last lead ball fell from his trembling fingers, sliding through the crevices in the rock. Nausea roiled in his stomach as he watched the wolves' sharp fangs rip over and over at Jed's shoulder and arm. With only a moment's hesitation, Jacob jumped from the rock and cracked the butt of his rifle across the remaining animal's skull. For the moment, the animal was dazed, staggering backward, its eyes wide and unfocused. Not waiting to find out if it would attack again, Jacob grabbed Jed's gun and, praying it was loaded, aimed, and fired at the confused beast. The animal fell to its knees, quivered, then toppled over.

Breathing hard, Jacob touched the blood-soaked animal before him, yellow eyes vacant and unblinking. He didn't hear the voices coming closer. Then he heard Opal Turner's scream.

"He got Jed's gun. He tried to kill him. Somebody get him." Jacob turned to stare first at her, then to the smoking gun in his hand, then to the moaning, wounded man on the ground.

"Help me move him to my wagon!" Doc Winslow barked out, as he moved to kneel beside Jed's body. Opal continued to scream that Jacob had tried to ambush Jed. The three burly trappers grabbed Jacob by the arms. One yanked the rifle from his hand. Jacob began to struggle.

"The wolves," he mumbled, then glaced around again to find the carcasses gone. He looked down at the hands holding him. They were covered with sticky blood. Jacob shook his head in confusion. Had they moved them? If so, why? All too soon, his questions were answered.

"This here man is dangerous. Best we take him to the fort with us." Dean Garrett spoke out loudly. Opal was pushing Doc Winslow away from her husband, rocking his blood-soaked body in her arms.

"Look, here is the bullet hole where that monster shot my husband."

The crowd moved closer, and a few of the folks turned

suspicious eyes on Jacob. Doc Winslow struggled to retrieve the body from Opal, but she only gripped Jed tighter, the consoling women making it more difficult.

"A mere bullet couldn't have made those," Doc Winslow began, but stopped as he and the crowd, which was rapidly becoming a mob, stared at Jacob's bloodied hands and shirt. While the trappers had been holding him, they had managed to smear the blood from their hands over his shirt. No one but them knew that it was animal blood, not Jed Turner's.

McCarthy and Flying Hawk came running to the gathering of angry people. Some of the men were shouting, "String him up! Shoot him!" while the women closed in around Opal or hurried the few children with them back to the wagons, murmuring about beasts.

In the confusion, Dean Garrett silently ordered his two companions to carefully move the poorly hidden carcasses farther away. Jacob had stopped struggling and watched in horror as the people he had known became an angry mob. In his many years in the South, he had seen or heard enough about lynchings to know that a mob knew no justice, only violent revenge.

"What in God's name is going on here?" Seamus McCarthy demanded, as he pushed his way through the crowd. The crowd pushed back. Flying Hawk pointed to the ledge where Jacob had lain just minutes before. Seamus jumped to the top of it, and addressed the crowd in a loud voice.

From his vantage point, he could see the restrained Jacob, although he didn't appear to be struggling, and he could see the blood-soaked Jed Turner wrapped in Opal's protective arms.

"For God's sake, or at least for Jed's sake, half of you go back to camp and give Jed some room." At these words, Opal sent up a plaintive howl, and the people began threatening again. Seamus stood undaunted, bellowing out commands. "Mrs. Turner, let the doctor look at your husband's wounds.

A lot of good he'll do anybody if *you* let him bleed to death. The rest of you women go back to your wagons."

For a moment, the crowd shifted restlessly, waiting for one of their ranks to lead. First Mrs. Winslow, then Sarah Foster turned to leave. Reluctantly, the other women followed. All but Opal.

Afraid of what the men might do to Jacob if he allowed him out of his sight, Seamus insisted he stay, and that a few men remain to guard him. Dean Garrett and his now returned companions offered their unbiased protection of the prisoner. This seemed to suit most of the men, who had been assured no decision would be made without a group consultation.

As the night grew later, only a small group remained: Doc Winslow, Seamus, Flying Hawk, Jacob, Opal, Jed, the three trappers, and four other men. A few of the men had left, returning with Doc's medical bag, some linen cloths for bandages, and some blankets.

Finally retrieving Jed's body from Opal, Doc investigated the wounds while the others waited breathlessly. Jacob's voice had grown hoarse from explaining about the wolves.

"Well," the doctor began nervously, feeling the importance of his words in the next few moments, "the wounds do look like they were caused by both a bullet and something sharp and tearing like a wolf's teeth."

"I ain't never known no wolf to carry no rifle before, and if it's like this nigger says, he shot at the wolves—three wolves—then where is the bodies?" Dean Garrett asked, as he stepped from behind Jacob. Jacob had stopped struggling a while ago, and Garrett felt certain the man wouldn't run, and well, if he did, he'd just shoot him. It didn't make a difference. He'd get the reward if he was dead or alive. He kind of wished the man would bolt. It would sure be a hell of a lot easier.

"I know, Doc. You don't have to say it. What about the

sharp tearing, or cutting wounds?" Dean paused in his rhetorical questioning for emphasis. The word *cutting* had not been lost on the gathering. Slowly, he produced a bloodied Bowie knife from behind his back. The men gasped, and Opal struggled to hide a smile. Garrett was absolutely brilliant. "While yous was all caterwauling, I found this here knife stuck in the back of the prisoner's trousers."

Jacob felt his knees go weak. It had been a plant. He was being set up. He had tried to do the humane thing by saving Turner's life, and now his hung in the balance. Looking from face to face, he knew he'd never receive a fair trial. These were white men. He was nothing to them. He thought of his Penny, and of Amanda, of all his hopes and dreams being crushed before they even bloomed.

"It ain't mine!" Jacob screamed, his voice trembling with panic and desperation. "I tell you, there were three wolves. I shot at them. I didn't bring my knife, just my gun." Jacob's voice faded off into a whisper as he stared into the disbelieving eyes around him. Only Seamus seemed convinced.

"Flying Hawk," Seamus said, without taking his eyes from Jacob's. Out of the shadows the Indian appeared. Seamus touched his eyes, his nose, then made a rapid hand movement. Flying Hawk slipped off into the darkness.

"What did you tell him?" Opal asked angrily, her voice quavering slightly with fear. Seamus caught her glance at Dean. Flying Hawk had been right. Mrs. Turner and the trappers had had a hand in this masquerade, and Jacob was both the prize and the scapegoat. It was all too convenient.

Dean Garrett smiled to himself. He wasn't a fool. He had ordered his men to hack the creatures into a million pieces and fling them to the four corners of the earth. As a matter of fact, the knife he now presented to McCarthy was one of the very tools used in the job. That stupid Indian would be lucky to find more then a single wolf limb, and wild animals would have done that, not a bullet, like Jacob claimed.

Garrett turned and smiled smugly at Jacob, and Jacob felt doomed, almost as if the lid on his casket were being nailed shut. Jacob shut his eyes and allowed his mind to drift back, trying to escape to a happier time. But it was no good. He could only remember hatred and trouble.

Rebecca, sweet Rebecca, had been driven to it by Old Man Whitingworth, tearing their child away from her bosom. Why? Because he hated who Jacob was. His bastard grandson. The old man could have handled it if his son had raped or abandoned Jacob's mother. But no, the young master, his father, had wanted to marry her, call her his wife. Jacob had found out the night he asked to buy Rebecca's freedom. Becca never had a chance. He should have refused to marry her or made her run away with him.

He thought of Whitingworth's long arm of vengence, seeking him out here in the western wilderness. The reward for his capture. This was what this had to be all about. He thought of Penny. Who would care for a murderer's child? There was a reward for her as well. Did these men know that, too? Damn his mother for not coming with him! She had chosen to stay. She said she loved his father. Rodney Whitingworth, Jr., had tricked him into believing he was a good man, giving Jacob his freedom, allowing him to save for his family's freedom, when all along he'd known his father, Rodney Whitingworth, Sr., would never let it happen. The old man had only one way to get back at his son, and it was Jacob's family that had suffered.

First the only real father he had ever known had been sold south to the hellish sugarcane fields of Louisiana, then Rollin had followed. Every time, his mother cried, but she never denied her love. Jacob drew in a deep, ragged breath. He hated them. He hated all white people. He hated himself because he had their blood. Amanda's beautiful face swam before his closed eyelids, her words of forgiveness and hope ringing through his ears. She was truly a good woman. She deserved better than him. A tight longing and regret burned in his chest. He never really had a chance. If there was a God, then Jacob's soul must have been sold to the devil, and he'd finally come to claim his own.

Twenty-four

Seamus knew Jacob was innocent. He had no proof, but it was a gut feeling, and his instincts were rarely wrong. It also didn't hurt to know that Opal and the trappers had planned to kidnap Jacob all along. What didn't figure was Jed Turner's role in all of this. Doc Winslow and Jed had been the only ones privy to the information about Jacob and Penny's escape. He hadn't really told them much, except what he thought was absolutely necessary in the event something happened to him. He had waited until he felt they were far enough into Indian Territory that there would be little anyone who had a mind to could do about it. He had really only wanted Winslow to know, but they'd gotten drunk, and Doc had let the cat out of the bag.

Now it was entirely possible that Jed had told his wife, and she had obviously told the trappers. But why had Jed been cut up? Had Jed refused to participate? Damn, the man was unconscious, and Doc said he might remain that way for a long time—or he might never come out of it. Seamus shuddered at the thought of Jed dying, the mystery unsolved. If that happened, the mob would want blood. And he had seen how Opal Turner could manipulate public sentiments. No matter what, he had to get Jacob out of here. He still felt somewhat responsible for the man, and he didn't want any of the resentment toward Jacob to turn on Amanda and Penny.

Doc Winslow and Opal had gone back with four of the men and the unconcious Jed to the Turners' wagon. Flying Hawk hadn't returned yet, and Jacob stood motionless, eyes shut between the remaining three trappers. Somehow he had to get Jacob away from these men.

"Shit, what a thing to happen," Seamus stated as he walked toward the trappers. He ran a hand through his unruly dark hair to show his exasperation. "Should have seen it coming. These two men have been at it for a long time." Seamus jerked a thumb in Jacob's direction. Jacob didn't move, and his eyes stayed shut. "Well, it could be a long time before Doc's through with Jed, and it's best to think on a full stomach and a little shut-eye."

Garrett eyed Seamus warily. "What's your idea? I ain't relinquishing the prisoner to your keeping, if that's what your thinkin'. Miss Opal done told me 'bout your black sympathies." Now Garrett grinned. "Heard you even been sampling a little black sympathy yourself." Seamus struggled to control the now familiar rage burning in his gut whenever Amanda was slandered. Jacob's eyes were still shut, so Seamus grinned back, disguising his disgust at the man's insinuations. Friendlier now, Garrett winked at Seamus. "Well, I don't see why we have to haul off the little lady if'n she suits your taste."

"And the child?" Seamus asked carelessly. Garrett frowned for a few seconds, and Seamus seized the opportunity. "Kids can be such brats. You can't imagine, but, well the lady has a certain fondness for the girl, and it might serve me better to keep her, if you know what I mean."

Garrett chewed on this for a moment, then decided McCarthy was probably right. Besides, how much could they get for a runt like her, anyhow? He smiled warmly at Seamus. He liked talking on this level. It was a level he understood.

"Shall we celebrate our, er, agreement then?" Seamus

asked, as he clapped a large hand on Garrett's scrawny shoulder. He saw Garrett glance back at the still silent Jacob.

"I ain't lettin' him out of my sight."

"I don't blame you," Seamus responded earnestly. "I'd have you take him away right now, if I could. The sooner I get my party back to normal and back on track, the better for me. I want to get past the Blue Mountains before snowfall." When Garrett nodded in sympathy, Seamus continued, "Let's tie the prisoner up, and then we can enjoy ourselves a meal, a fire, and maybe a little whiskey." Seamus saw the glowing looks of eager anticipation in the other trappers' eyes. Smiling broadly, Garrett agreed. "Then wait right here, and I'll be back in a minute." Seamus headed off toward the camp, glancing back over and over again, hoping they wouldn't do something stupid like make a run for it. Well, damn their souls if they did. He'd turn them all in as accomplices in both Jacob's escape and Jed's attack.

Doc Winslow grudgingly gave Seamus two of his bottles of Scotch whiskey. He complained that there would be great use for them as anesthesia on the remainder of the journey. Seamus had remained unbending, reminding the doctor how the money to buy the whiskey had come from the party's pooled funds, and they might not take too lightly to the fact the supply was already one bottle short, and there had been no medical need thus far for its use.

As he was leaving the Winslow campsite, Mrs. Winslow approached Seamus with a plate of hot food. "Can I help?" she asked. When Seamus didn't answer, but studied her closely, she continued, "I don't trust Opal, and I don't believe Jacob harmed Jed Turner. I'm inclined to believe Jacob's story, though I don't know where those wolves are." When Mrs. Winslow kept her steady blue eyes on Seamus, he responded slowly.

"Suppose Jacob were to take a little ride alone. Say to a

nearby fort?'' Mrs. Winslow nodded, waiting for him to continue. "Could you pack him a few things?" Mrs. Winslow nodded, then spoke.

"The child?" Seamus shook his head, and Mrs. Winslow smiled a warm, maternal smile. "Then I'll be putting her to bed in our wagon. Tell Jacob his baby will be well taken care of for, well, for however long it takes." Seamus smiled at the small woman.

Seamus was relieved to see that Garrett and his men were where he had left them. The silent black man had been tied with several feet of rope. His feet and wrists had also been bound. On his own, Jacob would never escape.

Purposefully, Seamus moved the men some distance from the prisoner. There wasn't much with which to make a fire, so Seamus handed round the bottles and placed the food from Mrs. Winslow between them.

"Never been able to make a stew from jerky taste so dang good," Garrett mumbled between bites of the food and fried bread. Seamus agreed, and looked guiltily over at the bent figure of Jacob. Mrs. Winslow had meant this food for Jacob, not his captors.

Suddenly, Seamus saw a movement in the long grass beside the rock. Then Flying Hawk stepped into the clearing, his hands empty. Seamus knew that didn't mean he hadn't found anything, but that he might be hiding something to share with Seamus later. Seamus regretted he'd probably never know what it was. The other three men looked back at Flying Hawk as Seamus started to sign rapidly and yell at the Indian.

"Go on, Flying Hawk. Everything's been settled. These men don't need you no more. Why don't you just go back to your own land? Go on, get lost!" Flying Hawk stood very still just outside the halo of the small fire Garrett had managed to start. He didn't look at any of the men, but studied Seamus's apt fingers. Garrett and his men grinned, nodding and adding their slurred derogatory remarks at him as well.

"Dumb Injun. Sometimes they can be so daft. Hope he understood we wanted him to get lost," one of the trappers said.

"I'm sure he did," said Seamus. "I signed it, too." The men smiled, and Seamus fervently hoped Flying Hawk had understood his message to get gear from the doctor's wife, cut Jacob loose, and take him far away, even to his homeland by the Walla Walla River. They'd never go that far looking for him. He'd find a way, once he arrived in Oregon, to get Penny to him.

Amanda had heard the news, and she broke into a run toward the distant fire where Jacob was being held. Several yards before, enshrouded in darkness, she nearly collided with Flying Hawk. His hands came out to steady her, and he shook his head slowly from side to side warning her from proceeding. A strangled cry fell from her lips as she tried to pull away.

"I must see him." Flying Hawk looked over his shoulder at the distant group of men. His eyes looked wary and doubtful when they came back to her. Amanda nodded vigorously. His shoulders slumped in resignation, and he motioned for her to follow him.

For an hour or more they crouched in the darkness, the damp grass soaking the hem of her skirt and petticoat. Finally, Flying Hawk rose and crept closer to the fire. Seamus, Garrett, and his men lay sprawled around the flames. Several empty whiskey bottles lay scattered around them. Amanda gazed at the scene with obvious distaste. Then her eyes and heart stopped. Off to the side, in the shadow of the rock outcrop, sat Jacob, bound and dejected. His proud, defiant stance was gone. In its place was a crumpled semblance of the man she knew. Forcing herself to move slowly, lest she waken the drunken men, she moved toward Jacob.

"Jacob?" The question came out soft and strained, cracking

on a sob. Although the word was no louder than a whisper, Jacob raised his head. His eyes were hollow and defeated, but they flickered with a small light when he saw her; then he looked away.

Fear and anquish crowded into Amanda's heart as she reached out to touch his cheek. There was no longer any time to wait to tell him all she felt.

"Jacob, please." Her long fingers caressed the scratchy surface of his unshaven jaw. "Please look at me." When he didn't turn, she moved closer, taking his head between her hands, and turning it to face her. "Jacob, oh, Jacob, what have they done to you?"

Looking at the tenderness and belief in his innocence in Amanda's eyes was almost more then Jacob could stand. He wanted to take her into his arms, to cry out that she was right, that he needed her. His wrists pulled at the tight ropes, then stilled. A sharp, unbearable pain stabbed through his heart. His dream had been stolen. Never again would he see his daughter, those he loved. He drew in a ragged breath and yanked his head from Amanda's hands. He could not bear to see the sadness, the promise of what might have been.

Suddenly, his wrist broke free. Flying Hawk's face came before his, a smug smirk on his face, and a knife glinting in the dying firelight.

"We must go, York son. No questions, now. Follow me." The last of the bindings fell from Jacob's ankles, and he scrambled to his feet. With a finger before his lips, Flying Hawk gathered the scraps of rope, stuffing them in a leather pouch at his side.

Jacob clenched and unclenched his fist, rejoicing in the renewed circulation. A reprieve—he had been given another chance. He would not squander it this time. Turning, he pulled Amanda into his arms, his mouth covering hers with a searing kiss. Over and over, his hands roamed her shoulders, back, and arms, as if memorizing her.

"I will find you. Wait for me. I . . . I . . ." Flying Hawk cut him off as he searched for words, his rough hands now cupping Amanda's face.

"So sorry, York son, but we must go, or it'll be too late." Jacob stepped back from Amanda, his hands still surrounding her face, his eyes pleading, then he pulled her to him and kissed her again. Garrett stirred, his leg striking an empty whiskey bottle. The trio tensed, then Jacob and Flying Hawk slipped off into the night.

For several minutes Amanda stood staring into the darkness after them, her fingers resting lightly on her kiss-swollen lips, her mind swirling with myriad emotions. One of Garrett's men groaned and rolled over. Glancing quickly over her shoulder, Amanda's senses returned. She must get back to the wagon. Looking one last time into the now empty darkness where Jacob had stood moments before, she silently promised him she'd wait.

All hell broke loose the next morning when the three trappers and Seamus awoke with hangovers to find Jacob gone. Seamus smiled when he realized that Flying Hawk had even taken the cut ropes, leaving no clue as to whether Jacob escaped or was kidnapped. But he quickly hid the smile and acted as angry as the others, organizing a search party.

The wagon train had been delayed due to Jed's injuries, and the diversion in searching for Jacob proved to be therapeutic to the restless men. Seamus was sure that neither Jacob nor a trace of him would be found. When Flying Hawk wanted to disappear, he was damn good at it.

As the bright sun reached its summit in the sky, Seamus dragged his shirt sleeve across his brow. It did him little good, as his shirt was soaked with sweat as well. For a moment he thought back to the morning before, to his conversation with Miss Smith. Had she really known what the weather would be? Or was it just a lucky guess?

As he rode over the flat, desolate land with the rest of the tired men, he mused over these questions. Perhaps he'd have to put her to the test. It would be great if Miss Smith could tell him when it was going to snow. He thought about Amanda for awhile, and he smiled. He was glad that she hadn't had to leave in the dark of the night as well. But she was still in danger, and now more than ever he had every intention of protecting her.

"You're out of your mind!" Amanda gasped, wide-eyed, at Seamus. He reached for one of her hands and she snatched it away. She had been badly shocked last night when she had been told that Jacob was being held for attacking Jed Turner, and that he would be held for murder if the man died. After seeing him and watching him flee with Flying Hawk, she had cried herself to sleep in the early morning hours. She was awakened by the angry cry of men outside the wagon, and the sound of pounding hooves. Peering out of Jacob's wagon, she watched the dozen or so men riding across the open prairie. Climbing down, she went in search of Mrs. Winslow, but was intercepted by Sarah Foster.

"Amanda, he's escaped or been kidnapped," the young woman gasped breathlessly as she ran to keep step with Amanda's stride.

"Now, why would he escape?" Amanda responded without slowing. "He didn't do anything wrong." The blood in Amanda's head pounded furiously, as she prayed she wouldn't give away his escape. She knew he hadn't harmed Jed, even though she'd seen his temper before, but he wasn't a physically violent man. Or was he? She thought momentarily of William Foster and his callous, harsh treatment of Sarah. When Sarah spoke, her words seemed to crash painfully down on Amanda.

"Amanda. Amanda, listen. Men aren't always what we

want or see them to be. Love can be blind." Amanda stopped and turned to gaze at her small friend. For the first time, she noticed the slightly swollen brow above Sarah's eye, and the purplish bruise just below her jaw. "I fell," Sarah said, and shrugged with embarrassment. Amanda knew she was lying. As she stood there in the middle of the wagon circle, Seamus walked up to her.

Dazed, Amanda let him lead her to his tent. She barely registered his words, but when she finally understood, she was shocked and outraged. He asked her to stay with him in his tent.

"It is for your own safety," Seamus responded gently, but with an edge of frustration. "I promise, I won't lay a hand on ye." He moved closer, laying his hands firmly on her shoulders, turning her to him. "I will protect ye, I gave me word." His voice was stern but filled with emotion, as his Irish brogue seeped into his words. Amanda struggled to break free, her voice high and uncontrolled.

"Just who do you think I need protection from? From Jacob? A man condemned before he was given a chance? Condemned by men like you?" Amanda could see that her words hit a raw spot, and she kept on with a vengeance. "Do you really believe he did it? Can you live with the fact that he may die or be captured? What of his child? Now she has no mother or father." Suddenly her anger gave way to tears, and she sobbed uncontrollably. Seamus pulled her gently to him, stroking her back with long, even strokes, reminding her of an earlier time when Jacob had comforted her this way. She began to cry harder, sure that her heart would break. She hadn't the strength to fight.

Seamus breathed deeply of her scent, his heart beating rapidly at the nearness of her. God, she loved Jacob, and Seamus was falling in love with her. For a moment, they clung to one another, each miserable in their thoughts. Then Seamus brusquely pushed her away. His voice was even, emotionless. Once again, he was the icy, impenetrable mountain.

"I don't believe he did it. I owe the man my life. He saved me from the fire in Saint Louis, and he'd didn't have to. I believe he was trying to save Jed's life. He's that kind of man." As he said these words, their meaning twisted painfully in his chest. Amanda was right to care about Jacob. Seamus did, too. Jacob was a good man in a world of too few good men.

Amanda was breathing shallow, hiccupy breaths as she listened to Seamus's story. She felt both relief at Jacob's probable bravery, and guilt at having had any doubt. As they talked, Seamus did not try to touch her, and Amanda was troubled by the distant demeanor he showed her now.

"I'm sorry for doubting you, Seamus. It's just that so much has happened." Amanda waved her hand wearily, and stared into the shielded blue eyes that seemed so impersonal. "We have both underestimated Opal's strength and hatred. I'll do what you think best. I will stay here . . ."

Seamus interrupted her, suddenly rising and pacing the few feet from where they sat to the fire. "No." Turning back around abruptly, he gazed off into the distance, his height and solid build making him look all the more like a mountain.

"But I thought . . ." Amanda began.

"You'll sleep in the wagon, and I'll move my tent nearer." Having spoken these words, Seamus helped her to her feet and then left. Amanda felt the chill of his icy eyes wash over her. Something had happened. Their relationship had changed. She stared after him, willing him to turn around. She needed him, needed his friendship. She said she was sorry for not trusting him. What more did he want? As she stood there, watching his retreating back, she realized that she didn't really want to know.

Twenty-five

It was early November when the original Winslow-Turner party descended upon the Willamette Valley. Their number had dwindled from one hundred twenty to ninety-eight, plus one due any day.

Sarah's husband, William, had abandoned her at the South Pass, deciding to take the California route with several of the other men. There, they had met a few would-be miners who had heard rumors of millions of dollars in gold lining the hills of California. Many of the men had promised to return rich to their families in the spring, but Billy promised no such thing. He took what gear he needed, all their money, and was gone. Sarah barely cried, but clung tighter to Amanda, sure that Amanda would know what to do when her baby arrived. Sarah never once doubted that she and Amanda would be together once they reached Oregon.

One whole family, a mother and her three children, had been wiped out by cholera just outside of Chimney Rock. The father, unable to bear his loss, had killed himself with his rifle at Fort Laramie. Several other members had been drowned in river crossings, and one woman died in childbirth. This terrified Sarah, and she became more reticent with each passing day, clinging more desperately to Amanda.

Amanda struggled to keep her optimism, lending an extra

hand when one was needed, helping the overworked doctor with the sick, and just being there, holding the hands of the dying or the bereft. Day after day, she spoke happily of the future land, the promised land—Oregon. But it was at night, when the last embers of the campfires died and she curled her exhausted body on top of blankets beneath the stars that she let the tears and her shattered hopes darken her eyes. This new world was not what she had seen in her girlhood dreams. Not that it wasn't breathtakingly beautiful. In that respect, it was more than she'd hoped for, but it was a heartless land of indifference. The barren deserts and perilous mountains had no sympathies for the weak and the young. Day after day, they passed grave markers attesting to the many lives that had been snuffed out before they'd even had a chance. And what of Jacob? Had he, too, perished? Was he buried somewhere, his grave perhaps unmarked, forgotten except in the lonely heart of his daughter—and Amanda? She couldn't bear to believe this was possible, and she clung to the hope that all would be well when they finally reached their destination. She had to believe. It was the only thing that allowed her to rise with a smile each morning and give hope to the others.

Now, as the early snows of November lay in patches in the hills around them, the travel-weary party looked down at the small valley town with something just short of euphoria. They had made it; not all of them, but enough to keep the dream alive.

"I'm having this baby in town, with a real bed beneath me," Sarah said, as she wrapped her arm around Amanda's waist and gazed down at the small spirals of smoke rising from the chimneys.

Other than the smoke, the town seemed deserted. Penny moved up along Amanda's other side, and took her hand.

"Do you think my daddy's waiting for us down there?"

Amanda squeezed the little hand tightly, but she didn't

answer. Again, her thoughts turned to Jacob, and she wondered where he was. She was glad he didn't know how close he had come to losing his daughter.

At Fort Laramie, Opal Turner tried once again to have Amanda and Penny taken captive to be returned to the South. Dean Garrett and the other trappers had tired of the chase and given up weeks before, but Opal was undaunted. She insisted that the captain of the fort honor the laws of the government he worked for and bring these Negroes to justice. She put on a remarkable show, playing the frightened meek wife who had almost been made a widow. She wept and prayed in front of the officials, saying she felt unsafe, and was afraid the murderous Jacob would return at any time to retrieve his daughter and whore, finish off her husband, and who knew who else. She reminded the soldiers that it was their duty to protect them, even if Mr. McCarthy would not.

This was a truly low point in the journey. It had been the only time in the whole trip when Amanda let her optimistic facade slip. She was utterly frightened. The captain of the fort took both her and Penny under house arrest until the matter could be resolved. Seamus became uncharacteristically outraged. His thundering words of protest could be heard echoing throughout the compound. She and Penny were kept in a small room with a single cot and a small, barred window. Seamus came to visit them often, telling them that only Doc Winslow and his wife would stand behind him. The rest of the party, although they liked Amanda and wished her no harm, were frightened that Jacob would indeed return to get her and his daughter. Opal had succeeded in rekindling fear and anger from the incident when her husband had been so savagely attacked.

Jed, who had just regained consciousness, was weak and sketchy with his description of the attack. He would only say that he remembered Jacob, fear, and pain. His gaze was elusive, refusing to meet those of his questioners. Opal, protective as a mother bear with her cub, refused to allow him to be interrogated and claimed it was unnecessary harassment. But the captain of the fort, Doc Winslow, and Seamus overruled her, and continued to question her suddenly taciturn husband. That was, until Seamus threatened the silent Southerner by shaking him roughly. Seamus was ordered from the room, and the fort guards were told to keep him out. Doc tried to find out more, but Jed refused to talk, saying he remembered nothing.

Amanda now turned to pull Penny closer, and in doing so, saw Opal staring at her. The hatred in her eyes was palpable, and Amanda shivered. Not once, but twice, Opal had been thwarted in her attempt to be rid of Amanda. Back at Fort Laramie, when Opal had been sure she would succeed, she came to visit Amanda and Penny in their prison. She brought a Bible and offered to pray with them for the salvation of their lost souls. Amanda screamed at her to get out, that surely she must be the spawn of the devil, for their Gods could not be the same. The woman gloated, her elegant face a distortion of evil. Then she called for the guard in a terrified voice, to save her from this blasphemous woman and feigned a swoon in his arms.

Amanda was miserable. Never had she been so out of control with anger, fear, and helplessness. It was Penny who had comforted her then. Together they curled on their cot and cried. If their bond had been strong before, the four days of confinement made it unbreakable.

To pass the hours, Amanda told Penny stories of England and Africa. She told of her Aunt Sondaba, and of their escape. She told her of the warrior twin she'd never known. Together they escaped the confines of the prison's four walls through her vivid stories.

What she hadn't known at the time was that Jed Turner, weak as he was, often came to sit outside their cell window and listened. He listened with a guilty conscience, and knew his silence, due to the fear of losing his wife's sexual favors, was terribly wrong. Once, he would had scoffed at the fate of a black man or woman, but that had changed. How could he allow his silence to condemn an innocent man who had saved his life. Then, on the fourth day, the captain came to see them. He apologized for their inconvenience and released them. Stumbling into the blinding bright sun, gripping Penny's little hand, she was swept into Seamus's powerful embrace. Then, as suddenly, he had released her.

Breaking eye contact with Opal now, she glanced around for Seamus. She found him standing tall and foreboding, the wintery wind whipping through his long, black locks, his profile strong and stern against the blue background of the mountains. She waited for him to turn to her, for she knew he was aware of her eyes on him. But instead, he frowned and turned back to his horse.

Seamus, too, wondered where Jacob was, and contemplated whether Amanda was thinking about him as well. Over the past six months, his feelings had grown for Amanda, and he had long ago given up denying them. He had been unable to stay away from her. Even when things seemed their most dismal, she was enthusiastic. He remembered her excitement at the Fourth of July celebration at Independence Rock. They had been a little behind schedule and didn't arrive until the twentieth of July, but she chipped right in and helped sew the twenty-eight stars on the makeshift flag the women made. It had even been the scarlet petticoat from her trunk that made up the stripes.

He looked over to where the two women and child stood and smiled. Sarah Foster was well to be rid of her husband. With Amanda's help, she had blossomed into a very promising young woman. He almost laughed at his choice of the word *blossom*. She did, indeed, look like a rose in full bloom, her belly huge with her unborn child, and her cheeks rosy from the exertion of walking fifteen miles a day with an extra thirty or so pounds.

She'd have no problem finding a new husband. Not in this female-deprived country. Besides, he had heard at Fort Hall that the government was considering giving land grants to anyone who would settle a tract of land for five years. It was said that a single man could get up to three hundred sixty acres, while a married man could get twice that. He chuckled again to himself. If the government wanted to populate the Oregon Territory so badly so the English couldn't get it by giving away free land, every man in the territory, young and old, would be on their knees begging Mrs. Foster to marry him. Hell, for that amount, he might even do so himself, baby or no. His smile died on his lips as his eyes wandered to Amanda. No, it wouldn't be Sarah Foster's door he'd be knocking on. He shut out those thoughts before he let them fully form in his mind and turned his gaze to the town below. He wasn't ready to settle down yet. He still wanted to travel, and that was no life for a woman. As if reading his thoughts, he felt Amanda's eyes upon him. He frowned hard, unable to understand the hard lump in his throat. It was the same lump he had felt that day at Fort Laramie when he had held her in his arms. He had been so desperate when he was unable to convince the captain that Jacob had never been found guilty, and that Amanda and the child were innocent of any wrongdoing. Even the calming techniques he had learned from the wise old Nez Percé Indian eluded him. He lost his head and threatened the captain. The captain had nearly thrown him and his party from the premises. Then, miraculously, Amanda had been released. He had rushed to her cell and held her so tightly. At the memory, his eyes stung, and a shiver of anguished longing washed over his arms and chest. He hadn't wanted to let her go, and in that moment of insanity, he had almost asked her to—to what? He didn't know. Almost as abruptly as he had grasped her, he had released her. He winced as he remembered how brusquely he dismissed her. Yet, even then she had been strong and resilient. She demanded an explanation. The captain told them how Mrs. Turner had come to withdraw her accusations and to apologize for the trouble she had caused.

Seamus's frown deepened now as he felt Amanda will him to meet her eyes. Quickly, he glanced at Opal Turner, and saw the enmity she directed at Amanda. He guessed that when she withdrew her plea in Fort Laramie, it had not been her choice, but only was done under some duress. What kind, he couldn't fathom. He only knew that when he had questioned both her and her husband, Jed only smiled knowingly at his wife, and she returned the look with daggers of hatred and resentment. Jed then told Seamus of the wolves and Jacob's bravery. The confused and evasive Jed Turner of the past week was gone. This new Jed was sure of his story, apologetic for his temporary loss of memory, lauding Jacob as a hero The captain of the fort was stunned at this turn of events, and pressed for information about the wolves' whereabouts after the incident. Jed wavered only slightly, saying he wasn't sure, but hinting at the possibility that Garrett and his men might know more then they had said. But since the trappers had long since disappeared, the case was dropped. Opal seemed to wilt and said nothing. As a matter of fact, she had caused no trouble the rest of the trip. The malice was still there, like a coiled snake ready to strike, but whatever secret her husband held over her head was enough to keep it at bay—for now.

Seamus lost no time in clearing Jacob's name among the wagon party, and the man became somewhat of a hero among the children. They encouraged Jed Turner to retell the story again and again around the campfire. Time after time, the wolves got bigger and meaner. Jacob was becoming a legend.

As Seamus placed his booted foot in his stirrup, he thought

about Jacob. He was no legend. He was a flesh-and-blood man, a good man who had been deprived of his freedom, his daughter, and a beautiful woman who cared for him. In two days they would be in Willamette. The way was clear, and the wagon train could make it on its own. It was time he found Jacob and returned to him what was rightfully his.

Twenty-six

Jacob swung down from the horse, and the Indians clapped. Although the November morning was cold, he was sweating profusely. Flying Hawk slapped him on the back, shaking the buckskin fringe that laid in neat rows across Jacob's thigh-length jacket. It was a present from Swimming Fish, Flying Hawk's little sister. She made no secret of her interest in him as a potential mate.

Jacob was overwhelmed with the warm reception he received among the small Cayuse tribe. They had accepted him openly and without reservation. Their only regard to the color of his skin was awe, almost reverence, not the hatred and condescension he had known for so many years. The women found his strength, size, and skill with horses very attractive, and since many of their men had been wiped out from a measles epidemic a few months back, they encouraged the chiefs to accept him into the tribe and choose a bride for him.

"You do fancy tricks, *Umapine*, my friend." Flying Hawk laughed and patted Jacob's arm again.

"I'd be happy to teach you a few." Jacob responded, his eyes merry as they surveyed the white and speckled Appaloosa horses that the Nez Percé bred so carefully and traded with the Cayuse. They were long limbed animals with eyes that looked unnervingly human.

He enjoyed the easy camaraderie he had with the Cayuse. They shared his respect and joy of horses and treated him as an equal. They also shared his mistrust and hatred of the white man, and this concerned him. Once again, he let his white heritage cloud his happiness. Would the tribe still accept him as a brother if they were to find out that his father had been a white man? A white man who, like the others who had come here, carried diseases that killed all but his own kind? A white man who forced them to offer up five young men as scapegoats to stand trial in the white man's justice system? Yet, they had accepted Seamus. They did not hold him responsible for his race. Was it possible to care for an individual regardless of his heritage?

Jacob was present when Flying Hawk was told of the measles epidemic, then the massacre at the Whitman Mission. It seemed that the outbreak of measles had arrived with one of the wagon party heading to Willamette, and subsequently wiped out hundreds of the Indian population. Flying Hawk had lost his mother and future wife. The young brave's face did not show any emotion, but a flame of vengence flickered in his dark eyes.

The chief went on to explain how some braves in the tribe had gone to the mission seeking vengeance on the white man, and they had killed the missionaries. Still, Flying Hawk's face showed nothing. Jacob swallowed back bitter bile at the images of innocent women and children lying in their own blood, no matter their race or color. But then he looked at the worn, haggard, scarred faces of the survivors of the measles outbreak around him. A great sadness enveloped him. The prejudice, the misunderstandings. He wondered if the races would ever be able to meld, or if they would be wiped out?

Only when the chief told Flying Hawk how the white man would only leave them in peace if they turned over the culprits involved to stand trial in Willamette had the young man responded.

"Then I will be one to stand trial, for I would have done the same had I been there. The white man has done nothing but destroy our land and claim as his that which belongs only to the earth."

The chief shook his head sadly, weary with the responsibility that weighed heavily on his shoulders. "No, my son. The men have been chosen." Turning his cracked leather face to the sky, a single tear escaped his dark eyes. "It is wrong, all so wrong. They do not understand what their coming and their new ways have done to our people. Now we both must suffer."

Jacob recalled Seamus's words about a wise old chief who had taught him restraint and honor, and he wondered if this were the man. At that time, he studied the lined old face carefully, awed at the man's forgiving nature. As if reading his thoughts, the ancient man turned to place a hand on Jacob's arm.

"You must help our Flying Hawk understand. It is sad, but our ways are changing. All white men are not bad, it is their ways that harm us. But there is no changing the future. They will continue to come. Like you, they seek this land of plenty. There is enough for all, but they do not share. They wish to own that which cannot be owned. Their numbers are like the waves of the ocean, never ceasing, and if we fight them, we will be knocked down time and time again. We must learn to flow with them if we are to stay afloat." Turning to the tribe, his voice rose, becoming stronger. "The Cayuse are strong. We sprang from the heart of the beaver, and for this reason we shall survive."

Jacob saw that the words brought little comfort to the young brave beside him, but he was able to see their wisdom. Now, he thought about himself, the other black people of this country, and wondered if they, too, would be able to float with the tide. Or were they shackled with too heavy a burden? He remembered Amanda's words, in what seemed a lifetime ago. He must survive, help change things, make his great-grandchildren glad he had been born.

Suddenly, his heart filled with a longing to see her, to hear her sweet voice. He needed her. She could help him believe in her ways, perhaps to believe there was a God in all this madness and suffering. Her visage rose before him like some angelic apparition. *She is all that is good,* he thought, and clasped that thought to his heart.

It had been nearly five months since he had last seen Amanda and Penny, and the fear that he might never see them again grew increasingly more intense as the days grew shorter and the nights colder.

After escaping that night back in June, when he had been falsely accused, he learned how rough the distance between Saint Louis and the Oregon Territory was. He saw hundreds of sun-bleached oxen and horse skulls. The trail, when they came down to the river, was littered with the debris of valuable belongings that had to be left behind, and more than he cared to remember, grave markers of women, children, and babies.

Now, standing here in the wintry sunshine, the urge to find his daughter and Amanda became overwhelming. He could wait no longer. The wagon party would be arriving soon. He didn't care if the whole town of Willamette believed he had tried to murder Jed Turner. He would risk anything to see his daughter, to hold her, to see Amanda just once more. These thoughts wrenched deep within his chest, causing an exquisite anguish and longing.

"What is it, my friend?" Flying Hawk asked, as his hand stilled on Jacob's back.

"I must go. It is time I find my daughter," Jacob responded, turning to look the other man in the eye. Flying Hawk was silent for a moment, the pain of his loss and the prospect of losing yet another friend flickering across his dark eyes. Then it was gone, replaced by a mischievous light.

"And your woman, I think," the young brave laughed, as he meshed his fingers together, like he had the night they met at Seamus's campfire. Jacob grinned, saying nothing. He felt a familiar tingling and wondered if Amanda had waited for him.

"Perhaps, Seamus friend think so, too?" Flying Hawk whispered in a loud voice to the other braves around him. Jacob stiffened, and the smile dropped from his face. His imagination began to race as a murderous scowl crossed his face. Just then, a loud thundering of hooves made the gathering turn. There was no mistaking the tall, dark-headed rider who came into view.

"Speak of the devil," Jacob muttered under his breath. He remained rooted while the others hurried toward the approaching figure. With a single graceful swoop of his leg, Seamus vaulted from his horse. He wrapped the closest brave in a bear hug. Glancing up, he caught Jacob's thunderous look and released his friend.

"I see you've kept him, black skin, black mood, and all." The grin on Seamus's face was one of sheer delight, and the Indians laughed. When Jacob's upper lip began to twitch in the semblance of a smile, Seamus laughed loudly, and covered the distance between them. "I was afraid I'd done something in my absence to warrant that welcome, and for the life of me, I couldn't figure it out." At these carelessly spoken words, Jacob tensed again.

"He thinks maybe you take his woman?" Flying Hawk offered, the earlier mischief still dancing in his eyes. Jacob growled at the brave, then quickly turned back to read Seamus's eyes. The big man's grin broadened, as he slapped a large paw on Jacob's back.

"Would if I could, but she won't have me." He turned to look at the gathering with mock serious eyes. "I guess I'm too much of a paleface for her." At this, the Indians hooted with laughter, and Jacob released a small grin. He stuck out his hand, and Seamus shook it. But, in a half-serious tone, Seamus spoke softly. "Mark my words, Jacob. If ye don't get a little sense and make a move on her, I just might."

Again, the Indians around them snorted with laughter. These strange customs of getting a woman were quite ridiculous. But this time Jacob didn't laugh. He didn't doubt Seamus was more than a little serious. It made him impatient to get started.

Twenty-seven

When the initial relief of arriving at their destination after five months on the trail had worn off, Amanda was shocked and disappointed by the small town of Willamette. She hadn't expected anything as grand as London or even New York, but she had thought it would be more like Saint Louis. It wasn't. It was barely more than two wide muddy troughs, flanked on either side by small, gray, weathered wooden buildings.

How was she ever going to support herself by doing book work? As if feeling her despair, Sarah and Penny scooted closer to her. This did nothing to relieve her anxiety, but only served to remind her that she had two, soon to be three, people depending on her.

In an effort to hide her ever-growing despondency, she turned it to anger toward Seamus. Some help he had turned out to be! He had promised to help her, and before she even knew it, he had taken off for God knows where. When or if she ever saw him again, she'd give him a piece of her mind. The uncertainty weighed heavily on her mind. *Please, dear God,* she prayed, *let him return soon, and let Jacob be here.*

As the wagons rumbled down the slushy streets, Amanda was struck by the lack of young men. Seamus had told her that women were scarce here in Oregon, but every one of the people waiting to greet them on the narrow boardwalks was female or too young to count. She scanned the scattering of faces until she met the rich brown eyes of a large black woman in a snug charcoal dress, wrapped in a thick ivory wool shawl. Amanda stopped the oxen and got down from the wagon.

"Welcome to Oregon," the woman said, deep dimples piercing her shining full cheeks. "Them there with you?" she asked kindly, her eyes indicating Sarah and Penny, still sitting upon the high buckboard seat of the wagon.

"Yes, they are. That is Mrs. Sarah Foster from Maine. This is Penny. Penny from Georgia, and we are looking for her father, Jacob. I'm sorry, I don't know his last name, but he is tall, of muscular build, and a very—attractive black man," Amanda responded, ducking her head self-consciously at the last few words. The woman nodded to both Penny and Sarah, then turned her gaze back to Amanda.

"Sorry, I don't know no Jacob. I'm Wanda. Wanda Richmond. And I didn't hear you tell your name, honey." The woman's voice was deep and rich, with a distinct southern drawl. Amanda flushed at the intimate endearment, and immediately felt she had found a friend. "Amanda. Amanda T. Smith," Amanda answered with a smile. The large woman grinned back and beckoned the three to follow her.

Unwilling to leave the tired oxen tied out front, blocking the street, Amanda left Penny and Sarah and drove the team to the end of the street, hobbling them in a nearby stretch of yellowing grass. Picking her way carefully up the muddy road, she despaired of keeping her hem clean.

Forty minutes later, she found the small wooden house behind the main structures of the street where Mrs. Richmond had taken Sarah and Penny. Knocking on the door, she entered an exceedingly warm room smelling strongly of lye soap.

"Welcome to Wanda's Laundry," Wanda bellowed with pride from a small table at the back.

Over weak hot tea and thick, buttery biscuits, Amanda

learned that Wanda took in laundry, and that her husband, Gregory, was a carpenter. He was always busy now, because almost every able-bodied male had gone to California in search of gold. Some of the letters that made it back promised Willamette would be a very wealthy town when the men returned.

"My Gregory would have gone, too, but we didn't want to risk leaving me here alone." The large woman sighed heavily and took another sip of tea before she leaned forward, her ample bosom resting on the small table. "You see, they don't really want no Negroes here in Oregon, but they overlook a few of us. There are always those who want to cause trouble, though." Wanda sat back with a stern shake of her head and took a small bite out of a golden-brown biscuit. "We thought about moving north, but I'm scared of the Indians. They're gonna hang five of them soon for scalping the missionaries up at the Whitman Mission." Amanda suppressed a shudder as Wanda said the words. She pushed away her plate of biscuits and saw Sarah blanch. Wanda continued nibbling on her biscuit and continued. "Gov'ment won't even allow no homesteading up near them vicious Cayuse." Amanda was stunned as she recalled the wonderful evening she had spent with Flying Hawk.

"Not all of them are vicious," Amanda blurted out. Wanda stopped eating, and her eyes narrowed to little slits.

"Mark my words, child. Them Indians have no faith in the good Lord, and they're nothing but savages." When she was sure the impact of her words had sunk in, she continued. "Some says blacks is safe, that they even made a black man chief of the Crows. A man named Beckworth. Yes, that's it, Jim Beckworth. Then there is that black man who done settled up north and grows wheat with no problems. I met him one time. He were a nice fellow name of George Bush. He got himself a big plot of land and made hisself a right rich man."

At these words, Amanda could barely contain her excitement. Seamus had been wrong. Black people could own land. She nearly wanted to clap with joy. Jacob would be so happy. Her mind began racing. Maybe he already had a plot of land.

"Then, anybody can own land?" Amanda asked, Indians and massacres nearly forgotten.

"Nope," Wanda responded evenly, continuing to eat another biscuit off the plate. "Mr. Bush's got a white wife, and white foster parents that done bought it for him." Noting the crushing look of disappointment that fell across Amanda's face, she put down her bread and patted Amanda's arm.

"There, there, honey. Don't you give up so easy." Wanda turned her gaze to Sarah and spoke bluntly. "You ain't got no man, do you?" When Sarah flushed and shook her head, Wanda brushed it off with a wave of her fingers. "No matter, then. You can put in the claim, and you two can be partners." Sitting back, Wanda looked critically at the three females sitting around her table. "Now, how you're gonna support yourselves, that's a horse of a different color." Her fleshy brow wrinkled into rolls of concentration, and she began tapping their bulges with a thick forefinger.

"I was hoping to do some bookkeeping," Amanda offered hopefully. The large woman's eyes flew open wide.

"You know your numbers and letters?" The disbelief in Wanda's voice was unmistakable. When Amanda nodded, the woman rubbed her hands together gleefully. "With half the town who knows how to read gone, you could be in business. Now, Miss Foster here is probably gonna have to front for ya, and her being so pregnant ain't very good, but I know a few businesswomen who won't mind." At this point Wanda rose and began pacing the small room's confines.

"Now, most work you'll have to do in trade, 'cause most folks ain't got much cash to spare. But that'll keep you with food for the winter." Wanda suddenly looked up, as if remembering the other women in the room. Her eyes became large, sparkling brown disks of excitement. "You could help me and do mine and my husband's numbers in exchange for him helping you build a nice little house." She paused only for a moment to wait for Amanda's nod of approval, then continued breathlessly.

"Maggie. That's it. I'll introduce you to Maggie. She's a good woman, and she'll pay you in cash. What with the soldiers and the trappers and the returning men from California, she'll have much need of your services." The excitement the big woman exuded was almost tangible in the small, steamy room.

"When can I meet Maggie?" Amanda asked, scooting her chair back with a screech across the wood plank floor. She was caught up in the excitement. Just when she had thought God had closed the door, he had opened a window of hope with Wanda Richmond.

"What kind of business does Maggie run?" Sarah asked, her face flushed with enthusiasm. "Some kind of mercantile? Maybe I could help, too." Suddenly. Wanda stopped moving, her short thick fingers coming together before her ample bossom. She looked first at Sarah, then at Amanda, then at Penny.

"A mercantile? Well, of a sort. You must remember that out here, to survive one must do what one must." With this vague explanation, Mrs. Richmond grabbed up her shawl and proceeded to the front door. At the door, she stopped and looked over her shoulder. "Perhaps Miss Foster would stay with Penny. Amanda, come with me, and we'll go talk to Maggie."

Sarah uttered a weak mewl of protest, then sat down again, as she gazed at her large protuding stomach. It would be better for Amanda to go alone. It would be more professional.

* * *

"You're in what profession?" Amanda nearly shouted, as she stood facing the redheaded woman.

"I like to think of it as arts and entertainment," the woman replied saucily, giving her bright, shoulder-length curls a jounce with one hand, as she placed the other on a tightly corseted waist. She seemed not the least bit embarrassed or upset at Amanda's obvious shock.

"Remember what I said, Miss Smith," Wanda whispered in a loud stage whisper. "Out here a body's gotta to do what they gots to."

Amanda whirled to look at her new friend. "You think this sort of thing is all right? You, who spoke of believing in the good Lord?" Amanda could feel the indignation rising in her chest as she struggled to keep her voice civil and controlled. "You thought I would consider working in a *house of joy?*"

"House of joy?" Maggie interrupted, a slow smile spreading across her carmine red lips. "Is that what you call it in England? I like it! I like it! Maggie's House of Joy."

Amanda turned back to her hostess, unable to disguise the look of shock and amazement. This woman wasn't the least bit uncomfortable with Amanda's outrage, but instead took the English word for whorehouse and put it to use.

With a smile still playing on her full lips, Maggie began circling Amanda. At first Amanda tried to rotate to keep her eyes level with Maggie's, refusing to be appraised like a prize piece of horseflesh, but she had to stop when she felt her skirts tangling, causing her to almost lose her balance.

"I demand that you stop this humiliating behavior," Amanda choked out, her cheeks burning with outrage.

"Honey, we're just trying to help you," Wanda said gently, and led Amanda to a worn velvet upholstered settee. "Think about that poor little girl and that very pregnant Miss Foster. They're countin' on you. They won't make it through the winter without some kind of shelter, and charity can only go so far."

The truth and kindness with which the words were spoken were all too much for Amanda. Resisting the urge to lay her head down on her arms and cry, she turned to Maggie with a fierce look of determination.

"Mrs. Richmond is right. I must do what I must do. How much are you willing to pay me for keeping your accounts?"

Maggie smiled ruefully, wet her bottom lip with her tongue, and began to *tsk* sadly.

"The Lord certainly saw to bless you in both departments, Miss Smith. You got brains and an exquisite body and face. Are you sure you won't consider becoming one of my girls? I'd pay you three times as much for those services. My customers would find you so exotic." Amanda felt her face burn hotter and started to rise. Maggie put out a long, bejeweled hand to stop her. "Don't be offended. You judge us too harshly." As the madam spoke the words, her face became weary and old for her years. "Most of the women here didn't choose to of their own free will. Many of them lost husbands and had no other means of survival. Wanda told me about your friend, Miss Foster. Without you, what would she do?" The words hit Amanda like a slap in the face, and she felt a surge of maternal protection for her young friend.

"I will do your book work only, if you'll still hire me, but you must promise me that you will never tempt Sarah with the other occupation you just offered me." With these words spoken, Amanda rose and stuck out her hand. Maggie took it willingly.

She liked this young woman. She had guts and determination.

Twenty-eight

Jacob was frustrated at the slow progress they were making. Heavy snow had fallen a week before, and it delayed them by at least four days. After his intitial reticence with Seamus, Jacob began to question him about the trip westward. He tried to keep his questions nonchalant when they concerned Amanda, but after a few days, he found that Seamus was more than willing to talk about her.

One day, they happened upon a small group of men herding a scraggly bunch of cattle. The animals looked thin and weak, and the men looked hardly better.

"Where you headed?" Seamus bellowed out to the head rider, his breath coming out in swirls of steam in the cold morning air. The man cocked his rifle, and rode closer for a look.

"And who might you be?" the man asked, the barrels of his gun poised at Seamus's chest. Seamus held up the empty palms of his gloved hands, and spoke in a warm, friendly tone.

"I'm Seamus McCarthy, and this here is Jacob Smith." The man eyed them carefully for a moment without speaking. A swarthy man with oily black hair joined him. They exchanged a few words in Spanish, and then studied Seamus and Jacob again. Seamus slowly lowered his hands to his thighs, his horse shifting ever so slightly beneath him. "It's awfully late to be herding up this way," Seamus said thoughtfully, then added, "Are you planning to take these cattle to Canada? Don't look as if they'd make it." These words spoken, the strange men scowled, then relaxed, their faces showing the lines of a rough journey.

"No, they won't make it to Canada. We was herding 'em up from California for the fort in Walla Walla, when we heard about the incident with the Cayuse. The fort and the missions been shut down?" The last words were spoken more as a question than a statement, and Seamus nodded his head.

When the man didn't continue, Seamus spoke. "We're heading to Willamette. You're welcome to travel with us. The fort there might buy the beef."

The man shook his head sadly. "Nope. They just had three wagon trains enter, and them folks were more than willing to sell their cattle."

Jacob had remained silent the whole time until now. The seed of an idea was taking hold in his mind. He cleared his voice and spoke slowly. "If you ain't gonna take the herd to Canada, and you ain't gonna take the herd back, what's you gonna do with them?" Jacob kept his face perfectly emotionless, struggling to keep the rising hope from his features. He heard Seamus's saddle creak as he turned to look at him, but Jacob didn't meet his eyes. He just kept them steady on the man he was addressing.

"Well," the man said thoughtfully, "I don't rightfully know." Placing one gloved hand on top of the other, and resting it on his saddlehorn, he turned to his partner. When the swarthy man lifted his shoulders in a shrug, the other man continued. "We've been wrestling with just that. We ran into some trouble a ways back. Andy was hurt, and we lost near a third of our herd."

Jacob looked past the man's shoulder and noticed for the

first time the third man in the distance, who was slouched in his saddle.

"How many you got?" Jacob asked, flicking his eyes over the herd and then back to the speaker.

"Bout sixty head," the man returned, a spark of hope flashing through his gray eyes. "You fellows in the market?"

"Maybe," Jacob responded. Seamus's gasp was audible.

"Fort Walla Walla was gonna pay us three dollars a head." The man paused, looked at his friend, at the injured Andy, and lastly at the straggly bunch of cattle. "But for you, two."

Jacob knew he was taking a gamble, but the sudden dream of owning his own ranch, of never having to toil in the backbreaking job of harvesting, like his ancestors had done for so many years as slaves, was too real.

"One and a half, cash here and now," Jacob countered. The two men looked at each other, exchanged a few more words in Spanish, and then the silent swarthy one spoke.

"For you, amigo, it is a deal." He stuck out his hand, and Jacob shook it with a broad grin. Then, carefully, he pulled a stack of bills from beneath his jacket. He heard Seamus gasp again, and his smile grew wider.

Jacob could not suppress his pure joy as he surveyed the first bit of property he had ever really owned. The hope that he had struggled to supress surged through his body, filling his lungs, swelling his chest, making him want to cry out, to raise his arms to the heavens with wild abandon. He wanted to sing with the fervor and the joy he had witnessed in the Negro religious gatherings of his youth. But this song would not be to God, but to this glorious land, to freedom. It would be his song, freedom's song.

"What in God's name has gotten into you, man?" Seamus asked, as he saw the three men ride off in haste, afraid that Jacob might change his mind.

"I'm gonna be a rancher. I'm gonna supply beef to the forts

at a cheaper rate than the ranchers in California can." Now he turned to Seamus with a earnest gleam in his eyes. "Don't you see, I won't have to trek them over thousands of miles, forcing them to become skinny, tough meat. I'll be right here." His face was wreathed in exultation as he spread his arms wide to encompass the terrain around him.

"But there ain't no fort in Walla Walla anymore. There ain't no mission, no fort. No mission, no buyer," Seamus nearly shouted in exasperation. "Besides, you have to own land to ranch, and the government ain't letting nobody settle in this land because of the massacre. Second..." Seamus's voice trailed off before he spoke the next words. Jacob frowned. He knew what Seamus was going to say. A black man couldn't buy property. Suddenly Jacob's face cleared, and he moved his horse closer to Seamus's.

"You could."

In response, Seamus shook his head. "I don't know nothing about these animals. I don't want to be tied down. The government won't—" Jacob interrupted him with a frustrated grunt.

"Don't you see? One, you don't have to know anything about these animals, I do. Second, you don't have to settle down. I just want you to lay the land claim for me. I give you a cut of the profits when there are some. And last, this land is perfect for grazing, and the government might make an exception for you because you know the Indians here. You speak their language. You could convince the authorities that it would be in the best interest of everyone. You know that eventually there will be forts and towns all over this land. We could be first. We could get the land for dirt cheap." This outpouring of his hope, and more words than he had ever spoken to this man at one time, left Jacob feeling drained as he waited for Seamus's response. Black eyes held blue in a long silence.

Finally, Seamus looked away, his eyes wandering over the landscape. Slowly, he began to speak. "We could try, I suppose. We could stop here for a while and build a compound for the animals. A house." He turned to Jacob, a smile on his face. Jacob felt his breath rush out him, unaware until that moment that he had been holding it.

"You'll try, then?" Jacob asked, a frozen place in his heart starting to thaw, a warm shimmer of hope beginning to burn. Seamus pulled off his glove and extended his hand. In the frosty air, warm palm rested against warm palm.

Twenty-nine

The tiny squalls filled the small room, then silenced abruptly as Sarah pulled Emanuel to her full breast. Amanda sighed wistfully as she moved closer to the mother and child and ran a finger through the soft, dark down on the infant's head. Sarah smiled, her face radiant with motherly love.

"I'll be back late, so don't wait up," Amanda said softly to Sarah as she crossed the small room and silently closed the cabin's door. It had been over a month since she and Sarah had moved into one of the small living quarters behind Maggie's House of Joy. She still missed Penny and longed for next Sunday when she would come into town.

She and Sarah realized that with the upcoming winter, the new baby, and no word from Jacob, they would have to stay with Maggie until spring, when they could build their own cabin. They decided it best that Penny go to live with Doc and Mrs. Winslow.

Penny resisted at first, sobbing into Amanda's skirt that she wanted to stay, but Amanda was adamant and promised she would visit often. She almost relented when the small girl flung her arms around her neck saying, "I love you so much. I wish you were my mother." But Amanda realized that she just couldn't allow the girl to live in the shadow of a whorehouse.

Now, as Amanda stepped out into the long shadows of the late afternoon, she pulled her shawl closer around her shoulders, lifted the corner of her skirt, and dashed for the back steps outside the big, two-story building. The muffled clatter of dishes and glasses could be heard from the small diner/bar below, as she opened the second-floor door. She slammed it tightly, shutting out the chilly December wind. The narrow hallway she entered was dimly lit, lined with closed doors. Turning her key into Maggie's bedroom/office, she listened to the sounds of the girls getting ready for their evening customers. As Christmas grew nearer, more and more of the soldiers, trappers, and mountain men visited the establishment more frequently. It made her sad to think of these lonely men, who probably were looking more for companionship than a bed partner.

Lighting the small oil lamp on the desk, she pulled out the ledgers from a dresser drawer next to it. She paused momentarily as she caught her reflection in the small gilt mirror above it. Her hair had grown long enough now to pull back in a single braid, and coil at least one round at the nape of her neck. She self-consciously tucked a small stray wisp of hair away from her temple. Her face had become gaunt since the last time she spent any time looking at her reflection. Her eyes seemed big and luminous, and her high cheekbones accentuated the hollows in her cheeks.

Just then she heard a giggle in the next room and a deep male voice murmuring something seductive. The woman giggled again. Then she heard the leather straps of the bed groan. A flutter of disgust mixed with excitement danced in the pit of Amanda's stomach. She glanced down at the pale blue ledger in her hand. Her eyes turned to the varied collection of bottles, vials, and brushes beside it. In the next room, the man moaned loudly, his voice harsh with desire as he cried for more. Amanda's breath quickened, and she fought to keep her mind from striving to know what was going on beyond the wall. Again, her eyes went to the collection of perfumes and cosmetics. Maggie had encouraged her to try them, to see what they could do for her beauty. Amanda slammed the drawer shut, her breath coming in short, heavy breaths, matching the loud panting coming from the room next door. Suddenly, the room was unbearably hot. She realized that the brothel's patrons were not the only ones who were lonely. The image of Jacob rose up before her. He was moaning her name, his shirt was unbuttoned to his waist, his dark chest gleamed with sweat, highlighting the play of muscles across its broad expanse.

Amanda sat down on the edge of the bed, trickles of perspiration dotting her forehead, upper lip, and collarbone. With unsteady hands, she unbuttoned the top five buttons of her bodice, fanning the ledger back and forth to cool her burning flesh. The moans next door became a duet of passion. She covered her ears, biting her bottom lip until she could taste the salty metallic taste of her blood.

What was happening to her? She had been sitting in this room week after week, listening to these same sounds, and they had filled her with disgust. Now they were doing strange things to her body, creating cravings. Cravings for what?

"Oh, Jacob, touch me again, here and oh—" The husky female voice filtered through the thin wall, filling the room with the music of wanton desire. The name. Amanda knew it wasn't her Jacob, but it was enough to release the longing and desire that had been building in her since the day he had crushed her to his chest, her body running the length of his, his eyes dark with desire as he said, "*I like you jes' like this.*" She remembered his all-consuming kisses the night he had escaped.

Feet on the floor, Amanda laid back on the bed, running her hand down the contours of her body. What would it feel like to have a man's, Jacob's, hands caress her body, suckle her breast? The tingling in the pit of her stomach dropped lower, becoming a real ache. She felt the crux of her legs growing warm and damp. She should stop her mind, get back to her work, stop these feelings before they overwhelmed her. She unbuttoned another button on her blouse and placed a tentative hand on her breast. Suddenly the door burst open. Jacob stood staring at her, his eyes filled with anger, disgust, and long-suffering desire.

Was this a dream? Amanda struggled to lift herself from the bed. The door shut, and Jacob was moving across the room, one hand unbuttoning his shirt, the other his breeches. Amanda lay mesmerized by the unfolding scene before her, her eyes soaking in the sight of him. Then he was on top of her, his breath hot upon her bared skin. Reality sank in as she struggled to get out from beneath him.

"Please, Jacob, what are you doing?" Amanda cried breathlessly, her heart pounding savagely, her voice weak and frightened. Jacob heard none of it, as he replaced her hand with his in the gaping bodice, exposing first one then two dusty, titillated breasts.

"Expecting another customer?" he spat angrily, as he gazed at the lovely sight of her body. He couldn't stand the thought of other men having gazed upon her as he was doing now. Jacob felt an anguished burning clutching his chest, searing his battered heart. He wanted to cry out in pain, pain at her betrayal. Instead, he wrenched at the hem of her skirt, pinning her legs between his. For six long months—no, even longer—he had thought of her as his pure, innocent Amanda. She had led him to believe she was that. She had deceived him. Why, he didn't know. But now he would have what he had so long denied himself. "Don't worry. I'll pay you what you're worth." The material of her skirt ripped with a tearing rent, and he felt the damp warm expanse of skin in the opening of her drawers. Jacob's hands were caressing, gentle but urgent. Amanda felt her body responding to the exquisite new sensation, but her mind rebelled at the rage and lack of respect motivating those hands, and she let out an ear-piercing scream. The door crashed open.

"Get him off of her." Maggie's bellowing voice filled the small room, as half a dozen hands yanked Jacob off Amanda. Amanda scrambled to the far corner of the bed, pulling her knees up to her bare chest, sobbing silently.

"Get out! Get out now!" Maggie screamed at Jacob, as two large, half-dressed men dragged him from the room. His eyes never left Amanda's. She was crying. For God's sake, the whore was crying.

Jacob turned to Maggie in disgust. "I was willing to pay."

Amanda burst forth into more sobs as the door closed in his face. He suddenly felt sick with anger, regret, self-loathing.

Seamus stood pale and stone-faced as he dragged Jacob down the wooden stairs. He had been visiting Sarah Foster when he heard the scream. He hoped to make a little sense of the things that had occurred since he'd left to find Jacob, but he hadn't gotten a chance.

He and Jacob had arrived in town about three hours ago, and first went to get a nickel bath and shave. Upon learning Penny was out of town staying with the Winslows, Jacob decided to locate Amanda. Seamus laughed at how nervous and shy he had become all of a sudden, and encouraged him to bring her a small present. They spent the next hour at the fort shopping for a small gold locket. There they ran into Opal Turner. Opal wasted no time in apologizing to Jacob about the unfortunate misunderstanding on the journey, and how she hoped there were no hard feelings. Her words seemed insincere, as did her eyes. It was then that she pulled them aside and whispered her deepest sympathy about the unfortunate turn of events with Miss Smith. She went on to say how

Amanda and Sarah had gone to work for the local whorehouse in town. In closing, she smiled smugly at Seamus, and reminded him that she always knew the girl was up to no good. As they watched the woman go, Seamus turned to see Jacob's face twisted in rage. Mistaking that the direction of his rage was at Mrs. Turner for her obvious lie, he encouraged Jacob to go check out Amanda's whereabouts while he sought out Mrs. Foster.

"What the hell was that all about?" Seamus whispered in a choked voice. He wanted to throttle the man. How could he be so stupid? Maybe Seamus had misjudged him. Maybe. He called on all his reserve of calm and indifference. He would hear both sides. Jacob attempted to shrug off Seamus's hand, but Seamus held tight.

"She's a whore, and still she wouldn't have me." Suddenly Jacob's large frame convulsed with sobs. "I, I—" The small gold locket fell from his grasp on to the frozen ground. Seamus struggled with the realization that Jacob had obviously seen something to convince himself that Amanda was one of Maggie's girls. Guilt and sadness washed over him. He led Jacob to his horse.

"Let's go see Penny." Seamus untied the horses, and they rode off into the starless night in silence.

Amanda sat on Maggie's bed with a patchwork quilt around her shoulders. The tears had stopped, but she was still shaking, and the hurt was deep.

"It's all right now. You drink this," Maggie admonished, as she handed Amanda a small glass full of whiskey. "I won't let that brute in here ever again. I never would have in the first place had I known. He just seemed so decent, said he knew you. That you'd be expecting him." The older woman stroked her chin as she looked at Amanda's bloodless face. Something wasn't right. Amanda hadn't wanted to send Maggie's thugs after him, and her crying had seemed more from a deep loss than from nearly being raped. "You want to talk about it?" Maggie asked as she shooed the other girls who had come running with their clients at the scream from the room. "I'm a real good listener."

Amanda looked away. She didn't want Maggie to see that her heart was breaking. She had been so sure that Jacob was different. Different than Sarah's husband. She shuddered. He had thought her a whore, no better than Opal Turner's gossip on the trail. He hadn't physically hurt her, and yet she felt as if her very life had been crushed. She wiped her eyes with the back of her hand and swallowed a deep sob. Then how could she still want him near her? Before he had come to her, she had wanted his weight and warmth. She had felt exhilarated in the dark desire and awe when he had gazed at her naked breast. She had tingled with sweet agony when his hand had caressed the sensitive skin of her thigh. Now she closed her eyes and willed the memories away. He had thought she was a whore, his for the taking, to be bought. Maggie sat patiently at the end of the bed.

"You're a virgin, ain't you?" Maggie asked softly. Amanda nodded and sniffled. The older woman's voice grew soft, almost reverent. "It can be a wonderful thing between a man and a woman. But they both gotta be willing." Maggie moved closer, her hand resting tentatively on Amanda's, clasped around the untouched whiskey. "Aside from all this, you care for that fellow, don't you?" Amanda could not meet Maggie's eyes, but only nodded. Maggie sighed heavily.

"Sometimes men get so stupid about these things. They think with their crotch instead of their heads." She rose to go, then turned. "You can stay here tonight if you want, but I don't think he'll be back."

"Maggie," Amanda whispered, new tears pooling in her eyes. "How can I love him after this? If he could do this, he surely doesn't care for me." The other woman came to her, wrapping her in her arms, pulling her cheek against her breasts. Amanda closed her eyes, breathing in the heavy smell of talc and cheap perfume.

"Oh, honey, men are so difficult to understand sometimes. I think that man does care for you. I could tell when he first came asking for you. He was all spruced up, with a look of fear, and puppy love all over his freshly shaven face. It's just that when he thought you were one of my girls, well, some men are sort of crazy when it comes to sharing what they consider is theirs. See, they think a whore ain't a woman with a real heart, because they can buy her affections and physical love, and they have to earn 'em with proper young ladies." Amanda heard a small catch in Maggie's voice as she said these words, and Amanda wondered if behind that painted smile was a broken heart.

"Then ask her to marry you if you can't stand the thought of another man with his paws on her," Seamus remarked, his voice clipped in exasperation. Jacob shook his head.

"I'd be better off to just forget her."

Seamus wrinkled his forehead in disgust.

"Why don't you go talk to her?"

Jacob rose from his seat by the Winslows' hearth. Slowly, he unfurled his large hands, one after the other, and studied them like some gypsy trying to see his future.

"It ain't no use. I'm sure she hates me now, even if she cared for me before. Besides, I can't marry a wh...a who...a woman like her. I got a little daughter to consider. Besides, I could never sleep with her without thinking about how many other men had before me." Suddenly he curled his hands shut into tight fists. For a moment he looked at them like he wanted to hit something, then they dropped limply to his sides.

The truth of the matter was that he wasn't going to be able

to forget about her. As he worked through the rest of the winter finishing his barn and the fences, he thought about Amanda daily. Sometimes, late at night when the cold winds howled through the open fields and towering pines, he would awaken drenched in sweat, his body and soul craving to recapture those few moments of closeness he had had with her before his escape with Flying Eagle. These nights he would hold the simple locket he had meant to give Amanda, rubbing his thumb over its golden smoothness. Several times he had become so frustrated, angry, and lonely, that he had thrown it across the room, or even out the door. But always he would retrieve it, as if the small piece of metal was somehow his last connection to her.

His heart no longer sang with joy over his budding ranch or his and his daughter's freedom. Penny had begun slinking around the house like a beaten hound, until he had finally agreed to let her go into town to visit Amanda and Sarah. He had tried to accompany her and Seamus once, but had become so despondent and depressed when the brothel had come into sight that he had begged off and gone to the fort instead.

The early months of the new year hadn't been easy for Amanda, either. She had gone through the days in a stupor, working from sunup until late into the night, never letting her mind wander to the broken dreams that had helped her through the long, treacherous journey west. She had thought that after her aunt's death she would never feel such grief and loss again, but she had been wrong.

She had been surprised when Penny had arrived unannounced with Seamus that early February day, but the brief gush of pleasure had been dimmed when she had glanced out the window to see Jacob's retreating back, his rejection clear. The sight had made her irate, allowing her outrage to diminish the pain.

Seamus and Sarah banged their collective heads against the

wall with exasperation at their friends' stubborn pride and self-imposed pain. But neither Amanda nor Jacob wanted to discuss the other, feeling that what could have been was lost, and that it was best not to speak of it.

Thirty

Winter passed, and the spring rains came. Willamette became crowded with men returning from the goldfields of California. And, so it seemed, the rumors had been true. The town was flooded with gold dust. Amanda's bookkeeping services were in much demand, and in early April, she, Sarah, and little Emanuel were able to move into their own small, snug cabin. Amanda started a garden, and after work, she tended it, cooing at the pudgy little baby rolling around on a blanket spread beneath the tamarack trees.

"Do you think you'll ever get married and have your own baby?" Sarah asked from the doorway, as she watched the woman and child. Amanda sat back on her heels, brushing the rich black dirt from her fingers. A wistful smile touched her lips.

"I don't know. Probably not." She leaned forward to touch one of the baby's pink toes. The child gurgled happily. "I'll just borrow yours for now." Sarah smiled, then frowned. Just as Seamus had forecast, the United States government had passed the Donation Land Grant Act, giving three hundred fifty acres of land free to any man who would claim it and settle it for five years. It also stipulated that a man and wife could get twice that. A week didn't go by when at least one would-be suitor didn't knock on their door. Even a few of the girls at Maggie's had received and accepted proposals of marriage.

Amanda looked up and noticed the troubled look on her friend's face. The child Sarah had been at the beginning of their journey in Independence, Missouri, was no longer visible. In a little less than a year, Sarah had turned into a woman, mind, body, and soul.

Amanda smiled. "If the right man comes around for you, things could change, but I will always be your friend." She turned to little Emanuel again. "And you'll always be my big boy, won't you?" The infant waved his fat little fists and cooed.

"I'm still a married woman, Amanda," Sarah said softly, and turned to reenter the small, one-room cabin. Amanda watched her leave. She felt sorry for her friend. Because of Emanuel, Sarah refused to annul her marriage. Once Amanda might have thought that it would have been herself that would have been the one to be planning a wedding, but now she had no dreams of becoming a bride. She stuck her small spade into the damp dirt, smelling the fresh scent of the rich, dark soil.

Seamus continued to come and visit. He made a pretense of bringing Penny to see them, and of scrutinizing Sarah's would-be suitors. Amanda had had a few, but she hadn't even entertained the notion and had sent them on their way. Now that spring was here, Seamus would be heading back east, and the visits from Penny would end. Amanda had only seen Jacob once since that awful visit in December, and he hadn't even spoken to her. Not that she had expected him to. He'd made it clear enough what he thought of her, or at least what he thought her to be. She felt a flush of indignation sting her cheeks. How could he have ever thought that she could have sunken so low, become so desperate, as to become one of Maggie's girls? Besides, hadn't he asked her to wait for him? She pursed her lips tightly in an angry pucker, her teeth gritted firmly behind them. She'd waited. Waited for what? His lack of faith in her, his physical abuse? No she didn't need a man so shallow and weak. Angry, bitter tears blurred her vision. Seamus and Sarah had both told her to go to Jacob, to explain. Seamus had said that Jacob wouldn't listen to anything he had to say, but might believe her, that Jacob was hurting, that he needed her.

Amanda squeezed her eyes shut, willing her damned tears to go away. Jacob need her? Her stomach tumbled, as it always did when she thought of him. Could she go to him and explain? What if he didn't believe her? Should she go to him and tell him that he had been wrong, that she wasn't what he thought her to be, that he had . . . that it could be like it was? But could it really? No, she thought as she jabbed her spade into the earth with an angry thrust. It was just as well to leave things as they were.

She had had this argument too many times in her head and in her heart, and her heart always lost. Despite the fact that Maggie had told her many men felt possessive of the women they loved, that did not justify or excuse Jacob's actions. What if Maggie had not been there to stop him? She shuddered at the thought of the irreparable damage that would have been done, yet sagged at the loss of physical intimacy she might never know. What then? What if circumstances had been different, and she'd had little choice, like some of the sad, unfortunate women she had since come to know, who had been forced to choose between starvation and prostitution?

No, if she ever married, she wanted it to be to a man who loved and accepted her for what she was, not what she'd done or hadn't done. Opening her eyes, Amanda raised her chin a notch, jutting it out slightly. She wanted a man who would think well of her, not condemn her before giving her a chance to defend herself. Amanda stiffened her spine, inhaling a deep breath, flaring her nostrils with umbrage. If the truth be told, she didn't want to have to defend herself at all. She shouldn't have to defend herself. *She* had done nothing wrong. It was Jacob who should come crawling, or at least on bended knee, asking for understanding, not the other way around. Jacob should be the one. She stopped, her shoulders sagging forward. Jacob would do nothing. Amanda told herself that tears did no good, that time healed all. She prayed silently that it was true. As if in apology for the angry thrusts she had directed at Mother Earth with her spade, she gently patted the upturned soil over a few seeds.

"Wish that I were that patch of dirt and received such tender care," Seamus called out, as he galloped into the clearing in front of their cabin. Amanda's face lit up with joy as Penny nearly vaulted from the horse. "Easy does it, half pint," Seamus said with a laugh, as he handed the wiggling girl down to Amanda's outstretched arms.

Amanda no longer blushed at the flirtatious way Seamus talked to her. In the beginning of the year, hat in hand, he had offered to marry her, to take her away from her life of sin. At first she had been outraged, then she had been amused. She told him that she worked for Maggie, but not as one of her girls. They had both laughed, and she had told him what a dear friend he was, but nothing more. Then she had been a fool to hope that Jacob would follow suit.

As the months went by and Jacob didn't come, she had at first been afraid that Seamus's and Penny's visits would cease, but he had continued to visit, bringing Penny and spending more and more time with Emanuel. He would talk to the baby in a deep Irish brogue, and Sarah would watch him with adoring eyes. She never said a word, but Amanda knew that had there been no Billy, and Seamus asked, there would be no doubt as to who Sarah would marry. But Seamus never asked, and no word of Billy ever came.

"I've missed you so, Penny!" Amanda cried, as she whirled

the little girl around in her arms.

"Good. Then you'll come take care of me," the little girl cried, wrapping her arms tightly around Amanda's neck. She turned a bright face, wreathed in smiles, to Seamus. "See. I told you everything would be all right."

Placing the little girl on the ground, Amanda turned serious eyes to Seamus. "Is Jacob all right?" Try as she might, Amanda couldn't keep the frightened concern from her voice.

"He's gone. Went to California to get a stud bull. The ones we got ain't good enough stock, or so Jacob says. Mrs. Winslow's been watching half pint here, and came down with a pox," Seamus said, as he swung down from his mount.

"Is it serious?" Amanda asked.

"No, but it's very contagious, the doc says. She has to be quarantined for a fortnight or so." Seamus stepped over to Penny and ruffled the frizzy curls on her head. "I just hope half pint didn't catch it. I had it once, so Doc says I'm immune." He paused again and looked past her head to Amanda. "Would you consider coming out? I don't think it would be a good idea to let her stay here with the baby and all." He looked pointedly at Emanuel trying desperately to roll over, but one arm kept getting in the way. "The doc says it ain't deadly, but might be hard on one so little." Amanda felt her chest tighten, and raised a hand to press against the uncomfortable pressure.

"Why can't *you?*" She demanded, slightly breathless as if she had been running instead of standing still. She couldn't go live in Jacob's house. What would he say? How would it look? Seamus shifted his large frame uncomfortably, his hands restlessly playing with the leather reins.

"I can't. I don't know." Seamus's glance fell to his hands, then out over his horse's profile, before it came back to her. "Damn, Amanda, I don't know about taking care of little girls and such." He waved his hand in a fluttering motion to indicate that elusive "and such." Amanda felt a little of the tension ease from her shoulders, as she saw it perch on his.

"Of course you do, and can," Amanda retorted in her strictest governessy way. She wasn't prepared for the barrage of tears that streamed down Penny's face.

"Seamus promised you'd come. He said you loved me and would take care of me. I . . . I wanted you to come see my house." The little girl pulled from Amanda's sudden grasp and ran to Seamus. Amanda stared at him with eyes full of accusation. Seamus glanced down at the small head of soft, springy curls that only reached just below his belt. He patted one of the thin brown arms that curled tightly around his thigh. He then looked up, his eyes a beseeching blue. He didn't need to say anything. Her body gave her away, as it slumped into resignation. *Jacob won't even be there,* she reminded herself silently.

Amanda looked past Seamus to the doorway where Sarah now stood, her heart in her eyes.

"You go on. Manny and I'll be fine. But let me pack you a little something before you go." Sarah bustled back into the kitchen, trying hard not to show her disappointment at losing Amanda for an indefinite amount of time and not being able to have Penny and Seamus stay for dinner. Amanda didn't argue, as she had never quite mastered the arts of the kitchen and left the cooking to Sarah.

The ride to Jacob's and Seamus's ranch took a little over two and a half hours. Amanda was amazed at the size of their cabin. It was actually two cabins connected by a breezeway. The main room held a loft, where Penny slept. The tamarack walls were lined with sweet-smelling cedar, and the hearth boasted a large stone fireplace with a small arched alcove above it to serve as an oven. Seamus showed her around the house and out back to a small spring house where the milk, eggs, and butter were stored. Amanda gulped in surprise. It had been ages since she had had real butter. As she walked around the small enclosure and watched the cool spring water pouring in, she spied another small, covered bucket.

"What's in here?"

Penny grinned from ear to ear. "We got cream. Mrs. Winslow made it special for me."

"Well, then," Amanda cried, "we shall have a right and proper English tea."

After tea, Seamus left for the Cayuse camp. He explained how he often spent time there or in town, seldom staying at the ranch. Only after he left, and she had put Penny to bed, did Amanda venture into the connecting room. Lighting a small oil lamp, she crossed the open breezeway to the other room. Carefully, she opened the heavy wooden door and held her breath. She didn't know what she expected to find, but it was a little unnerving entering the private room of the man she had cared for, and still cared so much about.

The room boasted one wide window, with a real pane of glass that looked out on the barn. Cautiously, she rested one hand against the cold pane. She felt the unevenness of the glass, and traced the small bubbles with her finger. She knew that Jacob somehow had managed to make the glass himself. She was in awe of the man's resourcefulness and abilities. Staring out into the moonlight-drenched landscape, she stared at her reflection in the window. Suddenly, she caught a flash of light reflected behind her. Turning, she saw a small golden locket resting on a crude night table next to the narrow bed. Putting the lantern down, she lifted the fine gold necklace. The metal was cool to the touch. She closed her fingers around the small heart shape, and wondered if it had belonged to his dead wife. Opening her hand, she flipped it over and saw the small letters, *A. T. S.* Her heart stood still, then beat unsteadily against her ribcage, threatening to explode.

Suddenly, the door opened, and a cold draft swirled into the already chilly room.

"What are you doing here?" In the dark shadows of the door frame, Jacob's features were dark and forbidding.

"I . . . I . . ." Amanda stuttered, completely unnerved by the sudden appearance of Jacob. Pushing past him into the passageway, she hurried back into the warm main room where Penny slept in the loft. "What are you doing home? I thought—"

Jacob cut her off. "Where's my daughter? Where is Mrs. Winslow?" He didn't wait for an answer, but scrambled up the steep ladder leading to the loft.

"Daddy? Daddy, I don't feel very good," Penny's sleepy voice whimpered in the darkness.

"My God, she's burning up," Jacob growled accusingly, as he carried his nightgown-clad daughter back down the ladder. Once he reached the light of the fire, both adults saw the large red bumps rising up along Penny's face and neck. Quickly, Amanda snatched her from Jacob, and ordered him across the room.

"Get out of here. She's got the chicken pox. Go wash your hands, and stay away. Maybe you haven't been exposed enough." Immediately, Amanda began cooing to the feverish child, laying her down on the makeshift bed in the corner. Jacob stood dazed for a moment, his travel-weary face uncomprehending.

"I won't. How do you know? I'm not leaving, you are!" Jacob barked, as he finally got his bearings.

Amanda glanced at him, then scowled. "Mrs. Winslow had to leave. She came down with the chicken pox. She exposed Penny, and now I've been exposed. No sense in exposing all of us. The quarantine period is a fortnight, so I suggest you take yourself to the other room and stay there. I'll leave your food outside your door. We will know if I've contracted the disease in a fortnight. Now, good night." With this terse lecture, Amanda turned to Penny and began bathing her forehead with a cool rag. When she didn't hear the door open, she looked up. Jacob was staring at her, a mixture of anger, confusion, fear, and hunger burning deep in his coal-black eyes.

"Go, now," Amanda ordered, her pulse beginning to leap frenetically.

"I'll sleep in the barn. You take the bedroom," Jacob mumbled in a soft voice, as he moved backward toward the door. "I'll go see the doctor in the morning." He had reached the door, and he still held Amanda's eyes. His hand rested on the latch, but did not move. In the silence, Penny moaned, and their eyes turned to the sweating child, then back to each other. "Thank you," Jacob whispered hoarsely, his words speaking more apologetically than in gratitude.

Before Amanda could respond, he was gone. Penny cried out for her daddy once again, then fell into a fitful sleep. Scooping up the warm body, Amanda carried her next door to the cool bedroom and tucked her into bed.

Jacob lay in the darkness on the hay in his barn. He could hear the cattle and horses moving restlessly in the silence. It had been months since they had had to share quarters with a human. Not since he had built his house in a frenzy after his disastrous visit to Amanda had he slept in the barn.

He thought of his solitary bed, and of Amanda sleeping in it. He wondered what she was thinking. Since his visit last December, he refused to allow her name to be mentioned in his house. He carried his hurt and betrayal like an albatross around his neck. Twice Seamus had tried to tell him about her, to explain about that terrible day, but Jacob stormed out, refusing to listen. He didn't want to be reminded of what he had almost done and of what had become of his Amanda.

In the darkness, he rose and slipped out of the barn. His horse nickered softly as he passed by. He froze as he saw a light in the window of his room. She had taken his advice. She had covered the window with her shawl, but her silhouette was unmistakable. Silently, he moved toward the light like a moth, unable to stay away, no matter the risk. As he drew nearer, he heard her singing. It was a sweet, melancholy song, her voice rich and melodious. He closed his eyes in the darkness and swayed to the tune.

After a while, the silhouette rose and stretched. Jacob watched in a daze as Amanda began to unbutton her buttons one by one. Unable to see anything but a simple silhouette, Jacob was still entranced. In his mind's eye he vividly recalled her glorious full breasts, dusky with dark, large nipples. The thought made him yearn for her even more. Amanda's silhouette stretched then, turning so her breasts were profiled. Then the light went out, and Jacob was left in the darkness, alone, loathing himself for wanting her so badly.

Night after night he tried to stay away, but night after night he was drawn to the singing, the silhouette, his desire. Every day he worked harder, trying to exhaust himself so he could sleep at night, but still he stood in the darkness, listening, watching, wanting.

By the tenth day, Penny was her old self again, and Amanda allowed her to go visit her father in the barn. Amanda cooked meals for them all, but she stayed clear of Jacob. She was afraid of exposing him, she told herself, but she knew she didn't trust herself to remain indifferent if they were to find themselves alone together.

She always requested Penny's company when she went to the spring house or the small vegetable garden. Sometimes, while Penny napped, Amanda would go to the bedroom window and watch Jacob toil in the sun. She'd watch him ride and rope his new calves for branding and break in his wild horses. She marveled at his fluid grace on the horse and cringed with pain for him when he was unseated. But he never turned to look at her. He never attempted to communicate with her.

As the second week drew to a close, she reluctantly packed her belongings. It was clear she had not contracted the pox, and there was no longer a reason for her to stay. Amanda tidied up the bedroom and stripped the sheets on the bed. As she ran a dust cloth along the furniture, she came across the small gold locket. Slowly, she picked it up again, reading the small letters engraved on the back.

"You can keep it if you want. It was meant for you. I just never got a chance to, well, let it be a sign of my appreciation for . . ." Jacob waved his one hand around him, then let it drop. "I reckon you're in the clear. If you want, I'll hook up the wagon." Jacob looked at his hands, looked at his boots, but didn't meet her eyes. Amanda wanted to cry, to ask him why things had gone so badly. She watched him shift from one foot to the other. She studied him, breathing in his warm, musky scent. The smell of honest sweat, horses, and sunshine was intoxicating. She watched the corded muscles of his forearms stretching and bunching as he turned the brim of his hat in his hands. Her gaze traveled upward to the small black curling hairs at the open neck of his shirt. As her eyes reached his profile, they darted out the window to search for that distant point on which his were fixed. She could find nothing. Her eyes wandered back to the stubble of growth on his strong jaw, thinning, then ending at the smooth curve of his bold cheekbone. He was a beautiful man.

Slowly, he raised his ebony eyes to hers, his long, thick eyelashes casting a slight shadow beneath his eyes, accentuating the dark circles of too many sleepless nights. For a moment their eyes met and held. Then the moment stretched on, and Amanda felt her lips go dry as she flicked her tongue along their perimeter. Jacob's eyes watched with a haunted, longing look. Amanda felt her breath catch in her throat. A burning fear and wanting squeezed her chest.

"Jacob, I . . ." she began, then didn't know how to finish. Jacob took a hesitant step forward, then stopped, one hand outstretched, barely touching the bare skin on her forearm. She felt the light touch as if it were a searing brand, and she pulled back. Jacob groaned and dropped his hand.

"I wouldn't ever hurt you. I never meant to frighten you. I just couldn't believe . . ." His voice trailed off, and his eyes searched for that elusive distant spot out the window.

Amanda swallowed hard, unsuccessfully. The lump lodged in her throat was still there. It burned, bringing tears to her eyes. "Jacob I want to—"

Suddenly Jacob cut her off, grabbing her hands in his rough calloused ones. "You can't leave. I mean, I want you to stay."

Amanda closed her eyes, waiting to hear the words that she longed to hear. That he needed her, he wanted her, he loved her, he wanted her to be his wife.

"Amanda, I need you. I want you like I never wanted a woman before. Stay with me. You could take care of Penny, be her teacher. You could have my room. I could come to you at night." Amanda's eyes snapped open. The throbbing in her chest and throat intensified. He wasn't promising her love, marriage, or a family. He wanted her to be his mistress. Ripping her hands from his, she pushed past him, fighting the tears that threatened to come. She ignored his tortured voice as he called after her. He didn't love her. No matter how much she loved and wanted him, she couldn't stay under those circumstances.

The next morning, Amanda departed. She rode silently next to Jacob, neither looking at the other. Penny chirped away happily as she leaned against the back of the buckboard seat. Jacob had removed the canvas and bows, and the wagon that had traveled hundreds of miles across the country now served as an open wagon.

When they arrived at Amanda's small cabin, Jacob's attempts to lift her down were ignored. Nearly tripping, she jumped to the ground, clenching her teeth when she landed wrong on her ankle. She politely but stiffly, bade father and daughter good-bye. Just then, Seamus emerged from the cabin's entrance.

"Well, ain't you a sight for sore eyes," he exclaimed happily, as he crushed Amanda in a bear hug.

She smiled weakly in return.

"When did you get back?" Seamus continued, looking at Jacob. Jacob remained stiff and silent, as he looked at Seamus's arm, which still remained around Amanda's waist.

"Bout thirteen days ago," Jacob offered in a toneless voice. Seamus raised one bushy black eyebrow, glanced down at Amanda, then back at Jacob. Neither of the two looked at each other, and both refused to meet his eyes. Removing his arm from Amanda's waist, he ran his long fingers through his unruly hair. It was obvious that the two of them had wasted a perfect opportunity.

"You staying for dinner?" Seamus asked, as he glanced back at Jacob. Again, Jacob grew stiff, his mouth in a grim line.

"No," he growled, and jumped back in the wagon and took off.

"Damn stubborn fool," Seamus muttered under his breath, and turned to follow Amanda back inside.

The ride back to the ranch was a quiet one. Penny tried to get her father to talk, but he only stared straight ahead in a determined silence. The next two days proved no better, and Penny felt forlorn and lonely. She followed Jacob listlessly around the ranch, getting in his way and causing him to yell at her more than once.

"Daddy?" Penny began, on the third afternoon, as she leaned on the split rail gate of the corral where Jacob was trying to get close to a yearling. The horse spooked, and skittered off to the far side of the pen.

"Jesus!" Jacob exploded, stripping his gloves off his hands and slapping them down with emphasis. "Can't you see I'm trying to work, honey? Can't you go play somewhere else?" His voice was tense with annoyance and frustration, and Penny began to cry at the harsh sound of it.

"Aw, baby, come here," Jacob coaxed apologetically. He squatted down and held open his arms. Penny slipped through the gap in the rail and clung to him, her tears wet and warm upon his neck. Slowly, soothingly, he stroked her back.

"Daddy, why can't Miss Amanda stay with us always? I miss her." The child continued sobbing until she finally pulled back, her bloodshot eyes meeting her father's. "Don't you like her no more? Why can't we talk about her? Why are you so mean to her? She loves you. I knows she does." These last words pieced Jacob's heart, and he clutched the child back to his chest.

"I don't know, honey. I just don't know."

That night Jacob tossed and turned restlessly in his bed. Turning, he saw the locket on the table by his bed. She hadn't taken it. He closed his eyes and wondered where Amanda was tonight. His heart turned painfully in his chest when he imagined her in the arms of another man. He saw Seamus's big arm around her tiny waist, and he quivered with resentment. He knew now that his big friend wouldn't sleep with her, but just that small intimacy drove him wild.

As he turned for the hundredth time, he knew that he could never forget her. She was a part of his life, and her memory gave him no peace. Rising, he went to the window and hummed the haunting tune he had heard her sing. He had to get her back here. She belonged with them. No matter what he had to offer, he couldn't go on like this. He loved her. Maybe someday he could forgive her, he could learn to live with her past, but for now he just had to have her here.

The next day, Jacob set out early. He and Penny ate a light breakfast, then climbed into the wagon. He wouldn't take just his horse, because he was determined he wouldn't return without Amanda.

"Daddy, you should bring her some flowers. Ladies like flowers," Penny suggested. Jacob stopped and gathered a handful of purple and yellow wildflowers. As the morning sun rose higher, the flowers drooped and withered, but still Penny clutched them in her tight little hands. When they stopped outside Amanda's cabin, Penny handed the flowers to Jacob. He took them, looking desolately down at their faded beauty.

"Daddy, just tell her some pretty words," Penny offered hopefully. Jacob met his daughter's eyes, fighting to hide his fear.

"You just go find Emanuel while I talk to her. I need to do this alone."

Penny nodded and let her father lift her down from the wagon.

Jacob tugged nervously at his shirt collar, smoothing his sweaty hands down the wrinkled front. He took two small steps toward the door, then ran his fingers across his cleanly shaven jaw. The door opened. His heart stopped. Sarah appeared.

"Why, Jacob, what brings you 'round visiting at this hour?" Sarah asked with genuine surprise. Jacob ducked his head self-consciously, fully aware that he'd never called at any hour before, much less an early one. But he appreciated that she didn't mention it.

"Is Miss Smith in?" Jacob croaked, then repeated the request again in a more even voice. Sarah smiled and glanced at the wilted flowers in his hand.

"Would you like me to get you some water for those?"

Jacob looked down in surprise at the wilted flowers that

were now crushed between his curled fingers. He looked up at Sarah beseechingly.

"Come in. I'll get a crock of water. Amanda's out back in the garden."

Jacob followed her lead, walking to the back door. A pleasant draft flowed through the house, cooling the perspiration that had made his shirt cling to his back. He stood silently, looking out at Amanda bent over her rows of small, green plants. She looked up as Sarah called to Penny to bring Manny in for a biscuit and milk. The door closed behind them, and Amanda and Jacob were alone in the yard.

Amanda had known he was there long before she had looked up. She had seen Penny first, but Seamus could have brought her. No, it was something else. She had felt his presence, and when the breeze had blown through the house, she caught the uniquely sensual smell of him. It was more heady than the sweetest flower in the garden. It reminded her of his warm skin, his strong embrace. She savored these few moments before she had to look up and acknowledge his presence. For a minute he stood with his back pressed to the door. She smiled. His collar was crooked, and his shirt front clung to him. He looked like a frightened lost boy. He smiled back and, encouraged, took two steps closer. She frowned as she recalled his hurtful words of the other night. Jacob stopped, waiting for some other sign that he could approach her.

Slowly, Amanda rose, wiping her hands on the apron around her waist. She knew she should have told him that what he believed was wrong. She had found out from Seamus that Jacob hadn't allowed him to explain. But it hurt too badly to know he thought her capable of sinking so low. It hurt to know that even if she had been forced to drop to those depths, he would feel her beneath loving. She closed her eyes tightly, then opened them to face him.

"Miss Smith, Amanda, I . . ." Jacob moved forward, grasping her hands in his, like he had the night at the ranch. Amanda steeled herself to the wave of emotion that washed over her, threatening to drag her under. His voice was desperate, pleading, naked with pain. "I was wrong to ask you to—I will marry you. Anything you want. I need, *we* need, er, Penny and I, we want you to come live with us."

Jacob saw her pull away before she even moved a muscle. He felt desperation encompass him. He had said the wrong thing again. He gripped her fingers more tightly, his knuckles pale with the effort.

"What I have is yours. I will ask nothing of you for now. I just . . ." He glanced about him, frantically looking for an argument to convince her of the rightness that she belonged with him. He looked back. Her eyes were closing. A single tear trickled down her ebony cheek. God, she was beautiful. He grabbed her chin and lowered his mouth to hers, first gently, then hungrily, pressing her hand against his heart.

Amanda heard a moan and wasn't sure if it was coming from her or from Jacob. She couldn't think, and her mind refused to focus. It felt so wonderful to be in his arms again, to feel his lips upon hers. His kiss deepened, becoming more demanding. With her hand pressed against his solid chest, she could feel the erratic beat of his heart. His tongue flicked across her lips, asking, pleading, demanding entrance. She parted them, and their tongues met, stroking one another.

Amanda felt her resistance giving way, and she yearned to tell him she would go with him, that she would be willing to take the chance, that maybe love would follow. She had to tell him, to let him know that there had never been anyone else, that he was wrong to think she had been one of Maggie's girls. She pulled back and met his eyes.

"Jacob, you have to know—" He silenced her with another kiss. His mouth moving softly against hers.

"I don't want to know. I don't need to know. It doesn't

matter. I want you, I need you. That's enough." His words dissolved into another breathtaking kiss, and Amanda almost allowed herself to ignore his words. But he had said nothing of love, only lust. He said that what he believed didn't matter, but he hadn't said he loved her.

She pulled away. She remembered Sarah and Billy, their all-consuming desire. But there had been no love. She wanted more from marriage than just the physical. She could not take a vow before the Lord with a lie. She shook her head sadly, slipping from Jacob's hands.

"I cannot marry you. I'm am no whore to give my body when there is no love." Amanda turned back to face Jacob, tears brimming in her eyes. "Can you say you love me?"

Jacob opened his mouth to say the words, then found he couldn't. He didn't understand her explanation that she was not a whore at Maggie's. He only heard that she was refusing him unless he said he loved her. He struggled again to say the words, then recalled the small room at Maggie's House of Joy where she had sat, her blouse unbuttoned, exposing the satiny cleavage of her breast, her lips full and rosy, wanton, inviting, and all for some paying customer. He clenched his fist and willed the memory away, but it was replaced by a dozen men's faces. He couldn't lie. He couldn't say the words.

"Oh, Amanda!" he cried out hoarsely, and she looked away.

"It wasn't meant to be. I love your daughter, and I will tutor her. I will help you raise her as if she were my own until you choose to . . . until another woman . . ." She left the sentence unfinished, the words too difficult to pass the tightening in her throat. She swallowed hard, unwilling to cry before this man who had ripped her heart from her chest.

Jacob stared down at his large hands, splaying them before him helplessly. It was over before it had really begun.

"Penny prepared—we were hoping you'd join us for dinner." Jacob didn't look up.

"Tell her I'll come just for tonight. I'll just be a few moments." Amanda hurried through the back door, leaving Jacob still clenching his fingers together.

The journey to the ranch was painful, as both Amanda and Jacob strove to keep the mood light. Jacob, then Amanda, tried to explain why it was not a good idea that Amanda stay indefinitely at the ranch, and that she was needed back with Sarah and the baby. Penny had been morose and difficult, saying it wasn't fair. As the miles stretched before them, Amanda wondered if she hadn't made a big mistake in agreeing to come for dinner.

When they arrived, Jacob went to the barn to tend to the cows and horses. There had been little rain and the grass was brittle and dry, so Jacob had to make sure that the animals were getting enough water from the reserve barrels.

Amanda was glad for the respite, and urged Penny to play out front while she set the table. At first, Penny refused, following Amanda around the kitchen, extolling all the virtues of their house over hers. When Amanda continued to ignore her cajoling, the child went outside.

Things weren't turning out as she had planned, and that made Penny angry.

"Stupid Daddy!" Penny called to the distant barn. But her small voice was lost over the distance. She plopped down on her back, and looked up at the fluffy white clouds. She didn't hear the small band of unfamiliar Indians until their dark shadows spread over her face.

Immediately, she sat up. Many of her father's and Seamus's Indian friends often came to visit. They called her *Umapine Temi*. Her father said that meant friend who is a girl. But she didn't know these men who sat so straight on their white and brown horses. They had arrived so silently, and they didn't smile. Penny looked around for her father. She couldn't see him. Standing up slowly, she smiled at the stern Indians.

"Umapine? Temi," Penny said, placing her hand over her heart. One of the Indians smiled, and spoke softly to the other. The speaker dismounted, and walked over to Penny. He continued to smile, so Penny didn't move. Seamus had taught her to remain calm and not to make any sudden movement when she met an Indian she didn't know. Frightened, she remained motionless. The Indian placed a hand on top of her head, then ran his hand over the tiny braid behind her ear. He grinned, and said something to his companions.

Suddenly, the brave grabbed her around the waist, and placed her on the horse in front of him. Penny let out a terrified scream. She had tried to follow the rules, but now they were taking her away. Another scream tore through the silence before the brave clamped his hand over her mouth.

Amanda heard the first scream, quickly followed by another, and her lungs refused to breathe. Gasping, she fled to the front porch, a large butcher knife in her hand. She screamed as she saw Penny being taken away.

Jacob first heard Penny's scream followed in rapid succession by another, then a more mature one. His daughter and Amanda were in trouble. He dropped the feed bag he had just filled and tore out of the barn. He almost collided head-on with the retreating Indians.

For a moment, they paused, staring first at Jacob, then at the little girl they had on the horse. Their eyes grew wider as Amanda hurried to Jacob's side. The one holding Penny hostage noted the large knife in Amanda's hands and scowled.

"Drop it," Jacob whispered loudly to Amanda, never taking his eyes off his daughter's captor. For a moment, Amanda hesitated, then slowly lowered the blade to the ground. The Indian nodded his approval. He barked some command to the other two braves, and one pulled Penny onto his horse.

Amanda lunged forward, but Jacob caught her arm. The Indian, marking himself as the leader, moved his horse closer to Jacob. He smiled at Amanda and uttered some words of praise. Jacob nodded.

"Do you know what he said?" Amanda demanded in a loud whisper. Jacob nodded, and signed rapidly with his hands. The Indian shook his head. Jacob signed again, this time pointing to his barn. The Indian paused, and looked thoughtful. Then he shook his head and reached over to run a hand over Penny's hair.

Amanda could see the muscles taut and coiled in Jacob's shoulders and back. Penny cringed when the hand touched her head.

"What did he say?" Amanda demanded again, this time not even bothering to whisper. The Indians gazed at her, then back at Jacob. Jacob hesitated, then spoke slowly, with barely suppressed anger.

"They say, I think, that they do not want my horses. They want the little black one who calls herself girlfriend. They like her hair. It will bring them luck." Amanda shuddered. Surely they would not scalp a child. If that were their plan, wouldn't they have done it already? Her mind began reeling, striving to find something, anything to get Penny back.

Suddenly, she had an idea. Amanda stooped to sweep up the large butcher knife. The Indians moved their horses back. Jacob grabbed her wrist.

"Are you crazy?" he hissed, his eyes filled with anger and frustration.

"Let me be," Amanda hissed back, and the lead Indian laughed and spoke in his strange language. Jacob released her wrist with a flourish.

"He says you are either a very brave or a very foolish woman. He wishes to see."

Amanda smiled grimly at the Indian, then began to unwind

the braid at the nape of her neck. The Indians watched in fascination as she sawed through the thick plait. Finished, she dropped the knife and presented it to the lead Indian.

"Tell him it is strong magic. Tell him it will," Amanda paused for a moment, and closed her eyes. She sniffed, and then opened them. "Tell him it will bring the rain." The Indian grabbed the hair and ran his fingers over the frayed ends. He turned to Jacob and repeated the word *rain*. Jacob nodded, his eyes furious with Amanda. He quickly signed, and the Indian nodded. The Indian then pointed at Amanda. Jacob shook his head.

"What now?" Amanda asked, her voice loud and clear.

"He says you are to go with him, and he will give Penny back. He says he likes brave women, especially ones with magical powers." Jacob spoke clearly, but his tone was heavy with sarcasm and anger.

"Tell him that it is my hair that carries the magical power, and that I will not go with him. If he insists, I will curse him." Amanda paused for a moment and then raised one finger. "Tell him to wait, and I will bring him more magic." With these words barely spoken, Amanda lifted her skirt and ran to the house. Jacob felt his heart drop like lead to the pit of his stomach. It was all over. Amanda had probably gotten some harebrained idea that she could get a rifle and pick them all off. He groaned in despair, and hopelessness. He looked lovingly at his daughter, then signed to the Indians what Amanda had said.

Amanda had brought something precious to show Penny. But to save the little girl she loved, Amanda knew she had to give up part of her heritage.

Several minutes later, Amanda emerged from the house carrying a large tan bundle. Breathlessly, she unfurled the large zebra hide with a flourish. The Indians were stunned as they gazed upon the black and white striped hide, the likes of which they had never seen before.

"Tell them that whoever possesses this magical horse's skin will travel to other worlds in the afterlife," Amanda called out in a dramatic voice. The Indians reluctantly dragged their eyes from the beautiful fur to read Jacob's translation. Jacob's hands worked frantically, his fingers stumbling over the unfamiliar terms. The lead Indian dismounted, and bent down to stroke the hide, his fingers lingering on the ropy tail. Folding the hide over his arm, he stared at Amanda for a long time. She stared back boldly. Finally, the Indian smiled and barked a command to his companions. The brave behind Penny gently lowered her to the ground. The Indian with the hide mounted his horse and said something to Jacob. He then laughed and said something else. Jacob nodded, his arms tight around his daughter, his eyes bright with unshed tears. Turning, the Indian smiled once more at Amanda and then rode off.

Jacob released a choking sob, burying his face in the soft curls the Indians had so prized on Penny's head. After a moment, he looked up at Amanda with a tear-stained face.

"Thank you. Thank you. I couldn't bear to think that I might have lost her."

Amanda reached out to touch Jacob's arm, and he pulled her into his embrace.

"The Indian was right. He said to hold on to you, that you are a woman of uncommon courage. A prize worth keeping." Jacob hugged Penny and Amanda tighter, unabashed at the tears coursing down his cheeks. "I was a fool, Amanda. Forgive me. I do love you, no matter what has come before. I love you for who you are, and I want us to be together always. I want you to be a part of our family." Amanda's heart soared with joy as she heard the words tumble out from Jacob's mouth, mixed with hiccuping sobs. She started to cry, too, and the three of them stood in the long shadows of the afternoon, hugging and kissing, and trying to hold on to each other.

Thirty-one

All three were too drained from the day's event to even contemplate the long drive back to town. Amanda agreed to stay for the night and go back in the morning.

That night, as Amanda snuggled alone into Jacob's bed, she smiled at his smell still lingering on the sheets. She thought about the future, about his strong, lean body lying next to hers. She knew he meant every word he said. He loved her. Tomorrow she would explain about Maggie's when Penny was out of earshot. She closed her eyes, thanked God for His blessings, and thanked her ancestors for their watchful eyes, giving her the strength and idea to use the hide. She drifted off into a peaceful slumber.

Jacob lay in the narrow bed under the loft. His heart was full of happiness, but he couldn't ease the worry from his mind. The Indians they had encountered today were not stupid, and if Amanda's promise of rain did not hold true, there would be hell to pay. They would not take kindly to being made fools. Throwing back his blanket, he rose from his bed. He figured the Indians would give it two days, three days at most. Then they would be back. He walked to the door, slipping into the starless night. He gazed around at his ranch. It was finally beginning to show progress. But now he would have to leave. He couldn't endanger his family. He gazed hopefully at the cloudy sky. Did he dare hope for rain? It had been dry for so long that it seemed like a long shot. Why had she promised rain? Jacob turned to go back inside, ashamed at berating Amanda for her desperate promise of rain, when suddenly he was pelted by a thick drop of water, then another and another, until he was scurrying for cover. For several long, joyous moments, he stood in the open breezeway marveling at the deluge.

As the wind shifted and the rain pelted against his face and bare chest, he turned again to go inside. He paused, his hand on the latch, then turned to look at the door to the bedroom opposite him. Slowly, he walked to it and lifted the latch. Amanda's eyes met his.

"How did you know?" Jacob asked, his voice filled with awe.

Amanda smiled. Sitting up, she patted the bed beside her. "It is a long story. It was a gift, bestowed by my ancestors, by God, by someone or something we can never understand."

They talked into the wee morning hours. They talked about life, their heritage, their hopes and dreams, their future children. Then they lay quietly side by side, each lost in their own thoughts, content to just be together. Jacob felt he had been purged of his hated past, no longer resentful of his mixed blood. He was who he was and what he chose to be. Amanda had made him see that. He pulled her closer, never having felt so much in love. He kissed her gently, then with more need. Amanda responded, and she didn't stop him this time when his fingers felt for the buttons on the nightshirt she had borrowed from him. He felt the rapid beat of her heart as his hand slid over the sweet swell of her breasts, then slid down to cup their fullness, bringing the tight dark buds of her nipples up to his hungry lips. Amanda moaned in pleasure, arching her back, giving him better access.

Jacob groaned softly, peeling back the linen fabric that covered her. Her breasts glowed luminescently in the lamplight. He feathered light kisses across her cheeks, then down her neck and breasts to her smooth, flat belly.

"You are more gorgeous than I remembered," Jacob whispered, as he eased the shirt up over her shoulders, his eyes worshiping her smooth, naked body. Amanda rolled her head to one side, her eyes heavy with the drugged feeling of passion. For a brief moment, she wondered at his words, then lost herself in his sensual, slow kisses.

Jacob moved lower over her satin flesh, his hands and mouth pausing only long enough to remove his remaining clothes. Amanda marveled at the sight of his powerfully built body. Frightened but curious, Amanda shifted her eyes to his narrow hips and proud show of manhood. Even as she quivered at the prospect, she ached for fulfillment.

Jacob's fingers stroked the curls surrounding her womanhood with light, feathery strokes. Amanda trembled, then felt a warm liquid release between her legs. Jacob's hand searched the damp, spreading the moisture over her throbbing mound. Slowly, he parted her legs, kneading the sensitive flesh between them. Amanda arched her back, and Jacob pushed her heels back toward her buttocks, lifting her hips high off the mattress. Bundling the blanket beneath her, he knelt between her legs. His voice was soft, gently urging her on. The words fell like sweet honey over her throbbing body, making her forget to be frightened.

"Please, Jacob, please," Amanda rasped out, her hips undulating, pushing upward, seeking. Jacob groaned and braced his arms alongside her head, as she turned to kiss the corded muscles standing out in relief. He plunged deep inside of her, and she was filled with a tearing pain. She bit into the skin on his arm to keep from crying out. Jacob froze, a look of anguish washing over his handsome features. Slowly he began to withdraw. In desperation, Amanda wrapped her long legs around his waist, drawing him back to her. The pain was gone, but the longing was still there, still fierce. Slowly, but steadily, her hips beat out a steady pulse. Jacob moaned, showering her face with a torrent of kisses before taking her lips in a long, searing kiss. Their bodies buckled, and they clung to each other, spent and exhausted, but magnificently satisfied.

After they had regained some semblance of composure, Jacob turned to Amanda. His face was pained and repentant.

"I didn't know. I hope I didn't hurt you. I thought—I would never have, if I'd only known."

Amanda kissed his lips to silence his futile apologies. When they parted, she whispered, "It was wonderful."

Jacob smoothed back the hair from her face and kissed her lightly.

"I love you, no matter what," Jacob paused, rolling his eyes over her face, devouring her with his gaze. "When can we be married? I want to have you with me always. I don't want to spend another night away from you."

Amanda pulled him closer and whispered huskily in his ear, "But this night isn't over yet."

Jacob groaned and kissed her giggles to silence.

Sarah cried as Seamus gave away the bride, but blushed when he proposed ten minutes later to her. Two days before Amanda and Jacob's wedding, word had reached Willamette that William Foster had been found drowned in a mud puddle outside a San Francisco saloon.

Begrudgingly, the minister agreed to marry the newlywed couple all over again, and make it a double wedding. Penny was thrilled to be the flower girl for not one, but two brides. She scattered the flower petals in her basket with relish and told anyone who would listen that one day she was going to marry her new mother's brother, and that he was a brave warrior in the wilds of Africa.

Maggie hosted the reception in the downstairs café/saloon. A large part of Willamette turned out, if not for the ceremony, at least for the free whiskey. As the tired brides and grooms piled into their wagons for the journey home, Maggie whispered into Jacob's ear. He grinned, and kissed the top of her red head.

"What did she say?" Amanda asked. Jacob glanced over his shoulder at his sleeping daughter in the bed of the wagon, then turned back to his bride.

"She said to go slowly and take my time, because it's your first time."

Amanda flushed and looked away, feeling very naughty and wanton. Jacob turned her face gently to his.

"Don't ever feel bad about what we've done. It was done in true love."

Amanda blushed again, but this time did not look away.

"That isn't why I was blushing. I was thinking you'd better not take your time, or I'll go crazy for wanting you."

Jacob's grin spread from ear to ear, as he slapped the reins down on the backs of the hoses, and yelled, "Yah."

Penny's sleepy voice could be heard from the back. "It's bumpy back here. What's the hurry?"

Amanda and Jacob just smiled at each other and urged the horses on faster.

Tales of passion and defiance from the wilds of Africa to the American frontier

Patricia Williams

__FREEDOM'S SONG 0-515-11631-9/$5.50

When Amanda Smith, born in Africa and raised in London, heads to the New World to aid the American slaves, she finds her people faced with dangers she never imagined. There she meets Jacob, a former slave on the run with the daughter he rescued from slavery, now bound for a life of freedom on the frontier. Nothing can change his bitterness at life, until Amanda shows him a passion to live for—and a new and dignified life to believe in.

__WARRIOR'S PRIZE 0-7865-0040-9/$4.99

When she first sees Cira, Monase is engulfed with desire—entranced by his lean, powerful body, his dark, glistening skin, his hard, glittering eyes. But passion quickly turns to fear when Monase realizes Cira is a warrior from the enemy's tribe. Even as she's given to Cira as a bride, Monase vows never to offer her spirit. But when a deadly battle and a jealous shaman threaten to destroy them, Cira and Monase become united in a furious passion that will never submit.

Payable in U.S. funds. No cash orders accepted. Postage & handling: $1.75 for one book, 75¢ for each additional. Maximum postage $5.50. Prices, postage and handling charges may change without notice. Visa, Amex, MasterCard call 1-800-788-6262, ext. 1, refer to ad #506

Or, check above books	Bill my: ☐ Visa ☐ MasterCard ☐ Amex	(expires)
and send this order form to: The Berkley Publishing Group	Card#_____	
390 Murray Hill Pkwy., Dept. B		($15 minimum)
East Rutherford, NJ 07073	Signature_____	
Please allow 6 weeks for delivery.	Or enclosed is my: ☐ check ☐ money order	
Name_____	Book Total $_____	
Address_____	Postage & Handling $_____	
City_____	Applicable Sales Tax $_____ (NY, NJ, PA, CA, GST Can.)	
State/ZIP_____	Total Amount Due $_____	

If you enjoyed this book, take advantage of this special offer. Subscribe now and...

Get a Historical

No Obligation

If you enjoy reading the very best in historical romantic fiction...romances that set back the hands of time to those by-gone days with strong virile heros and passionate heroines ...then you'll want to subscribe to the True Value Historical Romance Home Subscription Service. Now that you have read one of the best historical romances around today, we're sure you'll want more of the same fiery passion, intimate romance and historical settings that set these books apart from all others.

Each month the editors of True Value select the four *very best* novels from America's leading publishers of romantic fiction. We have made arrangements for you to preview them in your home *Free* for 10 days. And with the first four books you receive, we'll send you a FREE book as our introductory gift. No Obligation!

FREE HOME DELIVERY

We will send you the four best and newest historical romances as soon as they are published to preview FREE for 10 days (in many cases you may even get them before they arrive in the book stores). If for any reason you decide not to keep them, just return them and owe nothing. But if you like them as much as we think you will, you'll pay just $4.00 each and save at *least* $.50 each off the cover price. (Your savings are *guaranteed* to be at least $2.00 each month.) There is NO postage and handling—or other hidden charges. There are no minimum number of books to buy and you may cancel at any time.

FREE Romance

(a $4.50 value)

Send in the Coupon Below

To get your FREE historical romance and start saving, fill out the coupon below and mail it today. As soon as we receive it we'll send you your FREE Book along with your first month's selections.

Mail To: True Value Home Subscription Services, Inc. P.O. Box 5235
120 Brighton Road, Clifton, New Jersey 07015-5235

YES! I want to start previewing the very best historical romances being published today. Send me my FREE book along with the first month's selections. I understand that I may look them over FREE for 10 days. If I'm not absolutely delighted I may return them and owe nothing. Otherwise I will pay the low price of just $4.00 each, a total $16.00 (at *least* an $18.00 value) and save at least $2.00. Then each month I will receive four brand new novels to preview as soon as they are published for the same low price. I can always return a shipment and I may cancel this subscription at any time with no obligation to buy even a single book. In any event the FREE book is mine to keep regardless.

Name _____

Street Address _____ Apt. No _____

City _____ State _____ Zip Code _____

Telephone _____

Signature _____
(if under 18 parent or guardian must sign)

Terms and prices subject to change. Orders subject to acceptance by True Value Home Subscription Services, Inc.

11631-9

> "A captivating story penned with unusual warmth and compassion...a wonderful read!"
> —Lori Copeland, author of <u>Promise Me Forever</u>

CATHERINE PALMER
Falcon Moon

Bostonian novelist Hannah Brownlow is determined to find her long-lost brother—even if she has to squeeze her hoop-skirts into a westward wagon...with an Indian. But the raven-haired Osage Luke Maples is nothing like the savages she had been warned about. And as Luke accompanies Hannah through the wilderness, the passion that surges between them is like nothing Hannah has ever experienced.

__FALCON MOON   0-7865-0045-X/$4.99

Also by Catherine Palmer

__OUTLAW HEART   1-55773-735-5/$4.99

__GUNMAN'S LADY   1-55773-893-9/$4.99

__RENEGADE FLAME   1-55773-952-8/$4.99

Payable in U.S. funds. No cash orders accepted. Postage & handling: $1.75 for one book, 75¢ for each additional. Maximum postage $5.50. Prices, postage and handling charges may change without notice. Visa, Amex, MasterCard call 1-800-788-6262, ext. 1, refer to ad # 514

Or, check above books and send this order form to: The Berkley Publishing Group 390 Murray Hill Pkwy., Dept. B East Rutherford, NJ 07073 Please allow 6 weeks for delivery.	Bill my: ☐ Visa ☐ MasterCard ☐ Amex (expires) Card#_____ ($15 minimum) Signature_____ Or enclosed is my: ☐ check ☐ money order
Name_____ Address_____ City_____ State/ZIP_____	Book Total $_____ Postage & Handling $_____ Applicable Sales Tax $_____ (NY, NJ, PA, CA, GST Can.) Total Amount Due $_____